Two fearsome shape

Like the clawed, half-open ~~~~~~~~~~~~~~~~~~~~~, one reached up from the deck, the other was suspended from the overhead. Each was the other's mirror image. Rising from the deck along the bulkheads were three arches, spaced at 120-degree intervals. They were broad at their bases and narrowed as they curved upward to meet at the top half of the device.

Xiong stared agape at the machine, which pulsed with ruby hues of power. It was a miniaturized replica of the artifacts found on Erilon and Ravanar. "Commander Terrell?"

After a few seconds, he received a stunned reply. *"Yes?"*

"Please tell me you're seeing this."

"Oh, we're seeing it, all right," Terrell said. *"We're just not believing it."*

"Believe it," Xiong said, swelling with the pride of true accomplishment. He was about to say something more, something congratulatory to his comrades aboard the *Sagittarius* . . . then a roar of static disrupted the comm channel.

Xiong scrambled to boost the gain on his transceiver to cut through the noise. Seconds later, one sound from the *Sagittarius* came through—loud, clear, and unmistakable.

Explosions.

STAR TREK®
VANGUARD

REAP THE WHIRLWIND
DAVID MACK

Based upon STAR TREK
created by Gene Roddenberry

POCKET BOOKS

New York London Toronto Sydney Jinoteur

POCKET BOOKS
A Division of Simon & Schuster, Inc.
1230 Avenue of the Americas
New York, NY 10020

This book is a work of fiction. Names, characters, places and incidents either are products of the author's imagination or are used fictitiously. Any resemblance to actual events or locales or persons, living or dead, is entirely coincidental.

This book is published by Pocket Books, a division of Simon & Schuster, Inc., under exclusive license from CBS Studios Inc.

First Pocket Books paperback edition June 2007

POCKET and colophon are registered trademarks of Simon & Schuster, Inc.

For information about special discounts for bulk purchases, please contact Simon & Schuster Special Sales at 1-800-456-6798 or business@simonandschuster.com.

Manufactured in the United States of America

10 9 8 7 6 5 4 3 2 1

ISBN-13: 978-1-4165-3414-3
ISBN-10:   1-4165-3414-8

*For all who have ever done the right thing
and paid for it with blood and tears*

HISTORIAN'S NOTE

Reap the Whirlwind takes place in 2266 (Old Calendar), beginning roughly six weeks after the end of *Summon the Thunder* and ending before the Original Series episode "The Corbomite Maneuver."

For they have sown the wind, and they shall reap the whirlwind.

—Hosea 8:7

THE FIRE
AND THE SONG

THE FIRST WORLD

Come to me. . . .

The Shedai Wanderer extended herself across the void, her thoughts like tendrils: filaments of consciousness in the darkness—seeking, probing, questing, longing for the touch of the Conduit Song, the harmony of the Voice that could not help but answer her call.

So many lie sleeping, she lamented. *So many linger in the shadows of oblivion, content to be liberated from mere being. Free of the past, reposed beneath scatterings of dust on worlds long abandoned. Ours was to rule, not fade away.*

Gulfs of space-time stretched away from the Wanderer, vast expanses of vacuum desolate and forlorn. The Song was feeble, a weak melody amid the cosmic noise and the rasp of background radiation. Even in the deepest recesses of the universe, there was no silence; peace was a luxury reserved for the grave. She knew that unless the Song could be amplified, the Others would remain lost to the formless night, dissipated essences.

Come closer. . . .

A single Voice could awaken a hundred Conduits and raise a hundred sleepers. To bring the Voices back to the center was the only way. And so the Shedai Wanderer reached out through the First Conduit and enlarged her sphere of thought-space, extended its range, sought out the ancient Voice.

The effort of reaching in all directions was taxing for the Wanderer, but the recent profound incursion of *Telinaruul* into the realm of the Shedai had convinced her that haste was needed. Already two groups of *Telinaruul* had shown that they were deliberately seeking out the Conduits of the Shedai and that they intended to plunder them for their secrets. The intruders' technology, though not equal to that of the Shedai, had proved formidable, and the *Telinaruul* were coming in numbers. No longer could the Wanderer face this threat alone. Though the planned era of the Second Age was still aeons in the future, she resolved to rouse the Others and summon them home.

Answer me. . . .

Then came the reply: *We hear you.*

It was not the obedient Voice as it once had been. Gone was its deferential, reverent tone—it had been replaced by suspicion and defiance. Its psychic timbre had changed, had grown deeper, sharper, more complex. Unmistakably, it was the *Kollotuul*—the Voice of the Shedai. The Wanderer abandoned the exhausting projection of her spherical thought-space and focused herself through the First Conduit toward the *Kollotuul*. **Follow my voice,** she commanded.

Day-moments elapsed like shallow breaths. The *Kollotuul* drew closer, bending the fabric of space-time around themselves much as the *Telinaruul* had done. A low drone of anxiety preceded them, cold and unyielding in its thinly veiled hostility.

The Wanderer abandoned the burden of her physical prison and roamed into the heavens above the atmosphere, cast her thoughts into space above the First World. Dispersed between its three moons, she perceived the approach of the *Kollotuul* from multiple vantages. Above the lush blue-green orb of the First World, the Voice's fragile shell slowed and entered a geostationary orbit above the planet's largest ocean. The vessel's trilateral symmetry gave it a blocky, wedge-like aspect; it looked solid and formidable. Its energy source, like others the Wanderer had recently encountered, was a matter-antimatter reactor. The ship was also heavily armed—with the same kinds of weapons that had destroyed the world on which she had chosen to sleep for the next two revolutions of the galaxy.

I must be cautious not to provoke them, she knew. *They must not be allowed to repeat their sin against our kind.* As if assessing the texture of a rough stone, she caressed their minds with her thoughts, taking their measure and counting their number. There were hundreds of them, all bold and bright and tempered in fire, bristling at her touch, more aware of her presence than she had remembered the *Kollotuul* being capable of. *These will not be yoked willingly to the First Conduit,* she realized. *They will resist and force me to break their will. . . . So be it.*

One singer among them burned brighter than the others; his thoughts colored those around him. *He is the leader,* the Wanderer concluded, and she took him first. Ringing tones of panic chorused inside the *Kollotuul*'s ship as a wrinkle of space-time enfolded its commander, moving with invisible power at the whim of the Wanderer. Clamorous alarm grew pitched as she snatched up the crew, taking some singly, others in groups. She shifted them instantaneously to the planet's surface, releasing them into the core of the First Conduit, whose dark energies were already pulsing to life. A flicker of time, and the *Kollotuul* were her prisoners, as helpless as their ancestors had been hundreds of millennia earlier, when the Maker had plucked them from a volcanic crevasse on a hothouse world with an atmosphere composed of caustic acids and high-pressure gases.

Even secure in her grip they struggled. She marveled at what they had become, at the fury they mustered. Strength would be important for her Voices, she knew. Subjects who were too weak would prove unable to survive the rigors of the First Conduit. But too much strength was potentially even worse; a Voice blessed with too great a capacity to resist could defy the will of the Shedai and use the Conduit's power for itself, as the *Kollotuul* had done long ago, during the Age of Grim Awareness. Complicating the matter was the fact that these were not the *Kollotuul* of old; they had evolved. A better name for them, the Wanderer speculated, might be *Kollotaan:* "new Voices." If the *Kollotuul* had evolved into *Kollotaan,* they might no longer be compatible with the Conduits.

There was only one way to know for certain.

The Shedai Wanderer selected the strongest of the Voices, their leader. Wrapping him in coils of fire from within the First

Conduit's core, she separated him from the others and bound him to a node, one that would speak to the farthest reaches of the Shedai's possessions. She focused herself through thought-space and projected the Song toward him with a simple command: **Amplify.**

He resisted, responding in measures equal to her effort. The harder she tried to force him to be her clarion calling out in her voice to distant stars, the more violently he defied her. The fires of the Conduit blazed hotter and darker, enveloping the *Kollotaan* leader, who thrashed in its grip and emitted piercing, metallic screeches of agony.

Speak with my voice, the Wanderer demanded.

Twisting and shrieking inside the lightless inferno of the First Conduit's strongest node, the leader did not surrender to the Wanderer's will. Whether he was merely unwilling or in fact unable to yield himself was unclear. Then the immensely powerful forces inside the Conduit reduced him to dust and vapor, and the question of whether his substance or his spirit had been the stronger was rendered immaterial.

Finding the right Voices for the Conduit would take time, the Wanderer now understood. Striking the necessary balance between strength and malleability would be a matter of simple trial and error.

She looked to the gathered mass of *Kollotaan*, selected the next-strongest specimen she could identify, and yoked him to the same node inside the First Conduit.

From the first lick of dark fire, the Voice filled the Conduit with an eerie, high-pitched wail of terrified noise. A jolt of agony brought it under control.

Speak with my voice, the Wanderer commanded. **Or die.**

PART ONE

THE BRINK OF SHADOW

1

Dr. Ezekiel Fisher reclined in the chair at the desk inside his quarters aboard Starbase 47. It was late for him to be awake, a few hours into the third duty shift. His coffee had become tepid during the hour he had spent composing his latest letter to his daughter, Jane, the youngest of his three children. The missive was almost finished, and he paused to read it over.

"Dear Jane," it began, prosaically enough. "I hope this letter finds you well, and that Neil and your boys are on the mend from that bout of Argelian flu you told me about. I've been keeping my vaccinations up to date, so here's hoping I don't meet any viruses more clever than myself.

"Life and work here on Vanguard remain busy; I know it must seem funny to hear me say that, since there's rarely any mention of us in the news—nothing, in fact, since the loss of the *Bombay*. As much as I wish I could tell you everything that I've seen out here, it'd be a waste of effort: all our outgoing mail is censored. . . . Such measures must seem draconian on a world like Mars, but the truth is that it's for the best. At least, I hope it is.

"What *can* I tell you? For starters, my retirement plan has been nixed. Jabilo M'Benga, my handpicked replacement, put in for starship duty. His reasons make sense, I suppose. As it turns out, I've had a couple of months to get used to the idea, which is pretty much what I'd expected. We're pretty far from home, and even in the core systems it would take time to get this kind of thing approved. First, he has to tell Starfleet he wants a transfer. Then Starfleet has to see what billets it has open and whether anybody else put in for them first. Then some joker with a lot of braid on his cuff has to give his okay and cut new orders, which might take a few days to reach us."

Fisher picked up the data slate on which he had composed the letter. He carried the slate in one hand and continued to read while he took his coffee into his kitchenette to dispose of it. "And just to convince you that I've started losing my marbles," the letter continued, "I'm actually reconsidering retirement altogether. I admit, I'd have thought that after more than fifty years in a Starfleet uniform, I'd have had my fill by now. Before I came out here with Diego last year, I was starting to think I'd seen everything, that the galaxy was out of surprises. But, as you never tire of reminding me, I was wrong."

He dumped his leftover coffee into the sink and ran the water for a moment, then resumed reading as he ambled to his sofa. "It's hard to say if I'll ever be allowed to write or talk about the things I've seen here. My guess is, probably not. It's not like I have a shortage of stories at this point, but this assignment would make for some you'd never forget. That's not why I'm thinking of staying on, though. Truth is, I'm beginning to see that this is one of the most important assignments I've ever been given. We're on to something out here, something big. Even if M'Benga wasn't planning on warping away to the great unknown, I'd probably want to stay on to see this through. At this point, any lingering regrets I have over his transfer are grounded in simply being sorry to lose such a fine physician from my staff and feeling pity for him—because he'll probably never know what he's missed."

A yawn stretched Fisher's brown, weathered face. He gently rubbed the fatigue from his eyes and stared back down at the data slate. The letter wasn't long; it had taken an hour to write, because every time he'd thought of something to say, he'd realized that it would never make it past the Starfleet censors. He couldn't tell Jane about his role in the analysis of an alien corpse with meta-genome-laced liquid crystal for blood or the bizarre effects that had been inflicted upon a Starfleet officer attacked by the creature. All the tense rumors of a brewing political eruption among the Klingons, the Tholians, and the Federation would be excised as a matter of diplomatic policy, no doubt on Jetanien's orders. Scratching absentmindedly at the gray tuft of beard on his chin, he pondered how to end the letter. After staring at an empty line along the bottom of the slate for a few minutes, he realized that an obvious and simple valediction would be just fine, so long as it was sincere.

"That's all for now. Tell Neil and the boys I miss you all, and I hope to visit you again on Mars very soon. Take care, and write back when time allows and the mood strikes. Love, Dad."

He tapped a few keys on the data slate and transmitted the letter into the station's queue for outgoing comm traffic. In a few hours it would likely meet with the approval of the censors and be on its way to Mars, one of thousands of messages bundled in a massive burst of unclassified data traffic leaving Vanguard. In a matter of hours, Jane would get the message, maybe at home or in her office between patients. Unlike his sons, Ely and Noah, Jane had followed him into medicine, though she had pointedly declined a career in Starfleet in order to open her own private practice in the rapidly growing Martian city of Cydonia. It was there she had met her husband, Neil, and where they were raising their sons, James and Seth.

As always, thinking of his children and grandchildren made him smile. *That's a good way to end the day,* he decided. He got up from the couch and shambled stiffly off to bed. Tomorrow would be busy; he needed all the rest he could get.

The *Starship Sagittarius* was coming home.

Anna Sandesjo lay in her bed. A tangle of scarlet sheets covered her lap. Her hands were folded on the pillow behind her head, beneath her splayed mane of cinnamon-hued hair. The scratches on her back were deep and fresh.

It was still early, before 0600 station time. At the foot of the bed, Lieutenant Commander T'Prynn was getting dressed. The lithe Vulcan woman donned her red minidress in movements slow and graceful, a stark contrast to the frenzy of attention she'd shown Sandesjo the evening before. T'Prynn's every motion captivated Sandesjo's attention.

"Did you sleep well, my love?" Sandesjo asked, even knowing that T'Prynn—who had tossed and turned for the past several hours in the throes of night terrors—would lie to her.

Pulling back her long sable hair and tying it into a ponytail, T'Prynn replied flatly, "My rest was adequate." She sat down on the edge of the bed and began putting on her boots.

Sandesjo sat up and let the sheets bundle in her lap. Watching T'Prynn prepare to leave was always difficult for her; it was a reminder of loneliness. "Do you have to go so soon?"

With one boot on, T'Prynn reached for the other as she replied over her shoulder, "Yes."

"Because of the *Sagittarius*."

"Yes," T'Prynn said.

News of the scout vessel's return to Starbase 47 had been buzzing for a couple of weeks. The ship's recall from a remote area of the Taurus Reach had been ordered not long after the destruction of Palgrenax. Though ship movements continued to be classified for members of the general public and personnel with no need to know, Sandesjo's assignment as a senior diplomatic attaché to Vanguard's ranking diplomat, Ambassador Jetanien, afforded her access to a variety of otherwise off-limits items of interest.

Standing up, T'Prynn smoothed the front of her minidress and turned to face Sandesjo, all dignity and poise: cold, composed, and aloof. At times like this, Sandesjo felt less like the Vulcan woman's lover and more like a stranger. "Thank you for allowing me to spend the night," T'Prynn said.

"Perhaps you'd let me spend a night in *your* quarters sometime," Sandesjo said, her tone blatantly suggestive. "Unless you're ashamed to be seen with me."

Subtly lifting her left eyebrow, T'Prynn said, "Shame is not a factor. The heat and gravity in my quarters are configured for Vulcan comfort. I think you would find them . . . unpleasant."

"Don't be fooled, my love," Sandesjo said with a flirtatious leer. "Just because I look human doesn't mean I'm as fragile as one. Qo'noS has its share of heat."

T'Prynn stepped over to the dresser and collected her communicator, which she tucked onto her belt. "I'm sure your Klingon physiology would bear the temperatures admirably," she said. "The aridity, however, might prove rather uncomfortable."

"I think I can handle it," Sandesjo said. To her dismay, rather than continue their repartee, T'Prynn started to move toward the door. "Don't go," Sandesjo blurted out. As soon as she said it, she regretted having done so; it was a grossly unprofessional expression of desire and weakness.

Slowly, T'Prynn turned and regarded Sandesjo with a stare of clinical detachment. "Why do you wish me to remain?"

"I always want you to stay," Sandesjo said. "You never do."

Raising her steeply arched eyebrows, T'Prynn replied, "An extremely illogical statement, Miss Sandesjo. You—"

"Anna," she interrupted. "Why don't you ever call me Anna? I think we deserve to be on a first-name basis, don't you?"

In a surprisingly sharp tone, T'Prynn shot back, "If we do, then perhaps you would prefer I called you by your *real* name, *Lurqal.*"

Hearing T'Prynn speak her Klingon name left Sandesjo momentarily shocked silent. Though Sandesjo's true identity had been known to T'Prynn for nearly a year, until now the Vulcan had never uttered it aloud. Suppressed by years of living under her cover identity, that name sounded foreign to Sandesjo. She had submerged so deeply into her cover that she had come to think of herself as Anna Sandesjo rather than as Lurqal.

Finally recovering her voice, she said, "If, when we are . . . *alone together,* you wish to call me Lurqal, I would not object."

After considering that for a moment, T'Prynn said, "Is our relationship the cause of your current distress?"

"Yes, it is," Sandesjo said, relieved to be able to speak plainly and without the qualifying preambles of diplomatic discourse. "Though I'd really like to know what our *relationship* is, exactly."

Cocking her head slightly, T'Prynn asked, "What aspect of its nature eludes you?"

"I don't know," Sandesjo said. "All of it? You've been sharing my bed for months, but I still don't know what to call you. My girlfriend? My lover? What am I to you? Just another intelligence asset? Something else? Or am I just your whore?"

The conversation seemed to make T'Prynn uncomfortable. She took a deep breath, closed her eyes, and lowered her head. "You are not my 'whore,'" she said, then looked up. "But defining our relationship is complicated. There are . . . professional issues to consider."

"Such a nice way of putting it," Sandesjo said bitterly. "Did you start sleeping with me to turn me into a double agent? Or was that just an added perk?"

Unfazed, T'Prynn answered, "Did you become a double agent out of principle or because I had exposed you as a spy? Were you motivated by love, lust, or self-preservation? I am not the only one whose motives in this matter are suspect."

Stung, Sandesjo looked away for a moment. Turning back to face T'Prynn, she said, "I just want to know how you *feel* about me." As T'Prynn began to answer, Sandesjo recognized the telltale signs of a verbal evasion taking shape. She threw aside the sheets, got out of bed, and moved quickly toward the Vulcan woman. "And don't you *dare* tell me you don't have emotions, or that they don't matter to you." Standing naked in front of T'Prynn, Sandesjo leaned close to her and dropped her voice to a husky whisper. "I see the hunger in your eyes when you come to me at night. I feel the fire in your kisses, the wild part of you that takes me by force . . . dominates me . . . *possesses* me. You burn for me just as I burn for you."

With a haughty and dismissive mien, T'Prynn said, "If you are so attuned to my inner life, why ask for my declaration?"

Sandesjo turned her head slightly, so that her lips barely brushed T'Prynn's as she said, "Because I love you."

She leaned forward to kiss T'Prynn, who pulled back and then stepped away, haltingly at first, then quickly, until she was out of the bedroom, out of the apartment suite, and gone beyond Sandesjo's reach.

Sandesjo's reflection gazed back at her from the mirror. She looked pale, timid, defenseless—*human*. Rage, sorrow, and humiliation swelled inside her. Of all the traits that Klingons despised, none was so reviled as weakness. In a single rash statement, she'd rendered her deepest feelings as bare as her body; it was the most vulnerable she had ever felt and the closest she had ever really come to knowing the taste of fear.

Turning away from herself, she lamented ever having met T'Prynn—and surrendering to love's bitter sting.

The passageway that circled Vanguard's hub and looked out on its enclosed docking bay bustled with activity. Two huge Federation colony transports, the *Terra Courser* and the *Centauri Star*, had made port in bays one and two only a few hours before the starbase's newest arrival, the *Starship Sagittarius*, had docked in bay four. Weaving adroitly and with long strides through the crowd of teeming two-way pedestrian traffic, Commodore Diego Reyes stole a glance out an observation window into the main docking bay.

Attending the *Sagittarius* was a swarm of small maintenance craft and several personnel in light-duty pressure suits, all of them scrambling into action, making minor repairs and erecting a cocoon of scaffolding and netting around the ship, in preparation for more extensive work. Alongside such massive vessels as the two transports, or its own larger cousins, such as the *Constitution*-class *U.S.S. Endeavour* or the refit *Daedalus*-class *U.S.S. Lovell*, the *Archer*-class scout ship looked almost like a toy. Another thing that made it stand out was how new it looked; its hull was pristine, its Zodiac-inspired ship's insignia still gleaming, every letter and digit in its registry as crisp as they'd been the day it had left spacedock. Its docking hatch, located at the outermost curve of its port primary hull, was attached to an extended gangway that led to a series of narrow passages. Those fed onto the main thoroughfare, where Reyes now moved at a quickstep.

Reyes arrived at the entrance to the bay four gangway just as a chief petty officer unlocked and opened the pressure hatch. As the portal slid aside, he saw the senior members of the *Sagittarius*'s crew on the other side, moving just as quickly as he had been. They all wore nondescript, olive-hued utility jumpsuits devoid of rank insignia.

In the lead was Captain Adelard Nassir, a Deltan man in his mid-fifties. Slight of build and bald of pate, Nassir projected calm and dignity in his every action, no matter how great or small. Beside him was his first officer, a taller and much brawnier brown-skinned human named Clark Terrell. The man was built like a boxer but talked like a scholar.

Close behind the two men were two women. Trailing the captain was a statuesque blonde, who Reyes remembered was the ship's chief medical officer, Dr. Lisa Babitz. He had met her only once, months ago, but she had made a lasting impression by taking the opportunity to disinfect the desk in his office.

Walking behind Terrell was a petite young redhead. Her name was Vanessa Theriault; she was the ship's science officer. As with Babitz, Reyes had met her only once, several months ago, after the ship had first been assigned to Starbase 47 as its outrider scout. Something that Theriault had in common with Babitz was a gift for making a strong first impression: at the end of her first mission briefing, she had presented Reyes with a gift—a knitted scarf that she had made herself, in her "spare time." He had yet to wear it and suspected he never would, but he still liked it.

Bringing up the back of the small formation was a lissome and pale-complexioned human woman with raven hair and a male Saurian who moved with fluid grace on bare webbed feet. These two Reyes had never met, but he recognized them from a past review of their service records. The woman was the ship's second officer, Lieutenant Commander Bridget McLellan, and the Saurian was the ship's newest field scout, a senior chief petty officer named Razka.

Theriault, Nassir, and Terrell were the only members of the ship's complement who were privy to the real objectives of Operation Vanguard. But because of the new orders Reyes had come to deliver, that was about to change. Soon the entire crew of the *Sagittarius*, all fourteen of them, would need to be briefed. *Knowing this bunch*, he speculated, *they'll be too excited to know they ought to be scared out of their minds*.

Captain Nassir nodded to Reyes as he crossed the last few meters of the gangway to join him. "Commodore," he said with a friendly smile. "Sorry we kept you waiting."

"Actually," Reyes said, "I just got here myself."

As he shook Reyes's hand, Nassir replied, "I was talking about the six weeks it took us to get back from Typerias."

"Oh, that," Reyes said, returning Nassir's grin. "If you ask me, I'd say you made pretty good time." Looking around, Reyes noticed that the other officers from the *Sagittarius* were beginning to crowd around himself and Nassir. To the group he said, "Welcome back, everyone. I've opened a tab for all of you up at Manón's. Head up and get something to eat. Your captain and I will be there shortly." To their credit, Reyes thought, they took his suggestion in stride and moved off toward a nearby bank of turbolifts. Reyes made a sideways nod of his head to Nassir. "Walk with me, Captain."

Nassir followed Reyes as he started a slow circuit of the deck. The lanky commodore walked more slowly than he normally did to make it easier for the shorter captain to keep pace with him.

In a confidential tone, Nassir said, "I presume you didn't bring us back from a deep-space recon because you missed us."

"Actually, I did miss you," Reyes joked. "But you're right, that's not the reason. The Klingons have been listening in on our comm traffic, so I had to play my cards close on this one." He let a group of enlisted men and women pass by in the opposite direction before he continued. "Did you read Xiong's report about Jinoteur?"

Concentration creased Nassir's brow for a moment. "The

star system that was generating a subspace signal," he said, swiftly recalling details. "It made your station go haywire, yes?"

"Crazy as a junkyard dog," Reyes said. "We looked at Jinoteur to see if we could find the cause, but we didn't see anything . . . until six weeks ago."

A smirk tugged at the corner of Nassir's thin mouth. "And now you want someone to take a closer look."

"*Much* closer," Reyes confirmed.

Nassir half-chuckled. "I have to say, sir, I'm flattered and a bit surprised you'd assign this to my crew. Typically, a plum like this would go to a big ship like the *Endeavour*—"

"Busy showing the flag out by Forcas," Reyes cut in.

The captain continued, "Of course, knowing the role the *Lovell* and her crew played in fixing your Jinoteur problem—"

"They're on extended colony support to Gamma Tauri IV."

Humility replaced pride in Nassir's expression. "I see," he said. "We're going because we're available."

"I'm just yanking your chain, Captain. I wouldn't have pulled you back across two sectors unless I had a damn good reason," Reyes said. "Truth is, the *Endeavour* and the *Lovell* are the wrong ships for this mission. The first one draws too much attention, and the other one, I swear to God, seems to *invent* disasters. I need you, your crew, and your ship to do what you do best: explore the unknown."

"Without getting noticed," Nassir added. "Or turning it into a problem."

Reyes glanced in the captain's direction. "Precisely."

Ahead of them, the observation lounge for bay one was coming into view around the curving bend of the corridor. Nassir asked, "Are we still handling this as need-to-know?"

"Not anymore," Reyes said. "Your whole crew has to be briefed before you ship out. You're also getting a sensor-grid upgrade and some new gear for your scouts."

"Not just a sneak-and-peek, then," Nassir said.

Shaking his head, Reyes replied, "Not this time. We want a full survey. But after Erilon, we're taking precautions."

Nassir nodded once. "Understandable," he said. "Terrible, what happened to Zhao. He was a great officer." With an almost paternal concern, he asked, "How's Khatami handling command?"

"Like she was born to it," Reyes said. "It's not the way anyone likes to get promoted, but she's making it work."

"Good," Nassir said. "I'm glad." He sighed, then changed topics. "When's our mission briefing?"

"Tomorrow at 0900," Reyes said. "I'll have Xiong meet with your people on the *Sagittarius*." Eyeing Nassir for his reaction, he added, "Incidentally, Xiong'll be going with you."

To Reyes's surprise, the news seemed to please the captain. "Excellent," Nassir said. "I rather enjoyed his last visit."

Amazing, Reyes mused. *An authority figure Xiong hasn't pissed off yet. Maybe there's hope for that kid, after all.* "Glad to hear it," Reyes said, as they started sidestepping through wave after wave of civilians, colonists from the *Terra Courser* who were pouring onto the docking bay thoroughfare. Eager to escape the press of bodies, Reyes said, "I've kept you from breakfast long enough, Captain. Ready to head up to Manón's?"

"Absolutely," Nassir said.

They cut left toward a nearby turbolift and were almost free of the crowd when a woman's voice called out sharply from several meters away. "Diego!"

Jeanne. Dread, like a sudden splash of cold water in his face, shocked Reyes to a halt. He tried not to clench his jaw but failed. Nassir, standing at his side, turned and looked behind them. Reyes asked, "She's coming this way, isn't she?"

"With a vengeance," Nassir said.

Reyes closed his eyes. He took a deep breath that did absolutely nothing to enhance his calm. Opening his eyes to confront the inevitable, he said to Nassir, "Go on ahead, Captain."

"Yes, sir," said Nassir, who advanced quickly toward the turbolift. The Deltan captain had always demonstrated a keen sense of when to make an exit—an option that Reyes was, at that moment, dismayed to find himself without. As Nassir entered the turbolift, Reyes turned and faced his ex-wife.

Like many natives of Luna, including Reyes himself, Jeanne Vinueza was tall and long-limbed—the result of spending part of her formative years in a low-gravity environment. Her chestnut hair was curly and spilled over her shoulders and upper back, longer than it had been when he'd last seen her more than six years earlier. As always, she was stylishly dressed and carried a metallic briefcase. She fixed him with her brown-eyed stare as she strode toward him. Other civilians scrambled to make a path for her, some stumbling almost comically out of her way.

Expecting a verbal onslaught, Reyes lowered his chin and chose to lean into the harangue. She stopped in front of him, eyes blazing, and planted her free hand on her hip. She remained as youthful-looking as ever; if Reyes hadn't known that she was nearly forty-five years old, he might have guessed her age to be thirty-five instead.

Neither of them said a word for several seconds. Then the gleam in her eyes changed from furious to mischievous, and her lips trembled before opening into a lopsided smile. "*Hola,* Diego," she said.

He was both relieved and annoyed. "Hi, Jeanne."

An awkward moment lingered as they wondered how to greet each other. Several clumsy attempts at a platonic embrace and kisses on both cheeks left Reyes feeling self-conscious. He pulled back from Jeanne and looked around to see if any members of Vanguard's crew were observing this embarrassing reunion. Hundreds of hastily averted glances made him conclude that everyone on the station was probably watching them.

"So," she began, clearly searching for words. "You're a commodore now. Impressive."

Holding up his wrist, he said, "Don't let a little extra braid fool you. I'm still a jerk."

"*Sí,*" she replied, "but an *impressive* jerk."

He marshaled a pained grin. "Please tell me you didn't spend eight weeks on a transport just to come out here and flatter me."

Turning businesslike, she said, "I'm just passing through, on my way out to Gamma Tauri IV."

That didn't sound right to Reyes. "Now, that's a surprise," he said. "Thought you always said you wouldn't be caught dead on a colony planet."

"True," she admitted. "I used to say that. But that was before I was offered the chance to be the leader of one."

"You're the president of the New Boulder colony?"

"Don't make it sound so glamorous," she said. "It's an appointed position with a contract, like a company executive. And my first item of business is a meeting with Ambassador Jetanien, Captain Desai, and your colonial administrator, Aole Miller." She looked over his shoulder at a chronometer on the wall. "Speaking of which, I'm running late." For a moment, she seemed on the verge of saying something else but then thought better of it. "Maybe I'll see you before I ship out," she said, inching away toward the turbolift.

"Maybe," he said. "You know where to find me."

A turbolift car arrived. Jeanne stepped in and squeezed into place among the other passengers. The doors closed, and Reyes was left brooding in the middle of the passageway.

Serves you right for not reading the damn colony briefings, Reyes berated himself. The *Lovell* and its team from the Corps of Engineers were currently deployed to Gamma Tauri IV — principally for colonial support but also to find another alien artifact like the ones that had been found on Ravanar and Erilon. If another such artifact was on the planet, as Xiong's research suggested, and it proved to be as much trouble as those previous discoveries, then everyone on Gamma Tauri IV was in danger.

Reyes had never been comfortable with Starfleet Command's decision to let civilian colonization efforts provide unwitting cover for its search for new samples of the Taurus meta-genome — an exceptionally complex string of alien DNA, whose discovery a few years earlier had sparked Starfleet's mad rush into this remote sector of local space, including the construction of Starbase 47 itself. The presence of a legitimate colony, however, was the best camouflage his people could ask for; it gave them countless valid reasons for being on Gamma Tauri IV. Defense, construction, various surveys, mapping, irrigation efforts, sewage treatment—any number of civil-engineering efforts would conceal the *Lovell* team's hunt for the meta-genome and another artifact. The risk, of course, was that one wrong move could put the entire colony in peril.

And now Jeanne would be in the middle of it.

He remained bitter toward her for the way she had ended their marriage seven years earlier; she had terminated it like a canceled contract, as if it had been nothing more than a simple partnership that had outlived its usefulness. Despite that, part of him still harbored affection for her. Even as he had cursed her name during the divorce, deep fires had smoldered in his heart for her, and he had tried more than once to fan them back to life; but where he had seen the possibility of rekindling their romance, Jeanne had seen only ashes.

I should tell her not to go, he insisted to himself. Then duty reminded him, *You can't tell her why. And unless she knows why, she won't listen to you. Maybe not even then.*

It had been a serious breach of orders for him to bring his two closest friends—Dr. Ezekiel Fisher and Captain Rana Desai, the station's presiding Judge Advocate General Corps officer—into the loop several weeks ago, but at least they were Starfleet officers, and he could make a case to Starfleet Command that they needed to know the truth in order to perform their duties.

Telling a civilian would be another matter. Revealing the truth about Operation Vanguard and its current mission on Gamma Tauri IV to Jeanne, no matter how noble his motives for doing so might be, would mean the end of his career once word got out. About that, he had no illusions. If he warned her, the truth eventually *would* come out, and when it did, he would spend the rest of his life in solitary confinement on the coldest landmass on the remotest planet within reach of the Federation.

It was nearly 0800; he had yet to get a cup of coffee, and the senior staff meeting was about to start. Normally, Reyes waited until after lunch to decide whether a day was a good one or not, but as he trudged toward a turbolift for the ride up to ops, he decided that any day that began with him being ambushed by his ex-wife couldn't possibly end well.

Jeanne Vinueza's esper skills were nowhere near as powerful or focused as those of Vulcans, but she had enough experience gauging emotions and picking up surface thoughts to know when she was being lied to. Looking across the wide gray table at the Chelon ambassador and two Starfleet officers, she was certain that at least one of them was hiding something.

It wasn't Aole Miller. Starbase 47's colonial administrator was an open book, all bonhomie, warmth, and untainted goodwill. Men like him were a rarity, in Vinueza's experience: good souls unblemished by pessimism or cynicism. Short and ebony-skinned, with a smooth-shaved head and a bright white smile, he was without a doubt the most truthful and forthcoming person in the chilly, utilitarian-looking conference room.

Ambassador Jetanien and Starfleet JAG officer Captain Rana Desai were another matter.

Jetanien held up a data slate in one scaly, clawed manus. "I've read your petition three times, Ms. Vinueza," he said. "And I still don't understand."

"You don't understand our petition?" Vinueza asked.

"I understand its contents perfectly," he said, setting down the slate. "What I fail to understand is why I'm reading it at all. Frankly, I find your case for refusing protectorate status incomprehensible."

Mimicking his archly patronizing tone, she replied, "Perhaps your colleague Captain Desai could explain it to you, Mr. Ambassador." She tried to glean some sense of his reaction, but his face, a leathery olive mask marked by a turtlelike beak and deep amber orbs for eyes, betrayed nothing. His thoughts were even more remote from her; Chelon brain waves were too dissimilar from those of most humanoids for Vinueza to read.

Jumping into the conversation, Miller seemed genuinely taken aback by the colonists' petition. "I respect your colony's right to independence," he said, leaning forward. "But declining official Starfleet protection in a sector targeted for conquest by the Klingons seems, well, unwise."

Desai added, "If it's a matter of preserving your world's legal autonomy, Ms. Vinueza, there are several exemptions available under the Federation's colonial charter for the Taurus Reach. Accepting our protection would not obligate you to anything that hasn't been ratified by a vote of your colony's residents."

There was no duplicity in Desai's surface thoughts, at least none that Vinueza could detect. Something felt off about the slim Indian woman's demeanor, however. A tinge of concern, a shadow of doubt, the hint of a secret lurked behind her words. *She isn't malicious,* Vinueza concluded, *but she's not being completely forthright, either.*

Vinueza replied, "It's not about our independence, Captain. Our concerns are based on the rising frequency of clashes between the Federation and the Klingon Empire. If we accept UFP protectorate status, we might as well paint a bull's-eye on our colony. Neutrality, both politically and economically, seems like the safest course to us. So with all respect, the people of New Boulder would rather not fly your banner over their new home."

"I daresay you would be hard-pressed to find a more ardent supporter of colonial self-rule than myself," Jetanien said. "However, I have to confess that I find your political risk assessment of the Taurus Reach somewhat lacking in nuance and marred by gross naïveté. Disavowing affiliation with the Federation, far from sparing you the notice of the Klingon Empire, will in fact bring you more swiftly to their attention as a soft target, one that they can encroach upon without fear of Starfleet interference or reprisal. I would beg you to reconsider and withdraw your petition."

She shook her head. "That's not an option, Mr. Ambassador. The colonists have already ratified this petition. As their representative, it's my responsibility to honor it."

"And as their leader," Jetanien countered, "it's your duty to prevent them from making a potentially fatal mistake. The people of New Boulder are your constituents, Ms. Vinueza, not your shareholders. You are not blindly yoked to their will."

Vinueza sighed softly and resisted the urge to reply before thinking through her response. Jetanien's remark about shareholders clearly had been intended to goad her, by casting aspersions on her previous tenure as the chief executive of an interstellar dilithium-mining corporation and implying that her experience in the much-maligned private sector was inapplicable to her new role as an officer of civil government. *The first one to get angry loses,* she reminded herself. *Don't take the bait.*

"I would not present a petition in bad faith, Mr. Ambassador," Vinueza said. "Nor would I advocate any measure that I felt would be to the detriment of those I represent. The New Boulder colony is an agricultural collective. Gamma Tauri IV has no dilithium, so I'm not worried the Klingons will show much interest in it. What does worry me is how interested Starfleet seems to be. You've clearly read my file, so you know about my esper skills. Well, every time I've talked to Starfleet Command about this colony, I've gotten the feeling that someone is hiding something. Bottom line? I don't trust you people."

"Ma'am, we just want to ensure the safety and success of your colony," Miller said. "The *Lovell* and a team from the Corps of Engineers have been there for the past four weeks, helping your people get their farms running, their water cleaned, and their backup generators operational. And I want to assure you that even if you refuse protectorate status, the *Lovell* and her team will stay on to assist you, no strings attached, until your colony is fully self-sufficient. Starfleet just wants to help."

Rising from her seat, Vinueza said, "Thank you, Commander, that's very generous." She picked up her briefcase and cast a suspicious glare at Jetanien and Desai. "But I suspect we'll be getting Starfleet's *help* whether we want it or not."

2

Ensign Brian O'Halloran grunted and struggled to keep his hands from slipping off of the enormous, prodigiously heavy component, the name of which had slipped his mind at about the same time as his back had slipped a disc. He was fairly certain that part of the problem was that his partner, Ensign Jeff Anderson, was sitting on a rock behind him instead of helping him hook up the humongous whatever-it-was to a juncture in the colony's new water main. As his knees began to wobble under the strain, O'Halloran pleaded, "Would it *kill* you to lend a hand?"

"Yes, it would," said Anderson, staring at the horizon. "It kills me that we're stuck here, pounding out this kind of grunt work, when there's a whole world full of other stuff we could be doing." Eyeing O'Halloran's predicament, he added, "You should put that down before you hurt yourself."

As if Anderson had spoken magic words, the clumsy hunk of heavy metal fell through O'Halloran's hands. He leaped backward, barely dodging clear in time to save his foot. "Great," he groused, wiping sweat from his brow. "It's probably broken."

"Stop complaining," Anderson said, brushing a bang of blond hair from his eyes. "You know the first rule of engineering: If it jams, force it. If it breaks, it had to be replaced anyway."

Pacing around the device, O'Halloran replied, "It didn't jam, I dropped it—because you weren't helping me." He stepped back and stroked his dark goatee as he studied the problem. "How the hell are we supposed to get it back in position?"

Anderson shrugged dismissively. "Who cares?" He gestured

at the sea-green dome of sky overhead. "Look at this perfect day. We've got sun, fresh air, our health, and a colony full of women less than a kilometer away. Gamma Tauri IV is our oyster, and you're worried about a . . ." He paused and squinted at the oddly shaped device. "What *is* that thing?"

"I don't know," O'Halloran said defensively. "I thought you knew what it was."

"And to think, we both have engineering degrees," Anderson deadpanned. "We should be ashamed of ourselves."

Circling the device again, O'Halloran wondered aloud, "How are we gonna move it? It's gotta weigh a few hundred kilograms, at least."

Folding his arms across his chest, Anderson replied, "What're you asking me for? You're the one who dropped it." O'Halloran lunged at his partner, who lifted his hands and backpedaled quickly out of reach. "Whoa! Hang on there! Just calm down, and I'll help you."

"Right," O'Halloran snapped. "I wouldn't be in this mess if you'd helped me like you were supposed to." He lifted his arms in frustrated surrender. "Why'd I let Parsons talk me into taking her shift? I'm not even supposed to be here today!"

"I know why you took her shift," Anderson said. "You're sweet on her and thought you could score some points."

"That's not true," O'Halloran protested.

Anderson nodded knowingly. "Yes it is. Four weeks we've been on this dirtball, hooking up sewers, digging ditches, and laying cable—and the whole time you've been mooning after her. It's pathetic, really. I'm almost ashamed to know you."

O'Halloran shook his head. "No, no, no."

"Yes, yes, yes, my friend. Which, incidentally, is what I think you're hoping to hear lovely Lieutenant Parsons shouting from your bunk one of these nights."

Trying again to lift the deadweight widget, O'Halloran said through clenched teeth, "You really have a one-track mind."

"Untrue," Anderson said. "Sometimes I think about hockey."

A sickening pain bloomed in O'Halloran's gut. He was

fairly certain that he'd burst an internal organ through sheer effort. Slumping forward onto the gigantic gadget, he mumbled, "Good luck finding enough ice for hockey on this dustball."

"Oh ye of little imagination," Anderson replied. "Four years of engineering classes at Starfleet Academy, and that's the best you can come up with? 'Good luck finding enough ice'? When we have eighty-five thousand liters of the most advanced commercial refrigerants known to man at our fingertips?"

Rolling his eyes, O'Halloran said, "Those are for the food warehouse. I don't think they'd appreciate us using them to make a hockey rink."

"Only because they lack the proper appreciation for the sport," Anderson said as he slumped down next to O'Halloran, who had seated himself against the side of the massive machine. "We could fix that."

Knocking on the device to hear the hollow echo inside, O'Halloran said, "We have to get this thing hooked up first."

Anderson scrunched his face into a grimace. "Says who?"

O'Halloran was aghast. "Says Lieutenant Commander al-Khaled. It was a direct order."

"And you're going to let that stand between you and what might be one of the most amazing afternoons of hockey in your entire life? That's no way to live, my friend."

Ahead of them, sparsely vegetated rolling hillsides shimmered under a brutal summer heat wave. O'Halloran squinted into the glare. "How long do you think the ice would even last?"

"I don't know," Anderson said. He counted on his fingers for a few seconds and mumbled under his breath before coming up with an answer. "About twelve minutes."

"Hardly seems worth it," O'Halloran said.

"Story of my life, pal. Story of my life."

Minutes melted away into a hazy afternoon, and the two young officers had almost begun to doze off when a deep voice boomed from above and behind them. "Break time, gentlemen?"

Both men scrambled to their feet and turned about-face

toward Lieutenant Commander Mahmud al-Khaled, the recently promoted second officer of the *Starship Lovell* and their S.C.E. team leader. The swarthy man looked immaculately put together and completely unfazed by the dry, sweltering heat that had settled over the New Boulder colony for the past several days.

O'Halloran spoke first, stammering all the way. "I—that is to say, we—we were working on the, um, on this, and we had a bit of trouble connecting the, uh, that, to the other, um—"

Al-Khaled asked Anderson, "Care to step in here?"

"I think what Ensign O'Halloran is trying to say, sir, is that this . . . thing . . . is really unbelievably heavy."

The lieutenant commander glanced at the device, then back at the two junior officers. "Of course it is, Anderson. That's why I told you to bring a couple of antigravs."

O'Halloran turned his head very slowly toward Anderson and whispered with genuine menace, "I am so going to kick your ass."

"I'd pay to see that," al-Khaled said with a smirk. "Later. I want this filtration unit running by 1800. Both of you double-time it back to camp, get that load-lifter, bring it back here, and get this done. As in *immediately.* Dismissed."

"Aye, sir," O'Halloran said with a nod. He grabbed Anderson's sleeve and pulled him along as he began jogging back toward camp, where the rest of the S.C.E. team's equipment was stored. For once, Anderson cooperated and jogged along.

The heat was merciless, and the fact that they had been ordered to jog back to camp made it seem even more brutal.

"Filtration unit," Anderson said, with a glibness that O'Halloran had always envied. "At least now we know what it is."

Between huffing breaths, O'Halloran gasped out, "I'll get you for this."

"Sure you will," Anderson said.

"I hate you," O'Halloran said.

Anderson took a deep breath while running, let it out slowly, and smiled at the sky. "Lovely day."

"Why does nothing bother you?"

As if perplexed by the question, Anderson replied, "Why should it?"

"Must be nice to be a sociopath," O'Halloran said.

"It has its moments," Anderson said. "So, seeing as we're running all the way back to camp—"

"No," O'Halloran said preemptively.

"—and we've already got all the refrigeration coolant—"

"No," he insisted again.

"Don't you want to teach the natives how to play hockey?"

Venting his irritation, O'Halloran snapped, "There are no natives here, you moron. This is a colony. These are colonists."

"See?" Anderson shot back. "This is why you never have any fun. You turn everything into a semantic argument."

"Those antigravs better be fully charged," O'Halloran grumbled.

His sarcasm still sharp, Anderson asked, "Yeah? Why?"

" 'Cause after we hook up the filtration unit, I'm gonna use 'em to haul your body out to the desert."

Lieutenant Commander Mahmud al-Khaled walked between the rows of prefab colony structures and tried to tell himself that the help he and his team were providing to the colonists of New Boulder made up for the danger that he wasn't telling them about.

All the buildings on this dusty main street looked alike. Built from identical kits and powered by a common generator, the drab gray boxes had been arranged in neat, orderly rows. *Anything for the illusion of order coming to chaos*, al-Khaled figured. Each of the shelters was numbered, with three leading digits to indicate the closest numbered cross-street and two more digits after a hyphen indicating the lot number. A few industrious souls had taken the added measure of hanging makeshift signs in front of their doors, announcing their trade: Hardware. Dentist. Plumbing. Mechanic.

The colony had grown quickly. Despite the generally arid equatorial climate on Gamma Tauri IV, its soil was quite rich;

with proper irrigation it held substantial promise as an agricultural resource. As an engineer, al-Khaled knew the value of dilithium crystals, but he also appreciated that sometimes people needed fruit, grain, or vegetables even more than another load of crystals to run a warp drive.

He reached back and palmed a sheen of sweat from the nape of his neck. It felt strange to him that it was so bare; he had been accustomed to wearing his hair longer and leaving it slightly unkempt, but the climate on Gamma Tauri IV had made the shorter, regulation-recommended hairstyle suddenly appealing. Heat normally didn't bother him very much; he suspected his Middle Eastern upbringing made him less sensitive to high temperatures.

It was a hazy day, and the moment he'd stepped out of his climate-controlled temporary shelter on the outskirts of the colony, the scorching summer air had struck him like a blowtorch. *It still beats being cooped up on the ship,* he decided. Even though he had come to think of the *Lovell* as his home, he enjoyed spending time planetside once in a while.

He turned a corner and continued off the colony's official street grid to a large building set slightly apart from the others: his team's local operations center. Except for the red pennant of the United Federation of Planets that was painted on the structure's façade and the Starfleet Corps of Engineers logo emblazoned on the door, it looked like any other prefab shelter erected by the colonists. It was surrounded by a haphazard collection of equipment: antigravs, four-wheeled and six-wheeled all-terrain vehicles for scouting the countryside, seismological and meteorological sensor gear, excavation vehicles, tool sheds packed with construction and drilling equipment, and a shuttlecraft for long-range recon.

As he approached the entrance, a deep *thunk* from inside the doorframe signaled the release of the door's magnetic locks. The portal slid aside with a soft hiss, and a low chatter of voices, some belonging to people inside the room, others being received over comms, became audible. Al-Khaled stepped inside. The door closed behind him.

The main room beyond the door was close and cluttered. Three rows of a dozen tables were pressed end to end, with an engineer or other specialist working on either side of each one. Every table was covered with maps of Gamma Tauri IV's sole landmass—an irregular crescent that stretched nearly two-thirds of the circumference of the globe, reached from subarctic to subantarctic latitudes, and occupied more than thirty-three percent of the planet's total surface area. Overlying these topographical renderings were various scans and survey results: subsurface water reservoirs, mineral resources, projected weather patterns, plans for expanded civil infrastructure emanating from the New Boulder colony. It was a massive effort to turn this world, which had been unoccupied by sentient life just three years ago, into a self-sufficient civilization that could eventually help feed others.

Moving through the packed room toward a nondescript door at its far end, al-Khaled saw his second-in-command of the S.C.E. team, Lieutenant Kurt Davis, moving with particular haste to intercept him. Davis's shaved head reflected the overhead lights, which cast harsh glares in the dimly lit, windowless workspace. His path and al-Khaled's intersected at the end of a row of tables. "Sir," Davis said, "Captain Okagawa is trying to reach you. He says he has news from Vanguard."

"I don't suppose he told you what the news was."

As he expected, Davis shook his head. "No. But it didn't sound good."

"It never is," al-Khaled replied. "Thanks, Kurt."

As al-Khaled began to step past him on his way to the unmarked door, Davis said, "Sir, I'd like permission to return to the *Lovell*."

The S.C.E. team leader turned back to face his second with a knowing grin. "Afraid your engine room won't be safe in Luciano's hands?"

"Not at all," Davis said. "Margaux knows if I get it back any different than I left it, she'll be floating home. I just want to go back because . . . well, I have nothing to do here." Gesturing at the roomful of specialists, he continued, "These people all know what they're doing, Mahmud. They don't need a babysitter. And besides, I'm a propulsion specialist; my skills aren't exactly in demand down here."

Al-Khaled sighed. Davis's request was reasonable, but he was reluctant to grant it. With his own attention consumed by the S.C.E.'s other, clandestine mission to Gamma Tauri IV, he had been unable to devote the time necessary for supervising the colony-support efforts; he had been relieved to know that Davis was filling that role while he had been occupied elsewhere. There was no way to explain the situation to Davis, however, without breaching the mission's security protocols.

"All right," al-Khaled said finally. "Finish your shift, then you can beam back up to the *Lovell*. I'll have Ghrex take over as beta-shift supervisor. But if there's an emergency, I might need you back on the double. Understood?"

"Perfectly," Davis said. "Thank you, sir."

"You're welcome."

Davis acknowledged the end of the conversation with a nod, then stepped away to continue moving through the room and making spot checks of the other specialists' work. Al-Khaled walked to a plain, dark gray door at the back of the room, endured a brief biometric identification scan of his left retina, and stepped through as the portal opened.

He descended a narrow double switchback of stairs to a much smaller command center. Though it looked spare and utilitarian, it was concealed by some of Starfleet's newest sensor-blocking materials and was equipped with its most advanced computers and sensor technology. The wall opposite the stairs was actually a massive display screen, which provided most of the pale blue light that filled the room. Facing it were eighteen people seated at two short rows of workstations, set one behind the other on raised tiers. Another map of Gamma Tauri IV was displayed on the wall screen; it was marked with a complex assortment of grid lines, color codes, symbols, and statistics.

Lieutenant T'Laen sat in the middle seat of the rear row of workstations, patiently sifting through scads of data on her monitor. Al-Khaled approached the Vulcan cautiously and stood behind her while waiting for her to pause in her work. Several seconds later she stopped and turned her chair toward him. "May I be of service, sir?"

"Do you have anything to report before I contact Captain Okagawa?" al-Khaled asked. He eschewed preambles or niceties when talking with T'Laen, who had no patience for inefficient communication styles.

Highlighting an area of the map on the main viewscreen, T'Laen replied, "We have completed our analysis of grids 2115 south through 2119 south. No contacts and no sign of ambient radiation. However, a biological survey team in grid 3642 north has confirmed the presence of a type-V life reading."

"Thank you, Lieutenant." The news quickened al-Khaled's pulse. A type-V life reading was the Operation Vanguard code for detection of the Taurus meta-genome, an incredibly complex genetic artifact that was composed of hundreds of millions of unique chromosomes linked by a series of common chemical markers, which Federation scientists currently speculated might act as a kind of checksum for the eventual recombination of all its various strands. So far, unique variants of the meta-genome had been found on such far-flung worlds as Ravanar IV and Erilon—and now Gamma Tauri IV. Though it wasn't what they had been sent here to find, it was a good sign that they were looking in the right place. So far, both of the ancient artifacts that had been uncovered by Starfleet explorers had been on worlds where the meta-genome had been found. Though it was too soon to be certain that the meta-genome and the artifacts would always be discovered in tandem, the correlation between their discoveries was enough to encourage al-Khaled.

Starfleet's attention had been drawn to Gamma Tauri IV by its most recent discoveries regarding alien technology captured on Erilon and by continuing research of the Erilon artifact itself. Building upon the work al-Khaled's team had done a couple of years earlier, during the construction of Starbase 47, a team on Vanguard had succeeded in creating a less powerful but more focused facsimile of the alien "carrier wave" that had been transmitted from the Jinoteur system and had interfered with many of the station's onboard systems. Hypothesizing a link among the carrier waves, the artifacts, and the alien entities that the *Endeavour* crew had tangled with in a handful of bloody encounters on Erilon, Xiong's team on Vanguard had begun sending pulses of the synthesized carrier wave toward a number of planets that fit their search profiles. Something about the response received from Gamma Tauri IV had moved it to the top of Xiong's list of exploration targets. Commodore Reyes had wasted no time detailing the *Lovell* and its team to the colony planet to assist in developing the settlement for the benefit of its residents and the Federation as a whole, but they had kept secret their ongoing search for another, possibly hidden alien artifact on the planet's surface.

Al-Khaled left T'Laen and walked into his office. The door hissed shut behind him. As he settled into his chair, he pressed a button on the desktop and opened a secure channel to the *Lovell*, which had been in orbit for the past four weeks, fabricating material and components that were then beamed or flown down to the planet's surface. The past week had been spent creating pipes for an irrigation system. *Must be a thrill a minute for the folks shipside,* al-Khaled mused with a grin.

His desktop viewscreen glowed to life inside its bulky gray metallic shell. The face of Captain Daniel Okagawa appeared. From the few background details visible on the tiny screen, al-Khaled surmised that the captain was in his private quarters aboard the ship. "Good afternoon, Captain," al-Khaled said. "Davis tells me you have news from Vanguard."

"Unfortunately, yes," Okagawa said. *"The word from the colonial admin office is that New Boulder's going indie."*

"Are you kidding? They refused protectorate status?"

"*Afraid so,*" Okagawa said. "*I don't have to tell you, this makes things a bit trickier.*"

As soon as al-Khaled could unclench his jaw, he asked, "Are they planning on kicking us out?"

"*Don't know yet,*" the captain said. "*I talked to Miller. He says the new boss doesn't sound like one of our bigger fans.*"

After taking a few seconds to consider the ramifications of the captain's news, al-Khaled said, "We've built a pretty good working relationship with the colonists, so I don't think we need to worry about any bad blood. After all, we're not really asking them for anything."

"*All true,*" Okagawa acknowledged.

"My only real concern," al-Khaled said, "is what happens when word gets out that this isn't a Federation colony."

Okagawa sighed. "*Let's deal with one disaster at a time, shall we? The new colony president is still on Vanguard while her ship refuels and takes on new passengers, but she'll probably be here inside of a week. We need to focus on making a good first impression and not ticking her off.*"

Al-Khaled nodded. "Okay, I can do that."

"*Two things you ought to know,*" Okagawa said. "*First, she's an esper—so watch what you think when she's around.*"

That provoked a dismayed groan from al-Khaled. "What else?"

"*Her name's Jeanne Vinueza,*" the captain said, then added in a sepulchral tone, "*and she's Commodore Reyes's ex-wife.*"

A wince and a frown. "Permission to resign?"

"*Denied,*" Okagawa said. "*And heaven have mercy on us all.*"

3

A few dozen strong *Kollotaan* was all the Wanderer had sought; now she had them. Bound to the nodes of the First Conduit, these had proved both strong enough to withstand the terrible stresses of amplifying the voice of the Shedai and tractable enough to do so without struggling to the point of death. More than a hundred of their kith had perished as the Wanderer refined her trials, and many dozens more had been returned wounded and broken to the Conduit's core, to be tended by the legion of the untested.

The Wanderer increased the power flowing into the Conduit. Eldritch fires surged inside the core, and its Song pitched higher and brighter, drowning out the panicked din of the *Kollotaan*. She projected her thoughts into the burning prison.

Unify, she commanded. **One Song. One Voice.**

Like a chorus yielding to the will of a conductor, the *Kollotaan* tuned themselves to the Song of the First Conduit, blending together into harmony. Some of them spoke in tones deep and resonant, others in pitches bright and piercing. Together they captured its eerie majesty and projected it into the void.

Its ineffable beauty permeated the Wanderer's being, and for a moment it made the agony of physical existence almost bearable, almost worthwhile.

It was time. She spoke.

Awaken.

The imperative resounded and swelled within the First Conduit, and the power of the command trembled the foundations of the First World. The Wanderer's directive left the Conduit, amplified by the *Kollotaan*.

Quantum frequencies vibrated in sympathy throughout the vast expanse of space as ancient Conduits stirred to life, their fires reignited by her urgent call. The Wanderer felt them pulse and respond in kind, echoing her summons into the endless dark, answering her invitation to return to the almighty embrace of the Shedai.

Awaken.

Light-years away, one consciousness stirred, then another. Crimson hues of anger sounded like brassy crashes of noise, disrupting the harmony of the Song.

It is not time, protested one. Raged another, **Why do you rouse me?** Violet waves of defiance surged back across cold, unfathomable distances. **Be silent. . . . Go back to the darkness.**

The Wanderer added the blinding whiteness of authority to her commandment and adjured the others, **Rise . . . and return.**

Resistance to her charge ran deep. None wished to endure the tribulations of the material realm again so soon after succumbing to oblivion. **An hour of trial is upon us,** the Wanderer warned. **Our legacy is imperiled. Awaken and come home.**

On a pelagic orb circling an unremarkable yellow star, deep below the shroud of its ocean primeval, a massive coral reef shrugged and broke free of the seabed. Creeping armies of bio-luminescent bottom-feeders skittered away, retreating into crevasses and trenches. Schools of fish wheeled and turned and fled into the refracted shadows. The coral shattered and fell apart, dissipating into a dusty cloud rent by swift thermal currents. Free of physical bonds, the Herald shifted from a solid state to a fluid one and propelled himself by will alone through the dense medium of the sea. The Song of the Conduit pealed brightly in his thoughts, undistorted by the watery haven he had chosen for his aeons-long slumber.

The summons was like a pulse, a life force, a beacon pulling him forward. The briny depths foamed and boiled at his passage, molecular bonds excited almost to breaking by the energy of his essence coursing unshielded toward his destination. Then the Conduit was before him, its obsidian glory revealed for the first time in countless millennia. Sediment and barnacles and coral all had been blasted away, pulverized by its sudden resurgence of vital power.

Rise, came the behest of the Wanderer. **And return.**

The Herald envisioned the First World and projected his essence into the Conduit for the instantaneous journey home.

Our legacy is imperiled.

The Avenger stirred with furious anger, her wrath inflamed. *The Wanderer would not speak such words lightly,* she knew. *Nor would she rouse us without cause. War is upon us.*

Gathering her strength to break free of this world's womb of fire was an arduous task. Secreted within its nickel-iron core, she had remained beyond the reach of all but the most omnipotent noncorporeal beings, none of whom had proved so rash as to disrupt her deathlike repose. Now she shaped herself into a subtle blade of excited particles and sliced her way upward.

The fluid outer core of the planet was relatively rich with light elements, such as sulfur and oxygen, which she penetrated with ease. Soon it thickened, impeding her ascent; she began her relentless drilling climb through the lower mantle of oxidized iron and silicate perovskite. Its resistance was considerable, but her impetus was greater. She punched through into the plastic magmas of the upper mantle, churning them with her rapid passage until at last she sped toward the crust and burst through, to the freedom of the surface.

Like a colossus of living smoke, she strode the face of this primitive world while plumes of magma jetted skyward behind her, laying waste to the landscape and plunging millions of helpless *Telinaruul* into blind flights of panic. Their cities collapsed beneath the tremor of tectonic shifts provoked by her rising. One after another they were swallowed in surges of lava, from scores of volcanoes spurred by the heat she had imparted to the upper mantle.

Molten rock and sulfurous plumes blanketed the planet as the Avenger moved openly over its landmasses and seas, the air alive with the lamentations of billions of *Telinaruul* who prayed to her for mercy, having taken her for the deity of apocalypse. She ignored their desperate petitions and cleaved the face of a mountain to reveal the Conduit that she had hidden there aeons earlier, before she had buried herself in the heart of this world, for a sleep that had been intended to last longer than any known biological species had ever lived.

Awaken and come home, implored the Wanderer.

Receive me, replied the Avenger. **I return.**

Individuals came at first, then duos and trios. With supreme patience, the Wanderer watched and waited and periodically repeated her adjuration: **Awaken and return**.

Shapes came alive and congregated as the returning Shedai took avatars for the Colloquium. Some animated tendrils of snaking energy, others drifted as flashing clouds, a few chose to emulate the corporeal forms worn by their ancestors.

The Herald had been the first to return, and he had added his own voice to the Wanderer's. Then had come the Sage, he who embodied the living memory of the Shedai, the sum of its wisdom. In tandem the Adjudicator and the Warden had emerged from the Conduit, each choosing shells exotic and complex. The First World turned and shuddered under the renewed power of the Shedai Colloquium, and as one day-moment passed into another their numbers swelled with the ranks of the Nameless, they who are Shedai. At last the one known as the Maker revealed herself, and upon her proclamation a census was taken.

The Wanderer did not need to listen as the count ensued. She knew that when the names of the gathered were known, one of their august number would be found absent.

Ever insolent, she brooded. Singling him out in her thoughts, she cast her voice once more to the empty reaches, seeking him out. **Return.**

• • •

Alone on an airless moon under the cold grace of starlight, the Shedai Apostate lay mingled with the regolith, his essence one with the fine powder of meteorites long ago turned to dust.

The Wanderer's voice called out, no longer a general appeal as before but a targeted imperative meant expressly for him. He did not dignify her entreaty with a reply. The aeons of silence had suited him well, and when, not so long ago, the first stuttered Songs of Conduits had drawn his attention, he had hoped that such disruptions were only the fleeting product of the artifacts' destruction, perhaps by an aggressive intelligence or some natural calamity. But soon the Song had become more frequent, more focused, and he had realized that the sleepers were rousing. *Just as I had warned them,* he reflected. *Rest is not for ones such as us. We should have embraced eternity, not tried to cheat it.*

Unlike the others, the Apostate had not slept these many aeons. Sequestered on the lifeless satellite of a barren planet, he had enjoyed a measure of privacy and peace that had been denied to him in all the ages before then. To be summoned at the whim of one such as the Wanderer galled him. *I am second only to the Maker,* he fumed. *Who is she to command me?*

The Colloquium gathers, came the Wanderer's thought-pulse. **The others are risen. Hie unto us. The Maker commands it.**

Indignation blackened the Apostate's thoughts. Never had the Colloquium heeded his counsel; there was no reason to expect that would change. His role as a voice of reason was ever vilified, his partisans permanently consigned to a vocal minority. Attempts to guide or ameliorate the Colloquium's harshest voices were inevitably futile. He resented being forced to endorse such a charade with his presence.

The Maker commands it.

Denying the summons was not an option. If he refused, the Colloquium would be forced to assail his thoughts until he relented. The longer he refused them, the more resentful the Maker would become and the longer this travesty would endure.

He propelled himself with an act of will through the vacuum, to the artifact that would grant him passage to a home and a legacy he had long ago renounced. Undisturbed for so long, the Conduit dominated the moonscape, its brilliantly reflective obsidian surface standing in stark contrast to the blanched gray vista of pockmarked desolation.

Desist, he commanded the Wanderer. **Prepare for my coming.**

Blinding flashes of thought-color racked Nezrene [The Emerald]. Unlike the fleeting touches of the Lattice, where minds might meet and share for a brief time before retreating into privacy, the surges of the Conduit were constant and overwhelming. It was like drowning in a sea of thoughts too great to comprehend.

Against her will, she found herself echoing and tuning the voice of another Shedai, from a distant node in a thought-space network far more complicated and robust than anything her own people had ever contemplated.

Prepare for my coming, said the voice. Its defining qualities were arrogance and power, with undertones of resentment and melancholy. As soon as the message was relayed, the radiant auras of the beings around her and the rest of the *Lanz't Tholis*'s crew shifted noticeably, taking on hues of fear and anticipation. Then a tide of malevolent consciousness passed through her, cold and terrible.

The Song of the Conduit faded then, and the luminous beings began to confer among themselves. Forcing herself to dim her troubled thought-colors from crimson to a muted violet, Nezrene reached out to the minds of her shipmates. *Commune with me,* she invited them. The ones trapped in the core of the machine did not answer her. They writhed in the searing darkness, bereft of even the enemy's voice. Those bonded to other nodes of the Conduit, however, replied with the kind of intimacy that normally came only during touch-communion or a private SubLink.

Waves of incandescent scarlet coursed along the mind-line of Tozskene [The Gold]. *They are Shedai.*

The Voice speaks, chimed Yirikene [The Azure]. *It speaks and compels us.*

We must resist it, counseled Nezrene. *We must break free.*

Dismay coruscated through the others' mind-lines. Destrene [The Gray] protested, *They disintegrated the commander and the subcommander. If we fight, they will destroy us as well.*

I am not content to remain a prisoner, Nezrene countered. She felt out of place assuming a leadership role among her shipmates. Before the *Lanz't Tholis* had been ensnared and its crew forcibly abducted into slavery, she had been just one of several tactical specialists. Though she was one of the more experienced members of the crew, she was merely one of the warrior caste and certainly was not worthy to assume the duties of one of its leaders. Adopting such a posture during a crisis of this magnitude felt like arrogant presumption to her, despite the obvious necessity of her doing so.

Tozskene, she instructed, *see if this shell that holds us will let you look into orbit; try to find the* Lanz't Tholis. *Destrene, monitor the Shedai and warn us if they return to work the machine again. Yirikene, I want to know if we can use this machine to send our own signal back to Tholia.* Flooding her thought-colors with reassuring shades of indigo and dark green, she added, *We might die trying to break free, but I will not live as a slave to the Shedai.*

4

Ambassador Lugok paced liked a caged *targ* through long, red slashes of dusk light that fell across the stone floor in front of Councillor Indizar's desk. "How long will it take for Sturka to come to his senses?" he wondered aloud. "Every day I'm on Qo'noS is a day wasted."

His hostess—the acting head of Imperial Intelligence, one of the more senior members of the Klingon High Council, and a noted ally of Chancellor Sturka and his chief advisor, Councillor Gorkon—tracked his perambulations with a dispassionate stare. "The Tholians provoked us," she said. "You know that better than anyone. Or have you lost your taste for battle, Lugok?"

"Meh," Lugok growled. "I don't care if Sturka wants to blunder into war with the Tholians. Recalling me and my delegation from the Federation starbase was a mistake."

Indizar cast a bemused grimace at him. "It hardly seems to have impeded your dialogue with the Chelon. You seem to have exchanged more words with him since leaving the station than you ever did while serving aboard it. If anything, distance has made you more productive."

Lugok's bark of laughter was laced with derision. "I'd hardly call encrypted back-channel communiqués through third parties *productive*. Real communication requires presence—the chance to look one's foe in the eye. My efforts are little more than a stopgap, a way to salvage what little progress we'd actually made."

The councillor lifted a polished stone carafe of bloodwine and refilled her onyx goblet as well as Lugok's. He lifted his goblet and downed a generous mouthful of the tart alcoholic beverage. Indizar watched him with a pointed stare. "Tell me, Lugok, are you under the delusion that I invited you here so that you could regale me with your litany of complaints?" She picked up her goblet and took a sip. "It's not as if diplomacy was my paramount reason for sending you to Vanguard."

He looked out the window and across the First City toward the Great Hall, took a deep breath, and swallowed a few expletives. All his hard-won status as a member of the Diplomatic Corps meant nothing to Indizar. *To her, I am just another field agent for Imperial Intelligence—and not a particularly valuable one.* He turned back to face her cool and level stare. "I presume this is about Lurqal."

Indizar leaned back in her chair. "In the brief time since your official delegation left Vanguard, the quality and quantity of usable intelligence she's provided have declined sharply. The last truly original piece of information she gave us was the tip about the Jinoteur system, but that was nearly two months ago. Since then her reports of ship movements have lagged behind intelligence we've obtained for ourselves. Tell me, why does an agent trained to operate self-sufficiently for years at a time suddenly become complacent when mere cutouts such as yourself and that *ha'DIbah* Turag are removed from the equation?" The tenor of her query gave Lugok the distinct impression that he was being held to blame.

"There could be many reasons, Councillor," he answered. "With decreased diplomatic activity aboard the station, her direct partici—"

"According to Turag," Indizar said, "Lurqal spends a great deal of time with the station's Vulcan intelligence officer. Have you considered the possibility that Lurqal might have been compromised?"

Lugok spat out his mouthful of bloodwine in contempt. "I read Turag's report. It's pure fantasy. He's never even *seen* Lurqal and the Vulcan together."

Nodding, the slender politician said, "I noticed that omission, but his circumstantial evidence is intriguing, to say the least. . . . Putting aside his imagination, how do you account for Lurqal's increasingly poor performance?"

With great reluctance, Lugok admitted, "I can't."

"Then we have a serious problem," Indizar said as she rose from her chair and circled the desk toward Lugok. "After the Palgrenax disaster, we can't afford any more mistakes in the Gonmog Sector." As she leaned close to Lugok, the musk of her perfume aroused his animal appetites. "I'm trusting you to correct Lurqal's performance. The outrider *Sagittarius* just returned to Vanguard, recalled from a great distance. I suspect it's being sent to Jinoteur. Make it clear to Lurqal that I want to know when it's going to ship out. I don't intend to let the Federation succeed where we have failed." The councillor backed off and returned to her seat behind her desk. "Dismissed, Lugok."

The ambassador nodded his farewell, took two steps backward from Indizar's desk, then turned on his heel and exited her office. As he walked to a turbolift, Indizar's offhand comment about the Palgrenax disaster continued to bother him. Her mention of that ill-fated planet had reminded Lugok of the risks that came with trying to seize control of the Gonmog Sector. Whatever had drawn the Empire's interest to that world, it had been guarded by something extremely powerful and deadly—a force that had wiped out a Klingon occupation army with ease before annihilating the planet itself. Though Lugok was not yet privy to all the details of what the Empire's scientific advance teams had discovered on Palgrenax, he was certain that it was connected to the Federation's unusually aggressive expansion into the region. *Whatever they found, they don't want us to have it,* he concluded. *That's reason enough to find it, at any cost.*

After a few minutes of walking to and riding in turbolifts, he returned to the lobby of the huge government administrative complex. Turag was waiting for him. The burly young warrior served publicly as Lugok's bodyguard, but like himself Turag was a covert operative of Imperial Intelligence. As Lugok marched past him on his way to the front entrance of the building, the younger Klingon fell into step beside him. Together they shoved their way through a throng of *QuchHa'*, descendants of a Klingon offshoot race whose ancestors had been mutated by an unusual genetic affliction more than a generation earlier. Frailer and smooth-headed like the humans, the *QuchHa'* were the Empire's war fodder, its most expendable class. Privileged scions such as Lugok abused them with impunity.

Turag smirked. "Did she say anything interesting?"

"Does she ever?" Lugok replied. He hated walking next to Turag, because the warrior's powerful physique only reminded Lugok of his own slowly expanding girth.

Keeping his voice down to avoid drawing attention, Turag asked, "So . . . what does she want from us now?"

"Lurqal's slipping," Lugok said, passing through the security checkpoint on his way outside. Large archways scanned him and Turag as they passed through them. Lugok nodded to the phalanx of guards lined up along one side of the checkpoint. None of them returned the gesture.

Outside, the heat and humidity were as thick and comforting as the womb. Streets were packed from corner to corner with bustling bodies, and a frantic buzz of hover-vehicle traffic filled the sky overhead. From several avenues away, Lugok caught the aroma of fresh *gagh* and *rokeg* blood pie. *Time for supper,* he decided, and quickened his stride. Turag stayed with him.

"Did Indizar read my report?" the bodyguard asked.

After a grunt of acknowledgment, Lugok said, "She puts more stock in it than I do, but she's far from convinced."

"What is our next plan of attack?"

Lugok turned right, toward the tantalizing smell of well-spiced *gagh*. "Indizar thinks Starfleet is sending its scout ship *Sagittarius* to Jinoteur, and she wants to know when. Relay that request to Lurqal. And make her understand that we won't tolerate any more mistakes."

Atop the roof of the Great Hall, protected by an invisible force field over the seat of the Klingon government, Councillor Indizar stood next to Councillor Gorkon and watched Chancellor Sturka stare into the setting sun.

"How much does Lugok know?" asked Sturka.

Indizar glanced at Gorkon, then replied, "Less than he thinks he does, but perhaps still more than he should."

Sturka issued a low growl of understanding. "Has Captain Kutal been debriefed about this morning's Jinoteur debacle?"

"Thoroughly," Gorkon replied. "His battle group met with overwhelming force when they entered the system. It's actually quite remarkable that the *Zin'za* escaped with only sixty-five-percent casualties." Gorkon tactfully omitted any mention of the fact that, while Kutal's ship had barely escaped the system, its three heavy-cruiser escorts had not been so fortunate. Also absent from his remarks was the fact that this was the second failed expedition to the Jinoteur system since its peculiar properties had first been reported by their spy on Vanguard.

"What of the Tholian vessel detected in the system?" Sturka said. "Did it participate in the attack on our ships?"

"No, my lord," Gorkon answered. "Captain Kutal reports that the ship was deserted—but he also said it was undamaged."

The chancellor gazed out, past the jagged rooftops of the First City, toward the *qIj'bIQ,* the dark river that cut like a wound through its center. Though the air was growing cooler with the approach of night, waves of heat continued to rise from the stone architecture of the Great Hall's roof. Overhead, the sky was hidden behind a ragged blanket of clouds. Along the dark band of the horizon, only the brightest stars were faintly visible through narrow rents in the sky.

"Most curious," Sturka said at last. "Indizar, did you say

that your people found something in the *Zin'za*'s sensor logs? Something from its mission to Palgrenax?"

"Yes, my lord," she said. "Immediately prior to that planet's self-immolation, the *Zin'za* detected a number of complex signals moving between various locations under the planet's surface—the same locations where it had detected extreme power spikes. Dr. Grinpa tells me that the data-traffic pattern was consistent with a coordinated weapons system and that it bears many similarities to Tholian signal encryptions—though it was many orders of magnitude more complex."

That spiel inspired Sturka to actually turn away from the cityscape and face her. "Interesting," he said. Then he looked at Gorkon. "Could the Tholians have been using the Gonmog Sector to develop a secret weapons program?" Directing the second half of his comment to both of them, he continued, "It would explain why they've harassed our ships and tried to force us from the sector."

Indizar shook her head. "I don't think so, Chancellor. All of Dr. Terath's reports about the artifacts and their environs suggest that they are hundreds of thousands of cycles old, or possibly even more ancient. And whatever attacked Governor Morqla and his troops on Palgrenax, it was not a Tholian."

"I would have to agree with Councillor Indizar, my lord," Gorkon said. "The Palgrenax attack on the *Zin'za* was more powerful and sophisticated than anything the Tholians can currently muster. However, their actions suggest they have knowledge of the weapons' potential, and they mean to deny us the opportunity to possess or investigate it."

Sturka walked slowly in a wide arc, gradually circling behind the two councillors as he ruminated aloud. "That would explain the Tholians' attack on the Federation starship *Bombay*. Gorkon, where did that happen?"

"Ravanar IV," Gorkon answered.

Nodding, the chancellor continued, "Yes, yes. And more recently, their battle cruiser, the *Endeavour*—it came back to the starbase with heavy damage."

"From Erilon," Indizar interjected.

The chancellor scratched pensively at his chin. "And what do both those planets have in common right now?"

"Permanent Starfleet ground installations," Gorkon said.

That drew a grin and a growl from the grizzled Klingon leader. "Not a coincidence, I'm sure. . . . Where is Starfleet's newest ground installation in the Gonmog Sector?"

"Ge'hoQ," Indizar said. "They call it Gamma Tauri IV."

As he paced back in front of Indizar and Gorkon, Sturka asked, "What do we know about that planet?"

"Qo'noS-class, though somewhat more arid. The Federation colonists are setting it up as an agricultural colony."

A stiff breeze fluttered Sturka's robe around him as he walked. "How big a presence does Starfleet have there?"

"Much larger than necessary," Indizar said, pleased to see that the chancellor's deductive powers remained as keen as ever. "It's worth noting that the Federation's banner won't be flying over that world. There have long been rumors of distrust of Starfleet among the colonists; my sources have confirmed that they refused protectorate status from the Federation."

"Good," Sturka said. He eyed Indizar. "How soon can we put our own people on the surface?"

"As soon as you give the order, my lord," she said. "A team of scientists and a group of 'farmers' are standing by aboard a transport being escorted by the cruiser *Che'leth*. They can reach Ge'hoQ in a few hours."

"Send them now," Sturka said to her. "As for Captain Kutal, let's send him some new cruiser escorts and put him back in the hunt. I want the *Zin'za* to make another sortie to Jinoteur."

"Yes, my lord," Indizar said. A cool breeze wafted across the rooftop from the northeast. It chilled her as it passed by. "The *Zin'za* is still in port making major repairs, but I'll have it ship out as soon as possible."

Gorkon glanced at her. "Mask its deployment orders well. It

would be best if Councillor Duras and his allies remained as uninformed about the Gonmog campaign as possible."

"That was already my assumption," she assured him.

Sturka halted his pacing in front of Indizar. "Have we received any new intelligence about Jinoteur from our agent on the starbase?"

Exhaling an angry sigh through her nostrils, the rankled councillor replied, "No, my lord. Since the recall of our diplomatic team, her communications have become less frequent and less precise. Corrective steps are being taken."

"See that they are," Sturka said. "Starfleet plans to send its outrider to Jinoteur, I'm certain of it. I want to know the moment the *Sagittarius* leaves port. When it gets to Jinoteur, I want its crew to find the *Zin'za* waiting for them."

Indizar nodded deferentially. "Yes, my lord. I've made Lugok aware of your wishes on this matter."

"I'm sure you have." The chancellor aimed a narrow-eyed sidelong glare at Gorkon. "You're thinking something, my old friend—I can see it in your eyes. Out with it."

A grim frown settled over Gorkon's stately features. "I battled Vanguard's commander a few times in the past, back when we were both starship captains. Considering the losses we have sustained in our expeditions to Jinoteur, I am forced to wonder whether Reyes deliberately leaked us the information about Jinoteur so that Starfleet could learn from our mistakes."

"If so," Sturka replied, "it would imply that our agent on Vanguard has been detected."

"Or compromised," Gorkon said. He and Sturka both looked at Indizar, as if to challenge her to rebut their suspicions.

Instead, she maintained her countenance of dispassionate calm and replied simply, "If either is true, she will die."

Hidden deep within the crushing fires of Tholia's deepest redoubt, the Ruling Conclave had gathered physically, something that had not been done in ages. Shielded from the psychic tides of anxiety that coursed through the Tholian Lattice, the elite members of the Political Castemoot reached out to one another and made contact with their faceted limbs. Each touch brought another mind-line into their telepathic circle of harmony.

Azrene [The Violet] offered her thoughts in troubled shades of crimson. *The Voice grows stronger, and still no word from the* Lanz't Tholis. *Reinforcements are in order.*

There can be no rescue effort, countered Radkene [The Sallow]. *Too many have we sacrificed in that place. No more.*

Strident flares of white conveyed the fury of Velrene [The Azure]. *The Voice must be silenced,* she insisted. *Sacrifice the* Lanz't Tholis *if we must, but it is past time for us to strike.*

Narskene [The Gold] tried to mask his fear in hues of calming indigo, but the rich scarlet of alarm betrayed his stoic words. *Mounting a larger expeditionary force to that place will only draw the attention of our enemies,* he opined.

May they all suffer the same fate as Palgrenax, interjected Eskrene [The Ruby], her words coruscating with antipathy and interspersed with fleeting images of the scattered, glowing debris of the Klingon-occupied world that had recently exploded.

Yazkene [The Emerald] darkened his mind-line with grim disapproval and conveyed his warning in dolorous chimes. *The Federation appears to be seeking out all that we have feared. The Klingons, not to be outdone, follow their lead. They must both be stopped.*

From Azrene and Narskene came scintillating pulses of alarm and objection. A flurry of images from the recent past flickered over Narskene's thought-facets, recapping dozens of abortive attacks on Klingon warships by Tholian vessels. Then, for emphasis, he added several dispiriting reminders that of six Tholian ships that had launched an ambush on the Starfleet frigate *Bombay,* four had been destroyed before the enemy ship was finally overcome and detonated its self-destruct ordnance.

Though Narskene had been content to let the images speak for themselves, Azrene summarized his intentions with her own vermilion passion. *We are not capable of fighting a war against the Klingon Empire and the Federation at the same time,* she warned. *Even to consider it is to court our own destruction.*

Indignant, sickly colors blazed around the mind-line of Falstrene [The Gray]. *We cannot cede the Shedai Sector to them!*

Agreed, seconded Velrene. *It is not necessary to wage war for the entire sector. We need only deny them access to the source of the Voice.*

Low and steady came Radkene's reply. *There is no evidence that the Federation or the Klingons even know of the Voice, or its source. They see only the shells, not the essence.*

The Federation's people are far more clever than you give them credit for being, counseled Eskrene. *They have already learned too much. If left unchecked, they will unlock the secrets of the Voice. We must act before that happens. The Voice must be silenced, this time forever.*

Sharp, discordant tones of dismay echoed through their private mind-link, all of them emanating from Narskene. *We assault the Voice at our peril,* he cautioned. *Already we have lost one battle cruiser.* Ancient, terrifying fragments of vague, genetically encoded species memories blinked across his thought-facets. *Look to the past. Remember the price our kind paid for freedom. What if challenging the Voice brings it here to Tholia?*

Panic swelled for a moment among the members of the Ruling Conclave, only to be suppressed by the dark and dominating mind-line of Yazkene. *If the Shedai come to Tholia,* he declared, *we will give them a fight such as they have never known.*

Madness! protested Azrene in strident tones of violet.

Narskene tinted his thought-colors to match Azrene's, then

added to Yazkene, *Only a fool would risk the wrath of the Shedai! Their coming would herald our destruction.*

I would rather their wrath than their rule, Yazkene countered with incandescent pride. *Better to be annihilated than subjugated. Mark my words, Narskene: Our people will not wear that yoke again. They will kill to prevent it and die before they accept it. It is time to face the truth: This is war.*

5

There were no clouds in the night sky above New Boulder, but Ensign O'Halloran was nonetheless convinced that at any moment a bolt of lightning would slice down from the heavens to smite him and Ensign Anderson. "I can't believe I let you talk me into this," he said to his friend, who also happened to be the one person on Gamma Tauri IV he most wanted to strangle. "What are you trying to do, start a riot?"

"Would you relax?" Anderson wrinkled his nose at O'Halloran as if he'd suddenly detected an unpleasant odor. "This is going to be the best night of your life if you don't screw it up. More important, it's gonna be the best night of *my* life if you don't screw it up. So don't screw it up."

Visions of painful public death haunted O'Halloran's thoughts. He and Anderson were walking from the far edge of the settlement to a low-profile establishment somewhere in its center. Rumors of a party had lured Anderson in search of the basement bar, and, as usual, O'Halloran had somehow gotten dragged along. "This is a bad idea," he said as the streets around them grew darker and less trafficked. "Let's go back."

"Yeah, that's a great idea," Anderson said. "Another night sitting on a mound of dirt around a campfire with a bunch of engineers." He punched O'Halloran in the shoulder. "Are you nuts? This isn't just any party we're talking about, it's a *colony* party: girls a couple hundred light-years from home who haven't seen a new face in months. And you know what they say about colony girls—they're up for *anything*."

"Spare me the details," O'Halloran groused.

Anderson shook his head. "Suit yourself, *kemosabe*. But this is as good as it gets. This is the Garden of Eden, this is Mecca, this is—" He paused in mid-sentence, stopped walking, and looked up. All traces of humor and irony vanished from his expression. O'Halloran followed his line of sight.

A flaring orange pinpoint of light across the sky grew brighter as it descended. "Meteor?" O'Halloran wondered aloud. Anderson said nothing; he just watched the speck of fiery brilliance grow larger and brighter as it drew closer to the surface. In a single dramatic arc the object leveled its flight and cruised directly toward the New Boulder colony.

Within seconds it neared to within several kilometers, slowing as it went but still cruising at supersonic speed. It flew over the settlement and was kilometers gone before a deafening boom of displaced air rattled the entire colony. O'Halloran looked around and saw that the streets were no longer empty. People had piled out of residential shelters and workspaces to see what had caused the commotion.

He looked at Anderson. "Did you see what it was?"

"Yup," Anderson said.

Exasperated by his friend's dearth of details, he replied, "So? What was it?" After a few more seconds of watching Anderson stare grimly toward the vanishing engine glow of the retreating ship, O'Halloran snapped, "Dammit, Jeff, say something!"

Anderson sighed heavily and looked at him. "There goes the neighborhood."

The emergency signal on his communicator all but knocked al-Khaled out of his bunk. He fumbled to grab the device from the floor next to his cot and flipped it open. "Al-Khaled here."

"We've got company," said Captain Okagawa. *"Get to ops on the double."*

"On my way," al-Khaled answered, already halfway out the door. Falling asleep in his uniform, normally a symptom of his absentmindedness or fatigue, all at once seemed prescient. No sooner had he stepped outside than all of New Boulder was shaken by a thunderous roar from overhead.

Minutes later he scrambled out of the switchback staircase and into the underground bunker, still winded from his hundred-meter sprint from the officers' barracks to the operations center. "Someone talk to me," he demanded.

"Klingon D-5 cruiser in orbit, sir," answered Lieutenant Christopher Gabbert, the night-shift room boss. "Based on her power signature, we've identified her as the *I.K.S. Che'leth*." It was Gabbert's job to watch over all the other stations and coordinate all departments' responses to whatever crisis might present itself.

"What buzzed the colony?" al-Khaled asked, slightly distracted by the sweat dampening his uniform jersey.

Gabbert called up several screens of sensor readings and flight telemetry detailing the path of the ship that had flown over the settlement. "Klingon transport," he said. "Big enough to carry about three thousand people and a whole lotta gear." The bearded operations specialist added, "Looks like they set down about fifty kliks away, near the Cardalian Mountains."

"Dammit," al-Khaled muttered. "Didn't take them long, did it? They moved in as soon as they heard the colony refused protectorate status."

Nodding in agreement, Gabbert said, "They've probably been hanging out somewhere between here and the Al Nath system, waiting for a chance to move in."

"Get the *Lovell* on the horn," al-Khaled said. "Secure channel."

With a nod to the communications officer, Gabbert delegated the task. Seconds later, an active channel beeped on Gabbert's master console, and he flipped the switch to the open position. The image of Captain Okagawa appeared on the main screen.

"Captain," al-Khaled said. "Everything okay up there?"

"Yeah, we're just peachy," Okagawa said with naked sarcasm. *"I was thinking of having the captain of the* Che'leth *over for a few drinks. What do you think? Sound like a good idea?"*

Gabbert mumbled, "I could sure use a drink right now."

Ignoring the room boss, al-Khaled focused on assessing

the situation. "Is the *Che'leth* making any threatening moves against you? Has its captain hailed you?"

"Negative," Okagawa said. *"They made orbit and released their transport. They're holding position on the far side of the planet. Looks like their colony team is right in your backyard, though. Everything all right down there?"*

"A little shaken from their fly-by, but no real problems. Not yet, anyway."

The salt-and-pepper-haired CO's brow creased with concern. *"Do you have a contingency plan for continuing the search?"*

"Yes, sir, but it won't be easy," al-Khaled admitted. "Judging by how fast they moved in once the colonists opened the door, it's a good bet the Klingons know why we're here."

"Count on it," Okagawa said. *"They'll watch every move you make, and they'll assume you're doing the same to them."*

"Understood," al-Khaled said. It was going to be a battle of wits from this point forward. Both teams would be launching multiple feints, diversionary operations to throw the other off the trail of whatever real finds they might be seeking to make. Whichever side proved better at bluffing and following clues at the same time would gain the advantage. One thing that would work in the Klingons' favor, however, was that their "colonists" were likely imposters, just a superficial cover for their military and scientific mission on the planet; unburdened by the need to provide material support to a real, working colony, the Klingons would be free to devote all their time and resources to outflanking al-Khaled's group. That was a challenge al-Khaled was prepared to face, but another matter worried him. "Sir, what are we supposed to do if the Klingon Empire makes a formal claim to this colony? Without protectorate status—"

"I know, Mahmud," Okagawa said, looking markedly more fatigued by the mere asking of the question. *"Unless you or one of your people feels like starting a war with the Klingons, you have to stay neutral down there. Just keep doing your job and stay out of the Klingons' way."*

"That's fine in theory," al-Khaled said. "But if the Klingons come after New Boulder, my team won't sit it out."

A pained look deepened the frown lines on Okagawa's face. *"You don't have any choice, Mahmud. Unless the Klingons take a shot at uniformed Starfleet personnel, we can't interfere."*

"Not even if the colonists ask for help?"

Okagawa considered that for a moment. *"If they send an SOS, we can respond. But it has to be an official request for aid from the colony leadership. Anything short of that, and we have to stay out of it. That's an order. Clear?"*

As disappointed as he was concerned, al-Khaled answered simply, "Yes, Captain." After a breath, he asked, "Do you want to file the report with Vanguard, sir, or should I?"

The captain closed his eyes and massaged his forehead with his fingertips for a moment before he said, *"I'll do it. You've got a lot on your plate. . . . Besides, I* already *have a headache."*

Less than four minutes after receiving an urgent bulletin about the Klingons' landing on Gamma Tauri IV, Ambassador Jetanien stepped out of a turbolift into Starbase 47's voluminous and quietly busy operations center. The enormous Chelon diplomat moved swiftly across the main deck toward Commodore Reyes's office, his immaculate scarlet robes fluttering dramatically behind him as he went. He tried to control the nervous rapid clicking of his beaklike proboscis, but it refused to be still.

In one web-fingered manus he carried a data slate loaded with the key details of the Klingons' brazen action; in the other he held a hard copy of his unabashedly belligerent official rebuke of Jeanne Vinueza for inciting such an outcome.

As Jetanien passed the supervisor's deck, the station's first officer, Commander Jon Cooper, looked down at him from the circular elevated platform. For a moment the fortyish officer looked as if he were going to say something, but then he shook his head and turned his attention to his station on the hub, an octagonal bank of terminals and control panels that dominated the middle of the supervisor's deck.

No one seemed willing to get in Jetanien's way until he approached within five meters of Reyes's office door. Then the diminutive but unyielding shape of Yeoman Toby Greenfield appeared in front of him. The top of her head was level with the middle of his chest. Looking up with proud determination, she said, "The commodore is in a classified briefing."

"This cannot wait," Jetanien said. He tried to walk around her, but she sidestepped adroitly into his path.

"You'll have to be announced first, Your Excellency," she said, her voice polite but firm. "Commodore Reyes's orders."

"Young lady, I don't have—"

"My rank is lieutenant, junior grade," Greenfield said. "You can call me Lieutenant Greenfield. Or, if you prefer, you may also address me as Yeoman Greenfield."

Flaring with impatience and imperiousness, Jetanien was about to launch into a verbal riposte when he noticed that Greenfield's declaration had drawn the attention of nearly every Starfleet officer and crewman on the deck. He clutched his chattering beak shut a moment, inhaled, then exhaled and bowed his head as he remembered his manners. "Quite right, Lieutenant. My apologies. It will not happen again."

Tilting her head in a half-nod, she replied, "Apology accepted, Your Excellency. Shall I announce your visit?"

"Please do, Lieutenant."

He waited while Greenfield moved to her console, inserted a small Feinberger transceiver into her ear, and opened an intercom line to Reyes's office. She spoke in whispers, nodded to herself while listening to a response, then removed the small device from her ear. As she pressed a control to unlock the office door, she glanced at Jetanien. "The commodore will see you now, Mr. Ambassador."

"Thank you, Lieutenant," he said, moving in long strides toward the door, which slid open at his approach.

Inside the office, Commodore Reyes was seated behind his desk, reclining with his right foot crossed over his left knee. Lieutenant Commander T'Prynn stood in front of the desk, hands folded together behind her back. Both watched Jetanien as he hurried in. As soon as he heard the door close behind him, muting the sounds of the operations center, he said to them, "We have a problem. The Klingons—"

"Just landed a colony ship on Gamma Tauri IV," Reyes cut in. "We know. T'Prynn's been tracking them and their escort, the *Che'leth,* since they shipped out of Somraw five weeks ago."

"How considerate of you both to keep me so well informed," Jetanien said. "Since the Klingons do not share our objective of preventing hostilities in the Taurus Reach, I recommend that we withdraw all uniformed Starfleet personnel from Gamma Tauri IV immediately and—"

"Whoa!" Reyes bellowed. "One disaster at a time, Jetanien. T'Prynn got here first. You'll just have to take a number and wait your turn."

Only now did Jetanien notice that the display screen on the wall beside Reyes's desk showed an orbital chart of the Jinoteur system. His already profound sense of foreboding deepened. "Have the Klingons lost another ship at Jinoteur?"

"Three ships, actually," T'Prynn said. "The lead vessel escaped but suffered significant losses. However, that is the least notable detail of today's sensor logs."

She picked up a data slate from Reyes's desk and offered it to Jetanien. He reflexively reached forward to take it, then remembered that both his hands were full. Fumbling in a diagonal reach, he handed his data slate to her and then accepted hers. Reyes watched the transaction with droll amusement. "What, nothing for me?"

Jetanien handed him the letter. "This is for your ex-wife."

"I'm not sure that counts," Reyes said, tossing the folded pages casually onto his desk.

Reviewing the information on T'Prynn's data slate, Jetanien adopted a more professional tone. "Forgive the interruption, Commander. Please proceed."

"Our reconnaissance probes have detected a Tholian ship in

orbit above the fourth planet of the Jinoteur system," T'Prynn reported. "Based on previous sensor readings, we estimate that it reached the planet between 0300 and 0500 station time today. Shortly afterward, four Klingon battle cruisers attempted to join it in orbit. They were immediately fired upon by artillery concealed on the planet's three moons."

As Jetanien studied the details on the data slate, he was troubled by the news. During a heated round of negotiations seven weeks earlier, the Tholian ambassador, Sesrene, had intimated that his people feared the Taurus Reach, that they had for ages avoided it because of something they called *Shedai*. "*Of all places*," Sesrene had confided, "*this is where we are not to be.*" Even more telling, not only did the Tholians wish to leave the Taurus Reach unclaimed, but it seemed vitally important to them that no one else lay claim to it, either.

The pieces of this ancient puzzle had begun to come together for Jetanien. Starfleet discovered the meta-genome and an alien artifact on Ravanar IV, and the Tholians wiped out the planet; the Klingons moved aggressively to claim worlds in the Taurus Reach, and the Tholians retaliated by launching a campaign of sneak attacks on Klingon ships.

On every planet on which Starfleet had found an artifact like the one on Ravanar, it also had found the meta-genome. With those discoveries had come terrible reprisals, by a powerful adversary unlike any the Federation had ever encountered before. Merciless and brutal, the obsidian entity had proved itself willing to obliterate entire planets in order to protect its secrets. Though Jetanien as yet had no proof for his hypothesis, he was certain that whatever else this foe proved to be, it was the force that the Tholians called *Shedai*.

At the heart of the entire mystery lay the Jinoteur system. It had been the source of bizarre carrier wave signals that had disrupted Vanguard's systems during construction a year earlier. Now, having looked more closely at the system, Starfleet had discovered that its planets' orbital mechanics were unlike anything else ever recorded in nature. All evidence currently available suggested that if the Taurus Reach mystery had a focal point, the Jinoteur system was it.

And now a Tholian heavy cruiser was there.

Jetanien put down the data slate on Reyes's desk. "Most troubling," he said. "Covertly enlightening the Klingons about Jinoteur was a calculated risk. Their impulsive nature has spared us a great many casualties and provided us with valuable intelligence. But the presence of the Tholians is . . . unexpected." He made a few clicking noises with his beak while he pondered the matter. "Why would the Tholians, after making a point of their aversion to the Taurus Reach and the thing they call *Shedai,* send a starship to Jinoteur?"

Reyes replied, "Maybe for the same reason that they sent six ships to destroy the artifact on Ravanar IV."

T'Prynn cocked one eyebrow into a high arch. "Doubtful, sir," she said. "If the Tholians had attempted an attack on Jinoteur IV, we would have detected radiation from a planetary barrage. Furthermore, to neutralize all the planets and satellites in the system would require more firepower than one ship could carry. Lastly, considering the violent responses the Klingons have suffered when entering the Jinoteur system, a single Tholian vessel would seem to have little hope of waging a successful assault."

Reyes pressed two fingers against his left temple while he considered T'Prynn's reasoning. "Good points," he said. "So answer me this: If the Tholians aren't there for a fight, what *are* they doing there?"

"At present I find their motives opaque, sir," T'Prynn said. "We lack sufficient information about their link to the metagenome and the artifacts to make an informed hypothesis regarding their purpose in the Jinoteur system. I do, however, find it interesting that the Tholian ship does not appear to have been fired upon—unlike the Klingons' vessels."

Crossing his arms in front of his chest, Jetanien said, "It seems that expediting our investigation of the Jinoteur system has become our chief priority."

Reyes frowned and fixed Jetanien with a dour look. "You think?" He uncrossed his legs and sat up straighter as he pulled his chair closer to his desk. "I canceled *Sagittarius*'s shore leave five minutes before you got here. As soon as we get them loaded and Xiong finishes their briefing, they'll be shipping out, probably by 2300."

"That might present a problem, sir," T'Prynn said. "Klingon fleet activity in this sector has doubled since the recall of their ambassador, and we know they monitor our deployments. It is likely they will try to intercept the *Sagittarius*."

"Relax, Commander," Reyes said with a grin. "I still know a few tricks the Klingons don't. By the time they realize our boat's shipped out, she'll be long gone."

"Splendid, Commodore," Jetanien said with vigor. "As you appear to have the Jinoteur crisis well in hand, perhaps you could now direct your formidable talents toward the less glamorous fiasco developing on Gamma Tauri IV."

Reyes's grin flattened, and his thick eyebrows pressed down over his eyes, imparting a long-suffering quality to his face. "Would you like to run this starbase, Ambassador?" Knowing that the question was rhetorical, Jetanien took the gentle chiding in stride. Apparently satisfied that he'd made his point, Reyes continued, "I pulled the *Endeavour* off the border twenty minutes ago. She's on her way to Gamma Tauri IV at maximum warp."

"From the border?" Jetanien fumed. "It will take them nearly a week to reach Gamma Tauri! And what, pray tell, will they do to improve the current situation once they arrive?"

The commodore pinched the bridge of his nose and closed his eyes, as though trying to will away a headache. "I don't know," he muttered. "Prevent the Klingons from killing everyone?" He lowered his hand and sighed. "Do you have a better idea?"

"Well, naturally," Jetanien said. He reached forward and tapped with two clawed digits on the letter he had given to Reyes minutes earlier. "Persuade your ex-wife to reverse her decision about protectorate status. If she signs the accord, we can order the Klingons off the planet."

A gallows-humor chuckle rattled from Reyes's throat. "You think it'd be that easy?" He shook his head. "Trust me, that's not how Jeanne does business."

T'Prynn sounded almost optimistic as she said, "Your past marital relationship might lend your opinion greater weight with Ms. Vinueza, sir. It might be worthwhile to at least open a dialogue before she departs the station."

"Spoken like someone who's never been married," Reyes said. For a moment Jetanien thought he saw T'Prynn wince.

Reyes, oblivious of T'Prynn's reaction to his offhand remark, looked back and forth at her and Jetanien. Ostensibly concluding that he was outnumbered, he pressed his palms on the desktop and said with grudging resolve, "Fine, I'll talk to her. But don't get your hopes up, Jetanien. Listening to reason was never Jeanne's strong suit."

"Perhaps you could improve her disposition by broaching the subject somewhere other than this gray dungeon cell you absurdly call an office," Jetanien said. "For instance, you might take Ms. Vinueza to dinner at Manón's."

"An excellent suggestion, Ambassador," T'Prynn said.

The commodore leaned back in his chair and glared at Jetanien and T'Prynn.

Confused by Reyes's reaction to the notion of dining with his former spouse, Jetanien asked, "Is there some reason you wouldn't wish to dine with Ms. Vinueza?"

"You mean aside from our divorce?" Reyes rolled his eyes. "Can't think of a thing."

Sitting at the bar in Tom Walker's place, an unpretentious drinking establishment in Stars Landing, Master Chief Petty Officer Mike "Mad Man" Ilucci had no complaints. The beer was cold, the up-tempo music from the overhead speakers was edgy and loud enough to keep other people from eavesdropping on him and his fellow engineers, and the joint was blissfully free of officers, who generally preferred to drink at Manón's cabaret.

To his left, Petty Officer First Class Salagho Threx, the senior engineer's mate, covered a shot glass of Martian whiskey with one beefy hand, slammed the bottom of the glass onto the bar, and dropped it into his pint of amber ale. Overflowing spirits ran down the side of the glass as the sinking whiskey foamed. Threx lifted the glass, booze sloshing over his hand, and guzzled it before the reaction ended. Suds from the ale clung to the tall, heavily muscled Denobulan's thick dark beard.

On Ilucci's right sat Crewman Torvin, a nerdy young Tiburonian engineer. He nursed his drink, a pale lavender concoction that Ilucci had never heard of. Bald and fragile-looking, Torvin was barely a year out of basic and still seemed intimidated by most of the universe. Ilucci gave him a friendly slap on the back. "Drink up, kid," he said. "No telling when we'll get shore leave again."

Torvin glanced up toward the speakers and winced. Like most Tiburonians, he had extremely acute auditory senses. It gave him an edge during sensitive diagnostic work, but it also meant that he sometimes found loud noises overwhelming. "Isn't there someplace quieter we can go, Master Chief?"

The chief engineer knocked back a mouthful of his beer and replied, "None that give Starfleet discounts. What's wrong? You don't like music?"

After a timid sip of his drink, Torvin muttered, "I like music. Are you telling me that noise is music? I thought it was a sonic pulse for scaring rodents."

Threx wiped white froth off his chin and said, "It's called rock and roll, Tor. You get used to it." Pushing his long, oily hair back behind his ears, he nodded to the bartender for a refill.

"Listen to Threx," Ilucci told Torvin. "He knows music."

The boyish engineer sat quietly, looking pensive while Ilucci finished his beer and called for another. Staring into his drink, he said, "I wonder if Sayna likes music."

Ilucci rolled his eyes. Threx shook his head. They had heard far too much about Torvin's unrequited love for the ship's pilot, a stunning young Andorian *zhen* named Celerasayna zh'Firro. Clasping the younger man's shoulder in a fraternal manner, Ilucci said, "You gotta let this go, buddy."

"I know," Torvin said, verging dangerously close to a whine. "But it's so hard, seeing her every day, and she's so—"

Shaking the younger man silent, Ilucci tried to bark some sense into him. "Let! It! Go!" Hooking a thumb over his shoulder at Threx, he continued, "You think it ain't hard for Threx to spend his days lusting after Niwara? The only female on the ship hairier than he is, and she won't even give him the time of day." He turned Torvin to face him. "You think I don't wish Theriault would throw a little love my way? Sure I do. But it's never gonna happen, Tor. They're officers, and we're not. To them we're just a bunch of sweaty tool-pushers. Get used to it."

Threx pointed at Ilucci and looked at Torvin. "What he said." Then he let loose a rafters-shaking belch and turned back to the bar.

Ilucci watched the burly Denobulan slam another shot of whiskey onto the bar and drop it into another pint of ale, enlarging the foamy pool on the bar counter in front of them. As Threx knocked back his boilermaker, Ilucci said to him, "Maybe you oughtta slow down. We've got a big day tomorrow."

Setting down his emptied mug, Threx replied through his sudsy whiskers, "I'm fine, Master Chief. I could take that boat apart by lunch and have it back together by dinner."

"Yeah," Ilucci said, picking up his beer. "Let's hope it doesn't come to *that*."

Sleeving the foam from his face, Threx asked, "Any idea where we're goin'?"

"Like they tell *me* anything?" Ilucci sipped his drink and set it down. "All I know is we're scheduled for a briefing with Xiong tomorrow at 0900, and we're supposed to clear out the cargo bay to make room for some new gear."

Talk of work seemed to engage Torvin's interest in a good way. "Did they mention swapping out the sensor modules?"

"Yeah," Ilucci said. "Why?"

"I want to make some upgrades on the starboard unit," Torvin said. "It was running a little sluggish, and I thought it sounded like a problem with the heat exchangers, so I crunched some numbers. Well, I was right, and I think I can improve—"

"Fine," Ilucci said. "Approved. Get it done."

"Aye, Master Chief," Torvin said, apparently aware that the chief's approval was also a directive to shut up.

Ilucci swiveled his chair away from the bar and tugged at his olive-drab jumpsuit to make it less snug around his portly midsection. He scratched at his beard for a moment while he surveyed the bar. Seconds later, his gaze fell upon a table where four women in civilian clothes sat together, huddled over their drinks: two humans, one a blonde, the other a brunette; a shorthaired Vulcan; and a smooth-headed beauty with an inviting smile who Ilucci hoped was a Deltan.

He got up from his chair and said to Threx and Torvin, "Gents—follow my lead, and let me do the talking."

As the trio sauntered across the bar toward the fetching foursome, Threx said under his breath to Torvin, "Take notes, kid. Nobody works an angle like the Master Chief."

They were halfway to the table of paradise when the bar's front door opened and Senior Chief Petty Officer Razka, the *Sagittarius*'s newest field scout, walked in. The wiry-looking Saurian scanned the room in one quick turn of his head and moved to intercept the three engineers. "Shore leave's over, guys," Razka said in his nasal rasp of a voice, scuttling Ilucci's plans for the evening.

"How can it be over?" Ilucci protested. "We just got here."

Razka's vertical eyelids blinked twice in quick succession as he replied, "Captain's orders. Back to the ship."

Ilucci's shoulders sagged in defeat. He heaved a tired sigh and wore his disgust openly on his scruffy face. "All right, boys," he said. "You heard the senior chief. Back to the boat."

As they left the bar, the Deltan woman waved at Ilucci and flashed him a pitying grin as consolation for the night that might have been. He returned her smile and fell into step beside Razka as they left the bar and hit the sidewalks of Stars Landing on their way back to the station's core.

"I hate officers," Ilucci muttered.

Razka glanced at Ilucci with gentle surprise. "I'm surprised to hear you say that, Master Chief. After all, the officers say such nice things about you."

"Really?"

"No," Razka said, and quickened his pace to leave Ilucci behind. Watching the reptilian scout's back, Ilucci kept his next complaint to himself. *I hate Saurians.*

Diego Reyes stood up as Manón led his ex-wife to his table. He honestly wasn't sure which of the two women looked more stunning to him. Manón was a member of an alien race that radiated gentle heat and possessed a delicate and preternatural beauty, at least by human standards. Jeanne, by contrast, was an athletic woman of intelligence, grace, and confidence—the exact same qualities that had attracted him to his current clandestine lover, Rana.

The radiant hostess and club proprietor lingered half a step behind Jeanne as Reyes circled the table to pull out her chair for her. Jeanne appeared to be in no hurry to sit down.

"*Hola,* Diego," she said, staring at his eyes. "You can relax, I didn't come to make a scene."

"Well, that's a relief," he said, struggling to remain cordial. Her ability to read his surface thoughts had always bothered him. Though he knew that she couldn't help it, every time it happened it felt like an invasion of his privacy. Blocking her from his thoughts was difficult and required a great deal of concentration—either to flood his mind with random mental noise or to quiet his surface thoughts altogether. Of the two, achieving peace was the more difficult option, so instead he found his thoughts agitated and muddled whenever he had to spend time with her.

After a few awkward seconds, he motioned to the chair. "Please, sit down."

Jeanne continued to eye him with suspicion as she settled into her seat. Reyes gently helped nudge it forward under her as she made herself comfortable at their table. They were located a few tables from the stage, where a quartet featuring Lieutenant Commander T'Prynn on piano was playing mellow, sophisticated jazz for the club's dinner guests. Jeanne turned her attention to the musicians while Reyes returned to his own seat. As soon as he was comfortable, Manón handed him a wine list and stepped away with a knowing smirk.

"Thank you for having dinner with me," he said.

Jeanne tapped an index finger on the table. "Well, I seem to have the time, so I figured, why not?" Narrowing her eyes, she added, "My transport was supposed to leave an hour ago, but it seems we've been delayed by the station's control center."

"I guess I'm just a lucky man," Reyes said as he read the wine list and cluttered his inner monologue with the names and years of one vintage after another. "I had a bottle of the '56 Camigliano last month; it was excellent."

Not yielding to his clumsy imitation of charm, she asked, "I don't suppose you had anything to do with delaying our departure, did you?"

"Not in the mood for a Brunello tonight, huh?" He could see that she wasn't going to let him off the hook. "Fine, you caught me. I wanted to make sure I had time to talk to you before you left. Doesn't mean we can't have a nice dinner."

She shook her head as she unfolded her linen napkin into her lap. "Still can't come at a problem straight, can you? There always has to be a secret, or a twist, or a bit of deception."

Smoothing his own napkin into his lap, he asked, "If I had asked you to come to my office, would you have shown up?"

"Of course not," Jeanne said with a venomous smile. "I'd have told you to go to hell. But at least that way we'd both have the pride of knowing we'd been up-front about it."

"Touché," Reyes said.

Manón returned to the table at that moment, clearly taking the emotional temperature of the former spouses before she said, "Can I offer you something from the bar before you order?"

Taking the initiative, Reyes said, "Bring us a bottle of that good Vulcan syrah, would you?"

"The '59 Saylok?" Manón asked for clarification.

"That's the one, thanks," Reyes confirmed. Manón nodded and left to procure the wine. The commodore looked at his dinner companion and said, "Where were we?"

Feigning a difficult search of her memories, she said, "Let's see . . . I was calling you a duplicitous, overly secretive jerk . . . and you were ordering wine."

"It's just like we're married again," he said with a sarcastic grin. A server in a black-and-white uniform appeared from the shadows, filled their water glasses, and vanished without a word.

Jeanne watched the server depart, then she asked Reyes, "Why don't you tell me what we're really doing here?"

"You're an esper," he said. "Don't you know?"

She swallowed a bitter chortle and wrinkled her grin into a grimace. "It doesn't take a telepath to guess this is about the protectorate treaty for my colony."

"Things are moving fast out here, Jeanne," Reyes said. "The Klingons have already set up shop on your happy little planet. And unless you let us give Gamma Tauri IV official status as a Federation territory, we won't be able to do a damn thing when the Klingons walk all over you."

"At least I know why the Klingons are there," she said. "Conquest is what they do. But if you want me to trust Starfleet, try telling me the truth."

"Everything I've told you *is* the truth," Reyes insisted.

She traced the rim of her water glass with a fingertip. "It's *part* of the truth, not *all* of it. Why is the Federation so interested in Gamma Tauri? There are lots of UFP colonies that need your support more than mine does. Cygnet's been asking for help finishing its spacedock for almost a year, but you've had your S.C.E. team digging ditches around New Boulder for a month."

"I prioritize based on need," Reyes said. "The president of Cygnet XIV assured me just last week that her people can finish their own spacedock. Your colony is trying to get a high-yield crop planted on one of the hottest M-class planets in the sector, and you're already behind schedule." He picked up his menu. "The seafood is very good here, by the way."

She stewed for a few seconds while he filled his mind with the appetizer list. Lifting her own menu, she asked, "Have you ever met a subject you didn't change?"

"Sure I have," he said. "I recommend the fried Vulcan mollusks. You'll love the pepper-aioli dip they come with."

Manón returned to the table with their bottle of wine. She showed the label to Reyes, who nodded his approval. While she worked at uncorking the bottle, Jeanne peeked over the top of her menu at Reyes. "I know there's something you're not telling me," she said, as if that would be news to him.

"Of course there's something I'm not telling you," Reyes shot back. "I'm a flag officer running a starbase in a frontier sector. I have three starships and more than three thousand people under my command. There are probably a *couple hundred* things I'm not telling you."

Conversation paused as Manón filled his glass a couple of centimeters deep with dark red wine. He placed his fingertips on the base of the broad tulip glass and jogged it in a small circle, swirling the wine inside the glass to aerate it. Then he lifted the glass, inhaled the wine's sweet, almost floral bouquet, and sampled a mouthful. Complex yet subtle, it was light enough to mesh with seafood but strong enough to be paired with meat. He swallowed, then said to the ravishing hostess, "Excellent, thank you."

Manón filled Jeanne's glass and then Reyes's and set the bottle on the table. "Are you ready to order?"

His ex-wife's glare told him all he needed to know. "Give us a minute," he said. Manón gave a small nod and stepped away to attend the seating of more dinner patrons.

"Diego," Jeanne said, "you and I both know we don't want to eat together. So do us both a favor and get to the point."

Words caught in his throat. Much of the bitterness of their divorce had stemmed from the fact that he hadn't wanted it. Ending their marriage had been Jeanne's idea, and he had fought against it. Even though he had known it was likely for the best, letting go of their shared life had been excruciating for him. For his own emotional self-preservation he had given free rein to his resentment of her, but deep down part of him really did just want to sit here tonight and have dinner with her, for old times' sake. *I'll be damned if I tell her that, though.*

"You just did," she said under her breath, and as soon as the words registered in his ears, he realized that they both were blushing, him for shame at being found out, her for knowing that his torch for her still smoldered, however weakly. She closed her menu and put it down on the table. "Just ask me to sign the protectorate agreement so I can refuse and get out of here."

Abruptly, the music from the stage faltered, the piano going silent first and the other instruments rapidly falling away after it. Reyes looked up as T'Prynn walked away from the piano without a word to anyone and marched out the door. *What the hell was* that *about?* Resolving to follow up with the intelligence officer later, he looked back at Jeanne.

"I won't ask you to sign the treaty," he said, calmly setting aside his own menu. "You made it clear the colonists don't want it, and I won't ask you to betray their trust."

She eyed him with a confused expression—a rare look for her, in his experience. "Then what is it you want?"

"Don't go to Gamma Tauri," he said, purging his mind of all words and images, leaving only his focused, sincere concern for her well-being. "When the *Terra Courser* ships out, stay here."

Jeanne's mood altered in response. The suspicion was gone, replaced by a genuine acceptance of what he was saying. "Why?"

"I can't tell you," he said, continuing to focus on imparting the verity of his words. "Not even vaguely. But you know I won't lie to you, I never have. . . . Don't go."

Fear softened the resolve in her eyes, but she shook her head. "I want to believe you, Diego," she said. "But how can I when you won't tell me why? I know you never lied to me, but I know you've kept things from me, too."

"Never anything that would hurt you," he said. "Only what I had to, for the uniform."

A cold and bitter glare returned to her gaze. "So you always said. But how could I ever *know,* Diego?"

"If you don't know that about me," he said, "then I guess we were never really married."

Stung by his words, she got up from her chair. "You want to know why I divorced you?" She flung her napkin into his lap. "It wasn't 'cause I stopped loving you. It was 'cause I realized you loved your secrets more than you loved me." She started to leave, then turned back. "I'm touched that you care enough to try to save me, Diego, but I'm hurt that you don't care enough to tell me the truth."

"It's not that simple, Jeanne."

"Sometimes it is."

He sat stunned as she turned and walked away, carrying herself with pride and power between the clustered tables and out the front door, into the faux twilight of the station's massive terrestrial enclosure.

Alone at his table, Reyes picked up his wine. He took a sip, then looked across the table and noticed that Jeanne had not picked up either her water or her wine. As Manón returned, he handed her the napkin that Jeanne had hurled at him.

Manón asked, "Dining alone this evening, Commodore?"

He frowned. "Why should tonight be any different?" The hostess offered a comforting smile and reached out to start clearing away the table's second place setting. "Wait," Reyes said, feeling the word burst from his mouth before he could stop it. *I'm tired of living like a prisoner on my own station,* he decided. *Jeanne was right. I keep too many secrets. Maybe it's time to let one of them out into the light.* "Do me a favor?" he said to Manón. "Contact the station's JAG office and see if Captain Desai is available to join me for dinner."

Raising a curious, slender eyebrow at the commodore's request, Manón inquired, "Shall I tell the captain this is a professional summons?"

"No," Reyes said. "Definitely not. Just tell her . . . it's my turn to buy dinner."

T'Prynn poured herself into the music, felt her troubled mind release itself in a flood tide of notes and chords, heard the song flow from the piano and force the hungry ghost of Sten's *katra* deeper into her mind for just a few minutes.

Opportunities to play had been scarce of late. Her duties had become all-consuming since the *Endeavour*'s mission to Erilon. Lacking the regular outlet of playing the piano to ease her agitated thoughts, she had become profoundly tense and withdrawn in recent weeks. Adding to her stress was Sandesjo's increasingly ardent attachment to her.

I see the hunger in your eyes when you come to me at night, Sandesjo had said, her words pointed with accusation. There had been no denying her observation; T'Prynn had known it was true. It was the honesty of it that most gave her pause. The first night she had ravished Sandesjo, the first time she had fed the fires of her tortured *katra* with the pleasures of the other woman's flesh, she had lied to herself; she had blamed Sten's *katra* for goading her, for pushing her to indulge her appetites as part of his campaign to undermine her psychic defenses. She had told herself the lie again, after the second and third nights she spent in Sandesjo's arms. But when she had continued to return to her from then on, she had known without a doubt that it was her own doing and not Sten's. Sandesjo's voice still haunted her: *You burn for me just as I burn for you.*

Music was T'Prynn's solace, her sacrament, her salve. It gave voice to her conflicted states, her surging passions, her darkening moods and fiery rages. As her fingers moved with fluid precision across the black and white keys of the piano, the resulting music gave her thoughts order and clarity, focus and tranquility . . . but only in fleeting doses too soon lost.

A rare break in her schedule had afforded her an hour to play tonight in Manón's, and she had taken advantage of it without hesitation. The scheduled quartet's regular piano player had graciously permitted her to sit in for the first set, and she had paid for his dinner as an expression of her gratitude.

From time to time she stole glances at the crowd, not to gauge their reactions to her music but just to remain aware of her surroundings; her profession demanded that she be ever attentive and take no detail for granted. Most of the patrons tonight were civilians. A fair number of station personnel filled in the gaps at the bar. The nondescript nature of tonight's audience made the VIP guest seated close to the stage all the more notable: Commodore Reyes. As T'Prynn neared the end of the slow-tempo Paul Tillotson classic "Chartreuse," she noted the arrival of the commodore's former wife, Jeanne Vinueza. The human woman's body language as Reyes greeted her suggested that she was not in a receptive or trusting frame of mind.

T'Prynn did not envy the commodore. She expected that his attempt to sway Ms. Vinueza's decision about the political independence of the Gamma Tauri colony would prove futile.

She was less than a minute into Gene Harris's arrangement of "Black and Blue" when it became apparent to her that the commodore's dinner was taking a turn for the embarrassing. Despite being unable to hear what had been said at the ex-couple's table, T'Prynn surmised that it had been connected to their now-defunct marital relationship.

She was considering trying to soften her attack on the keys and mute her playing slightly so that she could eavesdrop when Manón seated another couple directly in her line of sight. As the hostess stepped clear, T'Prynn saw that the female diner was Anna Sandesjo. At the table with her was a civilian man, whom T'Prynn recognized as Roger Shear, an executive for a Mars-based mining concern that had been aggressively expanding its holdings by buying up hard-to-work claims in the Taurus Reach. The openness of Sandesjo's pose toward the man, coupled with her submissively lowered chin and the way she idly stroked locks of her auburn hair behind her ear, made it obvious that she was flirting with him. From T'Prynn's elevated vantage point on the stage, he appeared quite mesmerized by Sandesjo's exhibitions.

Sten's elbow crushes against my temple—

A jolt of psychosomatic pain tore through T'Prynn's head. Her hands stopped on the piano's keyboard, halted by the ferocity and power of Sten's focused *katra* attack.

Willpower alone kept her eyes open, though her face tensed with the effort of masking her agony. Without preamble or apology she closed the keyboard cover, pushed the bench away from the baby grand, stood, and walked off the stage without another look at Sandesjo. Every step brought another stabbing psychic assault, pushing her deeper into herself. Only her most consuming effort enabled her to see the narrow stretch of path ahead of her as she hurried across the manicured lawn of Vanguard's vast terrestrial enclosure.

I feel Sten's pain as the blade of my lirpa *takes three of his fingertips.*

Meters fell away under her long strides. Sten's attacks came more quickly than they ever had before.

A kick to my solar plexus leaves me begging for air.

I hear Sten's teeth crack as my knee slams his jaw shut.

Rising through the middle of the expansive, circular park that occupied the interior volume of the station's upper primary hull, the broad cylindrical core of the starbase was all that T'Prynn could focus on. One labored step after another, she marched herself toward the bank of turbolifts where the core met the enclosure's lowest level.

He buries the blunt end of his lirpa *in my abdomen. My dagger slashes the tendon above his knee.*

She didn't know how or why Sten's mental battery had become suddenly so emboldened, particularly when she was playing music that normally kept his *katra* at bay. She stumbled into an empty turbolift car and grasped its control handle. Her mind flashed for one brief moment on the image of Sandesjo flirting with the man in the cabaret; the memory vanished in a flurry of psionic jabs that coaxed a low whimper from her throat.

Sten's demand echoed in her deepest thoughts as it had for fifty-three horrible, strife-ridden years: *Submit!*

Her answer was as it had ever been: *Never.*

6

Lieutenant Ming Xiong grinned as he jogged down the passageway with his overstuffed duffel bouncing on his back, in a hurry to reach the gangway to the *Sagittarius*.

It had been more than two months since he had last set foot on the *Archer*-class scout vessel. He had served on several ships during his twelve years in Starfleet, but this small outrider, with its close quarters and tight-knit crew, was his favorite. On his last visit, Captain Nassir had given him a going-away gift: a green utility jumpsuit like the ones worn by the crew, with his name stenciled on its chest flap. As simple as it had appeared to be, its presentation had marked him as an honorary member of their spacefaring family. He was one of them. Wearing it now, he felt freer than he had in months.

As he neared the bay four gangway, he peered out an observation window into the cavernous docking bay. The tiny starship was concealed inside a metallic cocoon, within which transpired a flurry of activity. Robotic crane arms were swapping out modular sensor packages from its primary hull. Technicians in environment suits moved across the ship's gleaming exterior, repairing minor bits of wear and tear. An auxiliary gangway had been extended from Vanguard's maintenance complex, which ringed the core of the station. Xiong knew, from the mission profile that he had helped write, that several pieces of brand-new classified equipment designed by him and the rest of the researchers in the Vault—the station's secret research facility—were even now being hurried aboard the diminutive vessel.

He nodded to the Vanguard security detail guarding the

gangway entrance and paused briefly to identify himself. The deck officer in charge verified Xiong's credentials with ops and waved him past, down the gangway to the *Sagittarius*. As soon as the trim young anthropology-and-archaeology officer turned a bend in the gangway and was out of the guards' sight, he resumed jogging, eager to reach his destination.

Seconds later he stepped through the ship's sole airlock hatch, which was located on the port side of its primary hull. Both its inner and outer doors were open, as was routine for ships docked in the main bay. Then he was inside, on the main deck. The *Sagittarius* had only three decks. Its lowest level, along the belly of the primary hull, was the cargo deck. Most of it had a ceiling so low that the taller members of the crew had to duck to move around; the rest was crawlspace, for storing a variety of gear, tools, and spare parts.

The main deck was the heart of the ship. It housed the bridge in a heavily shielded forward compartment. On either side of the bridge were quarters for the captain and the first officer, the only two members of the crew who had the honor of private accommodations. By privilege of rank, the captain's berthing was the one closer to the ship's only head and shower, which everyone onboard shared. Four crew compartments— two to starboard, two to port, all recently reconfigured— housed the other twelve members of the ship's complement. At the broad aft curve of the slightly pointed oval were the common galley and the sickbay. Next to the XO's quarters was the ship's lab.

The crew spaces on the main deck ringed its outer edge. The core was completely packed with computer mainframes, sensor hardware, and a hefty complement of miniaturized probes.

Engineering and a little-used transporter bay occupied most of the space on the top deck. There also were a few access points to a number of tight crawlways used for making emergency repairs on such systems as the sensors and the ship's two phaser emitters. A self-contained probe-launching apparatus dominated the forward portion of the deck. Forward of the transporter bay was a hatch for descending into the ship's computer core for hands-on repairs.

Because the ship was too small to require a turbolift system, movement between the decks was achieved by traversing steep, wide-planked metal ladders. Passages between the cargo deck and the main deck were made amidships either to port or to starboard; traffic between the main deck and the top deck was limited to a single aft ladder, which terminated in the transporter bay.

And, just as Xiong had remembered, the entire ship looked immaculate and smelled sweetly, antiseptically clean. *I guess Dr. Babitz's war with germs marches on,* he mused.

His attention was drawn momentarily aft by the sounds of metal crashing against metal, followed by a string of bellowed profanities and vulgarities in several languages. *Sounds like a bad time to drop in on the master chief.*

A feminine voice came from close behind him: "Welcome back, Ming."

Xiong turned to face Lieutenant Commander McLellan, the second officer. He smiled and set down his duffel. "Bridy Mac!"

The raven-haired woman gave him a brief but friendly hug. "You're early," she said.

"I wanted to get settled before the briefing," he said.

She reached out, pinched a loose bit of his jumpsuit's sleeve, and smiled. "Looks like you're already blending in."

"Captain Nassir did tell me to wear it the next time I came back," Xiong said. "Is everybody back onboard already?"

McLellan replied, "We're in full scramble, trying to load up before we ship out." She motioned for him to follow her. "Come on, you can bunk with Ilucci again." He picked up his duffel and followed her aft. She moved with swift and graceful strides befitting her experience as a marathon runner. As he caught up to her, she said in a confidential hush, "I went below and took a look at the new toys you sent us. Crazy stuff."

"Hot off the workbench," he said. "All prototypes."

"Experimental gear? Classified briefings? We're gettin' into something interesting, aren't we?"

Xiong couldn't help but chuckle ruefully. "Trust me, Bridy Mac—you have no idea."

"All right," Captain Nassir said to his gathered crew, "everyone settle. We've got a lot to cover and not much time."

Even though the galley of the *Sagittarius* doubled as its conference room, it was barely large enough to accommodate the entire crew at once. Xiong waited patiently while the group came to order. It still pleased him to see that everyone wore the same style of olive-drab coverall with simple insignia. No one's uniforms had special markings, not even the captain's.

Xiong stood in front of the compartment's one wall monitor. Standing to his left were Nassir and Commander Terrell. Vanessa Theriault and Bridy Mac stood together to Xiong's right, along with a comely young Andorian *zhen,* the ship's helm officer and navigator, Lieutenant Celerasayna zh'Firro.

Seated at the table closest to Xiong were the engineers; all were noncommissioned officers except for one enlisted man. Ilucci sat up front. Behind Ilucci, Threx used a metal pick to clean between his teeth. The sight disturbed Xiong, who reminded himself that the brawny Denobulan had worse habits. Opposite Ilucci were Torvin and Petty Officer Second Class Karen Cahow, a tomboyish blond polymath.

Behind them, at the next table, were the ship's field scouts, who doubled as its security detail. The lead scout and head of security was Lieutenant Sorak—a lean, tough-looking, white-haired Vulcan man who had recently turned one hundred eighteen years old. With him were Razka and Lieutenant Niwara, a female Caitian whose reputation as a loner was well earned.

Dr. Lisa Babitz and her right-hand man, Vietnamese-born medical technician Ensign Nguyen Tan Bao, sat at the farthest table. Babitz had the impeccable posture of someone who feared that any surface she touched would be rife with germs. Tan Bao, on the other hand, was casually sprawled, leaning back on his elbows, his long, thick hair spilling over his shoulders and framing his boyish face.

Within ten seconds of Nassir's request, the crew of the *Sagittarius* fell quiet and turned their attention to Xiong.

"The first thing you need to know is where we're going," Xiong said. He pushed a yellow data card into a wall slot to call up a star map on the viewer. "Our destination is the fourth planet in the Jinoteur system, about six days from here at your best speed. The Klingons have tried to go there twice, and they've taken a couple of heavy beatings from automated defense systems on the planet's three moons. We kept a close eye on them both times, and we're hoping to learn from their mistakes.

"The reason we're shipping out early is that we detected a Tholian ship there. Unlike the Klingons, the Tholians haven't been shot at. We don't know why—but we've got a few ideas." Xiong paused as he saw the Vulcan head of security raise his hand. "Question?"

"Yes, Lieutenant," Sorak said. "What is the strategic importance of the Jinoteur system? Why are we—as well as the Klingons and the Tholians—interested in it?"

Leave it to a Vulcan to ask a simple question that demands a complicated answer. "Its overall strategic role is not yet fully understood," Xiong replied. "But we believe it to be the element that reconciles a number of mysterious discoveries made recently throughout the Taurus Reach." He inserted a red data card into a second wall slot connected to the monitor. An image of the Taurus meta-genome appeared on screen. From the back of the room he heard Dr. Babitz gasp softly.

"This," Xiong said, "is the Taurus meta-genome. It's a complex genetic artifact, containing hundreds of millions of chromosomes' worth of chemical information. Only the smallest part of it seems to be used to create living organisms. Most of it appears to be a remarkably complex form of data encryption." He pushed a few buttons next to the screen to pull different information from the data card. As the image onscreen changed, he continued, "Variants of the meta-genome have been found on three planets so far: Ravanar IV, Erilon, and Gamma Tauri IV."

He ejected the red data card and inserted a blue one. Side-by-side images of huge, obsidian artifacts appeared onscreen. The longer Xiong had studied them, the more he had come to think that they resembled giant, black-glass spiders suspended over their mirror-reflection counterparts. "On Ravanar IV and Erilon, we also discovered these artifacts. Our best estimates indicate that they could be hundreds of thousands of years old. The Tholians destroyed the artifact at Ravanar, but the crews of the *Endeavour* and the *Lovell* secured the larger one on Erilon for further study. We've barely begun to figure out what these things do, but at least one of their functions is to serve as the command-and-control hub for a planetary defense system."

Another raised hand drew Xiong's attention to Ilucci. He nodded to the chief engineer. "Go ahead, Master Chief."

"You said the Tholians destroyed the artifact at Ravanar?" Xiong replied, "Yes."

With palpable ire, Ilucci asked, "Does that mean the Tholians really did destroy the *Bombay*?"

For a moment Xiong wondered if he ought to evade the question somehow, but then he decided to play it head-on. *Commodore Reyes said to give them the truth. They might as well get all of it.* "Yes," Xiong said. "The Tholians ambushed the *Bombay* and destroyed it. Certain elements within Starfleet sabotaged the reporting of the incident to give the Federation Council an excuse not to go to war, so that we could continue our covert mission to unlock the secrets of the meta-genome."

Despite lowering his voice, Threx's sarcasm was heard by all as he muttered, "Oh, that's just great."

"Lock that down," Ilucci snapped in a harsh whisper.

Xiong sorted through his collection of data cards, chose two more, and put them into available slots beside the monitor. He thumbed a switch to activate the first of them. Probe-captured images of glowing, rocky debris filled the screen. "The planet Palgrenax," he said. "Or what's left of it. Our best intel suggests the Klingons found something like the artifacts on Erilon and

Ravanar IV. As with the *Endeavour* at Erilon, a Klingon cruiser in orbit of Palgrenax was fired upon by a planet-based weapons system. The Klingons responded with force—and apparently triggered a response that caused whatever they were fighting to blow up the planet."

Once again, Sorak raised his hand. After Xiong pointed to him, the Vulcan asked, "Can you tell us who or what the Klingons might have been fighting?"

Unable to prevent the grim shift in his countenance, Xiong said in a grave tone, "Yes, I can." He activated the second new data card and looked at the monitor. "This."

Moving images stuttered across the screen. Footage recorded with tricorders during the first and second battles against the black entities on Erilon showed the lethal killing machines from a variety of perspectives. More than two meters tall and vaguely humanoid in shape, they streaked across a bleak gray winterscape, churning up vaporized snow and ice as they went. Their arms ended in conical points that, in more than one image sequence, proved capable of tearing humanoids in half or skewering them with a single blow. A repeated motif of the montage was the utter ineffectiveness of phasers against the beings, who looked as if they were formed from volcanic glass.

The video ended abruptly, leaving the *Sagittarius*'s galley heavy with stunned silence. The normally unflappable Commander Terrell gave voice to the group's shared horror: "Holy shit."

"Yeah, that about sums it up," Xiong said without irony. "We were able to hold them off for a while with force fields, but the best defense proved to be a crude energy-dampening field. That enabled us to recover the body of one of them, which we found out contains large quantities of the meta-genome."

Sensing that it would be best to move on rather than let the crew dwell too long on the images of carnage from Erilon, he reactivated the Jinoteur star-system map on the monitor. "Now for the link. When Starbase 47 was still under construction, an alien carrier-wave signal was found to be interfering with several critical onboard systems. Lieutenant Farber from the *Lovell* was able to stop the carrier wave by transmitting a response on the same frequency. We've since learned that strings of data inside the carrier wave match certain sequences common to all varieties of the meta-genome. Duplicating it has given us leads on several worlds within the Taurus Reach that might merit further study." He pointed at the star map. "About two months ago, my team and I pinpointed the Jinoteur system as the source of the original carrier wave. When we took a closer look at the system, we discovered that it's . . . well, *not normal.*"

Xiong called up a more detailed, computer-generated animation of the system, with each planet and satellite following a track of a different color. He narrated as the animation's focus shifted and reoriented itself. "Jinoteur is a large white star with five planets, no two of which occupy the same orbital plane. That alone might not have been remarkable, except for how extremely they diverge from the ecliptic." Pointing out the wildly different paths of the planets around their star, he continued, "The orbital planes of the first and fifth planets are nearly perpendicular. The second and third planets follow paths almost equal in their offset from the ecliptic—but tilted at complementary angles. The fourth planet is the closest to level with the star's equator.

Entering instructions to the computer via the wall-mounted control panel, he continued as the animation zoomed in on the fourth planet. "The first three planets in the system have two satellites each. The fourth planet has three, and the fifth planet, a gas giant, has four. In every case, the orbital planes of each planet's moons are exactly parallel to one another and perpendicular to that of their planet, with the result being that none of the moons can ever come between their host planet and the star. Even weirder, every satellite exhibits the same rotational peculiarity: the same side always faces outward, away from the center of the system. For even one satellite in a star system to do that would be unusual. For all thirteen moons in the same star system to do so suggests deliberate manipulation—especially since we've detected artificial structures on the outward-facing hemispheres of each moon."

Razka, the Saurian scout, interjected, "Sounds like a defensive system."

"Yes," Xiong said. "That was our conclusion, too. Which is why we let the Klingons go in first. Turns out we were right." Turning to Captain Nassir, he added, "The planet-based weapons systems at Erilon and Palgrenax were extremely powerful, sir. The ones at Jinoteur are even deadlier. We might have a way to make your ship look less like a target to whatever's guarding the system, but you should still be cautious."

"I think you can count on that, Lieutenant," Nassir said with a modest grin. "Now, why don't you tell us about the new equipment you and your team packed into our cargo bay?"

"Aye, sir," Xiong said, happy to oblige. "Analysis of the Shedai body we—"

"Excuse me," said McLellan. "The *what* body?"

Ah, yes, Xiong realized. *Forgot that part.* "Shedai," he said. "It was a term the Tholian ambassador used several weeks ago during a meeting with Ambassador Jetanien. We think that it might be a proper name having to do with the entities we encountered on Erilon. For lack of a better term, it's what we're calling them." McLellan nodded her understanding, so Xiong pressed on. "As I was saying, analysis of the Shedai body has enabled us to make some educated guesses about what kind of signals and stimuli it might respond to."

He removed the data cards currently loaded in the control panel for the monitor and loaded in four new yellow cards. He switched images quickly while he talked, extolling the virtues of each piece of technology that appeared onscreen. "Some of what we've been working on are upgrades to your deflectors and shield emitters, to make you less noticeable to the Shedai.

"Beyond that, we're working on signal-based lures, which'll draw the Shedai's attention but interfere with their perception; and signal dampeners, to keep you from being noticed during close encounters. We've also modified some hand phasers, which might help us defend ourselves better than we did on Erilon." Shutting down the monitor, he added, "Best of all, my team kept all these items simple to use and lightweight, to make them more easily field-deployable. The specs are all available on your main computer." He looked around. "Any questions?"

Bridy Mac met Xiong's seeking gaze. "You said the word 'Shedai' came from the Tholian ambassador. What's the link between the Tholians and the Shedai?"

"We're not really sure yet," Xiong admitted. "We've noted some similarities between Tholian crystalline physiology and the crystal-lattice structure of the Shedai body we captured. Also, the Shedai seem capable of making a direct neural link with their technology inside the artifacts; it might be similar to Tholian touch-telepathy, or it might be something completely different. Part of why we need to go to Jinoteur is to get more hard data." Around him, a few people were nodding. The rest seemed lost in their own thoughts. "If there are no other questions . . .?" No one spoke. "Captain," he said as he stepped to the sideline and yielded the floor.

Nassir moved in front of the monitor and addressed the room, at once relaxed and authoritative. "Our first order of business," he said, "is to leave port and start our journey without being detected by the Klingon patrol ships cruising this sector. Thanks to Commodore Reyes, we have a plan for doing precisely that." He used the control panel to summon an image from the docking bay outside the ship. "The colony ship *Terra Courser* leaves Vanguard in twenty-one minutes. We'll be leaving with her, hugging her belly all the way out of spacedock. That's where we'll stay until she goes to warp. Then we'll follow her, using a few of Ilucci's trademark warp shadows to make ourselves look like a subspace echo on the trailing edge of her warp eddy. The *Terra Courser* will change her bearing at Arinex, but we'll keep going straight till we reach Jinoteur."

Helm officer zh'Firro asked, "Is there a risk of the *Terra Courser*'s crew detecting our presence? If they signal Vanguard for assistance, we'll be exposed."

"Their bridge crew is running interference for us," Nassir said. "They know they're helping us fake out the Klingons, but that's all." A few thumbed buttons on the control panel summoned an image of the Tholian ship above Jinoteur IV. "Our first assignment after reaching Jinoteur is to determine what that Tholian ship is doing there. If it's hostile, we'll be cutting this party short—that's a battleship, people; I'd rather not tangle with it if I don't have to.

"On the other hand, if it's neutral, or if we can get past it, our orders from Commodore Reyes are to mount a full survey of the planet's surface. That includes mapping, geological survey, collecting bio samples, the whole drill." Nassir looked to Sorak. "Lieutenant, familiarize yourself and your scouts with the new gear from Vanguard. If the Shedai are waiting for us on Jinoteur, let's be ready to meet them head-on."

"Understood, sir," Sorak said.

Turning to Ilucci, the captain said, "Master Chief, our energy signature needs to match the *Terra Courser*'s perfectly when we leave spacedock in twenty minutes."

"You got it," Ilucci said, and his engineering team nodded in agreement.

"Ensign Theriault," Nassir said to the young science officer. "Work with Lieutenant Xiong. Learn everything you can about the Shedai. Be ready to join the field scouts when we do our survey on Jinoteur." Theriault nodded without saying a word.

"Dr. Babitz," Nassir continued. "We have several forensic reports and autopsy files of interest from Dr. Fisher. I suggest you review them in detail with Mr. Tan Bao."

"Aye, sir," Babitz said.

The captain clapped his hands together. "Mr. Terrell, Bridy Mac, Sayna, join me on the bridge. It's time to go. Dismissed." Everyone rose from their seats and quickly exited the galley, making haste for their duty stations.

Xiong watched the crew snap into action. Nassir paused beside him and said, "Care to join us on the bridge, Ming?"

"Yes, sir," Xiong said. "I'd love to."

Nassir gave him a paternal slap on the back. "Glad you're back for this one," he said with a restrained grin that betrayed his excitement. "This is what being in Starfleet's all about."

Most of the time Xiong found himself at odds with his commanding officers, but this time he couldn't have agreed more.

Dr. Jabilo M'Benga toweled his hands dry as he exited the scrub-out room beside the operating theater. He had endured a long day of treating emergency cases. Now the last of his critical patients was on the way to recovery, and M'Benga was free to deal with the mountain of paperwork that had accumulated in his office.

In the past twenty-four hours, M'Benga had seen a variety of cases, each one coming on the heels of the last. A civilian cargo handler had suffered internal injuries after being pinned under a falling stack of filled crates, which had been knocked over by a colleague's inept control of a load-lifter; a mechanic in Vanguard's starship-maintenance complex had accidentally amputated three of his fingers by failing to obey proper safety protocols for storing his plasma cutter; one of the station's operations officers had slipped on a diving board in the Stars Landing natatorium, breaking her left ulna and giving herself a concussion and an intracranial hemorrhage; and a nine-year-old girl from the colony ship *Centauri Star* had been rushed into the ER in a state of anaphylactic shock after discovering the hard way that she was allergic to Ktarian eggs.

In other words, a slow day in Vanguard Hospital.

A hot cup of coffee and a warm raspberry croissant were in the forefront of M'Benga's thoughts as he walked through the parting doors of the ER and into the brightly lit blue-gray corridor outside. He turned right toward the turbolift that would take him back to his office. Before the ER doors closed behind him, the nasal drone of a nurse's voice squawked over the hospital's intercom. *"Code Two in the ER. Repeat, Code Two."*

M'Benga turned about-face and sprinted back inside. Code Two meant that one of the station's senior officers was in need of medical assistance. Code One would have meant that Commodore Reyes himself was in distress.

He scrambled past nurses and patients, weaving his way toward the main admissions area for the ER. Despite having been at the far side of the complex when he'd heard the call half a minute earlier, he was still the first doctor to arrive. A nurse and a medical technician had gathered around a crumpled form on the floor, a dark-haired female Vulcan officer in a red minidress. Pushing his way into the circle, M'Benga lifted his medical tricorder and started running a standard diagnostic scan on the unconscious Lieutenant Commander T'Prynn. "Nurse Martinez, report," he said.

Martinez continued her own tricorder scan as she answered. "She walked in and collapsed, Doctor. Her pulse, body temperature, and neural activity are all elevated." The young brunette adjusted her tricorder. "There's no sign of injury, but synaptic patterns in her somatosensory cortex are consistent with extreme pain."

The data on M'Benga's tricorder screen confirmed Martinez's report. He looked up to see that other members of the hospital's staff had belatedly joined the huddle around T'Prynn. "Someone get me a stretcher," he said. "We need to move her to a biobed." As the people around him hurried to fulfill his request, he puzzled over T'Prynn's bio readings. They were unlike anything he had seen during his residency on Vulcan. Despite his wealth of experience in treating Vulcan-specific afflictions, he was at a loss to pinpoint the nature of T'Prynn's malady.

"Stretcher comin' in," said Dr. Gonzalo Robles, who was assisted by a fourth-year Andorian medical student named Sherivan sh'Ness. Martinez and the med tech stepped aside while Robles and sh'Ness eased the stretcher under T'Prynn. M'Benga helped them straighten the Vulcan woman atop the stretcher. He beckoned to another doctor. "Steinberg, give us a hand here." To the group he declared, "Let's move her to exam one." With six sets of hands on the stretcher, they lifted

T'Prynn easily from the floor and carried her in a well-practiced march to a nearby exam room. Gently they set the stretcher on the biobed. Martinez, sh'Ness, and Robles worked in concert to lift T'Prynn just enough to slide the stretcher out from under her. M'Benga activated the biobed and watched the fluctuations in T'Prynn's vital signs.

"Nurse," M'Benga said. "Prep five cc of asinolyathin." Martinez nodded and moved to a pharmaceutical cabinet to load up a hypospray. Robles and Steinberg hovered on the other side of T'Prynn's bed, while sh'Ness and the medical technician watched from a few meters away.

Robles eyed the cardiac indicator on the display board above the bed. "Look at that," he said with amazement. "It's like she's in the middle of a workout." He pointed at the pain-level indicator. "Good Lord, her pain reading's off the chart."

"Weird," Steinberg said, folding his arms over his chest. "I've never seen a Vulcan have an anxiety reaction like this."

As he accepted the hypo from Nurse Martinez, M'Benga said to the two physicians, "Her condition is *not* the result of anxiety. Of that I am quite certain." He injected the light dosage of analgesic medicine into T'Prynn's jugular vein. In less than two seconds, the pain indicator on the board dropped from its maximum level to within a few notches of normal. "That seems to have dealt with the symptom," M'Benga noted, "but as for the cause, we'll have to run some—"

T'Prynn's hand shot up and locked around his throat. Her grip was viselike, and her open eyes were ablaze with fury. The speed of her attack caught everyone in the room off-guard. It took a very long second for Steinberg and Robles to start scrambling around the bed to M'Benga's aid. Martinez overcame her surprise and rushed forward to restrain T'Prynn while the medical technician hurried to a wall panel to summon security. The medical student remained paralyzed with fear in the doorway.

Before anyone could finish what they were racing to do, T'Prynn let go of M'Benga's throat. The fire in her eyes abated, and she took a deep breath. Everyone stopped and waited to see what she would do next. M'Benga coughed twice, then gasped for air as he massaged his throat.

In a calm but alarmingly uninflected tone, T'Prynn said, "Please forgive me, Doctor. My reaction was one of reflex." Her eyes traveled from Martinez to the other two doctors. "There is no cause for concern," she said to them. "It is not necessary to restrain me. I am in control of my actions."

Still trying to work the burn out of his esophagus, M'Benga found T'Prynn's declaration a bit hard to believe. If his guess was correct, she was masking her symptoms. To confront her about it in front of others, however, would be both improper and fruitless. Matters such as this required tremendous tact when dealing with a patient of any species, but especially so when interacting with a Vulcan. To the others in the room, M'Benga said with his injured rasp of a voice, "Leave us, please."

The other doctors and the medical technician left quickly, taking the shocked medical student with them. Nurse Martinez hesitated, but M'Benga gave her a reassuring nod and said, "Close the door." With obvious reluctance, she did as he asked, and he was alone in the exam room with T'Prynn.

She sat up and turned to drop her legs over the edge of the bed. He watched her with a clinical eye, seeking any of a number of subtle cues that were particular to Vulcan body language. In addition to a few signs of hidden discomfort, he detected ephemeral micro-expressions that reinforced his suspicion: a tensing near the mandibular joint, a twinge at the corner of her left eye, an inward curl of her upper lip. "You are in profound distress," he said to her. "Please relate your symptoms to me."

"I am merely fatigued," she said, and he knew it was a lie. Stoic prevarications by patients were not uncommon, but in his experience Vulcans were unlikely to tell such naked falsehoods.

"Lieutenant Commander," he said sternly, "minutes ago you collapsed in my ER. Your vital signs were highly irregular and not consistent with a diagnosis of fatigue."

She met his stare. "What *is* your diagnosis, Doctor?"

"Though it doesn't account for your unusually high pain indications, your other symptoms are consistent with the peak stages of *Pon farr*."

T'Prynn pushed herself to a standing position and wavered slightly as she replied, "Absurd."

M'Benga asked, "Are you close to your natural cycle?"

"No," she said. "I am not."

He lifted his eyebrows and tilted his head in a gesture of concession. "I see," he said. Thinking back over the reams of medical literature he had studied in ShiKahr, he said, "There have been cases of premature *Pon farr*. Some were caused by external triggers, such as—"

"Thank you, Doctor," she said, trying to move past him. "But I am not undergoing *Pon farr*."

Interposing himself between T'Prynn and the door, he said, "Wait a moment, Commander. Making a diagnosis is my job. I still need to ask you some questions. How old were you when you first experienced the *Pon farr* impulse?"

"That is a private matter," she said.

He held up his hands to ward off her protest. "I know. But how can I be certain you're not suffering premature *Pon farr* if I don't even know when your normal cycle would kick in?"

"I have already told you, this is not *Pon farr*."

Sensing that she would become only less cooperative if he continued on his present tack, he tried a different approach. "Very well. That still begs the question: Why did you collapse tonight? Was it something you ate? Something you drank? Did you experience any kind of unusual stress?"

His last inquiry provoked another fleeting twinge near her temple, but she kept her eyes locked with his. "As I said, Doctor: I am suffering from fatigue. If you will excuse me, I would prefer to recuperate in my quarters." She stepped around him and headed for the door.

"I haven't discharged you, Commander," he said. "If you leave now, you're doing so against medical advice."

As she stepped through the door, she said, "So be it." Then she was gone, and the door closed after her. Alone in the exam room, M'Benga realized that everything had happened so quickly that no one had been able to create a chart for T'Prynn. Now that she had left the hospital without answering even simple questions regarding her medical history, he would be forced to track them down himself through her official Starfleet medical records. *Wonderful,* he thought cynically. *More paperwork.*

"Commodore," came Yeoman Greenfield's summons over the intercom. *"The* Terra Courser*'s about to leave spacedock."*

Reyes put down the data slate he had been perusing but not really absorbing, got up from his desk, and walked out to the shadowy operations center. The vast circular space loomed high and wide around him as he made his way up to the elevated supervisors' deck in its center. Faint comm chatter and the muted voices of Vanguard's flight-control team gave the command area a steady undercurrent of focused activity. Scores of eyes were turned upward, away from the pale blue glow of dozens of work screens, toward the center's enormous display monitors, which formed an unbroken ring of moving images along the top third of the compartment's nine-meter-high bulkheads.

Commander Jon Cooper looked up from his post at the hub as Reyes climbed the steps and bounded onto the supervisors' deck. "Commodore," Cooper said, straightening his posture. "What can we do for you?"

Lifting his arm and pointing at the bay one monitor, Reyes said, "Just came to observe a departure, Commander. As you were." Reyes folded his hands behind his back and stood at ease while he watched the colony ship clear its moorings. Cooper made a show of working for a moment at his duty station before sidling over to a workstation beside Reyes. In a covert tone of voice he said, "The *Sagittarius* is in position, sir."

"Good work, Coop. I want you to send a message for me."

Tapping keys, Cooper said quietly, "Go ahead, sir."

"Send to Starfleet Command, marked urgent: *Sagittarius*

departure delayed. Require reinforcements for escort. . . . That's all. Send it on scrambler India Tango Nine."

Reyes hoped that the Klingons were not yet aware that Starfleet knew that its IT9 cipher had been broken. For now it could be used to feed the Klingons disinformation.

Cooper confirmed the order with a nod to the communications officer, Lieutenant Dunbar. "Message transmitted, sir."

That ought to throw the Klingons off the scent for a few hours, Reyes mused. *As long as the pilots on the* Sagittarius *and the* Terra Courser *don't do anything stupid, we might just catch a break.* Watching the bulky colony transport inch its way out of Vanguard's spacedock, he tried not to think about the fact that the *Sagittarius* would have less than three meters' clearance above and below as it snuck out beneath the *Terra Courser*'s massive bulk. One miscalculation, and all that would be left of the state-of-the-art Starfleet scout ship would be a streak of paint on the transport's belly and some mangled hull plates.

They'll be fine, he told himself. The station's tractor-beam systems were guiding both ships out of spacedock, with the main computer making any necessary adjustments to speed or direction. Pilot error was all but eliminated from the equation. Despite knowing that, dread still twisted in Reyes's gut.

He wondered if there was any way the *Sagittarius* or her crew could possibly be ready for what was ahead of them on Jinoteur. With each new discovery Starfleet made in the Taurus Reach, the stakes of that exploration seemed to increase. Ravanar, Erilon, and Palgrenax had been stepping stones to something larger, and Reyes was convinced that the *something* was Jinoteur. *Whatever we woke up is willing to destroy starships and blow up planets to keep us in the dark,* he brooded. *How's it going to react when we show up on its doorstep?*

Reyes knew he had just sent Captain Nassir and his crew into grave danger, but watching the *Terra Courser* clear the docking bay doors into open space, he knew that the people he was truly frightened for were the colonists on Gamma Tauri IV, and most of all their leader, the woman who had broken his heart seven years ago. *We should warn them,* protested his conscience. *At least Nassir's people know they're in danger.* His sense of duty shot back, *There's no way to evacuate the colonists without compromising Operation Vanguard. You can't tell them about the threat without revealing everything—and once it's public, every moron with a stardrive will come runnin', guns blazin', lookin' to get rich quick or die trying. Emphasis on the "die trying."*

On the monitor above and ahead of him, the docking bay doors began to creep shut as the *Terra Courser* engaged its impulse engines and cruised away from the station. Before the doors closed, Reyes caught a glimpse of the *Sagittarius* tucked under the hulking transport, like a tiny white remora hugging a shark's belly. Then the pale gray doors met, and the image on that screen changed to the majestic nebula that dominated one angle of the starscape outside the station.

Cooper checked the reports forwarded to his station by a handful of subordinates and reported discreetly to Reyes, "The jump to warp went perfectly, sir. The *Terra Courser* and her shadow are away."

The commodore nodded and stared at the dark sprawl of space and stars, not brave enough to imagine what was in store for the crew of either ship. *"Vaya con Dios,"* he said softly. Then he returned to his office—walking, as always, under a dark cloud of concern for those he had just placed in harm's way.

"What do you mean it's gone?" raged Turag, his ire palpable even across a long-range subspace channel. *"We told you to watch its every move! How could you have missed its departure?"*

Sandesjo struggled to keep her temper in check. Lambasting her Imperial Intelligence handler with vulgarities might draw attention in the Federation Embassy office, even from behind the closed door of her private office. "Starfleet normally announces arrivals and departures," she said. "This time there was no announcement. Furthermore, Jetanien was left out of the loop. Reyes concealed the *Sagittarius*'s deployment from all nonessential personnel, including the station's diplomatic staff."

"A sorry excuse, Lurqal," Turag said, sneering through her true name as if it were a slur. *"You have eyes. Couldn't you see the ship was no longer in the hangar?"*

I'm just going to throttle him, she fumed. Quieting her thoughts, she replied, "The *Sagittarius* is a very small ship, Turag. After it reached port, the maintenance crew covered it with scaffolding while making repairs. Apparently, the ship navigated clear of the scaffolding, which was left in place to create the illusion that the vessel was still in spacedock."

"An answer for everything," Turag said. *"How convenient. How could the* Sagittarius *have left undetected by our fleet?"*

"Not all our warriors are as cunning and alert as you are, Turag," she said with syrupy insincerity. "The *Sagittarius* probably left at the same time as the *Terra Courser* and used her for cover—much as she deceived the crew of the *Heghpu'rav* into thinking she was a battle cruiser."

Assuming your guess is right," Turag said, *"how much of a lead would they have?"*

"Two days and nineteen hours," Sandesjo said.

Turag pounded his fist on the tabletop in front of his monitor. "Jay'va! *They could be halfway to Jinoteur by now!"* He pointed an accusing finger at her. *"Every week your reports grow shorter and less useful. Now you've let a major Starfleet deployment slip past you. This is the last time, Lurqal. Fail us again, and you'll be making your excuses to* Fek'lhr!"

A jab of his index finger cut the channel. The screen hidden inside Sandesjo's briefcase went dark. With a calmness of motion that belied her distress, she shut the briefcase and slid it under her desk. Her mouth was dry and tasted sour.

For a few minutes she sat with her face hidden in her hands. Solid intelligence had become harder to obtain in the weeks since the death of Captain Zhao on Erilon, but Sandesjo's privileged position still made available a great deal of useful information. During her first several months aboard Starbase 47 she had mined the Federation Embassy's records repeatedly for items of interest that could be passed along to Turag and Lugok. Though that supply of internal memoranda was far from exhausted, she had become tired of sifting through it for material to pad out her reports. It had come to feel like busywork. More to the point, she had lost interest— in that task and in her mission.

She had tried to convince herself that she could serve her Klingon masters and T'Prynn at the same time without betraying either one. T'Prynn had never asked her to surrender information that would endanger Klingon lives, though the Vulcan had asked her to omit items from her reports that could place Starfleet personnel at risk. On occasion, the Vulcan had asked Sandesjo to pass along particular items of interest to the Klingons. Sometimes it was accurate intelligence of dubious strategic value; sometimes it was disinformation. Caught between Turag on one side and T'Prynn on the other, Sandesjo had tried to treat her predicament like a game, or like a high-wire act.

The time for games was over. Turag could sense that she was not delivering useful intelligence. She would need to give him exclusive information of genuine value to safeguard her deep-cover assignment, lest her own people move against her.

My own people, she thought ruefully. *Do I still have the right to call them that? I've lain down with the enemy and fallen in love. . . . I'm a traitor.*

Accepting that as true meant letting go of a comforting lie. She had told herself for months that her loyalties had been "divided" or her motives "conflicted." The truth of the matter, she now knew, was that she had been turned. Whether the deciding factor had been falling in love with T'Prynn or simply remaining too long submerged in an assumed identity, she was uncertain. Regardless, she admitted to herself that it was a fact: her only interest in serving the Empire was to serve herself, so that she could remain in T'Prynn's good graces—and in her bed. Likewise, she harbored no illusions of loyalty to the Federation. Its ideals and values held little interest for her.

Her true loyalty was to T'Prynn. If the only way to remain with her lover was to give Turag intel that would harm the Federation, Sandesjo had no reservations about doing so. If placating T'Prynn meant betraying crucial secrets of the Empire and sending Klingon warriors to their deaths, she resolved to act without remorse. All would be expendable in love's name.

I will burn in Gre'thor for this, warned the faltering voice of Sandesjo's conscience, but she paid it no heed.

Her love demanded blood, and it would not be denied.

Dr. Fisher sipped his coffee and knocked on the open door to his colleague's office. "You asked to see me?"

Looking up from behind several orderly stacks of data slates, Dr. M'Benga's face brightened when he recognized Fisher. "Yes, sir," he said. "Do you have a minute? Please come in."

M'Benga kept his office well organized and very clean.

Fisher approved. He slouched into a comfortable, padded leather chair in front of M'Benga's desk. It had been quite some time since he had been the one sitting in front of another physician. "What's on your mind, Doctor?"

The younger man handed Fisher a data slate. "A few days ago I treated Lieutenant Commander T'Prynn in the ER," he said. "She presented to the triage nurse with a nonspecific report of pain, then lost consciousness. I revived her with a low dosage of asinolyathin."

Scanning the information on the slate, Fisher remarked, "You've got a few gaps in your patient profile, Doctor."

"Yes, sir," M'Benga said. "T'Prynn left AMA before I could take a history or compare her readings to baseline data."

Fisher chuckled. "The higher the rank, the more difficult the patient." He set down the data slate on M'Benga's desk. "You can just request her file from Starfleet Medical, you know."

"I'm aware of that, sir," M'Benga said. "That's why I called you. I requested T'Prynn's records and was denied."

That made Fisher sit up straight. "Denied?"

"Yes, sir. Starfleet Medical informed me that I don't have sufficient security clearance to review her file."

The older doctor put down his coffee mug on the desk and grabbed the data slate that showed T'Prynn's incomplete workup. "Did you tell them she'd collapsed?"

"Yes, sir," M'Benga said, his manner far more calm and professional than Fisher expected his own would be under the circumstances. "They still refused to release her records."

Fisher studied the unusual bio readings taken during T'Prynn's ER visit and tried to make sense of them. "Doesn't add up," he said. "Why would medical records be classified?" He tapped the face of the data slate. "Quite a fever she was running. Any sign of viral infection?"

"Not that we found," M'Benga said. "No sign of injury, either. But lots of pain response in her somatosensory cortex. My first diagnosis was premature *Pon farr.*"

Nodding slowly, Fisher said, "That fits with the elevated temperature and pulse. But I don't see the pain connection. That sort of thing usually happens when they can't get back to Vulcan to mate. Are we sure it's not her usual cycle?"

"I asked," M'Benga said. "She insisted it's not time. Then she left."

"And you didn't stop her?" Before the other man could answer, Fisher continued, "This isn't some backwater private practice, Jabilo, this is a Starfleet starbase." As he got up from the chair, he felt his temper rise with him. "You were the attending physician, and she was your patient. Order her to the ER for a follow-up exam and a complete history. Make it clear that if she refuses *any part* of that order, I'll suspend her from duty immediately. Clear?"

"Yes, Doctor," M'Benga said, standing up with Fisher.

Collecting his coffee mug from the desk, Fisher added, "As for her medical records being classified? We'll see about that."

The spray from the shower nozzle was warm and forceful on the top of Diego Reyes's head. Jets of white water pushed through his graying hair and tingled his scalp, ran in long rivulets over his shoulders and down his torso. He reached up and massaged the back of his neck. Surrounded by the white noise of the running water, secluded briefly from the burdens of command, he reminded himself to breathe. With his eyes closed, he could almost imagine himself somewhere else.

Reyes pressed his palms against the tiled wall in front of him and bowed his head beneath the falling cone of water. Fatigue imbued his limbs with a leaden quality. *I wish I could sleep for a year,* he thought. *There's never time to think, no time to read, no chance to catch up. This is no way to live.*

Cool air wafted across his back. Even with his eyes shut and his head submerged in spray, he recognized the sensation. "Hello, Rana," he said with a bemused grin.

"You've been in here almost an hour," Desai said as she slipped into the shower behind him. She slid her arms around his waist and pressed her body against his back. "Hiding from me?"

"Why would I do that?" he said with a grin, adjusting the shower nozzle to toss some water over his shoulder at Desai.

She laid her head in the valley between his shoulder blades. Her soft London accent gave her voice an especially wistful quality. "I don't know. Maybe you were regretting taking us public the other night in Manón's?"

"Not at all," he said. "Switch?" In response to his offer, she shuffled around him to step under the main thrust of the spray, while he moved behind her. The water added weight and shine to her short but lustrous black hair. Thanks to the difference in their heights, a generous portion of the water angled over her and continued to pelt Reyes's chest.

Desai took half a step back and pressed her hands against her head. With a backward push she squeezed the excess water from her hair. "What're you still doing in here?" she asked with a coquettish grin. "Trying to use up Vanguard's hot water?"

"Just wanted a quiet place to think," he said.

Her delicate tan fingers explored his wet, steel-gray chest hair. "About work?" she pried. "Or about Jeanne?"

"They're kind of the same thing now," he said. "If something happens to her—"

"It won't be your fault," Desai said, her mien both firm and comforting. "You didn't send colonists to Gamma Tauri."

"No," he said, cupping his hand to collect a palmful of water. "But I didn't warn them, either."

"You couldn't." She rested her head on his chest. "They've been there almost a year, Diego. Did you know that planet was part of your mission when they set up their camp?"

"Of course not," he said. He pressed his handful of water to his face. Wiping his eyes clear, he continued, "I'd never put civilians at risk just to cover an op. But now that they're there, I can't force-evac them just 'cause Xiong and his white-coat brigade think we *might* find something useful under the surface." He sighed heavily, feeling the pressure of his command reasserting itself. "And by the time we know for a fact that they need evac, it'll probably be too late."

She traced her fingernails up and down along the flanks of his back. "They have the *Lovell* and the Starfleet team on the surface, and the *Endeavour* will be there in a few days. If anything goes wrong, they'll protect the colony."

"Sure," Reyes said glumly. "But if they end up defending it from the Klingons, it'll mean war. And I can't let that happen." He stepped back from the spray. "A bigger problem is what'll happen if Jeanne talks to one of our people on Gamma Tauri. She's too good an esper not to know they're hiding something."

Shutting off the water, Desai said, "We'll burn that bridge when we come to it." She turned to face him and slid open the translucent stall door. Cool air rushed in, creating thick clouds of water vapor that rolled around them. "For now, you have to trust the people under you to do their jobs." She stepped out of the stall, grabbed two towels, and handed one to Reyes. "Dry off and come to bed," she said. She wrapped her towel around herself and padded away toward the bedroom.

Reyes tied his towel around his waist and stepped out of the stall. He stopped in front of the sink and looked at himself in the mirror, despairing at the dark canals that concern had etched into his face over the past thirty years. His father's favorite saying echoed in his memory: "By the age of fifty, we all have the face we deserve." Eyeing his own weathered, grim countenance and the deep, dark crescents of fatigue beneath his doleful eyes, Reyes decided that his father had been right.

Desai called to him from the other room. "If you're not in bed in sixty seconds, I'm going to sleep."

"I'll be right there," he answered. Knowing she would

make good on her teasing threat, he turned out the bathroom light and exited to his bedroom, where Desai was already ensconced under the covers. *These are the good times,* he reminded himself as he climbed into bed beside his girlfriend. *Enjoy it while it lasts. . . . Because it always ends sooner than you think.*

8

A choir of cacophony. Too many voices clamoring to set the tone. To the Apostate it was beneath contempt. He seethed with resentment that his placid aeons of silent reflection had been stolen for this manic chaos. Saying nothing, he held himself at a remove from the din of the Shedai Colloquium.

The hour has come, declared the Maker. **Earlier than we expected, we must reclaim what is ours.** Thunder punctuated her call to action. The atmosphere of the First World churned around the Colloquium, hurling forks of lightning and deluges of rain upon the convocation.

The Wanderer shared ephemeral visions of her battles with two different kinds of *Telinaruul,* one ending in defeat, the other in the calculated sacrifice of a treasured world. **The *Telinaruul* grew strong while we slept,** she cautioned. **No longer confined to their planets, they harness subtle fires and traverse the stars. They are dangerous.** Images etched in strokes of lightning depicted a shattered Conduit on a smoldering orb. **The work of the *Kollotaan,*** explained the Wanderer. **They have grown more defiant, more difficult to yoke—but also stronger and more focused. We must subdue them. Properly dominated, they will serve us well. The reach of the Conduits will grow tenfold.**

Thousands of swelling pulses of agreement outnumbered the few rumbles of discontent—all of which, the Apostate noted, came from his partisans. Though the Apostate believed the Wanderer's grandiose vision to be hopeless, he kept his own counsel as the Warden injected himself into the gathering's discussion. **In numbers the *Telinaruul* hold an advantage,** counseled the defender of the Shedai. **If we are to subdue them, we must avoid a war of attrition. Overwhelming force is our best option.**

Burning with fires older than the First World itself, the Avenger added her opinion. **One demonstration will not be enough,** she insisted. **If the *Telinaruul* are as powerful as the Wanderer claims, they will need to feel our wrath many times before they learn to obey.**

Our strength is not yet equal to such a task, warned the Maker. **To challenge the *Telinaruul* with sufficient authority we must be prepared to marshal the entirety of our power. It is time to rekindle our Conduits and seed them with the *Kollotaan*.**

Assent coursed through the Colloquium, burying the minority of dissident voices consigned to its periphery. The Herald sounded a cautionary note: **The *Kollotaan* will resist.**

Those who do will be destroyed, replied the Maker. **Those who remain will echo our voice—and help us teach the *Telinaruul* to fear a new master.**

PART TWO

THE BRIGHT FACE OF DANGER

9

"Dropping out of warp in thirty seconds," reported Lieutenant zh'Firro. The Andorian pilot checked her readings. "We will slow to sublight approximately one hundred million kilometers from the fourth planet."

"Very good," said Captain Nassir. "Bridy Mac, get ready to power up those new mods." Throwing a sardonic glare in Xiong's direction, he added, "And let's hope they work."

The second officer nodded from the tactical station on Nassir's left. "Aye, sir." She started flipping switches and bringing the new stealth systems online. Nassir had listened to Xiong explaining to Bridy Mac that the new screens were like a dampening field for Shedai sensor frequencies. It all had sounded very reassuring until the young lieutenant admitted that the technology had never been tested in the field.

Not until now, Nassir thought, grinning at his own gallows humor. "Theriault, can you get a reading on that Tholian ship?"

"I think so," she responded. Her attention was focused into the blue glow from her sensor hood. "Main power is online. . . . No sign of damage." She recoiled slightly from the hood, adjusted her controls, and looked again at the sensor display. "No life signs, sir. It's a derelict."

Nassir glanced at Commander Terrell, who stood to the right of the captain's chair. The first officer affected a dubious expression. "Interesting," he said to Nassir.

"Exactly the word I'd choose," Nassir said with gentle sarcasm. "Where do you think they are? On the planet?"

Terrell shrugged. "Not exactly their kind of environment." In an ominous tone he added, "For all we know, they're still on their ship." Nassir took his XO's meaning clearly: *Maybe the Tholians are dead.* He looked left to Xiong. "Your opinion?"

Xiong peered at the main viewscreen, where the slow pull of starlight retracted into the placid vista of a starfield. "Hard to say, sir. Tholians have environment suits that could let them explore the surface, but it doesn't make sense that they'd send the entire crew. But seeing as their ship hasn't been fired upon, it's possible they're here as guests—which could mean that their hosts have prepared a habitat for them on the surface."

"Optimism," Nassir said. "How refreshing. Either way, this simplifies a few things. At least now we don't need their permission to make orbit." He leaned forward. "Sayna," he said, addressing the helm officer by her preferred nickname. "Take us in, full impulse."

Entering the commands, zh'Firro replied, "Full impulse, aye. Estimating twenty-one minutes to orbit."

He craned his head to look past Terrell, toward the science station. "Theriault, keep one eye on the planet and one on the Tholian ship. If either one makes so much as a blip—"

"Send up a red flag," Theriault cut in, knowing his orders by rote. "Aye, sir."

The captain swiveled his chair toward tactical. "Bridy Mac, arm phasers, just in case." McLellan acknowledged the order with a nod. Nassir turned back toward the main viewer and sighed with amazement. "I still can't get over how damned odd this system's orbital mechanics are," he said. "What kind of technology would it take to manipulate a solar system like this?"

Theriault looked up from the science station. There was a note of concern in her voice. "Actually, sir, I don't think this system was *manipulated* at all."

Nassir couldn't contain his look of surprise. "You don't think this aberration happened *naturally,* do you?"

"No, sir," said Theriault. "What I mean is, maybe someone

made this system like this from the beginning." With a tilt of her head toward the main viewer, she said, "Permission to put my data onscreen, sir?"

"Granted," Nassir said. As a low aside to Terrell, he added, "This ought to be interesting."

"Exactly the word I'd choose," Terrell joked, parroting the captain's earlier retort.

A computer-generated image of the Jinoteur system appeared on the main viewer. "In most star systems," Theriault said, "there's at least a small degree of variation in the apparent geological ages of the various planetary bodies. Gas giants form quickly, terrestrial planets more slowly, and so on. In this part of the galaxy, a Class F main sequence star like Jinoteur would be about four billion years old. So its planets ought to be anywhere from four billion to three-point-five billion years old. But they're not." She switched the image to a series of side-by-side graphs. "Every planet and satellite in this system is approximately half a million years old."

That caught the attention of everyone on the bridge. McLellan turned from the tactical station, zh'Firro looked up from the helm, and Nassir, Terrell, and Xiong all lifted their eyebrows in wonder. Xiong found his voice first. "Half a million years? With a thriving M-class ecosystem on the fourth planet? How's that even possible?"

The redhead held out her empty hands and said, "I just found the what and the when, sir. The who, how, and why are gonna take a *little* bit longer."

"Good job, Ensign," Nassir said. "Keep working on it, and let me know what you find." The captain looked at Xiong and Terrell. "Now, call me nosy, but I'd like to have a look inside that Tholian cruiser."

Xiong smiled. "So would I, sir. I studied Tholian physiology at the academy, and I visited their habitat on Vanguard after they recalled their diplomats—but I've never had a chance to see an environment of their own making."

"Sounds like we have a volunteer," Terrell said to Nassir.

With an approving grin, Nassir replied, "It certainly does." He added to Xiong, "I hear it can get pretty hot in one of those ships."

"Yes, sir," Xiong said. "The pressure's pretty intense, too. I'll need a heavy-duty environment suit, or else I won't be able to move once I'm there."

Terrell said, "Let's head up to the top deck and see the master chief. I'm sure he can rig you something for the job."

Nassir nodded his approval. As the two men left the bridge, the captain focused his attention on the main viewer, which was still packed with Theriault's surprising findings about the planets of the Jinoteur system. *The Shedai made an entire star system from scratch, and we think we're smart enough to play with their toys?* Doubt deepened the creases of his brow. *I hope we know what we're doing out here.*

Xiong had been standing on the transporter pad for nearly twenty minutes while Ilucci, Threx, and Cahow constructed his heavy-duty EVA suit around him from the boots up. Most of the labor had been devoted to installing a set of amplifying servomotors that would enable Xiong to move freely in the crushing pressure of the Tholian ship's interior, and they had integrated a tricorder into the suit itself, to record all critical data of his visit. Just as they began securing his helmet and visor, the captain's voice filtered down from the ceiling speaker. *"We're entering orbit, Ming,"* Nassir said. *"Are you about ready?"*

Ilucci gave Xiong a thumbs-up. Xiong answered, "Yes, sir. As soon as I get my helmet on, I'm good to go."

"All right, then," Nassir said. *"Clark, Bridy Mac's relaying safe transport coordinates to you now."*

"Understood, sir," Terrell said, moving behind the transport console. To the engineers he said, "Okay, suit him up. It's time." His hands moved quickly over the transporter controls as he powered up the system. "Coordinates locked in."

Cahow and Threx stood on either side of Xiong and lowered

the bulky headpiece of the suit into place. While they verified its built-in audiovisual uplink, Ilucci paced around them, giving orders like an artisan overseeing apprentices. With the helmet on, their voices sounded deeply muffled. The only sounds Xiong could hear clearly were the harsh tides of his own breathing and the quickening beat of his heart.

A short, low crackle inside the helmet preceded the activation of its comm circuit. Through his broad faceplate he saw Terrell speaking to him, but he heard his thinly reproduced voice inside the helmet. *"Ilucci says you're all set."* He smiled with warm humor. *"Still sure you want to do this?"*

"I've been waiting my whole life to do this," Xiong said. "Energize when ready, sir."

Terrell said, *"We'll leave your channel open. If you get in any trouble, just holler, and I'll beam you back."*

"Will do," Xiong replied as the engineers cleared the transporter pad and turned to watch his departure.

"Good luck," said Terrell.

As Terrell gently pushed the sliders that engaged the dematerialization sequence, Ilucci quipped loudly enough for Xiong to hear, *"I'll keep the bunk warm for ya."*

A blizzard of dreamlike whiteness filled Xiong's vision, and when it cleared he stood in a deep golden haze.

The interior of the Tholian ship shimmered in the searing heat and intense pressure. Xiong tried taking a step forward and found the resistance disorienting. An attempt to lift his arm and control its movement side-to-side resulted in several seconds of clumsy flailing. Even simple locomotion promised to be profoundly awkward.

"Xiong to *Sagittarius*," he said, hoping that the open channel was working. "Do you read me?"

Terrell's reply sounded scratchy and distant. *"Loud and clear,"* he said. *"Everything okay over there?"*

"So far," Xiong said. He regrouped and focused on standing still. "Acclimating is a bit harder than I expected. The habitat on Vanguard wasn't this hot—or this dense." Bending and turning slowly from the waist, he took in his surroundings. To either side of him a long, broad corridor curved away out of sight.

The passageway's overhead was high above him, arched and ribbed, as if the interior of the ship had been organically grown; it looked almost mismatched with the vessel's rigidly, trisymmetrically angular exterior. Every surface he could see—decks, bulkheads, portals—appeared to be composed of the same smooth volcanic glass. "Is the visual coming through okay?"

"It's a little choppy," Terrell replied, *"but we get the idea. If you head to your left, that should take you toward their command center."*

"Copy that." In careful, halting steps he worked his way toward the forward section of the vessel. Periodically he found crystalline formations protruding from the bulkheads. Their smooth, sheared-off surfaces danced with light from within. The structures bore an uncanny resemblance to the control panel that Xiong had seen the Shedai warrior use in the underground facility on Erilon several weeks earlier.

Everything about this looks familiar, he realized. From the techno-organic nature of the environment to its nearly uniform composition of metallicized obsidian, it reminded him of the massive artifacts on Ravanar and Erilon: black, insectile, and intrinsically frightening. Every biomechanoid-looking interface strengthened his conviction that whatever the Shedai turned out to be, their link to the Tholians was fundamental and ancient.

Moving through the superheated soup was getting easier. His motions took on a fluid, flowing quality. He didn't walk through the ship so much as he floated through it, riding its thick currents of rising warmth from one crest to the next. A wide, shallow arch in the bulkhead on his right led into a vast open space in the heart of the ship. *"Sagittarius,* I'm taking a detour to check this out."

"By all means," came Terrell's bemused reply.

Xiong stepped through the gap onto a broad walkway, careful to mind his step because the catwalk had no safety railing. The concave ceiling was close and gleaming with reflected crimson light from below. On the other side of the wide-open compartment, another walkway stretched along the starboard bulkhead. Both looked down upon a massive energy-generation complex. Its systems throbbed heartily. "Can't make out what kind of stardrive they're using," Xiong said. "The power source is matter-antimatter, but that's no warp drive."

Ilucci's voice chimed in on the comm inside his helmet. *"Good eye,"* said the master chief. *"Can you see a safe way down to the main engineering deck? I'd love a closer look at that."*

"Feel free to put on a suit and come join me," Xiong said.

A grim chortle mixed with the static. *"No, thanks,"* Ilucci said. *"I know some like it hot, but I ain't one of 'em."*

After taking a long look around the compartment, Xiong was stumped about how the Tholians accessed the lower level. "I can't see any way down from here," he reported. "I'm moving on toward the command deck."

"Copy that," Terrell said. *"Take your time. Check out anything of interest along the way."*

Half swimming, half walking back through the main passage, Xiong replied, "That's what I'm here for." Arriving at a Y-shaped intersection where a central passage split to port and starboard, Xiong sidestepped around a third branch of the passage that descended on a steep slope into the belly of the ship. "I think I might have a way to reach the lower deck after all, Master Chief. I'll check it out on the way back."

"Thanks, Ming," Ilucci said.

The main corridor ahead of him stretched away to a point obscured by heat shimmer. "Damn, this ship is big," Xiong muttered as he bounced and bobbed through the gelatinous atmosphere. Sweat beaded heavily on his forehead, and he felt perspiration travel crooked paths down his spine. "Master Chief, I think the heat exchangers on this suit of yours need a little more work. I feel like I'm getting slow-roasted."

Ilucci replied, *"What'd you expect? It's over 200 degrees Celsius in there. If it weren't for me, you'd be a casserole by now."*

"I'm just saying it's a bit warmer than you said it'd be."

In the background of the comm channel, Threx grumbled, *"I told him he oughtta strip down before we put the suit on him."*

Xiong rolled his eyes even though no one was there to see it. "Thanks, Threx, but a few of us come from cultures that still have nudity taboos, especially in front of members of the opposite sex."

"You didn't have to be modest on my account," Cahow teased.

"I don't think you should be ashamed of your body," Threx said. *"But then, I'm not the one sweating like a* plorgha *inside a Tholian battleship."* Mixed laughter warbled over the comm.

Meter after meter of the black-glass corridor passed by as Xiong worked his way forward. The main deck split into two upward slopes, which rejoined at the apex of an angled, oval-shaped opening for a downward passage. Tactical scans of Tholian ships encountered in recent years suggested the command deck was at the terminus of the upward slope.

Something at the end of the lower passage, however, caught Xiong's eye. He started toward it.

Terrell's inquiry conveyed confusion. *"Uh, Ming? Isn't the command deck on the upper—"*

"I have to see something," Xiong said. "Give me a minute."

"All right," Terrell said. *"It's your show."*

The deeper Ming descended, the darker the passage became, until the only illumination came from the compartment at its end. A ruddy glow bled from it into the thick, shimmering air. Bladelike protrusions of obsidian filled the center of the compartment. The closer he approached, the more familiar the shapes became. Then he emerged from the passage into the lower forward compartment and marveled at the biomechanoid device that dominated the cavernous space.

Two fearsome shapes, dark and symmetrical. Like the clawed, half-opened hands of a giant, one reached up from the deck, the other was suspended from the overhead. Each was the other's mirror image. Rising from the deck along the bulkheads were three arches, spaced at 120-degree intervals. They were broad at their bases and narrowed as they curved upward to meet at the top half of the device.

Xiong stared agape at the device, which pulsed with ruby hues of power. It was a miniaturized replica of the artifacts found on Erilon and Ravanar. "Commander Terrell?"

After a few seconds, he received a stunned reply. *"Yes?"*

"Please tell me you're seeing this."

"Oh, we're seeing it, all right," Terrell said. *"We're just not believing it."*

"Believe it," Xiong said, swelling with the pride of true accomplishment. He was about to say something more, something congratulatory to his comrades aboard the *Sagittarius* . . . then a roar of static disrupted the comm channel.

Xiong scrambled to boost the gain on his transceiver to cut through the noise. Seconds later, one sound from the *Sagittarius* came through—loud, clear, and unmistakable.

Explosions.

Claret waves of indignation propagated through the Colloquium. **Signals in orbit,** reported the Shedai Warden. *Telinaruul* **have boarded the** *Kollotaan* **spacecraft.**

Suspicion and recrimination resonated in the Adjudicator's query: **How did they breach our defenses?**

A dampening field, answered the Wanderer. **Like the one that wounded me, but more sophisticated.**

The *Telinaruul* **learn quickly,** observed the Sage.

Unity without hesitation from the legions of the Nameless: **Destroy them.** Their pronouncement was seconded by the

Avenger, who advised the Maker, **The trespassers must be exterminated.**

The Maker channeled hundreds of disparate wills through the focal node of the First Conduit. The collective power of the Shedai was being marshaled and directed skyward. Spectral light shimmered inside the Conduit's core, and the *Kollotaan* screeched in agony as the dark fires surged in response to Shedai fury.

At the threshold of unleashing their reprisal, one word brought the Colloquium to a stunned halt.

Hold, commanded the Apostate.

Cold anxiety rippled through the Apostate's partisans, all of whom were counted among the ranks of the *Serrataal,* the Enumerated Ones. The Myrmidon drifted closer to the Apostate's side in a display of solidarity, and he was followed quickly by the Thaumaturge.

The Maker swelled, expanding her bearing to majestic proportions, and lorded over the Apostate, who found her old tricks less than impressive. **Explain yourself,** she commanded.

Attacking the *Telinaruul* serves no purpose, argued the Apostate. **Destroy one ship, and many more will follow. Their numbers will only increase.**

We will bring them to heel soon enough, countered the Avenger. **Once we have mastered them, none will dare attempt our sanctum again. *Telinaruul* respond best to fear. You know this.**

I know that you believe it, the Apostate retorted. **And that you lack the wisdom to craft a new strategy.** To the Nameless he continued, **The *Telinaruul* have changed. We must change as well.**

Protests fused into a wall of angry noise. The Apostate paid no heed to the dismay of the Nameless, but the anger of the *Serrataal* was equally vigorous. **We do not change,** insisted the Maker. **We are Shedai.**

The Apostate projected his dissent with conviction. **What if** the *Telinaruul* can be engaged without conflict? Reasoned with?

Countless voices scoffed at his suggestion. The Wanderer retorted venomously, **One does not "reason" with beasts. They have trespassed in our domain and must suffer correction.**

The Apostate wheeled in a cloud of fury upon the Wanderer. She recoiled in fear as his voice trembled the Colloquium. **We gave up our domain for the peace of oblivion aeons ago. All these stars we abandoned, all these worlds we forsook.**

Nothing was surrendered, the Maker declared. **The seeds of our new genesis were planted. Our slumber was earned; now it has been disturbed by the petty ambitions of the ephemeral.**

Bitter sarcasm came easily to the Apostate. **The ephemeral,** he repeated, deriding the Maker before refocusing his ire on the Wanderer. *Brief flickers of life,* **you call them. You mock them, yet they have bested you twice. It seems the** *Telinaruul* **have risen in stature since last we reigned supreme.**

The Wanderer quaked with fury, her desire to work violence on him apparent, but he knew that she would not attack; she could not. He was the Apostate, ancient when she was made.

Defying the will of the Maker, however, was another matter. Oldest of the *Serrataal*, she ruled without compromise. **This is not the time for paralysis**, she declaimed. **Nor is it the hour for debate. The enemy is upon us. We must act with dispatch.**

Light poured from the Conduit and cohered into an illusion of the *Telinaruul* ship in orbit, holding at close station to the *Kollotaan* ship the Wanderer had lured to the First World. The Maker directed all her thought toward the tiny spacecraft and bade her legion of faithful to join with her in smiting it.

Despite the Apostate's defiant objection, the Colloquium's

majority had made its decision and stood poised to deliver its
judgment. As he turned his own thought-line to the fray, the defensive batteries on the triplet satellites of the First World
charged in a flicker of time and opened fire.

Supervising three separate mission initiatives at once had Commander Clark Terrell feeling a bit distracted.

On the main viewer of the *Sagittarius*'s bridge was a real-
time visual feed from Lieutenant Xiong aboard the derelict
Tholian battleship. At that moment, Xiong was working his
way forward in a central corridor.

At a station on Terrell's right, Ensign Theriault had started a
general sensor sweep of the surface of the fourth planet. The
young woman was deeply engrossed in her work.

On the other side of the bridge, McLellan was running
close-up, passive visual scans of the artificial structures on the
planet's three satellites. For the third time in five minutes, she
waved Terrell over. "Sir, have a look at this."

"What've you got, Bridy Mac?"

The compact screen above her station showed a densely
packed array of mechanical apertures. "It looks like a staggered
firing array," she explained. "Part of the reason for the delay
between shots at Erilon and Ravanar might have been that
those weapons needed time to build up charges in a prefire
chamber." She toggled a few keys on her control panel. The
image shifted to a series of graphs, some rendered as wave-
forms, others as topographical overlays for the moons' surfaces. "Based on the power signatures we picked up, I think
this thing has dozens of prefire chambers, and they're always
primed. Each one charges while the others around it are firing."

"You're saying we'd be looking at a continuous barrage?"

McLellan nodded. "Yes, sir. These things could wipe out an
attack fleet in no time."

Terrell sighed and moved back toward the center of the
bridge. "Wonderful," he muttered. He settled at the left side of
the captain's chair and said to Nassir, "You heard?"

"I wish I hadn't," Nassir said. "Theriault, anything notable on the surface?"

"Passive scans aren't getting much," Theriault said. "There's a lot of unusual interference. It might be part of the planet's natural magnetic field. I'm developing a canceling frequency to help us see through it."

"Very good," Nassir said. "Keep us posted."

Terrell nodded and smiled approvingly at Theriault, who returned the gesture and returned to work.

On the main viewer, the visual feed showed that Xiong had reached a point where the passage diverged. Ahead of him was an angled, oval-shaped tunnel that led down to a lower deck of the Tholian ship. The deck he stood on split into two paths that ascended around that passage's opening and converged above it.

The image came to a stop for a moment, then proceeded down the lower corridor. Terrell gave a quick nod to McLellan, who unmuted the outgoing channel. "Uh, Ming?" Terrell inquired uncertainly. "Isn't the command deck on the upper—"

"*I have to see something,*" Xiong replied over the comm. "*Give me a minute.*"

Terrell looked to his captain, who urbanely arched one eyebrow. "All right," Terrell said. "It's your show."

Nassir leaned toward Terrell and whispered, "Clark? What's he doing?" The most truthful answer Terrell could give him was a slow shake of his head and a shrug.

A wave of McLellan's hand snared Terrell's attention again. He walked over to her station, wearing an expression that he hoped would convey to the second officer how weary he was becoming of this particular ritual. "Yes?" he prompted her.

She spoke in a nervous whisper. "Shedai signals, sir. Origin unknown, but they're being relayed to all three moons."

"Have they detected us? Are they arming to fire?"

Switching her controls frantically, she shook her head and answered, "I don't know. I think those weapons are *always* ready to fire. Maybe this is just routine activity, but I—"

"Raise shields," Terrell said. "Now." He turned and moved quickly back to the center of the bridge. "Sayna, stand by for evasive maneuvers. Theriault, are you reading any signal traffic on the surface? Any energy readings?"

"Nothing unusual, sir," Theriault responded, "but I'm still getting interference, lots of it."

Nassir cut in, "Clark, look at the screen."

Terrell turned his head and saw the image that had his captain's jaw hanging half open. Xiong had found a compartment inside the Tholian ship that contained a near-perfect, small-scale replica of one of the Shedai artifacts.

Xiong's voice wavered with apprehension and crackled from static on the channel. *"Commander Terrell?"*

It took Terrell a few seconds to answer, "Yes?"

"Please tell me you're seeing this."

"Oh, we're seeing it, all right," Terrell said. "We're just not believing it."

"Believe it," Xiong said.

Blasts rocked the *Sagittarius*. A fountain of flames, sparks, and debris erupted from an unmanned aft duty station. Lights failed as the inertial dampeners cut out. In the darkness, Terrell didn't see the corner of the port console until he hit it chin-first.

Nassir lifted his voice above the thunderous din, but he still sounded calm. "Sayna, put us between the Tholian ship and the planet's moons!" He thumbed the intraship comm on the arm of his chair. "Engineering, damage report!"

"Containment failure!" Ilucci shouted back, his anger more evident than his fear. *"Had to dump our antimatter!"*

Terrell pulled himself back to his feet. "Master Chief! Can you beam Xiong back?"

"Negative," Ilucci said. *"Transporter's down!"*

From the tactical station, McLellan called out, "Shields buckling, Captain!"

A roaring boom pinned zh'Firro to the helm and threw the rest of the bridge crew forward. Over the comm, Ilucci yelled, *"Dorsal shields are gone!"*

"Sayna," Nassir said as he pulled himself back fully into his chair. "Get us out of here!"

Zh'Firro looked over her shoulder. "We can't get out of firing range in time on impulse."

"The planet," Terrell cut in. "Let's see if they feel like shooting at themselves."

Nassir confirmed the order. "Sayna, take us down—evasive pattern Bravo. Bridy Mac, send an SOS to Vanguard." He activated the shipwide comm channel. "All hands, this is the captain. Brace for emergency landing. Bridge out." More explosions rattled the tiny ship as he closed the channel. Radiant phosphors rained down from sparking systems overhead.

On the main viewer, the blue-green sphere of Jinoteur IV grew larger until the curve of its horizon passed beyond the edge of the screen, and all that was left was the broad canvas of its surface. Golden plumes blazed ahead of the ship as it penetrated the atmosphere. Turbulence quaked the *Sagittarius* and rattled its damaged hull with deafening bangs of metal against metal.

Zh'Firro glanced back at Nassir. "Landing gear's jammed. Airspeed dropping. Land or water, sir?"

The captain and the first officer looked at each other.

"A hard landing might breach the hull," Terrell warned.

Nassir countered, "Breach on a water landing, we'll sink like a rock."

"All right," Terrell said as the deck rumbled violently beneath him. "Split the difference."

Nassir nodded and said to zh'Firro, "Aim for a beach."

Terrell presented a stoic mien as the ship plummeted toward the planet's surface, but as the engines whined and the hull clattered and moaned, he couldn't help but grind his teeth as McLellan issued the distress call.

"Vanguard, this is *Sagittarius*! We're attempting an emergency landing on the fourth planet. We need antimatter! Repeat, we need antimatter! Stand by for final coordinates!"

As the ship dropped below a thick layer of storm clouds,

features of the landscape appeared, first hurtling closer, then blurring under the ship as zh'Firro fought to level their flight. "Impulse power fading, Captain," she said. "We're losing helm response."

At the science station, Theriault clung to her chair and stared at the main viewscreen, mesmerized by the rising menace of Jinoteur's rainswept surface.

"Theriault," Nassir said. "How far to the coastline?"

His order was enough to snap her out of her fear trance. She turned and gazed down into the blue light of the readout under the sensor hood. "Twenty-three hundred kilometers."

The *Sagittarius* dipped abruptly to starboard, and the pitch of the engines' whine began a swift, steady decline. Terrell leaned on Nassir's chair and advised him, "We won't make it."

"Ensign," Nassir said to Theriault. "What's the nearest body of shallow water? Quickly."

She threw a few switches without lifting her eyes from her sensor readout. "Twenty-one kilometers, bearing two-eight-point-one-six."

"Helm, make that your course," Nassir said. Blue-green blurs whipped along the bottom edge of the viewscreen as the *Sagittarius* skimmed the top of a jungle forest's canopy. The captain looked up at the grim-faced Terrell and smiled. "Look on the bright side. Now we can do the planetary survey."

With a sardonic grimace, Terrell replied, "Yes, sir. That was my first thought as well."

"Cheer up, Clark," the captain said. "It could always be worse, right?"

Terrell chortled. "Yes, sir. If there's one thing I've learned in Starfleet, it's that nothing is so bad that it can't get worse."

"That's the spirit," Nassir said.

The *Sagittarius* slammed through a dense swath of forest toward a flat, muddy brown streak winding through the jungle. Even through the duranium hull, Terrell heard the rapid, sharp cracks of hundreds of trees snapping from high-speed impact.

As the ship nose-dived, Terrell could only hope that the dark brown surface directly ahead of it was water.

After the sound of the explosions faded from Xiong's helmet comm, there had been nothing on the channel except silence. Several attempts to hail the *Sagittarius* by increasing the power to the suit's transceiver had proved fruitless. He checked the chronometer mounted on the left forearm of his suit. Contact with the ship had been lost for more than six minutes.

Xiong stood in the shadow of the unusual alien machinery he had discovered aboard the Tholian ship. It seemed to waver and ripple while he looked at it. The pressure and heat inside the ship made everything look like a mirage.

He glanced at the air and power gauges on his right forearm. *Enough air for another ten hours,* he noted. *About the same reserve in battery power. Ten hours to find a way out of this.* Seeds of anxiety that were nestled in his gut threatened to bloom into a fully developed panic at any moment. *Stay calm,* he reminded himself. *Review the facts.*

To the best of Xiong's knowledge, the nearest Starfleet ship to Jinoteur was at least twelve days away, perhaps more. There were a few well-trafficked star systems close by, but most of them were under Klingon control. A Starfleet rescue seemed unlikely to arrive before his suit ran out of air and power.

Maybe the Tholians have transporter technology, he thought. *If I can figure out how to work it, I could beam down to the surface.* Before he could get his hopes up, his inner pessimist spoke up. *What if they don't have transporters? Even if they do, would you even recognize one if you saw it? And how are you going to run it by yourself?* Dismay started turning into paralysis. He looked around the compartment and studied the various interface surfaces and noted that there were no buttons, levers, or switches that he recognized. *Maybe they interface directly with their technology, the way that Shedai did on Erilon.*

If so, jury-rigging my way off this ship just got a hell of a lot harder.

A triple-beep tone over the comm channel indicated that an encrypted Starfleet distress signal was being received. Xiong poked at the large frequency toggle on the arm of his suit until he locked in the secure emergency channel. McLellan's voice crackled over the comm.

"Vanguard, this is Sagittarius! *We're attempting an emergency landing on the fourth planet. We need antimatter. Repeat, we need antimatter! Stand by for final coordinates!"*

Knowing the ship hadn't been destroyed reassured Xiong slightly, but he still had his own predicament to cope with. He started walking back up the sloped passage. His next destination would be the ship's command center. *I might not understand things up there any better than the ones down here,* he figured, *but it's the best place to start looking for a way out.*

Before this mission, Xiong had seen Tholian bodies autopsied, he had studied several theories about their social structure and technology, and he had on a few occasions interacted with live Tholians who were garbed in amber-hued silk envirosuits. Not one iota of that experience had prepared him to be trapped alone inside one of their battleships.

First time for everything, he told himself as he reached the intersection and doubled back toward the bridge. *I just hope this doesn't turn out to be my first time getting myself killed.*

The Maker's rage burned like the heart of a blue star. **The ship should have been destroyed instantly! How did it survive?**

Fear and recrimination pulsed through the legion of the Nameless, who recoiled and thought only of evading the Maker's wrath. The Avenger and the Warden, denied the haven of retreat, stood together in the face of the Maker's fury.

The *Telinaruul* **ship had unique defenses,** the Warden insisted. **They came prepared to thwart us.**

Absurd. Blue-spark images raced through the air, drawn with the fires of the First Conduit, directed by the Maker's will. **Our power should have vaporized that speck of metal. Instead it has trespassed on the surface, defiled our sanctum. How?**

Hostile speculations buzzed through the shared mind-line of the Colloquium, but there was no sound but the distant crash of thunder and the soft slashing of rain outside the Colloquium.

The front rank of the *Serrataal* parted for the Wanderer, who approached the Maker, wrapped in hues of submission and fealty. **I sensed resistance in our mind-line,** the Wanderer said. **When the moment came to work our will upon the** ***Telinaruul,*** **one among us opposed the will of the others. We have been betrayed.**

The Maker reviewed the mind-line, relived the attack on the ship, this time opening her senses to the subtleties in the ebb and flow of power through the First Conduit. It was as the Wanderer had said. A defiant will had undermined the others, had diluted and diffused their power, enabling the ship to survive.

When she turned to confront the Apostate, he did not flinch or avert his focus. He stood proudly even as she accused him.

You interceded for the ***Telinaruul,*** declared the Maker.

I did. There was no shame in him for what he had done.

A series of violent images communicated the Maker's wishes to the Avenger, whose corporeal avatar dissociated, freeing her essence to speed its overland journey to the downed ship.

To the Apostate the Maker explained, **You have only delayed the inevitable and prolonged the** ***Telinaruul*****'s suffering. Never have we permitted their kind upon the First World. Their presence will not be tolerated now.** She summoned the others to join in her rebuke of the Apostate and marshaled their combined strength as if it were her own. One-third of the *Serrataal* refused her entreaty; they seemed poised to oppose her until the Apostate signaled his surrender to her

judgment, which she pronounced without delay. **I banish you
from our Colloquium. Return only when you are ready to
don the colors of a penitent.**

As the Apostate's physical form dissolved into separating
tendrils of dark vapor, his reply resonated ominously throughout the Colloquium: **That day will never come.**

10

Captain Nassir turned his chair aft as he heard the door to the bridge open. Ankle-deep dirty water surged between Master Chief Ilucci's feet and across the deck onto the bridge. "We've got a hull breach topside," Ilucci said as he stepped inside, water dripping from his sodden coverall.

"Amply demonstrated, Master Chief," Nassir said. "Are your people all right?"

Ilucci answered as he surveyed the damage to the bridge's overloaded consoles. "Torvin's hurt. He'll live, but Doc Babitz says he'll be down for a few hours."

The captain nodded. An injured crewman wasn't good news, but he was relieved that Torvin's injuries appeared to be the extent of serious casualties from the attack and the crash. "Keep me posted, Master Chief. And get that breach sealed."

"Will do, Skipper." Ilucci pulled an access panel off the starboard bulkhead and poked his head inside the gap.

Nassir got up from his chair and sloshed across the shallow flood to McLellan. "Bridy Mac, bring Sorak's team and Medic Tan Bao to the cargo bay. We'll meet you there." McLellan gave a curt nod and made a quick exit. The captain looked to the rest of the bridge crew. "Everyone else, with me."

He led them off the bridge to the port ladder, then down to the cargo bay. Only a few trickles of water had yet found their way to the ship's lowest deck. As soon as the rest of the bridge team had finished descending the ladder, Nassir began issuing directions. "Clark, Sayna, break out the lures Xiong brought aboard. Theriault, help me unpack the signal dampeners."

They opened the crates and had their contents ready to go by the time McLellan and the field scouts clambered down into the cargo bay. Sorak, as usual, skipped any preamble and cut to business. "Captain, a large energy reading is moving toward us, from the north. It will reach us in less than ten minutes."

"I expected as much," Nassir said. "Here's the situation. Without main power, the ship can't defend itself. Whatever's coming at us, we need to lure it away from here, with these decoys Xiong developed. We'll split into pairs and head in different directions." He pointed as he named each person. "Sorak with me. McLellan with Tan Bao. Theriault and Niwara. Razka, go with zh'Firro."

Nodding at the devices sitting in the open crates, Nassir continued, "One person from each pair take a decoy, the other take a signal dampener. Get as far from the ship as fast as you can; draw the thing's attention. If it gets too close, activate the decoy's propulsion circuit and let it go. Then use the dampener to hide yourselves. Clear?" The landing party nodded.

The captain turned to Terrell. "Clark, you'll have the conn. Stay with Dr. Babitz and the engineers. Once we're ashore, have Ilucci seal the top deck and scuttle the ship. You should have enough battery power to run a dampening field for about a half-hour. If we're lucky, the thing'll be gone by then."

Terrell made a rueful frown. "And if it's not?"

Nassir slapped Terrell's shoulder. "You'll think of something," he said. "You're clever that way." He picked up a fist-sized decoy device. It weighed roughly one kilogram. He had no idea what might be in it to make it so heavy. "All right, everyone," he said, motioning with the device toward the ladder. "Time's a factor. Grab a pack, and get moving."

As the head of the ship's security team, Lieutenant Sorak was the first to climb up the ladder and out the ship's wide topside hatch. He was greeted by warm, humid air, a storm-blackened sky flickering with far-off electrical activity, and gray curtains of rain that swept across the ship's half-submerged hull and churned up white froth on the surface of the river.

Sorak moved a few paces from the hatchway, lifted his tricorder, and crouched. He scanned the perimeter while the rest of the landing party climbed quickly out of the ship into the squall. Nassir was the first one to follow him out. The captain joined Sorak and dropped to one knee at his side.

"Any movement?" Nassir asked.

Sorak continued to watch his tricorder readout. "Not yet, sir. The storm is generating intense interference, on several wavelengths. It might not be an entirely natural phenomenon."

"Keep an eye on it," Nassir said. He turned to the rest of the group. "Sorak and I will head north. The rest of you, pick a direction and go. Move out." He pivoted back toward the river and said to Sorak, "Stow your gear; we're going."

Nassir eased himself over the curved edge of the hull into the brown water that surrounded the ship. Sorak turned off his tricorder, secured it inside his watertight backpack along with the dormant signal dampener, and followed the captain into the river.

It was warm, slow-moving, and thick with mud. Swimming while wearing boots and a backpack was awkward. The boots made it difficult for Sorak to propel himself efficiently, and the backpack was pure drag. He and the captain had the greatest distance to swim; fortunately, the ship had landed in a narrow bend of the river.

Sorak used a variation of the crawl stroke that kept his head above water, so that he could keep the captain in sight. The current was strong enough to pull them both slightly eastward of their intended landing point. After a minute of hard swimming, both men scrambled onto the muddy riverbank.

The Vulcan scout helped the captain to his feet. Nassir nodded his thanks and opened his own watertight pack to retrieve his communicator. He flipped open its gold grille and sent a hailing signal. "Nassir to all landing party personnel, check in."

Staring back across the river, all that Sorak could see was silver veils of rain. He retrieved his phaser from his pack.

The others responded quickly. McLellan and Tan Bao

checked in first, followed by Theriault and Niwara, then Razka and zh'Firro. "Good luck, everyone," Nassir said. "And Godspeed. *Sagittarius,* did you copy all that?"

"Affirmative, sir," Terrell replied, his normally rich voice sounding hollowed out by the communicator's speaker.

"Take her down, Clark," the captain ordered. "And stay there till I give the word."

"Aye, sir," Terrell said. *"Be careful out there.* Sagittarius *out."* The channel clicked and went quiet. Out in the river, the water boiled and churned as the ship's maneuvering thrusters fired and nudged it toward the center of the river, into deeper water. Dirty foam surrounded the ship, which vanished into the muck. Seconds later the foam dispersed, and the water once again became still and uniformly beige.

Sorak watched the captain hesitate on the riverbank and stare at the river with a melancholy expression. "Captain," Sorak said with polite insistence. "We have to go."

"Yes, we do," Nassir said. He turned his back on the river and jogged, then sprinted, into the dense, dark jungle.

Sorak followed him. As he neared the tree line, the sky above turned black as night, and a crack of thunder shook the ground. Then he was under the cover of the rain forest, heading north at a full run with the captain.

Completing the *Kolinahr,* the Vulcan ritual of shedding all emotion to achieve an intellect of pure logic, had taught Sorak that fear was a paralyzing emotion, an impediment to rational action. Being immune to fear, however, did not mean becoming oblivious of peril. Shadows in the forest had begun to pursue himself and the captain.

He poised his finger over the trigger of his phaser and quickened his pace, determined to place himself between the captain and whatever danger they now were running toward.

"Wait up!" shouted zh'Firro. Razka halted and turned back to let the Andorian *zhen* catch up to him. She was quicker on her feet than most humanoids he had met, but she had been unable to keep pace with the Saurian field scout in an environment so similar to that of his native world.

He breathed in the jungle. It was rich with the odor of decaying vegetation and the sickly sweet fragrance of exotic flora. Rainwater drizzled in steady streams through the multilayered forest canopy, and the ground was slippery with several centimeters of mud. His broad and leathery webbed feet were bare and felt more comfortable in the rough, root-covered terrain than on the smooth metal decks of the ship.

Cannonades of thunder concussed the air and swayed the tropical forest. In the rocking movements of the trees, Razka caught hints of movement. A nebulous presence was stalking them. He blinked his inner eyelid into place and surveyed the forestscape with his thermal vision.

He smelled the change in the air before he saw it. Darkness cold and foul was spreading like a slow poison through the jungle. Something terrible was descending from above, and it was coming down all around them.

Zh'Firro stumbled to a halt beside him and looked up, following his line of vision. "What is it?" she asked.

"A trap, Lieutenant," he said. "It's called a trap."

Rain hissed through the forest of azure, piercing wind-whipped boughs in drizzles and mists. High overhead, tree limbs snapped in the gale. On the muddy jungle floor, coltish legs carried McLellan through narrow slivers between lichen-draped trees. Tan Bao was right behind her, his own stride unflagging. McLellan figured it hadn't been coincidence that the captain had teamed her up with the medic, who was the only runner on the ship likely to be able to keep pace with an experienced marathoner such as herself.

She opened up her lead and hurtled down an uneven slope. The sky above was ink-black and stuttering with bright blue lightning. Racing through a rainstorm felt like a lark, like a child's foolish tempting of fate.

Directly ahead an electric bolt lanced down and blasted a

tree to smoking cinders. A thunderclap threw McLellan backward. She collided with Tan Bao, and they fell in a heap on the
muddy slope. Overhead the strike had torn a burning cavity in
the forest canopy. Dark sheets of rain hammered down.

Then another blast of lightning struck, closer this time. Its
crash was like a spike driven into her eardrums, its heat like a
furnace blast in her face. An indigo afterimage on her retinas left
her blind for a few seconds.

Before her vision had cleared, Tan Bao pulled her to her feet.
Her thunderstruck ears could barely hear him shout, "Run!" He
kept his grip on her jumpsuit sleeve and yanked her forward.
Sprinting blind into a violet darkness, she lunged headlong
through clusters of vines. Her feet slid and slipped in the mud.
Shapes came back a few at a time, in visual hiccups, strobes of
movement. At first she thought it was an artifact of the flash that
made her see shadows following them.

Fiery bolts slammed through the jungle, setting it ablaze,
while the maelstrom tattered the treetops and rained heavy debris onto the ground. Panic left McLellan short of breath, gasp-
ing. She swallowed a mouthful of air, and the compression in
her ears cleared with a painful pop. All she could hear was the
apocalyptic percussion of constant thunder.

Then a chilling, primal noise wailed from the sky. It was part
roar, part droning howl—the hunting cry of a leviathan.

From every direction, the predatory shadows closed in, gain-
ing speed with every meter of ground McLellan and Tan Bao
covered. Then a blast of fire rent a new gash in the jungle ahead
of her, and she realized that the leviathan and the shadows were
one and the same.

Icy wind slashed through the humid jungle air, gusting into
Vanessa Theriault's face. A tentacle of shimmering liquid
snaked out of the trees ahead of her and rushed in her direction.
She froze for the space of a breath, mesmerized as the dark fluid
sparkled with motes of power. Then Niwara tackled her to the
ground as the appendage struck like a viper.

It blurred past them and split the trunk of an ancient jungle tree. In the millisecond before impact, the tentacle's tip had sharpened to a swordlike point and transformed into a razor-edged blade of gleaming obsidian.

The tentacle ripped free of the tree, leaving behind a crystalline residue in the wound, like a scar of black glass.

Niwara and Theriault scrambled to their feet and resumed running, trying to continue on their easterly course away from the ship. A midnight blur lunged from Theriault's left. She ducked. Another tentacle, another bifurcated tree. Within seconds, more tentacles were invading the forest, probing, searching, taking every opportunity to attack.

Stands of trees to either side of her and Niwara were uprooted and blithely tossed skyward, enabling Theriault to see that the tendrils all originated in the storm cloud overhead. Flashes of lightning struck in tandem with more descending tendrils of jet-black liquid. This was not like the fearsome black golem that had assaulted the teams on Erilon; this was something of an entirely different order—larger, more versatile, and more powerful.

Liquefying vapors turned into stoneglass daggers and jabbed from multiple directions. Theriault sidestepped one, dodged another, somersaulted over a third. Tumbling back to her feet, she saw Niwara pivot clear of a deadly thrust. As Niwara sprinted toward Theriault, another tentacle raced up behind the Caitian woman. Pointing, Theriault cried, "Look out!"

Niwara hurled herself to the ground, and the saw-toothed blade grazed her golden mane before burying itself into the muddy ground. The Caitian rolled clear and backpedaled toward Theriault. "Keep going!" she shouted, drawing her phaser and laying down covering fire. She turned around when she reached Theriault, slapped her back, and started sprinting as fast as her broad paws could carry her. Theriault paced the longer-legged scout by virtue of sheer terror.

Shadows were tearing the jungle to pieces, and it was only a matter of time before she and Niwara ran out of room to run.

•   •   •

Eerie wails echoed across a coal-colored sky. Keening bellows of bloodlust, atonal and resonant, resounded off nearby hills, and there was nothing but the pandemonium of thunder and the searing fury of lightning ripping the jungle asunder.

Chaotic frequencies and shockingly strong electrical fields buffeted Celerasayna zh'Firro's antennae. Her Andorian senses were overwhelmed by emanations from the unnatural storm cloud. Its every pulse resonated inside her mind, filled her with panic, clouded her thoughts with confusion and fear.

There was no place she could hide from its psychic onslaught. All she could do was run.

Liquid knives arced out of the darkness and tested her reflexes. She outran one strike and weaved left past another. An abrupt halt spared her from an uppercut that would have decapitated her. Razka tugged her arm and yanked her clear of a stab in the back. Two of the tentacles collided and shattered each other in a flare of indigo flames.

They emerged into a wide-open clearing of sheared-off tree stumps and charred, smoking ground. Above, the ebon cloud loomed over the jungle, a Colossus with hundreds of fluidic limbs seeking out its prey. It was like the darkest passages of the Codices come to life—a physical incarnation of Chaerazaelos, the eternal storm of torments that awaited those who dared to appear unWhole before Uzaveh the Infinite. Zh'Firro stood in the open, staring slack-jawed at what she took to be the embodiment of annihilation, and lost herself in its terrible majesty.

A scaly hand slapped her face. The stinging warmth of the hit registered and raised her ire. Then she saw Razka standing in front of her. "Snap out of it, sir! Start running!"

One moment Captain Nassir and Sorak zigzagged at a full run through the claustrophobically close jungle forest, evading lethally agile tentacles lunging out of every shadow, and the next they stumbled clear of the tree line onto a broad, open slope that overlooked a lush terrain of steep, rolling hills. In the sky a few kilometers distant Nassir saw the edge of the massive storm cloud that lurked overhead and, beyond it, clear sky.

Behind them, a dozen serpentine coils were smashing through the forest and were about to overtake them.

"End of the line," he said to Sorak, pulling off his pack. As he reached inside for the decoy, he said to the Vulcan, "Prep the dampener."

He was grateful that Xiong and his team on Vanguard had simplified the use of the decoy. With so little time to deploy it, the less Nassir needed to remember, the better. Rain pelted the sphere in his hands. He engaged its autopropulsion module and pointed it in the direction he wanted it to go. Then he pressed the button under his index finger.

The device leaped from his hands and shot away into the sky, quickly becoming little more than a speck sailing over and beyond the crest of the next hill, speeding away toward the horizon. "Activate the dampener," he said. Sorak switched on his device. Nassir snapped, "Hit the deck!"

He and Sorak dropped to the ground as the tentacles erupted from the trees and raced over them—and continued into the distance, chasing after the still-flying decoy. Nassir gave silent thanks to Xiong and his cadre of scientists, pulled his communicator from his belt, and flipped it open. With the press of a single switch he sent a triple beep to the rest of the landing party. That would be their cue to release their decoys and activate their signal dampeners.

He just hoped that the rest of the landing party was still alive to receive the order.

McLellan and Tan Bao flailed clumsily with their packs as they ran, their bodies able to do two things at once with speed but not with grace. She fumbled the decoy, which bobbled inside the pack with every running footfall she landed, while Tan Bao struggled to get a grip on the dampener.

As soon as her hand gripped the fist-sized device, she let her pack fall away in the mud behind her. Tan Bao did likewise as he pulled the dampener free.

Flashes of lightning to her left gave McLellan enough light to find the controls of the decoy. One touch was enough to arm its propulsion circuit. Another would send it on its way. It was only another five meters to a narrow break in the canopy cover.

An impact against the back of her knee was so swift and the cut so clean that she didn't realize what had happened until the lower portion of her right leg fell away and she pitched forward onto her face. She fumbled the decoy, which rolled ahead of her and sank halfway into the mud.

Then the pain hit. Cold fire coursed through her leg. She looked down and saw the crystalline residue spreading over her wound, a scab of glass. The tentacle that had severed her leg reared up, momentarily a vapor as it coiled to strike.

The dampener, fully activated, rolled to a stop beside her, and the tentacle wavered, as if it had lost track of its prey. Then it steadied and fixed itself on a new target: Tan Bao. The medic dived toward the decoy, reaching for it with one hand while brandishing his phaser in the other. He slid across the muddy ground as the tentacle snapped forward. His hand closed on the decoy, and he fired his phaser at full power into the jungle canopy. The tentacle liquefied and solidified on target for his heart. He dropped his phaser, lifted the decoy, and activated its propulsion circuit.

The decoy shot up and away through the hole he'd blasted in the canopy. He flattened himself on the ground, face pressed into the mud, as the tentacle curved up away from his back and out through the smoldering channel in the foliage, hurtling after the decoy. A rumble of thunder shook the ground. Then there was only the white noise of rain.

Tan Bao pulled his face from the muck. He gasped for breath, checked to make certain there were no more tendrils stalking them, and scrambled over to McLellan. She took his arm in a fierce grip. "It hurts, Tan," she said through gritted teeth. Tears of agony rolled from her eyes. "God help me, it hurts! *Do something*."

"You have to let go of my arm," he said. "I need to get back to my pack. I have a field kit in there." He pried at her fingers. "I'll be right back, Bridy, I promise."

It took all her strength to let go of him. She covered her face with her mud-caked hands and listened to his sprinting steps squishing across the wet ground. Fighting for breath and clarity, she focused on the sound of him coming back, getting closer. Then the hiss of a hypospray brought a warm sensation to her body, and she felt weightless. She remained half-conscious while he examined her with his medical tricorder.

"The good news," he said, "is that whatever that thing did to your leg, it stopped the bleeding."

Anticipating the second half of his report, she asked, "What's the bad news?"

"Whatever that stuff is . . . it's alive."

"Come on!" Niwara shouted to Theriault, who was a few paces behind her. "We're almost there!"

The jungle teemed with scores of tentacles. Adding to Niwara and Theriault's numerous disadvantages, they had been forced to retreat uphill for the last hundred meters.

A crystalline blade cut across Niwara's path and embedded itself in a tree. The liquid part of the tentacle disengaged from the crystal blade, leaving it behind as it recoiled for another strike. The nimble Caitian ducked under the stuck shaft of black glass and dodged right, nearly colliding with Theriault, who had caught up to her.

Ahead the darkness of the forest gave way to light and air, a clearing open enough to release the decoy. The two officers jumped through a wall of thick blue-green fronds—and nearly plunged over the edge of a cliff into a vine-choked ravine, thirty meters above a run of white-water rapids.

Niwara regained her balance first, then she reached out and steadied Theriault. They teetered for a moment on the crumbling edge of the cliff. "Activate the dampener," Niwara said as she readied the decoy. Seconds later, the dampener powered up with a low hum, and Niwara released the decoy into the sky. The jungle canopy echoed with the snaps of breaking limbs as the tentacles shot upward in pursuit.

Mission accomplished, Niwara congratulated herself.

A shimmering blur barreled out of the forest behind them— a straggling tentacle in belated pursuit. It slammed them aside as it passed between them and sped away toward the horizon.

The impact hurled Niwara and Theriault off the cliff.

Niwara's left paw shot out, seeking the cliff's edge. Her right paw reached for Theriault. Catching the edge, she arrested her own fall, but she could only watch as her shipmate tumbled down the ravine. Vines snapped as the young science officer plummeted through them, desperately grasping for handholds. Then she splashed down into a muddy froth of fast-moving current and was swept away.

The Caitian scout pulled herself back on top of the cliff and looked down at the rushing waters. Overhead, the storm began to split apart. Something deep inside it unleashed another horn-like, groaning cry.

As she listened to its unearthly howl echo off the distant hillsides, Niwara felt as if it knew of her failure to protect Theriault . . . and that it was mocking her.

Razka let go of the decoy into the clearing full of stumps, and it zoomed on a long arc for the horizon. Lieutenant zh'Firro huddled close to him, the dampener humming softly in her hands. Crouched down at the tree line, they watched dozens of writhing coils blaze dark trails across the sky.

Looking up, he noted that the storm cloud was beginning to break apart. Pieces of it were heading in each direction, following the decoys. Watching the stormhead split itself and retreat, Razka grinned. *Divide and conquer,* he mused with satisfaction.

"We should head back to the rendezvous," zh'Firro said.

"Yes, sir," Razka answered. He took point and began retracing their steps through the jungle. It would be a roundabout route back, but it held the least likelihood of becoming lost.

As they walked, zh'Firro looked up at the clearing sky. Her focus seemed to be deep, as though she were looking into a great distance. "I wonder if Xiong's okay up there," she said. "He's all alone on that Tholian ship. What's he going to do when he runs out of air?"

"I'm sure he'll think of something," Razka said, pressing ahead to follow the trail. "He's quite clever . . . for a human."

"Is that supposed to be a compliment?" zh'Firro asked.

Razka cocked his head in amusement. "I guess that depends on your opinion of humans," he said.

11

The Apostate was correct, noted the Herald. **The *Telinaruul* are elusive. Perhaps the Avenger's slumber robbed her of skills.**

His words bordered on heresy. Agitating the others—particularly the Nameless—had always been the Herald's favored sport, and the Wanderer had long held him in contempt because of it. The Herald was a rogue, a dangerously random element; it was impossible for her to tell whether his loyalties belonged to the Maker or to the Apostate, or if he had any loyalty at all. Had the choice been hers, she would have expelled him from the *Serrataal* and forced him to be counted among the Nameless.

Alas, the choice was not hers, and the Maker suffered his insolence with aplomb.

Commanding the Colloquium's attention with a brief harmonic vibration of her mind-line, the Maker reassured them, **The intruders will be dealt with. They may have misdirected the Avenger, but their respite will be temporary.**

Acceding to the Maker's cautious optimism, the gathered Shedai cooled the colors flowing through their shared thought-space. The Adjudicator took advantage of the collective pause. **The *Telinaruul* have sullied our world. We should make an example of one of theirs.**

Other matters press upon us, the Wanderer interjected. **First we must teach them to respect what is ours.** She harnessed a sphere of violet fire from the First Conduit and illustrated her point: a remote star group, a precious world of life, a hidden Conduit . . . and a surface infested by *Telinaruul*. **Even now they seek to unlock our secrets. They have come in**

numbers to Avainenoran and are searching for its Conduit. That world must be washed clean with their blood.

The Maker attuned herself to the First Conduit and tested its bond to the Conduit on Avainenoran. **It is distant. There are many** *Telinaruul* **on the surface . . . and two starships in orbit.** Her aura clouded with doubt. **Such vessels did not exist when the foundation of our domain was laid.** She went quiet, apparently considering the matter with great care. **To act with sufficient force and celerity will be taxing and perilous.**

Alarmed, the Wanderer responded with bitter indignation. **The more they learn,** she declared, **the more dangerous they become. They must not capture another Conduit.**

Brooding silence answered the Wanderer's argument. Finally, the Maker's mind-line resolved to a bright golden hue of determination, and she set the future in motion. **We must gather strength to manage a great transit. When the next day-moment begins for the** *Telinaruul* **on Avainenoran, let them awaken to a battalion of the Nameless bearing our grim tidings.**

12

Commodore Reyes stood next to Lieutenant Commander T'Prynn at the hub. On the other side of the octagonal console were Commander Cooper and Ambassador Jetanien. Reyes had been in his office when Cooper, as the officer of the watch, had received the distress signal from the *Sagittarius*. Within seconds of hearing Cooper's summons, Reyes had been at the XO's side on the supervisor's deck. Less than two minutes later, both T'Prynn and Jetanien had arrived in the operations center at Reyes's request.

T'Prynn and Jetanien listened closely as they finished their second replay of the downed ship's last transmission. *"Repeat, we need antimatter! Stand by for final coordinates."*

Reyes asked Cooper, "Did we get the coordinates?"

"Yes, sir," Cooper said. "In a compressed data burst."

Jetanien made nervous clicking noises with his beaklike proboscis. "Do we know who or what attacked them?"

"Most likely they were fired on by the weapons emplacements we detected previously," T'Prynn said. "An earlier report from the *Sagittarius* indicated the Tholian vessel was derelict, and long-range sensors have detected no other ships in the system."

"See how long that lasts," Reyes said with a worried frown. "It's a good bet the Klingons got this message before we did."

Cooper shook his head. "Wouldn't do 'em much good. It was sent on a secure channel."

"Son," Reyes said with weary cynicism, "how many Klingon codes have we broken in the last three months?"

Grasping the gist of Reyes's rhetorical query, Cooper lowered his eyes and lifted his eyebrows. "Point taken."

Reyes leaned forward and planted both his broad hands on the console. Studying the star chart on the screen in the middle of the hub, he asked the group, "What do the Klingons have in that area right now?"

"One heavy battle cruiser," T'Prynn said, pointing out a star system very close to Jinoteur. "The *Zin'za,* currently finishing repairs after its last mission to Jinoteur." Indicating another star system, one far away in Klingon space, she added, "Three more cruisers have been assigned as its combat escorts, but they shipped out of Ogat less than three days ago. They will not reach the *Zin'za* for another eleven days."

The commodore sighed heavily. "The *Zin'za*'s less than twelve hours from Jinoteur at maximum warp." He looked across the hub at Jetanien. "If they reach the *Sagittarius* before we can, this ball might wind up in *your* court." He looked at T'Prynn. "How soon do you expect the *Zin'za* to ship out?"

"In less than five hours," T'Prynn said.

Cooper called up a Starfleet deployment grid and superimposed it over the star chart. "The *Endeavour* and the *Lovell* are at least twelve days from Jinoteur," he said. "We have plenty of antimatter fuel pods here on Vanguard, but the fastest ship that could haul one would still take almost a week to get out there."

"Thank you for apprising us of the staggeringly obvious, Commander," Jetanien said gruffly. He clicked his beak three times in quick succession. "If we require a remedial primer on the difference between hot and cold, we will be sure to enlist your sage counsel once again."

Reyes eyed Jetanien warily. "Somebody woke up on the wrong side of the rock today." He knew that he was letting Jetanien off easily. Ever since the collapse of the Chelon's diplomatic summit with the Klingons and the Tholians seven weeks earlier, the inscrutable diplomat had fluctuated between bursts of grouchiness and long intervals of sullen withdrawal. Reyes was concerned that more had been at stake in those negotiations for Jetanien personally than he had been willing to admit.

"What I was going to say, before I was interrupted," Cooper

continued after the passage of an awkward silence, "is that we might be able to track down a few friendlies in the systems around Jinoteur and have one of them haul out a fuel pod."

"Civilians," Reyes mumbled, hoping that another option would suddenly appear but knowing that it probably wouldn't. "I can't believe we'd even *think* of sending civilians in there."

T'Prynn said, "There might be an alternative, Commodore. However, it might necessitate a few . . . compromises."

Her choice of words raised Reyes's hackles. The last few months had taught him the hard way that T'Prynn's idea of what constituted a "compromise" often proved to be more ruthless than he found palatable. "What are you suggesting, Commander?"

"Even with the help of local parties, delivering antimatter to the *Sagittarius* will take at least twenty-two hours. Because that timetable cannot be shortened, our only option is to ensure that the Klingons' timetable is extended."

Furtive glances were volleyed among Reyes, Cooper, and Jetanien. Cooper looked askance at T'Prynn. "Are you talking about delaying the *Zin'za*'s deployment from Borzha II?"

"I am," T'Prynn said.

Jetanien made a deep rumbling noise before he asked with grave suspicion, "And how, exactly, do you propose to do that?"

She turned and fixed her cold, calculating stare on Reyes. "That," she said, "is where the compromise comes into play."

Moments of genuine privacy were rare for Ganz. Surrounded daily by his retinue of henchmen and female companions, he was obliged to appear aloof, unassailable, and in control. Managing the public perception of his image was an ongoing concern. He could not afford to be witnessed in a moment of candor. To lose control of himself in front of others would be to lose control over those he employed and to lose face in front of those with whom he did business. A careless laugh, a display of temper, any sign of hesitation or regret could undermine everything that he had worked for so long to build. Keeping his moods in check was difficult for him. He was a passionate man, prone as often to anger as to levity. Playing the role of a cipher was the hardest skill he had ever mastered—and possibly the most vital.

Spending his days and most of his evenings on display made his daily few hours of solitude aboard the *Omari-Ekon* precious; he savored them for their simplicity. Crisp, cool, clean sheets. Relief from the driving noise and narcotic odors of the game floor. The passionate embrace of the only woman who ever saw the inside of his bedroom, even though no one ever saw them within five meters of each other outside of it.

Neera sat in front of the vanity on Ganz's right, pulling a jade-handled brush through her thick sable hair. She worked the brush in long, seductive strokes that had an all but hypnotic effect on Ganz. Her skin was a slightly brighter shade of green than his own, and her eyes were a pale aqua—an unusual color for an Orion woman. Though he knew it was wrong to let himself love her, she was irresistible to him. Outside, managing the male and female companions who worked aboard the ship, she was savvy and subtle and cunning. When distracting the gamblers at the tables or screening new arrivals to see whether they harbored bad intentions, she could instinctively adapt to whatever they desired her to be: coy one moment, brazen the next; meek and innocent for one man, a salacious flirt for another, a warm and caring heart for the ones who needed confidants.

There was no denying the effect she had on him, and it unnerved him. On his upward climb to affluence and power he had learned that there was only one universal principle in business: fear. His goal had always been to instill fear in those below him, while managing his fear of those who sought to undermine him—and there were many individuals and groups that fell into the latter category. Superiors, rivals, competitors, governments. There was always a reason to be afraid when so much stood to be won or lost on every decision he made, but he had become a self-made merchant prince of Orion by obeying one simple rule:

Never show fear to anyone. *Especially,* he thought with a self-deprecating grin, *not to the woman you sleep with.*

She noticed his stare in the mirror. Her reflection looked back at him with a soft, caring expression. "Finally awake?"

"I was having a dream," he said. "Then I realized you weren't in it, so I decided to wake up instead."

Holding a lock of her hair in a firm grip, she worked the brush through some tangles at its end. "Ready for another night of impressing the masses?"

He rolled onto his side to face her more directly. "I'm just hoping the tables do better than break even tonight."

"I spoke to Danac about that," she said. "He understands that he's supposed to finish the night with a profit."

"Good. I'll have Zett watch him, just in case."

A sour look darkened Neera's face. "I know Zett's quite good at what he does," she said, "but I don't like him."

"Neither do I," Ganz admitted. "But we're not supposed to *like* him. His job is to keep people in line, not win them over."

Neera put down her brush and half-turned in his direction. "You need to keep a shorter leash on him," she said. "He has an unhealthy obsession with that drunkard Quinn. I don't want it disrupting business."

Never show fear to the woman you're sleeping with . . . especially when she's your boss.

"Sure, Zett holds grudges, but he's disciplined," Ganz said. "He won't act unless I tell him to. He knows Quinn is useful to me."

"Quinn is a liability," Neera replied. "Too angry to be an underling, too volatile to be a middleman, and not smart enough to stay bought. He could be trouble."

Ganz sat up on the edge of the bed. "All true," he said. "But like I said, he's *useful.* He gets jobs done that other people can't."

"That's no reason to trust him," Neera said.

He got up. "I don't trust *anybody.*" Walking over to her, he continued, "Someone with muscle's pulling his strings from the other side. I don't know who; maybe one of the other bosses, maybe Starfleet. I don't care, really. Smuggling gets harder every day, but whoever's backing him makes it possible."

"The only reason smuggling is difficult for us is that we're docked at a Federation starbase," Neera said. "If we made port in one of the neutral star systems nearby, we could move much more freely."

With a firm but tender grip, Ganz started massaging Neera's shoulders. "You're right. . . . But how long do you think we'd last without armed escorts? And how much do you think it'd cost to hire them?" She closed her eyes and relaxed into his kneading hands. "I'd rather deal with a few delays and do our business from here. As long as we're docked at Vanguard, no one'll come gunning for us."

In a teasing voice she quipped, "You'd give up your liberty in the name of security?" She smirked. "Some might call that a foolish bargain."

"No liberties when you're dead," he replied.

Her personal comm device, which had been sitting among her assortment of cosmetics containers on the vanity, beeped softly. She picked it up, flipped it open, and pressed it to her ear. "Go ahead," she said to the person on the other end. After listening carefully for several seconds, she said simply, "I understand," then flipped the device closed. Setting the device back on the vanity, she met Ganz's questioning gaze in the mirror. "Get dressed," she said.

Not wishing to comply too easily, Ganz asked, "Why?"

"Because there's just one problem with relying on Starfleet's protection," Neera said, rising from the vanity. "Every now and then, they want something." Turning to face him, she added, "Commodore Reyes would like to see you."

The last time Ganz had met with Reyes, the Orion merchant prince had come away with a clear understanding: his ship could remain berthed at Vanguard only so long as its illicit trades remained confined to its interior and his clientele remained free of Starfleet personnel. Reyes's terms had been reasonable, though the brusque manner in which he had detailed them had left Ganz wanting to separate the commodore's head from his neck.

Ganz arrived at the rear service entrance of a building in Stars Landing, the crescent-shaped residential development inside Vanguard's massive terrestrial enclosure. As the invitation had specified, the door was unlocked. The burly Orion opened the door and slipped inside.

A narrow hallway led past some storage rooms and a pantry before opening into a large professional kitchen. Waiting there for him was Manón, the establishment's owner and namesake. "Right on time," she said, offering Ganz a courteous nod. She was one of the few women whom Ganz considered comparable in beauty to his own beloved Neera, though the two women could not be more different. Neera was dark, athletic, and almost feral in her mien. Manón was pale, delicate, and refined; her elegantly shaped crest of multicolored hair and almond-shaped eyes were arresting, and as he neared within a meter of her, he sensed an aura of physical warmth emanating from her.

Manón's tasteful turquoise-colored wrap billowed gently around her as she led him out of the kitchen into the main room of her club. The main room had an open floor plan, so that every seat had a clear line of sight to its stage. Despite the height of the ceiling, the room's use of recessed lighting and strategically placed shadows contributed to a more intimate ambience. The opaque front doors were closed and, Ganz presumed, locked; there was no sign of any of the club's staff.

Standing beside a table in the middle of the club was Commodore Reyes. The lanky human Starfleet officer regarded Ganz with a stern expression.

His hostess turned and said to him, "There are drinks on the table. . . . I'll wait for you in the kitchen. Let me know when you're ready to be shown out." At that, she returned to the kitchen, leaving the Orion with the man who had summoned him.

Ganz crossed the room in casual strides and joined Reyes at the table. "Commodore," he said in a neutral tone. "You called?"

With a downward nod of his chin, Reyes said, "Have a seat." The commodore sat down.

Ganz settled into a chair but kept a cautious watch on the human. On the table were two glasses, both filled with the same bubbly, pale golden liquid. Neither man seemed interested in drinking, however.

Eager to get to business, Ganz asked, "What's on your mind, Commodore?" He hoped that none of his people had done anything rash to violate the terms of his truce with Reyes.

"A business proposition," Reyes said. "There's a ticking clock on this deal, so let me tell you what I want first, and we can work out a price second."

Masking his intense interest, Ganz said, "I'm listening."

"There's a Klingon heavy cruiser in port at Borzha II," Reyes said. "The *Zin'za*. She's making final repairs and getting ready to ship out ASAP. I want your people on Borzha II to keep that ship in port for another twenty-four hours."

The Orion suppressed a single low chortle. "Tangling with the Klingons is bad for business," he said. "If you want the ship destroyed, do it yourself."

"I don't want it destroyed," Reyes shot back. "I just want it stuck in port for an extra day."

Ganz didn't like the sound of this. "My people aren't proxy fighters, Commodore, they're smugglers. Thieves, not soldiers."

"That's why they're perfect for this," Reyes said. "I don't want them to *fight* the Klingons, just *mess* with them a little. Some light sabotage. Steal a few critical moving parts the *Zin'za* can't go to warp without."

The merchant prince scowled. "Sabotage is risky business. It took a long time to get my people jobs inside a Klingon starport. I don't want to risk them just so you can beat the Klingons to a few more balls of rock at the ass end of space."

"This is bigger than that," Reyes said. "One of my ships is

down, in the Jinoteur system." Ganz relaxed his posture as the commodore continued. "The Klingons picked up the *Sagittarius*'s mayday, and the *Zin'za* is being sent to neutralize them. We're sending help to the *Sagittarius,* but the *Zin'za* is closer and faster. I need the *Zin'za* to have some major malfunctions R.F.N., understand? That ship needs to stay stuck in port for at least another twenty-four hours, or my people are dead."

Ganz nodded. The rules of the game had just changed in his favor. "How much hurt do you want me to put on the *Zin'za?* I could arrange an accident that would take them out for good."

"Don't go that far," Reyes said. "Just foul the machinery. I want a delay, not an interstellar incident. To use a cliché, make it look like an accident."

"All right," Ganz said. "I presume you don't want to know the details." Reyes shook his head, so Ganz continued, "That brings us to the matter of compensation."

"You've heard what I want," Reyes said. "What do you want?"

The Orion considered the matter carefully. He had many needs of varying degrees of importance, but he was capable of satisfying most of them without Starfleet's help or knowledge. One pending project had been stymied several times in the past few weeks, however, and this seemed like an opportune time to set it right.

"Two weeks from now," Ganz said, "I'll need you to do me a favor. For a period of seventy-two hours, I'll want all Starfleet sensor sweeps and patrols suspended in Sector Tango-4119. For three days that'll be a blind spot. Do that, and we have a deal."

Now it was Reyes's turn to glare suspiciously across the table. "Two conditions will have to apply."

"Your proposal didn't mention conditions," Ganz said.

"It didn't rule them out, either," Reyes said. "Condition one: no piracy. If even one ship, one person, or one piece of cargo gets hassled or goes missing from Tango-4119, I'll have that big green head of yours on a plate."

The burly Orion admired Reyes's boldness. "Your second condition?"

"If I find out you helped an enemy act against Federation interests while we were turning a blind eye, your head won't be the *first* body part I put on the plate."

Ganz smirked at Reyes. "If you ever leave Starfleet, you'd be quite a businessman." Turning serious, he added, "We won't be helping your enemies, and there won't be any piracy. My word is my contract: if Starfleet complies with my request, there won't be any problems, and there won't be any complaints."

The commodore extended his hand across the table. Ganz took it and shook the human's hand firmly. Reyes said, "Deal."

"Deal," echoed Ganz. He released Reyes's hand and got up from the table. "If you'll excuse me . . ." The commodore nodded, and Ganz left the table, moving quickly toward the kitchen to make his clandestine exit out the back of the building. He tried not to betray his profound satisfaction by grinning, but keeping a straight face was difficult.

This was the best deal he'd made in a very long time.

Reyes slumped into the comfort of his padded, high-backed chair, relieved to be once more in the privacy of his own office. His meeting with Ganz had left him edgy and irritable; treating the Orion as an equal had galled him. In terms of power and influence, Ganz was clearly a formidable political actor, but Reyes could not help but feel sullied at having brokered a deal with an unrepentant criminal.

The desk-mounted intercom buzzed. Thumbing the switch, Reyes asked gruffly, "What is it?"

His gamma-shift yeoman, Midshipman Finneran, answered over the comm, *"Lieutenant Commander T'Prynn to see you, sir."*

"Fine," he said wearily. He unlocked the office's door.

T'Prynn entered from the operations center and stopped on the other side of Reyes's desk. Matter-of-factly she said, "I trust your meeting with Mr. Ganz produced the desired result."

The commodore let out a disgruntled sigh. "If by 'desired result' you mean a sick feeling in my gut, then yes." He rubbed his eyes. "Has there been any further contact with the ship?"

"Not yet," T'Prynn said. "However, I have procured an antimatter fuel pod for the *Sagittarius* from a vendor on Nejev III. It's a civilian component, but one that can easily be adapted to the *Sagittarius*'s systems."

He let go of a deep breath. "Well, that's something, at least. Who's taking it to the ship?"

"I have left urgent instructions with a trusted asset known to be on the planet," she said. "I am still awaiting his confirmation that the message has been received."

The evasiveness of T'Prynn's reply rankled him. It was not the first time she had given him a vague answer to a simple question, but the fate of one of his ships hinged on every detail. Half-truths and artful omissions would not be enough to satisfy his curiosity. "Commander," he said, "exactly who is this *asset*? Whom are we trusting to save our ship?"

After a brief but clearly conflicted hesitation, T'Prynn answered, "Cervantes Quinn, sir."

"Please tell me you're kidding."

She lifted her left eyebrow. "Mr. Quinn is on Nejev III conducting legitimate private business. His ship has a cargo hold large enough to carry the fuel pod and is fast enough to beat the *Zin'za* to Jinoteur—provided Mr. Ganz lives up to his end of the bargain." Driving home her point, she added in an arch tone, "He is also our only ally close enough to reach the *Sagittarius* in time."

And I thought dealing with the crime lord was the low point of this mess. Reyes massaged the ache from his brow. "Doesn't Quinn travel with Pennington, the reporter?"

She lowered her eyes in a gesture of concession. "Yes," she said. Looking up again, she continued, "His involvement is unavoidable. Under the circumstances, I think we should consider it a necessary risk."

Reyes couldn't help it; he laughed. It was the mirthless chortle of a condemned man. "After all we've done to keep a lid on this mission," he said, still chuckling with grim amusement, "we're sending a reporter to Jinoteur." He laughed harder and barely managed to add, "That's just great."

"Hysteria is not a productive response, sir."

His hilarity tapered off gradually, and the dire nature of the situation pressed in on him once more. "We're sending a drunk and a reporter to save the *Sagittarius*," he said, and shook his head with disappointment. "Why not tell Nassir to set his ship's autodestruct sequence and save your boys the trip?"

"Despite his outward appearance, Quinn is a resourceful field operative," T'Prynn said. "As for the risk of allowing Pennington to have access to Jinoteur . . . managing his perceptions of what he sees on the planet's surface is a task that can be dealt with after the *Sagittarius* has been rescued."

Reyes sighed. "I hope you're right about them."

"Sir, I assure you, there is no cause for concern. Quinn may not be Starfleet, but he knows what he's doing."

"What the hell are you doing?" Pennington shouted. He hoped Quinn could hear him over the whine of plasma bolts flying overhead and the violent shuddering of the dilapidated hovercraft in which they'd fled Quinn's latest deal-gone-wrong.

Quinn snapped, "I'm driving, newsboy. Shoot back or shut up!"

A dark cityscape blurred past them. Nejev III was a heavily populated planet, the homeworld of a peculiar animal-vegetable hybrid species known as the Brassicans. Pennington had meant to learn more about them than that superficial detail, but everyone had started shooting before he'd had the chance.

Wind stung his face as Quinn banked the open-topped hovercar through a diving turn. The vehicle's overtaxed engine screamed almost as loudly as Pennington himself when Quinn wrenched the craft out of its descent. They sped under a series of covered walkways that bridged the gap between two massive skyscrapers. In the distance, over the whine of the engine and the roar of the frigid wind, Pennington heard sirens.

"More company," he shouted over the din.

"I hear 'em, newsboy," Quinn growled. The scruffy, white-haired scoundrel threw a nervous look over his shoulder at their pursuers and dodged another fusillade of plasma shots. "If you get the urge to do something useful, feel free to give it a try!"

They cut through a dense artery of traffic, leaving a flurry of randomly scattered vehicles in their pursuers' path. The obstacle only slowed the chasing hovercars, but it gave Quinn and Pennington enough of a lead that Quinn was able to accelerate through two quick right turns, double back through the open core of a large building, and make another right turn that merged them back into airway traffic.

Blending in with the flow of the hovercars around them, Quinn slowed down and settled into the middle of a thick pack of vehicles. Ahead of them, city patrol fliers raced across their path, lights flashing and sirens wailing, then vanished into the nighttime canyons of the city.

After a couple of minutes of coasting along with ordinary traffic, there was no sign of pursuit, by either the police or Quinn's aggrieved clients. Pennington sat up and stretched his legs, which had been tucked anxiously against the edge of his seat. "Nicely done, mate."

"Nothin' to it," Quinn said. "Like my pappy always said, two wrongs don't make a right, but three rights do make a left."

As they neared the coastline, Quinn veered north. It took a moment for Pennington to notice that they were heading away from the city's spaceport. "Aren't we going back to the ship?"

"What for?" Quinn said. "No point leaving without a cargo or a fare. Flying empty's just a waste of fuel."

Still paranoid that the men who had been shooting at them earlier might reappear, Pennington said, "After what happened, I figured you'd want to get off this rock as soon as possible."

"Nah," Quinn said. "Getting shot at? Occupational hazard. It happens. Besides, it's not like they know where we parked. Might as well scare up a job before we breeze out."

For once, the grungy middle-aged pilot made sense. "All right," Pennington said. Nodding toward the seedy-looking sector of the city they had cruised into, he asked, "What kind of job are we going to get here?"

"Ain't here to get a job," Quinn said. "We're here to get drunk. And if you can learn to stop runnin' your mouth all the time, we might get lucky, too." He slowed the hovercar and guided it to a shaky landing on a dark street crowded with the drunk, the indigent, and the shifty. In other words, amid a throng of people just like Quinn.

Quinn vaulted out of the driver's seat and walked around the front of the vehicle toward a dive bar, which pulsed with annoyingly shrill synthetic music. Two enormous, vaguely reptilian bouncers loitered beside the entrance.

Pennington sat in the passenger seat, exhausted. All he had really wanted to do after evading the gunmen was to get back to Quinn's ship, the *Rocinante*, and tumble into his hammock for some much-needed rest. "Go on without me," he muttered.

"Come on, newsboy," Quinn said. "I know you're not into having fun, but you oughtta try it, just to see what all the fuss is about."

Too tired to argue, Pennington pulled himself out of the hovercar and followed Quinn toward the bar. As they neared the door, one of the bouncers pointed at the hovercar. "You can't park that here," he said.

"We didn't park it," Quinn said, slipping the bouncer a few notes of the local currency. "We abandoned it."

The bouncer pocketed the cash and opened the door. "I understand, sir. Have a good time."

He and Quinn pushed through the crowd inside the dim, smoke-filled, and deafeningly loud bar. Pennington could barely shout loudly enough to be heard, never mind to convey how irritated he was. "Did you just give away our hovercar?"

"I gave away *a* hovercar," Quinn yelled back. "And seeing as we stole it to make our getaway, the sooner we're rid of it, the better." He bellied up to the bar and caught the female bartender's eye. He pointed at a bottle on the shelf, held up two fingers, then pointed at Tim, who squeezed in next to him.

"Well, that's just great," Tim said. "How the hell are we supposed to get back to the ship?"

Quinn accepted the drinks from the bartender, tendered some more local paper currency, then held up two fingers again and directed the bartender's attention to a pair of attractive young alien women at the other end of the bar. As the bartender nodded and moved off to refill the women's empty drink glasses, Quinn gave Pennington a brotherly slap on the back. "Relax, Tim. These things have a way of working themselves out—if you just stay calm and keep drinking."

13

Captain Nassir huddled with Sorak and Razka around Niwara and her tricorder. Circled around them was the rest of the landing party except for McLellan and Tan Bao. Everyone was drenched and caked with mud from their desperate sprints through the jungle. The warm rain had slowed to a steady drizzle in the hour since they'd crash-landed, but there was still enough precipitation that Niwara had to wipe a sheen of droplets from the tricorder's screen every few seconds while the captain and the landing party studied the area map.

"There's no telling how far downriver Theriault might be by now," Razka observed. "Our scan's accurate only to ten kliks. After that, we're making educated guesses."

Sorak pointed at the screen. "This much is clear: the landscape slopes downward to the north. It is reasonable to deduce that the river therefore continues in that direction."

"Agreed," Nassir said. "Assuming she survived the fall, the river's our best hope of finding her. If she makes it to either bank, and she's able to walk, she can follow the river back to us. If not, it'll give us something to follow."

Niwara said softly, "I volunteer for the search mission, Captain. I was the one who lost her; I should go find her."

"You didn't lose anyone," Nassir reassured her. "Accidents happen, you know that. And considering what we were up against, things could have been a lot . . ." Words failed him as he saw Tan Bao emerge from the tree line, supporting McLellan's weight while she hopped along on her one remaining foot. Her right leg had been cut off just below the knee, and the severed limb protruded from Tan Bao's backpack.

Tan Bao's voice cracked with strain and exhaustion. "Little help?" Razka and Sorak both ran to his aid and relieved him of McLellan's weight. The two scouts draped her arms across their shoulders and swiftly spirited her back to the circled landing party. The bedraggled medic jogged behind them and dropped to one knee beside McLellan as the scouts carefully set her down.

"Report," Nassir said to Tan Bao, who was busy scanning McLellan with his medical tricorder.

"The Shedai . . . whatever it was, it did this," Tan Bao said, gesturing at McLellan's leg. "I can't explain what this glasslike substance is, or why it seems to happen to every living organism the Shedai attacked. The good news is that it cauterized her wound, so she hasn't lost much blood." He packed up his tricorder and looked anxiously at Nassir. "We need to get her to sickbay, sir."

Nassir plucked his communicator from his belt and opened it with a flick of his wrist. "Nassir to *Sagittarius*."

Terrell answered, *"Go ahead, Captain."*

"Raise the ship. We have wounded. And grab two full packs—I need you to lead a search and rescue."

"Understood," Terrell said. *"Stay clear of the north bank; we're coming up."*

The rest of the landing party began backing away from the riverbank. "Acknowledged," Nassir said, following the others.

Seconds later the sepia-colored river boiled with white foam. Large waves formed in the middle and radiated ashore. The narrow bulge of the secondary hull emerged from the froth, followed by the rest of the oval-shaped primary hull. The ship hovered a moment, as if it were afloat. Then it drifted slowly toward the landing party until the port side of the primary hull scraped against the sandy bank and came to a halt.

A mechanical whirring and a loud hiss accompanied the opening of the top hatch. Terrell climbed out, followed by Dr. Babitz. Ilucci and Threx handed a stretcher up to Babitz, passed two large backpacks up to Terrell, then followed the two officers topside and began inspecting the hull.

Babitz ran to McLellan and set down the stretcher. She and Tan Bao spoke to each other in a quiet but steady stream of medical jargon. Terrell strapped on one pack and carried the other toward Nassir and the landing party. Setting down the second pack, the first officer said, "Orders, Captain?"

"Proceed downstream with Lieutenant Niwara and find Ensign Theriault," Nassir said. "Niwara has the coordinates where Theriault went into the river. She'll lead you there."

Niwara nodded to Terrell and tucked her small pack inside the new, larger one that Terrell had brought.

From several meters away, Ilucci called out, "Whoa! What happened to Vanessa? I mean . . . to Ensign Theriault?" The engineer balked at Nassir and Terrell's matching glares of reproof, then added in an apologetic tone, "Sirs."

"I'll brief you later, Master Chief," Nassir said, allowing his chief engineer to save face. "Right now, we need to move."

Terrell asked, "How long do we have to find her?"

"Until we get some antimatter," Nassir said. "Or until something else goes wrong."

The first officer flashed a disarmingly wry grin. "Not long, then. Understood." He stepped quickly toward the river and called out, "Niwara, with me. Double quick-time." The Caitian woman fell in beside Terrell, and together they jogged briskly along the riverbank, headed downstream.

Nassir turned to see Sorak and Razka helping Babitz and Tan Bao carry McLellan back aboard the *Sagittarius*. He fell in with zh'Firro and followed the stretcher bearers as they marched up onto the hull of the ship toward the topside hatch. The engineers were the first ones back inside the ship. At the edge of the hatch, the captain and zh'Firro took over for Babitz and Tan Bao while they climbed back inside the ship. Then the stretcher team carefully lowered McLellan into the waiting hands of the medical staff and engineers Ilucci and Threx.

Nassir watched the sky and the jungle for movement while

the rest of his crew descended the ladder to the top deck. He grabbed the rungs and slid back down, the last one back inside. "Seal the hatch, Master Chief," he said. "We're taking her back down."

In the span of just two hours, Ming Xiong had concluded that Tholian shipbuilders must be very fond of nooks, crawlspaces, and tight areas. Aside from main engineering, the compartment housing the miniaturized Shedai artifact, and the bridge, most of the interior spaces aboard the Tholian battleship were cramped and difficult for him to navigate.

Following the loss of contact with the *Sagittarius,* Xiong had spent his first hour of solitude on the Tholians' bridge. Sending a message had been his first intention. Unfortunately, all the duty stations had looked alike. *For all I know,* he had reminded himself, *they might be identical until configured by their user for a specific purpose.*

Accessing the ship's command and control systems had proved all but impossible. None of the apparent interfaces had responded to his poking and prodding. He had worried that he might accidentally fire the weapons or initiate a self-destruct mechanism while trying to send a distress signal to Vanguard, but his complete failure to make any of the consoles acknowledge his input had relieved him of that concern. His best guess was that the Tholians employed biometric security measures, ensuring that their systems could be operated only by Tholians.

After leaving the bridge, he had begun a methodical search of the ship, one compartment at a time, looking for anything that he could recognize as useful. Most of the ship's passages narrowed into dead ends. He had probed several compartments packed with rows of honeycomb-like cells. Based on similar structures he had seen in the diplomatic habitat on Vanguard, he surmised that those were quarters for the crew.

An hour of mind-numbingly repetitive search protocols had brought him to a passageway lined with narrow, hexagonal apertures. Confident that the openings were wide enough to permit passage of his bulky pressure suit, he floated through one into a compact space that led to another dead end.

Tumbling awkwardly forward, he was instantly aware that the confined area had zero gravity. Eyeing its glassy black surfaces, he saw that they bore numerous small protrusions. He looked more closely at the edges inside the hexagonal opening. Multiple layers of what resembled hull plating and recessed mechanisms gave him the impression that this was an escape pod.

He decided with a satisfied smile that this was useful. *Now I just need to figure out how to release it from the ship, control its descent to the planet, and escape from it once I get there.* His hands glided over its various contours and raised surfaces. As on the bridge, nothing reacted to his touch. Stymied again, he let himself float while he formed a plan of action. *Two ways to make this work,* he concluded. *Trick the ship into thinking I'm a Tholian so I can access the controls, or bypass the regular interface and make one of my own.*

Xiong examined every square centimeter of the pod's interior, looking for a way to access what was inside its bulkheads. As far as he could see, there were no removable panels. *Damn,* he thought with a shake of his head. *I'd hate to be an engineer on a Tholian ship.*

Questions formed quickly in his thoughts. How did the Tholian engineers make repairs to internal systems without access panels? Did they have some means of cutting through this obsidian surface and then making it whole again when their work was done? Might the ship's bulkheads be like a mineralized form of smart polymer, capable of being retracted, reinforced, or reshaped by the application of properly modulated energy?

Looking at his multiple reflections on the black surfaces inside the pod, Xiong felt a surge of intuition: *Somewhere on this ship, there is a tool that opens up these bulkheads.* Climbing out of the pod back into the passageway beyond, he promised himself, *Wherever that tool is, I'm going to find it.*

•   •   •

Following the muddy river's twisting path had proved to be the long way from the *Sagittarius* to the point where Theriault had plunged from a cliff into the rapids. Terrell had wanted to take a more direct route through the jungle, but Niwara had resisted. The rain, she'd said, had almost certainly obscured the trail that she and Theriault made during their flight from the Shedai attack, and she didn't want to risk becoming disoriented while leading Terrell to the scene of the accident.

They had passed a high waterfall not long after leaving the ship. Since then they had traversed the top of the cliff. At most points along their winding route, there was less than two meters' clearance between the edge and the tree line. Every few meters, Terrell snuck a look down into the ravine. It was choked with dry, tangled vines that stretched from one side to the other. They formed a thick layer of natural netting over the churning rapids below. He asked Niwara, "Were there vines like these where Theriault fell?"

"Yes, sir," the Caitian scout replied. "Without them I doubt she would have survived the fall."

Terrell hoped that Theriault's ride down the river proved as fortuitous. "How much farther?"

"A few meters more," Niwara said. She pointed at a bend in the gorge. "That's where Ensign Theriault fell."

He looked ahead and noted the gap that the science officer's plunge had torn in the vines. When they reached the spot, Terrell said, "Hold up. We'll run our first scan from here." He lifted the tricorder slung at his side and powered it up. He set it to zero in on Theriault's communicator signal. Within seconds it registered a lock. "Got her," he said. "Bearing oh-eight-point-two, distance roughly twenty-one-point-six kilometers. She's moving, about three meters per second. It's a good bet she's still in the river."

"It's been two hours," Niwara said. "I hope for her sake she's a strong swimmer."

Returning the tricorder to his hip, he replied, "Only one way to find out, Lieutenant. Take us downriver."

Niwara continued forward along the cliff trail, and Terrell followed a few meters behind her. He hoped that Theriault was still alive and conscious, and that she could halt her journey on the river soon. Moving on foot, he and Niwara would only fall farther behind Theriault the longer she remained in the river.

As for whether the young science officer would be able to survive for two hours or more trapped in a raging current, he could only pray for the best and keep walking in slow pursuit.

Dr. Lisa Babitz hated germs. Most people she had ever known weren't fond of infectious bacteria, but the blond surgeon reviled them with a passion that bordered on the pathological.

Keeping every surface of the interior of the *Sagittarius* clean and disinfected had been a challenge since her first day aboard, due in no small part to the habits of her crewmates. In the few short years that they had served together, she had learned to tolerate Ilucci's penchant for eating with hands unwashed after working in engineering, Threx's knack for leaving thick wads of shed body hair in the single shower that the entire crew shared, and even Lieutenant Niwara's disturbing method of cleaning herself. In return, they had come to ignore her practice of conspicuously sanitizing every crew compartment on the ship at least once every other day.

Now there was mud in her sickbay.

There was mud, and trampled vegetation, and puddles of dirty water, tracked in long paths throughout the ship.

Worst of all, Lieutenant Commander McLellan, who was lying anesthetized on the biobed in front of her, and medical technician Tan Bao, who was standing on the other side of the bed, both were mummified in brown sludge. Just looking at them plagued Babitz with sensations of phantom insects creeping across her skin. She took a deep breath and searched in vain for calm.

Struggling to keep her tone professional, she instructed Tan Bao, "Cut away the fabric above the wound." Tan Bao carefully sliced away several centimeters of the soiled green fabric. Babitz squinted at the unusual substance that had aggregated over McLellan's wound. "Can you wash that?" she asked Tan Bao. "I want to get a clear look at it."

"Yes, Doctor," Tan Bao said, and he set to work rinsing the dirt and debris from McLellan's leg. While he worked, Babitz reviewed the data from Tan Bao's tricorder. The molecular structure of the crystalline substance on McLellan's leg was very similar to one that Babitz had noted in an autopsy file Xiong had provided as part of her preparation for the mission.

Tan Bao interrupted her ruminations. "Doctor? The wound's clean and ready for examination." He stepped back to give Babitz more light.

She leaned down and eyed the dark, glasslike substance. "Hand me a two-millimeter biopsy punch," she said. Tan Bao passed her the instrument, and she positioned it with care and precision above the thickest portion of the crystalline scab. With a quick jab, the punch penetrated its surface and came away with a tiny chunk of the substance lodged inside its circular cavity. She handed it back to Tan Bao. "Run a full-spectrum scan on this." The technician nodded and carried the sample away to a compact analyzer on the other side of sickbay.

Babitz turned her attention to McLellan's severed limb. The lower half of the woman's right leg was cocooned in the peculiar crystal. She set it on the sickbay's second biobed, from which she had only minutes earlier ejected engineer Torvin. A pallet of scanners mounted above the bed hummed as she powered them up. The indicators shifted on the bed's display board. Babitz lifted her own tricorder and downloaded more complete results from the sickbay computer.

The severed leg showed no evidence of putrefaction. It had been all but completely mineralized by contact with the alien crystalline substance. *Like petrified wood*, Babitz thought. *Except almost instantaneous.* Impatient to verify her findings, she called up the autopsy report she had remembered from her pre-mission briefing. It took only seconds to find it.

Drs. Fisher and M'Benga had conducted an autopsy on the body of a Denobulan named Bohanon. According to the file, the man had been killed on Erilon during an encounter with a Shedai entity, slain instantly. His body had been returned in stasis to Vanguard, but as soon as it had been taken out of stasis for analysis something remarkable had occurred. Anabolic activity had been detected on all the exposed internal tissues contacted by the Shedai combatant. Some kind of alien bio-residue had started to transform the Denobulan's organic tissues into a substance resembling a crystalline lattice. Fisher had noted that the process was short-lived, penetrating only a few millimeters into the surrounding tissue—but he also had speculated that the process might not be so abbreviated in a living subject.

Working quickly, Babitz placed McLellan's crystallized leg into a stasis module, then returned to the woman's side and initiated a new scan on the stump of her right leg.

She was still comparing her results to Tan Bao's original scan of McLellan's injury when the technician looked up from the analyzer and swiveled his chair to face her. "It's a living crystal matrix," he said with amazement. "A mineral composite with anabolic properties." He added more ominously, "Just like what the Vanguard team found in that thing they brought back from Erilon, except . . . *alive*."

"That's not all, Tan," Babitz said. "It's spreading. Two hours ago, this substance penetrated two millimeters up her thigh. Now it's twenty-two millimeters along. If it continues at this rate, it'll start hitting vital organs in less than thirty-six hours. And in forty-eight . . . she'll be dead."

Theriault had lost any sense of how long she had been in the water. It had carried her through multiple sets of rapids, across clusters of half-submerged boulders, over sudden plunges into rock-bottomed shallows. Her entire body was covered with scrapes and bruises.

Her fall from the cliff had seemed to happen in slow motion. Succumbing to gravity's pull, her senses had sharpened, and she had seen all the vines between her and the river. Her hands had grasped in vain at every one within reach, and they all had snapped under the force of her plummeting body.

Striking the water had been a stunning blow. Disoriented from the impact and the irresistible pull of the current, Theriault had spent several seconds fighting her way to the surface. Her first instinct had been to swim for one bank or the other, but the rocky walls of the winding ravine had offered her no handholds, no means of pulling herself from the water.

Little by little, the clifftops had drawn closer, the ravine had narrowed, and the water had gained speed. Now it emerged from the rocky gorge into a lush rain forest of azure. The river was wider here, and though Theriault now could see flat river-banks on either side of her, she was too weak to fight across the current to reach them. It took all her flagging strength to keep her head above the surface, to gasp for breath without swallowing the silt-rich water.

The jungle was eerily quiet. There was no sound except her own labored breath and the splashing of her exhausted limbs. *Have to conserve my energy,* she reminded herself. *Rest before I hit more rapids.* She took a deep breath, then closed her eyes and rolled facedown into the river. Relaxing her arms first and then her legs, she let her limbs dangle beneath her as she floated limp in the current, letting it take her without a fight. After struggling for so long, she relished being able to rest her weary body, even if just for a minute.

When she couldn't hold her breath any longer, she rolled gently onto her back and exhaled, drew another long breath, then returned to her "dead man's float" pose, drifting down-stream like a corpse. Every time she held her breath she counted the seconds carefully to sixty. Then she counted the minutes each time she rolled over for a breath. Fifteen minutes passed quickly, then thirty minutes. She used the time to plan her next move. *Once I reach shore, I should follow the river back,* she decided, recalling her survival training. *The captain will send someone to look for me, and that's where they'll start.*

As her strength recovered, she took the opportunity to make an inventory of her equipment. The strap of her tricorder had broken shortly after her first run-in with submerged rocks in the rapids. Her fingers found only an empty loop of fabric where her communicator should have been. Only her small hand phaser was still securely in place. *Figures,* she thought. *My least favorite piece of equipment is the only one I've got left.*

Rolling onto her back at the thirty-five-minute mark, she started to wonder if she might be recovered enough to make an attempt for land. Then she heard the soft wash of white noise getting louder ahead of her. Twisting herself to face forward, she saw light low on the horizon and realized that the landscape was beginning another steep decline. She was drifting toward another run of rapids, and there would be no time to reach land.

The water around Theriault became turbulent, and where the river narrowed it churned itself white with violence and swallowed her whole. Adrenaline coursed through her body as she kicked and flailed against the water, unable to find air, unable to see, hearing nothing but the roar of water crashing over rocks and against itself.

Then she ricocheted off one enormous rock, caromed off another, scraped roughly along the bottom, and broke free for a fleeting moment. She had just long enough to pull one desperate breath of air and realize that the river was racing down a steep gradient and disappearing into a broad, cavelike opening in the side of a hill.

Panic fueled her frantic attempts to defy the current and strike out for the riverbank, which was dozens of meters out of reach. A dip of the riverbed dunked her underwater, and her head struck a rock as she was towed past. Dazed and blinking painful colors from her vision, she suddenly found herself in the dark. The river had gone underground and taken her with it.

No more points of reference, no more parallax along the riverbank to gauge her motion. Pure blackness engulfed her, frigid, merciless, and endless. Inside the subterranean channel the roar of the water echoed back upon itself, a deafening wash of noise so mighty that she no longer heard her own frightened splutters and gasps.

She kicked downward, hoping to hit a shallow patch or a sandbar, anything that might let her stop her inexorable forward motion, but the river hurtled through the stygian depths, its embrace deep and cold. Keeping track of time was a lost cause now. There was only fear and darkness. Then, as she bobbed upward for air, her head collided with the rocky roof of the cavern. Reaching up, she felt it close above her, slick with slime. The river's passage through the underdark was running out of breathing room.

There was no way to hang on to anything. Every surface she grasped was coated in the same slippery mess, and the roof grew closer by the minute. Theriault kicked as hard as she could to keep her mouth and nose above the water, but the tunnel dipped and curved without warning in the blackness, and she had to cough out one mouthful of water after another. With the space above her narrowing to a sliver, she sucked in one full chest of air, then submerged and let the current carry her away.

Watery silence, no air to breathe. Just the rapid beating of her own heart growing slower as her lungs filled with carbon dioxide. Holding in the expiring breath was too much effort. She let it go slowly, a few bubbles at a time, reluctant to exhale because she knew that her body would reflexively try to inhale immediately afterward . . . and she knew that would not be possible.

One bubble at a time, one breath escaping, then another, like a prison break from her lungs. Letting go of her last breath was a relief, a surrender, an admission that it was time for the end to begin. A final push, and her chest was empty.

She resisted. Tried to will herself not to breathe in. Squeezed her eyes and prayed that she could just fade away without having to feel the water invading her lungs.

Her chest expanded, and she choked down on the reflex, fought it. It was too strong. Defying her will, her body breathed in. The water flooded her sinus, gagged her, assaulted her. A spasm sealed her airway, and water poured down her throat into her stomach. Terror overcame her training, and she kicked and twisted wildly, desperate to discover some hidden pocket of air, irrationally hoping to find one more fresh breath with her hands.

Involuntarily gulping water, she lost all sensation of her body. Darkness melted into vivid colors, bursts of turquoise and crimson, emerald and chartreuse. A siren's song called to her.

Then she was free, released into open air.

She was falling, shot out of the stone tunnel by a jet of water and plummeting beside an ivory cascade of spray, toward a cerulean pool fifty meters below. Unable to scream or even breathe through her spasm-sealed airway, she marshaled her wits long enough to tumble into a feet-first position, pinch her nose shut, and cover her mouth before she made impact.

Her body sliced through the water like a blade, sank in a straight line, and came to a stop in the deep pool. Fighting against the weight of the water and the pull of gravity, Theriault kicked and stroked her way to the surface. For several seconds, she struggled to tread water and pull in a breath. Despite being free of the underground river, her body was still trapped in its panicked state. Then her throat relaxed, and she coughed out huge mouthfuls of icy water, clearing the way for the sweetest breath of air she had ever tasted.

Floating in the still waters of the enormous pool, she turned slowly and surveyed the space that yawned around her. It was a staggeringly huge cavern, two kilometers wide and a few hundred meters tall. All around the cavern, massive jets of water erupted from natural-looking tunnels in the walls and fell in majestic plumes to the deep, wide pool. Multiple entrances to a labyrinth of other caves gave the cavern's walls a honeycombed appearance. The pool emptied into a vast, high-ceilinged tunnel that led deeper underground. High overhead, the dome of the cavern's ceiling was open, revealing a sky streaked with the painterly hues of a subtropical sunset.

Using slow, steady strokes, Theriault swam to shore, crawled onto the sandy ground, and collapsed. She was grateful to be free of the water, to be tasting air, to be alive. It took her several minutes to notice that she was shivering violently. Looking at her hands, she saw that they were almost blue. *Hypothermia,* she realized. *Have to work fast, before I lose consciousness.* She looked around and spotted several large rocks. In her exhausted, battered state, dragging several heavy stones into a line beside a small nook in the cavern wall was a labor of desperation. She assembled enough to make a row as long as she was tall, then crawled into the nook behind the rocks and drew her phaser.

A quick check of the device confirmed that its outer casing was intact. She hoped that it was as waterproof as its specs claimed, and she primed it to fire.

Short, controlled bursts on a low setting swiftly turned each rock orange-hot. *That'll do,* she decided.

She tucked her phaser back onto her belt and let herself start to drift off. Basking in the warm glow of the rocks, she decided that, though her phaser used to be her least favorite piece of equipment, it had just become her new best friend.

14

between a banister and the wall, but he'd rather die with you. He said, "I don't think I really want to come in here."

"Trust your instincts," said one of the other. "My advice: Support the extraction process." O'Halloran replied, "You sound to me sadder than so many empty columns."

O'Connor, Mac Anderson, said, grinned. "Thinking maybe it wants you into the future."

"Guess I think I was no idea how much can't," O'Halloran

"*Kepler* to base," Ensign O'Halloran said, keeping one eye on the shuttlecraft's flight controls and the other on the smoke rising from Gamma Tauri IV's parched landscape.

"*Go ahead, Kepler,*" replied Commander al-Khaled.

Circling the landing site specified in his orders, O'Halloran reported, "We're nearing the coordinates now. Lotta smoke down there, sir. Lotsa debris, too."

"*Can you tell what it's from?*"

Squinting against the glare of early morning light low on the horizon, O'Halloran said, "Negative. Not reading any metal, no bodies, no fuel. Doesn't look like a crash or a battle site."

"*Find a clear spot to put down,*" al-Khaled said. "*Stand by for dust-off if the survey team gets in trouble.*"

Guiding the shuttlecraft into a slow descent, O'Halloran said, "Roger that, base. Putting down in sixty. *Kepler* out."

Slouched in the copilot's seat, Ensign Anderson had one foot propped on the edge of his console and both hands folded behind his head. With a nonchalance that vexed O'Halloran to no end, he said, "What do you think we're gonna find down there?"

"*We* aren't gonna find anything," O'Halloran said, "because we're staying in the shuttle, as ordered."

"Wow, that's a really boring life choice you've made, my friend." Gesturing at the sunbaked vista outside the cockpit, he added, "For all you know, the mysteries of the universe are down there, waiting to be found, and you're gonna stay in the ship."

O'Halloran watched the ground slip under the shuttlecraft as he made a banking turn. "I'd love to debate this with you," he said, "but I'm kind of busy with the landing."

"That's your problem—you don't multitask," Anderson said.

Engaging the vertical thrusters, O'Halloran replied, "Your problem is you never shut up long enough to think."

"Of course not," Anderson said, unfazed. "Thinking too much is what gets you into trouble."

"No one's asking you to think too much, Jeff." O'Halloran leveled the shuttlecraft with the ground. "I just want you try *thinking*." He set the craft down with a soft bump and released the rear hatchway. It lowered with a smooth mechanical whine and served as a ramp for the rest of the team to file out of the shuttlecraft. Anderson got up from the copilot's chair. O'Halloran looked up at him. "Where do you think you're going?"

Pointing aft, Anderson said, "To check out the big hole in the ground." He started walking toward the ramp.

"Sit down," O'Halloran said.

Flashing a grin over his shoulder, Anderson replied, "You have to outrank someone to give them orders, Bri."

"Dammit," O'Halloran muttered. He hurried through the postflight checks and secured the controls. For a moment he hesitated, torn between obeying orders and indulging his curiosity. Knowing he would probably regret it, he got up and followed his annoying friend out of the shuttlecraft, jogging to catch up with the survey team.

Lieutenant Donovan Adams led the survey team away from the *Kepler,* across a dusty plain littered with huge, irregular chunks of blackened glass and fine coal-colored dust. The enormous, jagged obsidian boulders looked as if they had fallen from the sky and embedded themselves in the ground. They radiated intense heat, and smoke wafted from their coating of smoldering resin. All around him, the ground had a scorched quality and stank of cordite.

"No life readings," he reported, watching his tricorder for any kind of fluctuation. Several meters ahead, the dusty soil sloped down to the edge of a circular pit. Its walls were burned black and coated in what looked like a thick layer of dusky, polished glass. Broad columns of smoke ascended from its depths and mushroomed into the sky. Searing heat stopped him more than five meters from the edge of the abyss, and he backed off. To the rest of the team he said, "It's too hot to go forward. Fan out around it."

Ensign Blaise Selby, the team's geologist, marveled at the data on her own tricorder. "The pit extends all the way down to the power source, Lieutenant. But the crystalline structures inside the pit are inconsistent with this area's geological profile. That's volcanic glass, sir, but there's no volcanic activity here."

Circumnavigating the pit, Adams noticed that the shuttlecraft pilots had followed the survey team. "What are you two doing out of the shuttle?"

"Uh, we just figured, um, you know, maybe you guys could use help with the, uh, stuff," stammered the fair-haired one.

Adams stared at them until they took the hint and turned back. Once they began plodding back to the *Kepler,* he turned his attention to the gaping maw of the inferno that lay before him. He looked to his science officer, Lieutenant sh'Neroth. "What could have made this? Energy beam?"

The Andorian *shen* shook her head, bobbling her antennae slightly. "A blast powerful enough to penetrate ten kilometers of bedrock would likely have continued into the atmosphere. We would have detected that. It also would not account for the crystalline residue."

Kattan and Ndufe, the team's security guards, stayed on opposite sides of the pit, circling it slowly, phasers drawn.

"Let's run a few more scans," Adams said. "I want to know if we've found a central hub or maybe a node in its defense—"

The jagged black-glass boulders split apart, stood up, and glowed with violet motes of energy inside their shells. The survey team was completely surrounded. At least two dozen of the giants rose from the field of smoke and ashes. Slinging his tricorder and drawing his phaser, Adams yelled to the others, "Get back to the shuttle!"

He made it all of three running steps before his legs were cut out from under him. His torso fell forward, and he landed face-first in the dust. Kattan and Ndufe each fired two shots before they were dismembered in flurries of blood and shadow. Selby's torso was hollowed out in one fearsome strike, and a blunt impact threw sh'Neroth backward toward the pit. Her body ignited as it plunged into the darkness.

Adams fumbled for his communicator and flipped it open. "Adams to shuttlecraft! Run! Lift—"

He barely felt the storm of blows that tore him to pieces.

O'Halloran flipped switches and prayed that the main thrusters wouldn't choose that moment to be temperamental.

Anderson stood at the open aft hatch, firing his phaser at the company of black goliaths advancing on the shuttlecraft. The screech of his weapon was constant, but every time O'Halloran looked back, the obsidian giants were moving faster and getting closer, and the phaser energy seemed to have no effect on them.

The engines thrummed to life, and O'Halloran skipped his preflight check and punched the liftoff thrusters. "Hang on!"

A roar of exhaust shrouded the shuttlecraft in a dust cloud. Anderson kept on firing blindly into the golden haze. The *Kepler* wobbled and then lurched forward, racing skyward away from the smoldering pit and its dark guardians.

O'Halloran pressed the button to close the aft hatch. He looked back as it shut with a gentle *thump*.

Anderson sat on the deck, his back against the bulkhead, his left hand clamped over the stump of his right arm, which was missing from a few centimeters below the shoulder. He grinned weakly. "Lost my phaser," he croaked. "Boy, am I gonna be in trouble."

•   •   •

"Security just finished their sweep of the site," Gabbert said to al-Khaled. "They found the bodies of the survey team . . . well, most of them. But no sign of the attackers."

Commander al-Khaled felt the cold grip of fear inside his stomach. He had seen what one Shedai entity was capable of on Erilon. He didn't want to imagine the threat posed by dozens of such beings—but if O'Halloran and Anderson's report was correct, then that's exactly what was loose on Gamma Tauri IV.

"Have them recover *everything*," al-Khaled said to his room boss. "Then get the samples beamed up to the *Lovell*. I want forensic scans relayed to Vanguard inside the hour."

"You got it," Gabbert said. He set to work whipping the rest of the top-secret operations managers into action. Al-Khaled checked the medical report on Ensign Anderson that had just come in from Dr. Rockey, the *Lovell*'s chief medical officer. Anderson's wound had been infected by some kind of peculiar crystalline substance, and it was spreading. Unless some way was found to halt its progress, it would kill the ensign in a matter of hours.

Shaking his head, al-Khaled wondered grimly, *What have we stirred up out here?*

Gabbert rejoined al-Khaled at the master console. "Ready for some more bad news?"

"Always," al-Khaled said. "I'm an engineer."

Nodding upward, Gabbert said, "Colony President Vinueza is upstairs. She wants to talk to you. Says it's urgent."

Al-Khaled groaned. Vinueza had arrived less than thirty-six hours ago, but in that short time the new colony president had made a lasting impression on him and the rest of his Starfleet contingent. The woman was boldly aggressive when she wanted something from them and impossibly stubborn when they needed anything from her. An advance file sent several days ago by Commodore Reyes had warned al-Khaled and his senior personnel about Vinueza's considerable esper talents. When dealing with politicians, al-Khaled was used to being careful about his every word. It was a far greater challenge to exercise the same caution about his every thought. So far he had managed not to compromise the security of Operation Vanguard, but he was fairly certain that Vinueza was now keenly aware of how much he admired her figure and how embarrassed he was that she knew.

"I'll be upstairs talking to the boss lady," al-Khaled said. "If I'm not back in an hour, it's because I've either shot the president or committed suicide, or both."

"I'd stop at the first one," Gabbert said as al-Khaled left, "but that's just me."

Because the ops center was a restricted area, the S.C.E. team maintained an administrative office adjacent to the main operations building. It was little more than a naked gray box consisting of four prefabricated polymer walls, a scrap-duranium ceiling, and a thermoconcrete floor. The desk was made from the same dull gray composite as the walls, and the chair behind it was just as uncomfortable as the guest chairs in front of it.

Al-Khaled entered through the office's back door and found Jeanne Vinueza, president of the New Boulder colony, standing in his path. Her arms were crossed in front of her chest, and she regarded him with a glare whose equal he hadn't seen since basic training nearly two decades earlier. "Commander," she said icily. "How nice of you to finally join me."

"I came as quickly as I could, Madam President," al-Khaled said. "It's been a busy—"

"Commander," she said, "my people have been asking for Starfleet's help for more than an hour. I know that a non-Federation colony probably doesn't rate high on your priority list, but when someone says they have an *emergency*—"

He held up his hand to interrupt. "Emergency?"

"Yes, Commander, an emergency. Our civil engineers were testing the aquifers out on the Ilium Range this morning. They've missed two check-ins, and they aren't answering hails."

She kept talking as al-Khaled stepped past her to stand in front of the wall-sized planetary map on the opposite wall. "Around noon the sheriff sent two of his deputies to check on them. Now we've lost contact with them, too."

Fighting to conceal his fears from Vinueza, al-Khaled reached toward the map and pressed his finger down on the Ilium Range. The first thing he noticed was its alarming proximity to the site where his survey team had been slaughtered less than ninety minutes earlier. "I'll send out a shuttle immediately," he said, afraid that he already knew what the rescue team would find.

Vinueza stepped up close behind his shoulder. A concerned look darkened her expression. She lowered her voice. "You're worried about something."

"Of course I am, Madam President," he said, quickly blanking his thoughts. "You've just reported two sets of disappearances in one day at the same site, less than fifty kilometers from the Klingons' colony. If I wasn't concerned, I'd be a fool."

She didn't look or sound convinced. "A lot of your people are on edge right now," she said. "I can feel it. Something's going on, Commander, and I demand you tell me what it is."

"Ma'am, if you were the president of a Federation colony, I might have clearance to tell you, but you're not, so I'm afraid I'll have to ask you to leave." Softening his tone, he added, "As soon as I know what happened to your people, I'll be in touch." He gestured with an outstretched arm toward the door.

"I don't like secrets, Commander," Vinueza warned.

"No one does, ma'am." He stepped ahead and opened the door for her, ending the discussion. "Please, Madam President. Don't make me call security."

Vinueza took her time walking to the door. As she slipped past him, she said in a seductively teasing voice, "You wouldn't call security on me, Commander. You think I'm much too hot for that." Her knowing smirk imprinted itself on his memory as the door closed. He held that image in his mind as he pulled his communicator from his belt and flipped it open.

"*Lovell,* this is al-Khaled. Do you read me?"

Captain Okagawa answered, "*We read you, Mahmud. Go ahead.*"

"Captain, have you beamed up the forensic samples from the attack on our survey team?"

"*Affirmative,*" Okagawa said. "*We just started compiling the data for Dr. Fisher on Vanguard. Why? What's happened?*"

Al-Khaled focused on breathing and staying calm. "We need to get a priority message out to Vanguard, right now. Tell the commodore that the 'storm' he warned us about is starting—and it looks like we're gonna get hit head-on."

Mogan had been a Klingon warrior his entire adult life, and he had been an agent of Imperial Intelligence for the past decade. He had fought countless battles, walked innumerable battle-fields . . . but this one was the first to give him pause.

The battle's result appeared to be entirely one-sided. More than a dozen Klingon reconnaissance agents had been slaughtered, dismembered like *lingta* in an abattoir. Severed limbs and heads lay scattered across the smoldering site at the base of a cliff. Twisted, mangled torsos rested in the blackened dirt beside bodies hollowed out by some terrible force. Every wounded appendage, every liberated skull, was sheathed in a crystalline shroud. Disruptor rifles had been reduced to splinters.

Halfway up the cliff, sixty *qams* above ground, an obsidian-walled tunnel looked as if it had been cored from the bedrock.

His platoon of *QuchHa'* fanned out behind him as he led them across the killing field, watchful for any sign of ambush or a trap. Bootsteps crunched on the gravel as a hot, westerly wind kicked up dust from the rocks and ambered the afternoon light. "Watch the flanks," he said to his men, who nodded and continued to swivel their heads slowly as they advanced, searching for any sign of Klingon survivors or enemies.

At the cliff Mogan stopped and looked back the way he had

come, toward the armored ground transport he and the rest of his men had used to get here from their base camp. "It's secure," he declared. Then his eyes sought out the team's scientist. "Dr. Kamron," he said. "Start your analysis."

Kamron, one of the few men under Mogan's command who was not one of the *QuchHa'*, kneeled amid a jumble of body parts and began scanning them with a handheld device. Next he chipped off pieces of the crystalline substance and inserted the fragments inside his scanning device for a more intensive analysis.

Mogan's eyes studied the distribution of debris, the patterns of scorch marks and bloodstains. He visualized the genesis of each bit of evidence and constructed in his imagination a reen-actment of the battle. To one of the nearby *QuchHa'* he said, pointing out details, "The attack began here. Multiple opponents. They came from above, from that hole in the cliff. The center of the formation was attacked first." He turned, backpedaled as he followed the clues, narrating as he went. "The front ranks turned, and the rear guard charged. A cross-fire. Their targets split up, broke toward the flanks." His eyes roamed the ground, sensing the direction and momentum of the combat. "Whatever attacked them did not prioritize among their targets. They killed whoever was closest." He reached the edge of the battle zone, where the ground ceased to smolder. Dropping to one knee, he scooped up a handful of the radiantly warm earth and sifted it between his fingers. "They were hit with overwhelming force. It was over in seconds."

His words provoked anxious looks among the *QuchHa'*, and not for the first time Mogan was angry and ashamed to think of these weaklings as Klingons. *Such as these are not fit for war,* he brooded, gazing with contempt on his weak-browed troops.

Dr. Kamron walked quickly toward Mogan, his mien stern. When he had closed to within a half-dozen paces, Mogan commanded him, "Report, Doctor."

"All members of the reconnaissance unit accounted for," Kamron said. "Time of death approximately one hour ago. All casualties inflicted by physical trauma. No sign of energy residue on any of our men."

Mogan pointed at the dark, glasslike substance that coated a nearby head. "What about *that* residue, Doctor?"

"Some kind of living crystal. Origin unknown." The scientist pointed up at the roughly circular opening in the cliff. "The same substance is up there, coating the walls of that tunnel. It does not match any natural elements or composites indigenous to this planet." Stepping close to Mogan, Kamron confided, "But it does resemble substances documented before . . . on Palgrenax."

"Thank you, Doctor," Mogan said. "I want your full report in six hours. For my eyes only, understood?"

With a nod, Kamron said, "Yes, sir," and drifted away.

Mogan paced around the perimeter of the battlefield. Allowing such a valuable asset as Palgrenax to fall under the control of an imbecile like Morqla had been a grave misstep by the Empire. It had led to the planet's destruction at the hands of an enemy and resulted in the loss of a valuable strategic resource— one that the Federation had already taken the lead in studying and possibly exploiting. Imperial Intelligence did not intend to let the mistakes of Palgrenax be repeated here, but the threat that had presented itself could not be ignored, either. Mogan had to act quickly.

He pulled his communicator from his belt and set it to a secure frequency. "Mogan to Hanigar."

Moments later, his Imperial Intelligence supervisor answered. *"This is Hanigar. Report."*

"Threat assessment complete," Mogan said. "Status positive. Recommend response protocol *Say'qul.*"

"Understood," Hanigar replied. *"I will relay your recommendation. Hanigar out."* The channel went dead, so Mogan closed his communicator and tucked it back on his belt. He was surprised at how little resistance Hanigar had offered to his suggestion that they summon reinforcements and eliminate the independent colony as a precursor to asserting absolute dominion

over the planet. Typically, Imperial Intelligence supervisors were loath to request aid from the Defense Force, preferring to handle sensitive operations independently. The exercise of brute force, however, was the Defense Force's singular specialty.

He called out to his troops, "Back to the transport! We're returning to base! Move!" He jogged behind them, barking orders to round up the laggards of the bunch. As he stepped aboard the transport and sealed the hatch behind him, he grinned at the knowledge that a military strike on the independent colony, no matter what flag its people lived under, would certainly draw the ire of the Federation and place the Empire's diplomats in politically untenable positions.

If there was one thing that Mogan loved above all else, it was finding anonymous ways to make politicians miserable.

Captain Daniel Okagawa prepared his report for transmission to Commodore Reyes on Vanguard. The past six days had been filled with low-key tension, the product of maneuvering survey teams around the Klingons' recon units, who clearly were seeking the same elusive artifacts that Starfleet had come to Gamma Tauri IV to find. In the past hour, however, the bad news had started to come in like a high tide dimmed with blood, and Okagawa suddenly found himself nostalgic for the days of merely simmering aggression.

He tabbed quickly through the layers of information on the data slate he'd been given for review. Casualty reports, complete with service records on each of the lost Starfleet personnel; brief dossiers on the nine civilian engineers, twenty-eight laborers, and two New Boulder peace officers slain at the aquifer dig; an after-action report by two ensigns who had barely escaped the slaughter of the survey team; several kiloquads of classified forensic data collected at the scene, for Dr. Fisher's personal review; and his own command report, for Vanguard's senior officers.

Nothing like a little bit of light bedtime reading for the commodore, Okagawa mused with dark humor.

An insistent beeping on a console behind him was silenced by the *Lovell*'s junior communications officer, Ensign Folanir Pzial. The young Rigelian placed a Feinberger receiver in one ear, then started flipping switches and inserting data cards in slots around his console. Whatever he was doing, he was working intensely and quickly, and it captured Okagawa's attention.

"Report, Ensign," Okagawa said.

Pzial held up his index finger to signal that he needed a moment. His bright red eyes were wide with surprise as he listened to whatever signal he had received. After a few more seconds, he looked up at Okagawa and said, "I've intercepted a coded Klingon signal, Captain. It's one of their newer ciphers, took me a few seconds to unscramble it." He flipped a few more switches on his console. "I'm still translating it. Sounds like they're using idiomatic code phrases."

Commander Araev zh'Rhun stepped behind Pzial and observed over his shoulder. The Andorian *zhen* squinted as she examined the data on Pzial's screens. "That encryption method is not generally used by the Klingon military," zh'Rhun said. "This signal is very likely being sent and received by agents of Imperial Intelligence."

"Their team on the ground is recommending something called 'Protocol *Say'Qul*,'" Pzial said. "Whatever that is. I can't find it in the Klingon language database."

Science Officer Xav joined zh'Rhun and hovered over Pzial's other shoulder. "In *tlhIngan,* words are sometimes compounded to create more complex terms," the Tellarite said. "Try breaking the word down into its components."

"Well, *Say'* has a few possible meanings," Pzial said, reading from a screen above his console. "It can be a verb, meaning to make something clean, or an adjective, meaning that something is clean." He switched to a different set of data. "*Qul* means 'research.' . . . I'm not sure putting those two words together makes much sense."

Xav scratched the back of his head. "Maybe it's a directive to purge their computers of sensitive information," he said. "Clean up their research?"

"It might be an order to remove their scientific personnel from the planet," zh'Rhun said.

Okagawa got up from his chair, tucked his data slate under his arm, and joined the press of bodies gathered around the communications station. Xav and zh'Rhun both moved half a step aside to make room for him. The communications officer ducked his head slightly as the captain leaned over him. "Pzial," Okagawa said, "scroll this list back a bit—one screen should be sufficient. I want to see something."

"Aye, sir," Pzial replied. The data on the overhead display paged back one screen's worth of data, showing more selections from a very limited Klingon-English translation menu.

Pointing at the screen, Okagawa asked Xav, "Why are these words not in alphabetical order?"

"But they are, sir," Xav said. "Our phonetic renderings of *tlhIngan* use the uppercase and lowercase *Q* characters to distinguish different pronunciations. In a translation dictionary, words that begin with the lowercase *Q* are listed before those that begin with the capital *Q*."

"So," Okagawa said, "for all we know, the word that Pzial transcribed from the Klingons' coded message might not be *Qul* but *qul*. The Klingon common noun for *'fire.'*" He looked at zh'Rhun. "Care to parse that into a familiar idiom, Commander?"

"Cleansing fire," the Andorian first officer said with a grim realization.

Walking back to his chair, Okagawa remarked, "Yeah. That sounds like the Klingons I know and love." He sat down. "Commander, what's the ETA for the *Endeavour*?"

"Twenty-five hours and forty-nine minutes," zh'Rhun said.

Okagawa shook his head. "This could be over by then." He signed the command authorization on his data slate and handed it to a yeoman, who carried it to the communications officer. "Pzial," the captain said, "add that intercepted signal to the report we're sending to Vanguard, and let them know what we think it means. After that, get al-Khaled back on the horn; tell him to pack up and bug out. I'm not letting trouble catch us with our pants down this time."

"Sir," zh'Rhun asked, "what about the colonists?"

He nodded. "We'll warn them," he said. "They've got their own ships, enough to carry a few thousand people. Anyone who wants a ride with us can come along," he said, "but no luggage, no gear, nothing. We can evac a few hundred guests if we dump our cargo. *Endeavour* can carry a couple thousand."

As if fearing reproach for stating the obvious, Xav said, "Captain, there are more than eleven thousand colonists on Gamma Tauri IV. Your evacuation scenario would leave nearly fifty percent of them stranded in the event of a disaster."

"I know, Xav," Okagawa said, staring at the reddish-brown world turning slowly on the main viewscreen. Something terrible was stirring on the surface of that world, and Okagawa had no idea how to stop it. All he could do was prepare to meet it head-on. "Commander," he said, "take the ship to yellow alert."

15

Commander BelHoQ was in search of perfection on the bridge of the Klingon battle cruiser *Zin'za*. As the first officer of one of its newest warships, he took pride in his job performance, and he expected nothing less than exemplary work from all those who served as members of his crew.

"Kreq," he said as he passed the communications officer. "Tell spacedock to prepare for our departure." Moving along to the weapons station, he slapped the shoulder of tactical officer Tonar. "Run a battle drill exactly thirty-one minutes after we go to warp," he instructed the lieutenant. "Don't announce it, just run it." Tonar nodded his understanding. BelHoQ moved on to the next free station and opened a channel to the engineering deck. "Engineering, bridge," he said. "Respond."

Lieutenant Ohq, the chief engineer, replied over the comm, *"What do you want, bridge?"*

"What I *want*, Ohq, is full power and all systems ready for launch in ten minutes," BelHoQ snapped. "And if I don't get it, there won't be a crawlspace on this ship deep enough or dark enough to keep me from feeding you to the captain's *targ*."

"The engines are ready for space, Commander," Ohq said, his tone all bluster and bravado. *"If you want to know where the delay is, try the cargo deck. Engineering out."*

Ohq cut the channel. The first officer permitted himself an admiring sneer for the chief engineer's fearless attitude. Then he patched in an intraship channel to the cargo bay. "Cargo bay, bridge! What's the holdup down there, you *taHqeqpu'*?"

His hail was met by a din of falling containers, shouting voices, and overtaxed machinery. The longer BelHoQ listened to the chaotic opera of ineptitude over the speaker, the angrier he became, and the harder the rest of the bridge crew laughed. The first officer's rage finally exploded from him, too potent to be restrained. "Urgoz, you damned *Qovpatlh!* If I have to go belowdecks to get an answer from you, no one will ever find your body!"

After a few more thuds of tumbling cargo, Urgoz, the cargo chief, spoke over the comm, sounding winded and harried. *"Sir."*

"What in *Gre'thor* is going on down there?" BelHoQ demanded.

A few huffs of breath preceded Urgoz's reply. *"Just a few problems, Commander. One of the new hands didn't secure the stacks as ordered. It's under—"* He was interrupted by another clanging ruckus that quickly gave way to silence. As if nothing had happened, Urgoz finished, *"It's under control, sir."*

BelHoQ stifled the laughing bridge officers with a glare. "How long before you're ready for space, Urgoz?"

"Twenty-five minutes," Urgoz said.

"You've got ten," BelHoQ said. "Don't be late. Bridge out." He cut the channel before he was forced to endure another one of Urgoz's pathetic excuses or simpering apologies. Just as he finished making a note in his duty log to cut the cargo crew's rations by a third for the next week as a punishment, Captain Kutal stepped onto the bridge. BelHoQ announced, "Captain on the bridge!"

All the officers and enlisted men snapped to attention and faced Kutal as he walked to his chair and sat down. "As you were," he growled. Everyone except BelHoQ resumed preparations for spacedock departure. The first officer moved to stand at the captain's left side.

"The knuckle-draggers in cargo are lagging again," he said. "Ready for space in fifteen minutes, sir."

Kutal grunted and glowered at the image of the spaceport on the main viewscreen. "The sooner the better," he confided to BelHoQ. "Been here too long as it is."

The *Zin'za* had been docked in orbit of Borzha II for more than a week, repairing the damage sustained on its last jaunt to the Jinoteur system. None of the crew, BelHoQ included, was eager to return to that star system. The captain did not seem to share the crew's lack of enthusiasm. Ever since the mission to Palgrenax, he had behaved like a man driven by restless demons. "Start prelaunch systems check," he ordered.

"Yes, sir," BelHoQ replied, and he nodded to the others, who had turned and looked at him for confirmation. They went back to work, their focus now entirely on their duties. The XO asked the captain, "Do I get to know why we cut our repairs two days short?"

Kutal cast a wary glance around the bridge, then replied in a low rasp, "A Starfleet scout ship sent a distress call from Jinoteur. We're to capture the ship for analysis and its crew for interrogation." He jerked a thumb toward Tonar. "Tell him only when he needs to know. Tell the others only when the mission is done."

"Understood, Captain."

A deep buzzing sound and a green warning light on the tactical console drew fiery stares from BelHoQ and the captain. The first officer stalked quickly across the bridge to Tonar's station. "Report," he commanded.

"Sensor malfunction," Tonar said. "Primary array offline, power spikes in the secondary array." He looked back at Bel-HoQ. "If we leave port now, we'll be flying blind, sir."

BelHoQ heard the captain's heavy footsteps approaching and felt their ominous vibrations through the deck. "Those systems were just repaired," Kutal said. "What's going on, BelHoQ?"

"Either *Fek'lhr* himself has defecated inside our sensor array," BelHoQ replied, "or Chief Engineer Ohq just earned himself forty jabs with a painstik."

Lieutenant Ohq had shoved aside a half-dozen mechanics to get at the damaged sensor array components. Word of the first officer's impending arrival in main engineering—a rare occurrence that usually presaged tremendous suffering for the person whose mistake had inspired the visit—had been called down from the upper decks, by mechanics cowed like *jeghpu'wI* while the commander made his livid passage to the midships ladder.

I will not relay secondhand reports, Ohq vowed as he twisted at the waist and pulled himself deeper inside the smoking jumble of slagged machinery behind the bulkhead. *When BelHoQ asks what happened, I'm going to have the answer.*

Ohq had been worried that some intricate system failure would have to be tracked down, at the expense of great effort and much time. Instead, he beheld the nexus of the problem in the sensor array and deduced the cause of the malfunction immediately. He called back to the mechanics, "One of you *toDSaHpu'* pass me a plasma cutter, now." A few seconds later the tool was pressed into his hand, and he bent his wrist at an awkward angle to get at a safe place to cut free the component that had caused the cascade failure.

In less than a minute he decoupled it from the part of the spaceframe with which it had fused. As it dislodged and fell into his hand, he heard BelHoQ bellow in the corridor behind him, "What's your excuse this time, Ohq?"

The chief engineer wriggled backward through the close-packed bundles of cable and protruding junction boxes. He landed on his feet, turned, and looked up at the grizzled black beard and wild mane of the first officer. "This," Ohq said, handing the damaged part to BelHoQ.

BelHoQ turned the misshapen hunk of metal one way and then the other. He thrust it back at Ohq. "What do you call this?"

"Sabotage, sir." He took back the half-melted glob. "We had a gravimetric flux compensator installed where a tachyon distortion filter should have been. They look identical on the outside except for the fact we color-code them and label them on every axis. Of course, someone could disguise one as the other pretty easily—until it breaks." He pointed out a dark red streak where the part's outer casing had split open. "That's the kragnite shielding—which is used only in the gravimetric flux compensator." He lobbed the device back to BelHoQ. "Somebody in the station's supply depot switched parts on us."

The first officer's fist closed white-knuckle tight around the fragged component. He stormed away grumbling foul curses and slamming the side of his fist against the bulkhead as he went.

Someone's about to get a painstik up the bIngDub, Ohq chuckled maliciously. *And for once it isn't me.*

"Could it have been a mistake?" asked Captain Kutal. "Or an error by one of Ohq's people? Kahless knows, his tool-pushers aren't exactly the brightest in the fleet."

BelHoQ slammed the ruined component down onto the captain's desk. The impact rang like a bell. "This was no accident! Whoever did this should be found and put to death in public, as a warning to others."

"I couldn't agree more," Kutal said. "But a manhunt on the scale you're proposing might take a day or more, and we don't have the time. Tell Ohq to expedite the repairs. As soon as we have the secondary array working, we can ship out. He can finish fixing the primary array en route."

Pacing in tight circles, BelHoQ scrunched his face with rage. "This sends a bad message to others, Captain. They will think we are weak, that we let crimes like this go unpunished. It will invite more of the same."

"Doubtful," Kutal said. "I suspect this will prove to be an isolated incident, intended to delay us from reaching the Starfleet ship. For all their noble talk, I wouldn't be surprised to find that Starfleet had a hand in this."

The first officer was grinding his jaw slowly, and his hands had curled into trembling fists. "We must make an example of the scum who did this!"

"Absolutely," Kutal said. "Flay them alive and quarter them. Set them on fire and put them out with a disruptor blast. You'll do so with my thanks." He rose from his chair and made certain that BelHoQ understood that his was to be the last word on the subject. "But not until *after* we get back. Until then, I want you focused on the mission and nothing else. Get back to the bridge, and keep a fire lit under Ohq until those sensors are working. . . . That is all. Dismissed."

A low rumble of protest rolled around inside BelHoQ's throat, but he nodded his understanding and marched out of Kutal's quarters. As the door closed, Kutal abandoned his own façade of calm and seethed to imagine what kind of lowly *petaQ* would resort to sabotage. It made him sick with rage to think of the damage his unseen foes had wrought on his ship. He calmed himself by daydreaming that one of them was human; then he envisioned his hands around the human's throat, squeezing and crushing until it all but turned to putty in his grip, and he kept on picturing that—until it finally, inevitably, brought a smile of murderous glee to his face. *That's more like it,* he thought as he left his quarters and returned to the bridge.

Pennington leaned against Quinn for support, and the pilot was leaning on Pennington. Arranged like a pair of crooked book-ends, they waved their drunken salutations at the two women who had just dropped them off in front of their docking bay at the Lamneth Starport. The attractive young ladies sped away in their hovercar and ascended swiftly back into the flow of traffic.

"Nice girls," Quinn said with only a hint of slurring.

Lolling his head to cast a cockeyed stare at the older man, Pennington said, "Maybe yours was. What was her name again?"

"Dunno," Quinn said from beneath a furrowed brow. "What was your girl's name?"

The journalist shook his head. "No idea." After a moment, he added, "I think she took my wallet."

"So did mine," Quinn said. He looked at Pennington and let out the snort of a suppressed laugh.

Even though he was angry, Pennington was starting to laugh, too. "Brilliant!" he hollered. They stumbled apart. "Men with guns are still looking for us, we don't have a job to get us off this rock, and now a couple of skanks have snicked our wallets!" Quinn laughed harder, which only annoyed Pennington more. "Don't you care?"

Forcing out his reply between guffaws, Quinn said, "Not really." A few hilarious gasps later he added, "Mine was empty." He straightened and brushed his fingers through his tangled mess of bone-white hair. "Relax, will ya? It'll be okay."

Pennington asked, "How will it?"

"I don't know," Quinn said with a shrug. "It's a mystery. You just have to roll with what comes. Most of the time, things get sorted out on their own."

Eyeing the pilot's disheveled state, Pennington quipped, "Well, that would certainly explain the paragon of wealth and success who stands before me now."

Miming a chest wound with exaggerated gestures, Quinn weaved and stumbled comically. "A hit, a palpable hit! You wound me, newsboy!" He tripped deliberately over his own feet and sprawled onto his back in a man-sized X pose on the tarmac. As Pennington strolled over and stood beside him, Quinn waved him away with mock pride. "Just leave me here. Sun'll be up soon."

"Get up, you ridiculous sod," Pennington said.

Quinn made a pillow of his folded hands. "Not until you admit you had fun tonight. Don't deny it. I was there."

Rolling his eyes, Pennington admitted, "Maybe a bit. Except for the getting shot at."

"What, are you kidding? That was the best part!" Quinn flashed a devilish grin and extended his hand to him. "Help me up, will ya?"

He reached down and lifted Quinn to his feet. "I'm wiped out, mate," he said. "Mind if we bag it for the night?"

"Not at all," Quinn said, slapping the dust from his trousers as he walked toward the entrance to the docking bay. "Tomorrow's another day, I reckon. We'll get some shuteye, start fresh first thing in the—" He checked his chrono and finished his sentence. "—afternoon. Brunch and Bloody Marys on me."

Despite himself, Pennington smiled. "You're all right, mate," he said. "For a pain in the ass."

"I'm a work in progress," Quinn said, unlocking the docking bay door. He let Pennington step past him, down the passage to the ship, and locked the portal behind them.

The mottled gray bulk of the tramp freighter *Rocinante* sat dark and quiet in the middle of an open-air landing pad. Beyond the vessel's large warp nacelles, its wingtips stood upright in their landing configuration; its narrow wedge-shaped fuselage was connected to the spaceport by a web of umbilical lines providing power, local communications, water supply, waste removal, and fuel.

After several weeks of hopping from one system to another with Quinn, Pennington had in the past week been entrusted with the ship's security codes. He could now lock and unlock the rear hatch, enabling him to come and go as he pleased while Quinn busied himself with the business of booking freight or passengers for each leg of their journey. With the slow precision of someone who had just mastered a code sequence—or someone who was just drunk enough to have trouble remembering it—he opened the ship's aft hatch. It lowered with a sickly whine of poorly maintained hydraulics and thick downward plumes of ghostly white vapor.

Pennington plodded with leaden steps up the ramp and lurched like dead weight into his hammock. Several seconds later Quinn clomped up the metal ramp into the main compartment and sealed the aft hatch behind them. Several recent brushes with unsavory types had left Quinn on the defensive. Where he had once taken security for granted, he now considered it to be chief among his concerns.

Quinn sat on his hammock and pulled off his boots. The stench of his sweaty socks had made Pennington gag during their first shared journey. After nearly two months in the man's company, Pennington still found the smell horrid, but he had developed enough resistance to it that his reaction was limited to wrinkling his nose and rolling over to face the bulkhead.

Just as he was prepared to be serenaded by the buzzsaw of Quinn's postbinge snoring, the pilot muttered a low string of curses and plodded off to the cockpit.

Twisting back around, Pennington called out, "What is it?"

"Message light's on," Quinn said. "Might be a job." Pennington listened to the sound of Quinn tapping buttons for a few seconds, then the grizzled pilot sighed. "Aw, crap."

Pennington rolled out of his hammock and stumbled into the cockpit with Quinn. "What's going on?"

"It's from T'Prynn," he said. "There's a Starfleet ship down on Jinoteur IV, needs a new fuel pod before the Klingons get there—and she wants us to bring it to 'em."

"Jinoteur?" The word jogged Pennington's memory. "That's where we jacked that Klingon probe for her, remember?"

"Yeah," Quinn said. "I remember. I bet it ain't a coincidence, either." He punched up a second screen of data. "She already bought the fuel pod from a vendor here on Nejev. Wants us to pick it up and hightail it to the *Sagittarius*." He stabbed at a control with his index finger and shut off the comm screen. "So much for making a profit on this run. Do me a favor, will ya? Go below and make as much room in the hold as you can. I'll call the vendor and tell them we're on our way."

"Sure, mate, you got it," Pennington said. He left the bridge in a hurry and made his way down to the hold, grinning the entire time. He wasn't the least bit happy that a Starfleet ship was in trouble, but he was ecstatic that he would be the first and only reporter there to cover it.

It had been a few months since T'Prynn had duped him into filing a story about the destruction of the *U.S.S. Bombay,* one that had borne all the earmarks of truth but had turned out to be a complete fabrication. He still had not fully deduced her motives for embarrassing the Federation News Service and himself with that intricate charade, nor had he forgiven her. Having been disgraced in the eyes of his peers, Pennington had spent the months since then filing anonymous filler for various news ser-

vices. Making matters worse, by filing many of his stories from
Vanguard, he had unwittingly condemned them to the limbo of
the Starfleet censor's office.

Now he had exclusive access to what promised to be a truly
compelling and eminently *newsworthy* event involving another
Starfleet ship—and this time his reporting would be firsthand,
as an eyewitness and participant. The sweetest detail of all, however, was that he had T'Prynn to thank for it.

Who says irony is dead? he mused as he set himself to work
making room in the *Rocinante*'s hold—and daydreaming about
the story that was about to resurrect his career.

16

"For that reason," Captain Okagawa said via the secure channel, *"we think the Klingons are preparing to eliminate the civilian colony on Gamma Tauri IV, as a precursor to assuming control over the entire planet. We've started evacuating our own people, but the colonists are another matter. My first concern was that we wouldn't have enough room for all of them. Now it seems the bigger problem is persuading them to leave at all."*

Dr. Fisher stood flanked by Ambassador Jetanien and Lieutenant Commander T'Prynn in front of Commodore Reyes's desk, listening to Okagawa's report. Having only recently been brought into the loop regarding Operation Vanguard, Fisher chose to stay quiet for the time being. He turned a red data card over and over in his hand while the meeting continued.

Jetanien asked Okagawa, "Have the Klingons made any overt threat against your ship or your people on the planet?"

"No, Your Excellency," Okagawa said. *"But I've put my ship on yellow alert anyway. 'Turn the other cheek' doesn't mean stand there and wait to get hit."*

Reyes nodded. "My sentiments exactly."

"Captain," T'Prynn said, "when did you detect the spike in energy readings on Gamma Tauri IV?"

"About three and a half hours ago."

T'Prynn looked at Jetanien and then Reyes as she said, "The signals group down in the Vault detected unusually intense activity on the Shedai carrier-wave frequency around that time. They claim the signal originated in the Jinoteur system."

"Then it would appear that the link between those two systems is more than merely circumstantial," Jetanien said as he began pacing slowly in the middle of the office. Looking at Captain Okagawa on the monitor, he continued, "Do you have an estimate on when Klingon reinforcements will arrive?"

Okagawa shook his head. *"Nothing definite. But considering how fast their colony ship moved in, I suspect their military can't be far behind."*

"Getting back to the situation on the planet," Reyes said, "how many civilians were killed at that aquifer dig?"

In the time it took Okagawa to look at his data slate for the answer, T'Prynn said, "Thirty-nine: nine engineers, twenty-eight workers, and two peace officers."

A few short clicks prefaced Jetanien's query. "Are we certain beyond a reasonable doubt that the Klingons aren't responsible for the attack on the colonists?"

"That's for Dr. Fisher to say," Okagawa said. *"We've sent all the forensic data we collected at the scene. As far as deciding what it all means—"*

Reyes cut in, "Point taken, Captain." Looking at Fisher, Reyes said, "We need your report on the double, Zeke, so consider it a rush job."

Fisher quipped with a weary smirk, "Aren't they all?"

"Captain," Reyes said, "continue evacuating our people. I'll have the *Endeavour* pick up the pace; they should be with you in less than twenty-one hours. That should be enough to make the Klingons think twice before taking a shot at you."

A troubled look lingered on Okagawa's face. *"What about the colonists, sir? If a Klingon battle cruiser on their doorstep doesn't convince them to leave, then what?"*

"Then nothing," Reyes said. His weathered face slackened with dour resignation. "If they won't ask for help, there's nothing we can do for them. Once you have our people aboard, pull back to safe distance and stay out of it."

"That seems pretty harsh," Fisher said, sounding more irate than he had intended. "Why not tell them the truth? That something really powerful is going to kill them if they don't get out of there?"

In an arch tone that rankled Fisher, Jetanien replied, "And how do you propose we explain our wealth of knowledge about their predicament, Doctor? The colonists would no doubt ask us to cite previous encounters with these entities. They would inquire about the nature of these beings: Are they intelligent? What do they want? Can they be bargained with? In every case we would find ourselves unable to answer, lest we divulge the entirety of Operation Vanguard."

"You say that like it's a bad thing," Fisher said. "Those colonists' lives are in danger. They have a right to know."

"Perhaps," said T'Prynn. "Perhaps not. Warning the colonists would expose our operation and grant the Klingons an undue advantage."

Suddenly, Fisher felt like the only sane person in the room. Indignant, he said to T'Prynn, "What advantage? The only reason the Klingons are on Gamma Tauri IV is because we are. They obviously know why we're there."

"Not necessarily," T'Prynn said. "They know that we are searching for *something*, but they might not know what. I suspect they made discoveries on Palgrenax that were similar to our own. But you misunderstand me. I am not speaking of a scientific or even a military advantage but a political one.

"If we betray our knowledge of the entities the Tholians call 'Shedai' in order to save the colonists on Gamma Tauri IV, the Klingons will manufacture a public outcry about our 'secret programs' to undermine civilians' trust in Starfleet and the Federation. Our ability to continue our investigation will be compromised, while the Klingons will be able to justify their own efforts as a reaction to our own."

Fisher was fuming as he looked to Reyes. "Am I hearing this right, Commodore? We'd let eleven thousand people die on Gamma Tauri to make sure the Klingons don't *embarrass* us?"

Reyes sighed. "It's a bit more complicated than that, Doctor. You've seen the potential in the meta-genome—hell, you showed us how to unlock part of it." He reclined regally in his chair. "Now, I could be wrong about this, but I'm pretty sure that whoever figures out the meta-genome first is gonna be holding all the cards in this game—and I'd rather not see them in the Klingons' hand, especially when we've got damned near all our chips on the table." He leaned forward and folded his hands in front of him on the desk. "So far we've been a little bit lucky, and we've bluffed our way out of a few tight spots—but if we show our cards early to save eleven thousand lives on Gamma Tauri, we might be throwing away eleven *billion* lives across the Federation by giving the game to the Klingons." Softening his tone, he added, "I'm not a monster, Zeke. I don't want to see those people come to harm. But I've had to get used to the fact that we're playing for much higher stakes than we've ever played before. I'm not trying to be dramatic, but we could be talking about the survival of the Federation."

Heavy silence fell over the room. Realizing that he was outnumbered by people just as stubborn as himself, Fisher grimaced and shook his head. "Rationalize it, explain it, justify it any way you like," he said. "It still adds up to letting innocent people die so we can keep our damn secrets."

A low rumbling sound percolated inside Jetanien's broad chest. Then the Chelon ambassador said, "May I make a suggestion, Commodore?"

"Please," Reyes said, sounding both weary and curious.

Jetanien grasped the lapels of his robe and said, "It is likely that the Shedai attacked the Starfleet survey personnel because they were armed and perceived as a threat. If so, it is possible that the unarmed civilian colonists will not be considered dangerous and will not be targeted by the Shedai. If Dr. Fisher's forensic analysis concludes that the colonists were killed by Klingon action, I propose that we treat the incident as a matter between third parties and remain neutral. But if he concludes that the colonists have been targeted by the Shedai, I recommend we either coax or coerce the colonists to evacuate, while taking steps to preserve operational security."

Reyes nodded. "Fair enough." He looked at Fisher. "Sound okay to you, Doctor?"

"I still think it stinks," Fisher said, glancing at the data card in his hand. "But I can live with it."

"Then you'd better get to work," Reyes said, "because your report'll decide what we do next."

Dr. M'Benga shivered slightly as he entered the chilly confines of the morgue. Located on the lowest level of Vanguard Hospital, the morgue was a place that M'Benga disliked visiting— not out of superstition but to avoid being reminded of those times when all his knowledge and all of Starfleet's formidable medical science simply wasn't enough, the times when death bested them.

Hunched over an angled viewer in front of the morgue's main computer bank, Dr. Ezekiel Fisher looked lost in his work, staring with unblinking intensity into the greenish illumination of the device's recessed screen. He didn't seem to register the sound of M'Benga's footsteps as the younger physician walked over to join him. Even after M'Benga was right next to him, Fisher continued staring into the viridian glow. A half-empty mug of coffee sat to Fisher's right; a semi-congealed swirl of artificial dairy product coated its surface. Fisher reached across the console without looking up, grabbed a blue data card from a stack of cards, and inserted it into a slot.

Trying to interrupt without breaking Fisher's chain of thought by speaking, M'Benga covered his closed mouth with his fist and made a few low, throat-clearing coughs.

Fisher peeked sideways at him. "I knew you were there, Jabilo," he said. "No need to be coy."

"My apologies, sir," M'Benga said. "I can see you're busy."

Rubbing his eyes with his thumb and forefinger, Fisher sighed. "What brings you downstairs?"

"T'Prynn's medical records," M'Benga said.

The chief medical officer turned his back to the console and leaned against its edge. "I sent them over two days ago. Did you get them?"

"Yes, sir," M'Benga said. "I reviewed them at length."

Crossing his arms, Fisher said, "And?"

"They're suspiciously perfect," M'Benga said. "From her adolescence through the present, her records paint her as the picture of health."

Fisher shrugged. "Vulcans take good care of themselves."

"Yes, sir, I know. I interned on Vulcan. So I know from experience that they suffer illnesses, just like everyone else. But according to T'Prynn, she's never been sick, and every injury she's ever suffered has been duty-related."

"You talked to her?" Fisher asked. "Did you have her come in for a physical and a history like I told you?"

M'Benga nodded. "Yes, I did. And I didn't find anything wrong . . . at first."

Suspicion creased Fisher's wrinkled brow. "Meaning?"

"When I compared the history she gave me with the file you sent over, they matched—*perfectly.* I know Vulcans often display eidetic memories, but how many know their own medical files word for word?" He offered Fisher the data slate he was carrying. "So I compared the data from her physical with her history. They don't line up." Pointing out several items, he continued, "She says she suffered dozens of minor injuries during her years of service in security and intelligence, but look at the numbers on those fractures and deep-tissue scars. Those injuries were all inflicted *at the same time*—approximately fifty to fifty-five years ago, either before or while she was a cadet."

Sounding confused and alarmed, Fisher mumbled, "She lied."

"There's more," M'Benga said. "Over the last two days, I've spoken to six doctors who were CMOs at her previous assignments. Most don't remember treating the kinds of injuries she reported, but three of them said they did treat her for symptoms similar to the ones that brought her into the ER six days ago. And they all found that their private records regarding T'Prynn had been . . . *expunged.*" Nodding at the data slate, he added, "Forgive the pun, sir, but her medical records have been doctored."

Fisher pulled a hand slowly and firmly over his gray goatee. "Exposing a lie is one thing, Jabilo. Getting the truth is another." He handed back the data slate. "Let me tell you what I found out from the brass at Starfleet Medical. Her files were sealed by someone at Starfleet Intelligence—someone with a much higher clearance than mine. The whitewashed version was the best I could do; if you really want to get her original medical file, you'll have to talk to someone above my pay grade."

"Someone like Commodore Reyes?"

A knowing smile pulled Fisher's mouth wide. "If you think you can get him to sign the order, be my guest."

M'Benga asked, "Could you help me convince him?"

"Sorry," Fisher said, turning back toward the console. "I have a lot to do and no time to do it. If you want to go tilting at windmills tonight, you're on your own."

"Thank you, Doctor," M'Benga said, hiding his irritation at being left to carry on alone. "I will."

Lines, circles, and arrows. That's all that Reyes could see after staring for too long at the sector chart on his office wall. Dots, rings, and washes of color. It was all bleeding together, turning into gibberish. Part of him suspected that the idea of borders in interstellar space had always been nonsense.

Arrowheads, trefoils, diamonds, and squares—ship markers were scattered far and wide across his map. Arrowheads were few and far between: those were Starfleet vessels. Slightly greater in number were the trefoils representing Klingon warships. The diamonds were scarcest of all, not because the Tholian vessels they represented didn't exist but because Reyes's team had no idea where they were. Cluttering the map were the squares: civilian ships. Freighters, tankers, colony vessels. Almost too many to count, but it was his team's job to protect them all.

Every day he tracked the activity in the sector like a hunter watching for a telltale warning sign in the brush or a rustle of movement in the tall grass. Sooner or later, either the Klingons or the Tholians would make their move to seize control of the Taurus Reach. *Assuming I do my job right,* he reminded himself, *I'll see it coming and be able to stop them.*

Reyes picked at his midnight snack. The lasagna had gone cold while he'd sat staring at the wall, and the salad had marinated in its red-wine vinaigrette to the point of nearly disintegrating. He tried forcing down another mouthful of lasagna, but it had been mediocre when it was hot and had since become all but inedible.

His intercom buzzed. He thumbed open the channel. "Yes?"

"Dr. M'Benga to see you, sir," said Yeoman Finneran.

He felt himself blink and recoil gently. *This is new.* "Send him in," he said. Grateful for an excuse to abandon his meal, he pushed the tray aside.

His office door opened, and M'Benga walked in. The doctor noticed the tray on Reyes's desk. "I didn't mean to interrupt your dinner, sir."

"I was finished," Reyes said, standing up to greet him. He circled around the desk and extended his hand. "You look familiar. Have we met before?"

"No, sir," M'Benga said.

Sifting through memories of recent events, Reyes flashed upon why M'Benga's name was familiar. Snapping his fingers, he said, "You put in for a transfer a few weeks back, didn't you?"

"About two months ago, actually," M'Benga said.

Reyes gestured to the chairs in front of his desk as he circled back behind it to his own. "Well, these things take time. If you're here about speeding up the process—"

"I'm not," M'Benga said. "I came to talk to you about Lieutenant Commander T'Prynn's medical records, sir."

Settling into his chair, Reyes knew this couldn't be good. "What about them, Doctor?"

"For starters," M'Benga said, "I'd like to know why they were redacted by Starfleet Intelligence. Regulations require us to maintain complete medical histories on all serving officers.

But someone at Starfleet Intelligence modified her records, removed critical information, and inserted fraudulent data. T'Prynn herself gave me false information when answering questions about her medical history. I want to know why."

Exercising care in his choice of words, Reyes said, "There are numerous reasons why Starfleet Intelligence might classify someone's records, Doctor." He slowly adjusted the monitor on his desktop so that he alone could see it. As he continued, he submitted a request for T'Prynn's medical records using his own security clearance. "What if our medical database was compromised? An enemy might data-mine those records to match dates and places with injuries, to identify undercover field operatives. Even years later, an agent's history might have to remain redacted to protect others."

M'Benga shook his head. "That still wouldn't explain the absence of accurate baseline data. Without that, it's impossible for us to tell the difference between chronic conditions and acute ones, and we have no basis for detecting anomalies in her vital statistics. Scans I made during her recent visit to the ER suggested some serious neurochemical imbalances, but I have no way to make a comparative analysis."

"What are you asking for, Doctor?"

"You have the rank and security clearance to override the classification order," M'Benga said. "I'm asking you to release Lieutenant Commander T'Prynn's authentic, unexpurgated medical record, if not to the main medical archive, then on a need-to-know basis. Sir, I have reason to believe she's suffering from a long-term condition that requires treatment, but I can't make an informed diagnosis until I have all the facts—and I need your help to get them."

T'Prynn's medical file appeared on Reyes's monitor; in a glance he noted that it looked remarkably spare in details. As the doctor had said, the file had been marked as classified by Starfleet Intelligence. What alarmed him, however, was the identity of the person who had classified it: T'Prynn herself.

There's got to be a regulation against that, Reyes figured.

Considering the serious nature of the doctor's allegations, he wondered whether he ought to inform M'Benga of T'Prynn's role in classifying her own medical history. The consequences loomed large in his deliberations. *No doubt Zeke'll want an investigation,* Reyes knew. *They could take T'Prynn off active duty, hold an inquest—hell, Starfleet Medical might even be able to have her court-martialed.* He thought of all the crises that were unfolding on every front at that moment: the *Sagittarius* downed on Jinoteur and dependent on one of T'Prynn's unofficial "assets" for its rescue; a clandestine sabotage-by-proxy operation on Borzha II that Reyes had set in motion from a plan drafted by T'Prynn; and the downward spiral into violence that was threatening to consume the New Boulder colony on Gamma Tauri IV, and hundreds of Starfleet personnel with it. Of all the possible moments to lose T'Prynn's counsel and expertise, this was one of the worst Reyes could imagine.

If she sealed her own records, she must have had a good reason, Reyes convinced himself. *You have to trust her.*

He blanked her information from his screen and looked up at M'Benga. "I'm sorry, Doctor. . . . Request denied."

17

Finding tools aboard the Tholian battleship had been both more and less difficult than Xiong had expected.

Several compartments off the main engineering deck were packed with a variety of devices, all formed of substances very similar to the glasslike compound of which the bulkheads were made. Large tools and small tools, some shaped like levers and others like hooks or forks, lined the bulkheads. Locating them had taken less than an hour.

Since then, Xiong had spent three hours trying to figure out what any of the devices did or how he might activate them. Pressing their surfaces at various points had been ineffectual. Touching them against bulkheads or machinery or each other had proved equally futile. He had tried pulling them apart, to no avail. In a moment that had been half inspiration and half desperation, he had probed the bulkheads of the engineering deck seeking apertures into which one or more of the devices might be inserted, only to find them solid, smooth, and unyielding.

Though he had long considered himself to be handy with tools, he had begun to realize that in his hands the Tholian gadgets were little more than a collection of exotic clubs. *I give up,* he decided, and he left the engineering deck.

After slogging up to the passageway intersection on the main deck above, he checked his air gauge. It showed less than five hours remaining. As much as he tried to convince himself that five hours would be plenty of time to find a way off the ship and safely to the planet's surface, he found it impossible to forget that he had already been there for five hours without making any significant progress whatsoever.

Stay calm, he told himself. *Keep it together. Keep moving.*

He worked his way aft, checking each open compartment for any sign of loose equipment. In the aft quarter of the ship he found another intersection that led to a higher deck, and he followed it. The obsidian bulkheads on the upper deck were dotted at irregular intervals with asymmetrical fixtures of corrugated metal. Xiong scrutinized one closely but was unable to determine what purpose, if any, it served.

Most of the compartments he inspected while passing by were packed with blocky crystalline pedestals, which were arranged around the rooms' perimeters or grouped in trilateral formations. He suspected that these might be analogous to any of several duty stations aboard a Federation starship, such as a fire-control center or an environmental support office. One extremely large compartment was heavily partitioned and seemed designed for quarantine procedures. *Either a sickbay or a science lab,* Xiong concluded, and he kept moving.

Then he passed a nondescript chamber. After doing a quick double-take he stopped and backed up. He entered slowly, as if sensing that there was something special about this place. It had the focused design and economical aesthetic that he knew Tholians associated with rituals. In its center were two wide crystalline platforms that appeared to be melded with the deck. On each platform was a meter-wide hexagon of a different kind of crystalline substance. To Xiong's surprise, the hexagon was only an empty frame with what appeared to be a handle attached to its central cross-brace. He extended one finger and tried to push it through the empty space in the frame. A flash-crackle of energy repulsed his hand and knocked him backward as it sent a loud burst of static over his helmet's transceiver.

Shake it off, he thought, staggering forward toward the platform once again. *You're all right; get it together, Ming.*

On his second approach he avoided the hexagons and focused on the peculiar, slender objects beside them. He crouched to examine the closer one. It appeared to be made of the obsidian bulkhead substance; roughly twenty-five centimeters long, it looked like a handle for a tool. As he tilted his head to look at it from a slightly lower angle, a glint of light on a microthin blade emanating from the object pierced the shimmering haze of the Tholian ship's superheated, hyperdense atmosphere.

Now he understood. It was a sword.

A difference of a few degrees could render the blade all but invisible. After studying it for a few minutes, Xiong deduced that it was likely composed of monofilaments. Its meter-long edge was likely so atomically fine that it could cut through nearly anything.

On a hunch, he grasped the haft of the weapon with great care, turned it in his grip so that the edge was poised to cut, and lowered its tip slowly to the deck. He barely felt the vibration of contact. Pivoting slowly, he watched a gouge appear in the black perfection of the obsidian floor. The glimmer of the blade came and went from his vision as he inscribed the cut in a half circle around himself. Lifting the monoblade from the deck, he grinned. *Yes, this'll do nicely.*

Carrying it back to the escape pod he had found was more nerve-racking than he had expected. Every time the unfamiliar atmosphere of the Tholian ship caused a slight wobble in his step, he worried that he might amputate a digit or a limb or his head with one careless turn of his wrist. Most of the time he couldn't really see the blade he was carrying, which made navigating corners and portals hazardous.

He stopped when he reached the hexagonal entrance to the escape pod. Space inside the pod was limited. One careless turn of the monoblade inside there could rupture its hull and render it useless. Worse, the interior of the pod was a zero-gravity environment, which would make it difficult to get the necessary leverage to control the blade's movement while cutting. It would take only one fumble to cut himself in half while using the blade to access the systems inside the pod's bulkhead.

He decided it was time for a change of strategy. Even if he

could open the bulkhead, he had no reason to think he would be able to fathom its inner workings. He chided himself, *What do you expect to find, Ming? Duotronic cables?*

A flicker of anger drove him to fantasize about skewering the pod with the monoblade. Then he stopped and considered the sorts of features that were often found in escape pods, regardless of the species for which it was made. Most relied on manual operation for launch, but on many ships there were conditions that would trigger the automatic release of escape pods. On Starfleet ships, some self-destruct sequences ejected escape pods as part of their protocol. In many cases, an ejection sequence could be triggered by fire . . . or by a sudden loss of hull integrity and air pressure.

Xiong set the monoblade on the deck between his feet and climbed carefully into the pod. Then, clinging to the edge of the portal, he reached out and picked up the sword. He looked around until he saw a part of the Tholian ship's hull that could be easily perforated without harming the escape pod—and he thrust the monoblade into it.

A groan of wrenching metal, the roar of escaping high-pressure fluids, the shattering of obsidian. Xiong fought the blowout effect caused by the explosive decompression and pushed himself back inside the escape pod. Grabbing any handholds he could find, he wedged himself inside the tiny space as the thunder of the disintegrating bulkhead was drowned out by the screech of venting gases.

An iris snapped shut over the pod's portal. Sudden acceleration hurled Xiong against the iris as the pod was blasted away from the Tholian battle cruiser. Seconds later its inertial dampeners kicked in, and he was once again floating freely inside the pod. Looking toward its far end, he saw that its black surface had become almost transparent, showing him the curve of the planet as it spread wide beneath him.

He was about to congratulate himself for his ingenuity when he realized that he had absolutely no means of controlling the pod's descent or landing. As a vast ocean rolled into view,

Xiong hoped that the pod's automated features extended to more than just its ejection sequence.

The tropics, he mused as the pod fell. *Assuming I survive the splashdown, this might be the start of a nice vacation.*

Niwara stood at the river's edge as Commander Terrell waded out into the rapids. An orange safety line from her pack was tied around his torso and secured to a thick tree trunk several meters behind her. She controlled the slack of the line as he moved into deeper water, anchoring him so that the current didn't sweep him away as it had Theriault. The bright orange rope chafed the pads of her paws as she fed out a few more meters of it to Terrell.

He called back to her, "How much farther?"

She glanced down at the screen of her tricorder, which lay flat on the ground by her feet. "Two more meters," Niwara said. "Then dive." Paying out some more line for the first officer, she wondered how he would find anything in the churning murk of muddy water. Opening his eyes underwater would be all but impossible. In every practical sense, he would be diving blind.

Terrell took a deep breath and submerged. Niwara monitored the slack in the line by touch while she watched her tricorder screen. It was centered on the signal from Theriault's communicator, which lay unmoving on the river bottom. Slowly the first officer's bio reading closed in on it, then stopped. A few seconds later he surfaced and gasped for breath while fighting to tread water against the current. "Am I close?" he asked.

"Half a meter more to your left when you dive," she said.

He nodded, took a few quick breaths, then ducked back under the water. When he surfaced again half a minute later, he had Theriault's communicator in his hand. "Reel me in," he said.

Hand over hand, Niwara helped pull Terrell back to the riverbank. He dragged himself out of the water and slumped to a sitting position. His body, bare except for some regulation-issue dark gray underwear, was covered in dirty water that dried quickly in the warm air, leaving him coated with sandy grit. His close-cropped wiry hair was packed with silt. He untied the safety line from his body.

Niwara asked, "Was there any sign of her?"

"No," Terrell said, shaking his head. "Just her communicator." He looked out at the river. "Probably got knocked loose when she went over those rocks." Niwara nodded and began undoing the knots that held the safety line to the tree trunk. As she expected, Terrell tried to put a positive spin on his discovery. "I'm just glad she wasn't down there," he said. He gazed into the distance, following the river's path into the jungle. "That means there's a chance she's still alive, somewhere downriver."

Although Niwara always hoped for the best, she made a point of preparing for the worst. *Theriault could be dead,* she admitted to herself. *Floating away, a slave to the current.* She knew not to say so aloud. Terrell had no patience for pessimism.

Terrell stood up and brushed off as much of the water and dirt from his body as he could. He retrieved his clothes, which he had placed in a neat pile several meters from the water. In less than a minute he was dressed. He rejoined Niwara, who coiled the last few meters of the safety line, knotted it around its middle, and stowed it in her pack. "We've got about an hour of daylight left," Terrell said. "We'll continue downriver till it gets dark. Then we'll make camp for the night."

"Aye, sir," Niwara said, putting on her pack. The first officer was right to recommend halting their trip downriver when darkness fell. Niwara could only hope that Theriault had found the opportunity to do likewise.

The top deck of the *U.S.S. Sagittarius* looked like a junkyard.

Master Chief Ilucci and his engineering team were surrounded by the disassembled components of several different systems, ranging from shield emitters to plasma conduits. Several pieces were scorched; a few had been warped by intense heat. Kneeling in the middle of it all was Threx. The brawny

Denobulan poked and prodded the item in his hand with various tools and sensors, then he chucked it over his shoulder. "Well, that one's dead," he said. "Toss me another."

Karen Cahow lobbed an identical component to him. "If we don't find a working regulator soon, we can forget about fixing the shields," she said.

"Two more pieces, and I can build a new one," Threx said.

Torvin stood with one of his enormous Tiburonian ears pressed against the impulse reactor and glared at the other engineers. He pressed his index finger to his lips in a shushing gesture. Cahow grinned with amusement at the boyish engineer's brazen rebuke of his superiors. Ilucci rolled his eyes; Threx simply glowered and turned away. They all stopped talking, however, giving Torvin a few moments to listen for whatever was going wrong inside the delicate reactor assembly.

After several seconds he pulled back from the machine. "It's the vectored exhaust director," he said despondently. "The inner and outer vanes are totally misaligned."

"All right," Ilucci said. "We can't fix that. Realign the warp-core EPS taps instead. I want to be ready to hook up the new fuel pod as soon as it gets here." *If it gets here,* he prevented himself from adding.

"You got it, Master Chief," Torvin said. He picked up his tools and went to work.

Ilucci kneeled beside the transporter emitter. The entire engineering team had taken half an hour to decouple it from its housing beneath the cargo deck and transfer it with antigravs to the top deck. Moving it back belowdecks and resecuring it was just one of many labor-intensive tasks the engineers had to look forward to this evening. First, however, Ilucci had to find some way to fix it. "Cahow," he called out. "We got any spare imaging scanners?"

"No," said the blond engineer. "But I can rig you one if you let me raid the dorsal sensors for parts."

It wasn't the answer he was hoping for; cannibalizing the array would create large gaps in the ship's scanning capabilities.

Weighing the value of restoring the transporter against the loss
of tactically useful data, Ilucci decided that it was a necessary
trade-off. "How long?"

"At least eight hours," she said.

He sighed. "Okay, get on it." She nodded, grabbed a box of
tools, and disappeared into the starboard forward crawlspace.

Ilucci walked over and joined Threx, who removed the housing from a metallic shaft the size of his forearm. Studying the
cables and circuitry inside, the Denobulan said, "This one looks
like it might be okay." He pointed at an oddly shaped device
near Ilucci's right foot. "Can you hand me that, Master Chief?"
Ilucci picked up the object and passed it to Threx, who test-
fitted it against the cylinder in his other hand. "Yeah, that'll do.
I can make a new regulator with these. Have the shields back by
morning."

"A hundred percent?" Ilucci asked.

Threx cocked his head sideways. "More like sixty-five."

"All right," Ilucci said. "Keep me posted." He watched Threx
shamble away with half-disassembled machine parts in each
hand and prepared himself for what promised to be a long night
of jury-rigged repairs.

One crisis at a time, he told himself. *That's how we do it.*

The escape pod was sheathed in fire. Plunging like a stone
through the atmosphere, it shook and spun around Xiong. He
ricocheted off the bulkheads, despite his best efforts to brace
himself with his outstretched arms and legs.

Images of the view outside the pod rippled over its every interior surface, creating the impression that the pod was little
more than a capsule of clear gelatin inside a flame. Then the fire
dissipated and faded away, yielding to a seascape that was half
day and half night.

Xiong saw the image distort where his hands and feet
touched the bulkhead. *Must be some kind of holographic projection,* he realized, amazed at the total panoramic visibility.
Though some aspects of Tholian technology had seemed infe-

rior when compared to that of the Federation, this was one achievement at which he marveled.

Below his feet the horizon flattened into the distance, and the ocean became all that he could see in any direction. Splashdown was only moments away.

No sound but the roar of wind, no light but the glow of two moons over the sea. The pod spiraled down, turning like the bit of a drill as it struck the water. Sudden deceleration hurled Xiong against the bottom of the pod. His impact was cushioned by the extreme density of the atmosphere inside the pod and the protective servomotors and shielding of his EVA gear.

Boiling plumes erupted around the pod as it sank. The distorted surface became distant and faded into blackness. *I survived splashdown,* Xiong thought as his helmet beacon activated. Then he noted with dismay that the pod remained sealed as it sank into the ocean.

His next dilemma became clear. After all the effort he had gone through to make the pod seal itself and eject from the Tholian ship, he now had to find some way to make it let him out. For a moment he wished that he had kept the monoblade, but then he remembered that in all the turbulence of reentry he would likely have filleted himself, or damaged the pod.

Think like a Tholian, he told himself. *You live in a high-pressure environment. You like it really hot. You need your escape pod to keep you alive for days or weeks until you're rescued.* The inevitable conclusion was exactly what he didn't want to contemplate. *They wouldn't* want *this thing to open,* he realized. *Not unless it landed in a Tholian-friendly environment—which is the one thing I'm trying to escape.*

Absolute darkness surrounded the pod. He couldn't tell whether he was looking at its natural obsidian surface or at a faithful representation of the lightless depths outside. Several challenges now demanded his attention: open the pod, return to the ocean's surface, and survive both events; then find some means of staying alive in a vast expanse of untraveled open water on an uninhabited planet.

All right, time to get creative. He activated his helmet beacon and eyed his surroundings. Seeing no other resources, he began looking at his environment suit. *What have I got?*

Taking stock of his heavily modified EVA gear, he replayed in his memory the process by which Ilucci and the engineers of the *Sagittarius* had built the suit around him. They had added several nonstandard components to the suit, in order to make it strong enough to survive inside the Tholian ship. Miniaturized structural integrity fields protected him from the pressure. Myo-electric servos enabled him to move through the dense, semi-fluid atmosphere. Additional power packs had been installed to drive the new components. And a tricorder had been built into the suit's bulky control block.

His inventory completed, he asked the next question. *What do I need to do?* Unfortunately, it seemed that the only way to open the pod and get back to the surface would be to blast open its bottom, releasing its superheated atmosphere and causing an explosive decompression whose exhaust would propel the pod upward. *Just one problem with detonating something inside the pod,* he realized. *Any blast strong enough to penetrate the bulkhead will cause an overpressure that'll turn me into salsa.*

He pondered whether a shaped charge might mitigate some of the blast effects before he realized that he still had no idea how to create an explosion in the first place. *Come on, Ming,* he thought, trying to boost his own morale. *First, figure out how to blow this thing open. Then worry about how to survive the blast. Solve one problem at a time.*

Of the various components in his suit, the ones that seemed to hold the most promise for generating explosive force were the power cells. They were composed primarily of sarium krellide and had been fully charged when he'd beamed over to the Tholian ship. Even after several hours of use, they were likely still at least half-charged. The key would be releasing all the energy of a power cell at once and directing its force against the bottom bulkhead. Thinking back to the engineering training he'd had at Starfleet Academy, he remembered all the things the instructors had warned him never to do when working with power cells.

Never, they had cautioned, *allow an ungrounded conductive wire to contact an exposed sarium krellide power cell.*

He searched the pockets of the EVA suit and found that all the standard-issue equipment was still there, including an insulated tether cable of three-ply kelvinium. It was insulated, of course, because kelvinium was superconductive and could be a hazard during EVA operations if left unprotected. Using a small wire cutter from the suit's repair kit, he stripped the insulation from the kelvinium tether cable and unwound its three-ply wire into separate, delicate filaments. Watching the gossamer-thin wires float in the dense, shimmering atmosphere of the pod, he began thinking about how to dislodge one of the suit's power cells without compromising the suit itself. The last thing he needed was to fill the inside of his suit with superheated, sulfur-rich gas.

There were only two power cells that he could reach: the ones located just behind each hip of the suit. They powered the servos in its legs. Disabling either one would make it very difficult for him to move until he reached an area of lower pressure. Because that was the cause for which the power cell was being sacrificed, he decided it was a fair trade.

After a few minutes of work, he had almost succeeded in freeing the power cell behind his right hip when the pod jolted to a stop. The impact pinned him against the bulkhead for a moment. *Guess I've really hit bottom,* he mused, then berated himself for the joke. He wondered briefly whether the presence of land under the pod would help or hinder his attempt to return to the surface.

The power cell detached from his suit. Holding it in his hands, he knew that he had the means of generating a fairly potent detonation. His next challenge was to direct its energy and protect himself at the same time.

You've made it this far, Ming. You're doing great. Reason it out. It's just physics. Just do the math.

The only thing he could think of was to make a force field. If he could generate a conical subspace field above the power cell before letting it make contact with kelvinium wire, all its explosive force would be directed downward, against the bottom bulkhead—and it would do so without causing an overpressure inside the pod. *All I need is a subspace field generator.*

The tricorder that the engineers had integrated with the suit contained a fairly powerful subspace transceiver assembly, used for relaying data back to a ship in orbit. Unfortunately, it was nestled in the back of the suit, at a place Xiong couldn't reach. *I wish I had a communicator,* he thought—and then he remembered the comm assembly attached to his helmet. Although the speakers and sensing unit were inside, the transceiver components were accessible from the outside. As he reached back and started disconnecting it, he knew he would have to work quickly once it was off. The internal components of the transceiver were fairly delicate, and they wouldn't last long exposed to the pod's superheated atmosphere.

All-or-nothing time. Guiding his hands by watching his dim reflection on the obsidian bulkhead, he detached the transceiver assembly from his helmet. He kneeled beside the power cell and set the circuit next to it. He powered down the transceiver and attached two filaments of kelvinium to it. He shaped the wires into a crude circle around the transceiver and the power cell.

The key to his plan would be the timing. He twisted the last piece of wire into a loose ball and made a few test drops away from the power cell, to see how long it would take the wire ball to fall from the top of the pod to the bottom; it took just less than three seconds, and he concluded it was because of the density of the pod's atmosphere.

Xiong pocketed the wire ball and checked the settings on the transceiver. He needed it to create a field strong enough to contain the blast but small enough that he would be outside its area of effect when he climbed up into the pod's corner. He made a few adjustments to its subspace field geometry, increased its power output to maximum, and calculated how long it would take the transceiver to power up and generate a subspace field.

The tricky part was that after reactivating the transceiver Xiong needed to be outside its subspace field; he also had to drop the wire ball from the correct height at the proper moment so that it would be *inside* the subspace field. If he dropped the ball too early, he would have no protection when the sarium krellide detonated; dropped too late, it would bounce off the subspace field—and because he would be unable to pierce the force field himself, he would be unable to shut it off to make a second attempt. If he dropped the ball off-target, he was dead.

He would get only one shot at this. If his math was off, or if his reflexes proved to be either too slow or too jumpy, his day would very soon take a turn for the worst.

Bending forward, he stretched his right arm down and forward toward the transceiver; he held his left arm above the power cell. Clutched in his left hand was the wire ball. Shaking with tension, he aligned his head above the power cell to fix his aim. Anxiety filled his gut with sick sensations.

Here goes.

His finger tapped the transceiver's power switch.

He pushed off with his left leg, lined up his left hand, and let go of the wire ball. It began to fall in slow motion.

Turning away, he scrambled with his one powered leg and both arms to pull himself up into the corner. Handholds and footholds seemed elusive, his fumbling grasps desperate and clumsy. The top of the pod, which had seemed suffocatingly close this past hour, now seemed far away, unreachable.

A flash of white and a boom like the eruption of a volcano. An impact pinned him to the top of the pod, and a steady roar and a *whoosh* surrounded him in the darkness. He was moving, the pod was rocketing upward, the explosive exhaust of its searing high-pressure gases enough to push it off the ocean bottom. As quickly as it had started, it slowed and stopped, and the pod pitched to one side.

Water flooded in, boiled into a mad froth, and slammed against Xiong's pressure suit, setting him afloat. Then he felt the pod pressing on him again, pulling him back down as it sank once more. *If it hits bottom and traps me inside, I'll be stuck for good.* He fought his way across the inside of the pod, finding the water as hard to move through as the Tholian atmosphere had been. His gloved hands found the jagged edge of the blasted-open bottom. He pulled himself through the opening and pushed free of the pod. As soon as he was clear it fell away beneath him, swallowed into the night of the ocean bottom.

He was deep enough that he saw no light from the surface, but stray bubbles of gas rising past him showed him, aglow in the light of his helmet, which way to go. Pointing himself upward, he used the forearm controls of his suit to create a slow, steady expulsion of carbon dioxide from his rebreather. Chasing his own escaping waste gas, he ascended swiftly, reassured that the same systems that had protected him aboard the Tholian ship would keep him safe from pressure effects on his journey back to the surface.

Several minutes later he saw the first glimmers of light above, and soon afterward he crested the surface. He checked the passive sensor gauges on the underside of his suit's forearm. The air tested as breathable and free of toxins; local gravity was just a few tenths of a percent greater than Earth standard. Bobbing along, he powered down the suit's servos and activated its exchanger to replenish its air tanks from the atmosphere.

The sea was calm beneath a pale sky and sparkling with the peach-colored light of a breaking dawn.

Flotation sequence functioning, he noted with a glance at his gauges. *Air supply increasing. So far so good.* He lowered the shade on his visor and, confident that he was momentarily out of danger, decided that he'd earned a few hours of rest.

As he drifted off, he murmured to himself with weary sarcasm, "Well . . . *that* was fun."

Theriault shivered awake. Her row of heated rocks had dimmed to a faint reddish hue, and only a faint aura of heat radiated from them. The shafts of amber daylight that had filled the cavern beyond her nook in the wall were gone now. Darkness had fallen.

She was unsure how long she had been asleep, but the fact that the rocks still had some of the heat she had phasered into them told her it could not have been long, perhaps a few hours. *Early evening,* she figured.

Her teeth chattered, and the flesh on her arms and legs was pimpled from a pervasive chill. She drew her phaser and extended her arm. Steadying her aim was difficult. Holding her breath helped slightly. A few short bursts per stone made them bright orange again, and when she'd finished, their soothing heat enveloped her once more. She tucked the phaser back onto her belt and retreated into the nook, ready to return to sleep.

As she lay basking in the ruddy glow, her thoughts turned to her ship and crewmates, and to her family at home on Mars . . . then she shuddered awake, fear animating her like an electric current. She was certain that she was not alone.

In the darkness beyond her glowing rocks, she saw only pale ripples of moonlight on the pond, heard only the susurrus of the waterfalls . . . but there was something else there, something intangible, moving like a breath in the night.

Hyperalert, she scanned the cavern, seeking out something that her fear told her could not be found against its will. Then a voice spoke to her without sound, its authority absolute, its form unseen but its presence undeniable.

Rest, it told her. **Your wounds are deeper than you know.**

Fear and pain put tremors in her voice. "Who are you?"

Sleep, the great voice said, and this time her body obeyed.

18

Despite being transmitted over a subspace channel across several light-years, Klingon Ambassador Lugok's rage was evident to Federation Envoy Akeylah Karumé. *"The Klingon Empire will not let such a brazen act of aggression go unavenged!"* Lugok bellowed, his fury verging on apoplexy. He was in as high a state of dudgeon as Karumé had ever seen.

For all of Lugok's raw volume, Ambassador Jetanien seemed entirely unimpressed. "Ambassador," the Chelon said with an air of disdainful hauteur, "has it escaped your notice that within hours of your team being attacked, a Starfleet survey team was slaughtered less than a hundred kilometers away? Or that more than three dozen civilian colonists fell victim to an almost identical mass homicide less than fifty kilometers from your people's own encampment on Gamma Tauri IV?"

"So you claim," Lugok said. *"They could be the victims of an accident. Our people were cut down like beasts!"*

Ignoring the instructions she had received from Jetanien before entering his office for the unofficial, "back-channel" meeting with Lugok, Karumé entered the verbal fray. "Quit your posturing," she berated the Klingon. "There's no one on this channel but us. What do you *really* want?"

"We want your people off that planet!"

Jetanien made some low clucking noises inside his beak. "I'm sure that you do."

Unfazed, Lugok continued, *"We want justice for our dead!"*

"What, in your estimation," Jetanien asked, "would constitute justice under these circumstances, Mr. Ambassador? No, wait. Don't tell me. Public beheadings? Perhaps something more old-fashioned, like a communal stoning?"

Lugok's face became a twisted grimace of disgust. *"You mock me,"* he said. *"You mock our dead. Have you no honor?"*

Karumé shot back, "Have you no common sense? All the evidence points to one attacker for all three incidents."

"The Federation would not be the first to make a false-flag attack on its own to hide a strike against another," Lugok said.

Puffed up with indignation, Jetanien boomed in reply, "Preposterous! Your ship in orbit has monitored every being in a Starfleet uniform on the planet since it arrived. How could we have perpetrated such an atrocity without being detected?"

The portly Klingon shook his index finger angrily at them. *"Absence of evidence is hardly proof of innocence. Who else had a motive to attack our troops? If it wasn't your people, it was the colonists!"*

"With what weapons?" asked Karumé. "They have barely enough small arms to outfit a handful of peace officers."

A bitter smile brought no levity to Lugok's manner. *"So you'll do nothing to punish your colonists?"*

"Technically, it's not our colony," Karumé said. "It refused the protectorate treaty, so we have no jurisdiction."

Lugok harrumphed. *"The presence of your Starfleet vessel robs that claim of credibility."*

Beside her, Jetanien made some dry scraping sounds with his beak. It was an affectation that she had learned was used to express annoyance. Whether he was irked at her, at Lugok, or at both of them, she had no idea.

"Ambassador," said Jetanien, "I propose we end this charade. We both know what attacked our survey teams and the colonists."

"What I know," retorted Lugok, *"is that the battle cruiser veS'Hov is on its way to discourage any further acts of aggression by Starfleet—or its pathetic civilian proxies."*

Adopting an equally combative tone, Jetanien replied, "Then

it's only fair to warn you that the *Starship Endeavour* will be arriving at Gamma Tauri in less than twenty hours—to discourage *your* people from taking any rash actions."

"Splendid, more guns," Karumé interjected, shaming both ambassadors to silence. "That'll solve everything."

Captain Kutal marched onto his bridge with long strides and a short fuse. "Enough excuses," he snapped at his first officer. "Ohq's had six hours to make repairs. Are we ready or not?"

Commander BelHoQ left an auxiliary tactical station to fall in beside the captain. "We have the backup sensor array func—"

"Yes or no?" Kutal glowered at BelHoQ. "Are we ready?"

BelHoQ struggled to suppress the snarl that was tugging at his mouth. "We can navigate," he said.

"That's a yes," Kutal said, dropping into his chair. "Helm, contact spaceport control. Tell them we're leaving."

As the helm officer began the departure protocol, BelHoQ stepped closer to the captain and advised him in a low voice, "Our main sensor array is still down, sir. We'll be at a disadvantage if we go into battle without it."

Regarding him with narrowed eyes, Kutal asked, "How long to get it working?"

"At least fifteen hours," BelHoQ said.

Kutal growled and faced forward. "We have to go now. Fix it on the way." At the forward console, the helmsman turned his chair to face the captain, who barked, "What is it?"

"The dockmaster reports a malfunction clearing moorings," the young pilot said. "Docking clamps have lost power on the station's side, and the supply umbilicals won't release."

The captain ignored his first officer's accusatory stare and issued orders quickly. "Tell them to release the clamps manually. Have Ohq send teams EVA to clear the umbilicals."

Lieutenant Krom, the second officer, turned from the ship's status console to report, "Pressure spike in umbilicals three, four, nine, and eleven, Captain. Power surge in life support."

Immediately, the overhead lights flickered, then paled. The gentle hum of the ship dropped to a low moan and then went silent. Kutal's jaw clenched as he waited for someone — anyone — to speak. "In the name of *Fek'lhr*," he shouted, "someone *report!*"

The first officer joined Krom and watched the console light up with warning signals. "Multiple pump malfunctions," he said. "Reflow valves jamming open . . ." Both sets of doors at the aft end of the bridge slid open. "Portals opening shipwide —"

"Seal off the cargo deck," Kutal ordered, to prevent the lower decks of the ship from being vented into space.

BelHoQ answered, "Only interior hatches are opening, sir. Outer doors secure."

Kutal decided he'd had enough. He slapped the button on the arm of his chair and opened a channel. "Bridge to engineering!"

Ohq's reply squawked from the speaker. *"Engineering here!"*

"What's going on down there?"

The chief engineer sounded terrified and irritated. *"Power spikes, probably a computer virus or —"* He stopped. Over the comm Kutal heard Ohq talking in angry whispers to someone else before he finished, *"Overpressure in the main recycling tank!"*

The bridge crew traded confused looks. Kutal directed a questioning glance at BelHoQ. "Overpressure in the *what?*"

He got his answer in the form of a deep boom followed by a low *whoosh* — and a gag-inducing stench. In the stuttering light he saw a cascade of dark sludge rush out of the lavatory in the port corridor. From the starboard head came a putrid spray of liquid-chemical waste and fluid excrement. It was a steady eruption: twin geysers of fetid slime coating the deck ankle deep and pouring down the passageways into every compartment, including the bridge.

Overpowered by the grotesque odor, Kreq and Krom doubled over and added their emesis to the deepening mess that de-

filed the bridge of the *Zin'za*. Tonar turned his back on his comrades and vomited across his tactical console.

BelHoQ looked down at the ship's status monitor, then back
at the captain. "Every lavatory on every deck, sir." He coughed
and struggled to breathe. "Apparently, the spaceport's waste system is backing up into ours."

Though Kutal was seething with a blood fury unlike any he
had ever felt before, his voice was deathly quiet as he said to
BelHoQ, "Seize the port. Find the saboteurs. Kill them. Now."

"I thought you said we didn't have time," BelHoQ replied.

Kutal shot him a murderous glare. "We'll *make* the time."

The Klingon soldiers' boots were still coated with foul-smelling
wet filth as they stormed through the Borzha II spaceport,
rounding up anyone and everyone who wasn't one of their own.

BelHoQ was in charge of the siege, and he orchestrated it
with brutal efficiency. His men left no compartment unsearched,
no locker unopened. A skeleton crew had been left aboard the
Zin'za with the captain, freeing most of the ship's more than
four hundred personnel to place the facility under control.

"Please," mewed Bohica, the spaceport's pathetic weakling
of an administrator. "There's no need to hold all these people, is
there? The galley staff hasn't done anything wrong."

"I've eaten in your commissary," BelHoQ said. "I assure
you, they have done *many* things wrong."

Scores of civilians were dragged past, kicking, protesting
their innocence, and cursing the Klingon troops. There was no
way for BelHoQ to know which ones were speaking the truth—
at least, not until the beatings commenced. Hidden details
would no doubt come to light once more coercive methods of
interrogation were initiated. Until then he would let his men
continue to gather evidence and segregate the suspects.

So far the search process had consumed nearly four hours of
his time. More than eight hundred people lived and worked
aboard the spaceport, and few had come willingly when his men
had begun rounding them up in the cargo bay for mass detention.

Content to direct the operation from the administrator's office, BelHoQ was having second thoughts about permitting Bohica to remain as a fair witness to the proceedings. For one thing, the man was an inveterate whiner. "This is outrageous," Bohica complained, standing in front of what had been, until four hours ago, his own desk. "This was not part of our agreement! If even *one* of my people is harmed, my world will have to rethink its decision to let you use our port!"

BelHoQ looked up from Krom's latest report and scowled at Bohica. "Was that supposed to be a threat?" Before the effete Borzhan could answer, BelHoQ picked up the heaviest knick-knack on the man's desk and threw it at him. The lumpy block of glazed ceramic caromed off Bohica's broad forehead, knocked his spectacles off his face, and dropped the man unconscious to the deck. BelHoQ waved over two of his soldiers and pointed at the administrator. "Take him below."

The warriors obeyed without speaking. As they dragged the Borzhan out of his office, Lieutenant Tonar walked in. "We have them, Commander. Three saboteurs."

He bared his fangs with anticipation. "Where?"

"They were in a secured docking bay, trying to sneak aboard an impounded ship." He walked to one of the office's security monitors and switched it to a different internal feed. An image of the docking bay appeared, showing the three prisoners and the heavily armed squad of Klingon troops that had captured them. "We checked their identities," he said as he walked back to the desk. "All three are wanted criminals who worked for the man who owned that ship." Tonar handed a printed report to BelHoQ, who looked it over. "Our men found evidence that the suspects have been living aboard the impounded vessel, in scan-shielded hidden compartments under the deck plates."

"Broon," said BelHoQ, reading the name of the ship's proprietor, a reputed arms dealer and interstellar racketeer who had been arrested several weeks earlier for possession of a stolen Imperial Klingon deep-space probe—one that had been de-

ployed to chart the Jinoteur system. "Interesting," the first officer said, thinking aloud. "It seems that Broon—or perhaps
whatever criminal syndicate he works for—has an interest in the
Jinoteur system. And they feel strongly enough about it to risk
sabotaging our ship." He cast a pointed stare at Tonar. "We *have*
linked them *directly* to the sabotage, yes?"

"Yes, sir," Tonar said. "A search of their ship uncovered several spare parts like the ones used to damage our sensor array—
including some in the process of being disguised and a few
failed pieces that look like early attempts."

BelHoQ nodded with satisfaction. Hard evidence and solid
indication of premeditated action. He couldn't have asked for
more, especially in so short a time. "Well done," he said.

"Do you or the captain wish to question them?" asked Tonar.

"No," he replied. "We've lost enough time as it is. File a
complete report—and make sure you record the execution."

The distant shrieks of disruptors echoed in the corridors.

"Sounds like Broon's boys just got dusted," said Delmark, a
nondescript Orion man with dark hair, a lean physique, and a
complexion of an especially deep hue of green.

His two comrades walked with him in a corridor above the
hangar deck. Tarris, an Elasian woman with caramel-colored
skin and snow-white hair, asked, "What if the Klingons keep in-
vestigating?" Her large, almond-shaped eyes harbored anxiety.
"It won't take a genius to realize those three couldn't have accessed the station's sewage-treatment system."

"The Klingons won't even think of that," said Laëchem, a
fair-haired Zibalian man with brilliant indigo and vermilion facial tattoos. "They have someone to blame, and now they have a
schedule to keep. As long as we don't hit them again, we should
be in the clear."

Delmark nodded. "I agree. It's time to lay low." Glancing out
an observation window at the Klingon battle cruiser *Zin'za,* he
added, "How long do you think it'll take them to swab out the
lower decks?"

"Weeks," Laëchem said with a smirk.

All three accomplices chuckled. They stifled their mirth as a squad of Klingon warriors double-timed past them, on their way back to the ship. Tarris remarked, "Looks like they're almost ready to go." She checked her chrono. "Only eleven hours late. . . . Ganz won't be happy about that."

"It's the best we can do," Delmark said. "Besides, I think he'll forgive us when he hears that one of his biggest rivals is both down for the count and taking the heat for our handiwork."

Much to Captain Kutal's relief, the *Zin'za* cleared moorings without further incident and navigated swiftly clear of commercial traffic in the Borzha system. Less than an hour after Bel-HoQ had imposed a much-deserved death sentence on the saboteurs, the Klingon warship was hurtling through space at maximum warp toward Jinoteur.

A disgusting reek permeated every compartment. Officers throughout the ship were much more vigilant than usual for any sign of insubordination. Any error, no matter how slight, by enlisted personnel would be sufficient excuse to put someone on a punishment detail. On every deck, teams of grumbling enlisted men moved about on all fours—scraping, scooping, scrubbing, spraying one *menIqam* at a time in what seemed like a futile effort to cleanse the ship of its repugnant stench.

The officers, at least, had the benefit of raiding the medical supplies for help. Each of the senior officers wore a smear of white ointment under his nose. The sharply medicinal salve was used by the ship's surgeon principally for blocking the smell of decay while he performed autopsies. Now that the interior of the *Zin'za* smelled like something that had crawled up the back end of a *targ* and died, the ointment had become the most popular substance on the ship.

As successful as the salve was in blocking the ship's pervasive stink, it also obliterated desirable odors. As Kutal and several of his top officers sat down in the mess hall, he expected his evening meal to lack much of its normal flavor.

Then the food slots opened, the officers saw their meals, and in unison Kutal and his men howled with rage.

Platters were heaped with spoiled *Pipius* claws, rotting *bregit* lung, and mold-covered heart of *targ*. Steins overflowed with sewage-tainted *warnog*. Dishes of *rokeg* blood pie crawled with bugs. Skewers of *zilm'kach* melted into orange slag.

The *gagh* was dead.

Kutal's men hurled their trays of inedible food against the walls. The crashing trays were not loud enough to drown out the chorus of Klingon vulgarities echoing through the ship.

Picking up a fistful of the expired serpent worms, Kutal looked at the ruined delicacy and shook his head in dismay at this final insult. "Who would be so *ruthless*?"

19

Through the dense silhouette of the Jinoteur forest, the sky paled with early morning light. Niwara gathered up the perimeter security devices that had helped protect the site next to the river, where she and Terrell had camped for the night. The first officer busied himself securing their packs for travel.

"How much longer do you want to continue downriver?" she asked, hoping that he would not be hasty to abandon the search.

He looked at the brown water flowing past, then peered downriver as if looking there for the answer. "As long as we can," he said, "or until the captain orders us back."

A gentle pass of Niwara's nimble paw powered down the last sensor device. It retracted into itself, becoming compact for storage and transport. She picked it up and tossed it into her secondary pack. At the riverside, Terrell adjusted the settings on his tricorder. "Still no sign of her," he said. He looked worried as he added, "And the interference is getting worse."

"What's it from?" She squinted at the shafts of white light that cut through the jungle at shallow angles. "Is it solar?"

Looking skyward, Terrell said, "I don't know." He put away the tricorder. "I can't tell if it's natural or artificial. All I can say for sure is that it's intense and it's everywhere."

Niwara cinched shut her spare pack and was about to walk over and claim her main pack from Terrell when a change in the air bristled her whiskers. An ozone smell and a galvanic tingle made the fur on her tail stand at attention. She stood absolutely still, searching with her ears, her eyes, and her nose. Terrell noticed her hyperalert state and remained quiet. With slow, cautious motions he reopened his pack, then drew his type-2 phaser from his belt. Together they waited.

Overhead, the sky was clear. A soft breeze rustled the foliage around them and brushed the surface of the river with small ripples across the current. There was no sign of danger, no matter where the Caitian scout directed her acute senses, yet she remained certain that something hostile was nearby.

Then she felt it. A cold breath announced its presence. The glow of dawn through the trees dimmed. Daylight faded.

Giant blades of dark flame appeared in mid-jab, lancing out of the jungle in lightning blurs of shimmering indigo. The beam from Terrell's phaser passed through them without resistance.

Niwara dodged the first thrusts and called out, "Run, sir!" Twisting to evade another death-stroke, she cried, "Take cover!" The bladelike projections behaved like serpents, attacking and recoiling repeatedly. One agonizing strike tore off part of her right shoulder and spun her around to see that Terrell was already under attack, surrounded and taking serious hits to his torso. A glancing blow across the back of his head stunned him. He dropped his phaser.

She sprinted toward him and leaped, knocking him backward into the river. Wounded and dazed, he submerged for a moment, then spluttered back to the surface. Niwara knew that merely submerging him would not be enough to protect him; he would need the signal dampener.

An overpowering blow swept her legs and hurled her into the air. Marshaling her species' natural agility, she rolled through her landing and somersaulted toward the pack that held their signal dampener. As she rolled to her feet, a pointed tentacle of crackling energy slammed into her abdomen and impaled her. Slashes of glowing violet severed her left front paw. She let herself pitch forward and landed on her right paw.

The pack was only a couple of meters away. Pulling with one arm and kicking with both legs, she fought against the agony in her gut, ignored the sharp impacts falling on her upper back, blocked out the burning sensation that began to consume her.

Sinister coils of scarlet fire entwined her legs and tried to drag her backward, but she refused to lose ground.

Centimeters now. Almost within reach . . .

Her fingers grasped the already opened pack and pulled it on its side toward her. She thrust her hand inside and grabbed the signal dampener. It activated with a simple push of a button. Extending her arm to throw the device to Terrell, she saw a blade of nightfire tensed above her.

She made the throw. It was a clumsy lob. The device barely made it to the river's edge, where it rolled over the caked mud and disappeared into the murky currents. In her last moment, she looked for Terrell, but he was already gone.

Then a storm of cutting blows fell upon Niwara and ended her suffering with oblivion.

Getting knocked into the river had been a boon and a curse. Coughing out the dirty water had racked Terrell's wounded body, but the momentary respite from the melee had given him a chance to collect his wits. He wished as quickly that it hadn't.

A quartet of fearsome tentacles congealed into existence from empty air directly above him. His feet slipped on the muddy riverbed. *Dammit, I'm off-balance, and I can't move worth a damn in the water.* Watching the tendrils assume the form of undulating spears, he braced for the worst.

The signal dampener thudded onto the mud in front of him. Niwara's arm was still curled from having made the throw. A barrage of glowing shapes stabbed at her in a frenzy of violence. As the device rolled down the sloped riverbank into the water, Terrell saw that it had been activated.

He dived after it.

There was nothing to see under the water, so Terrell made his best guess and searched with his hands, making broad overlapping circles ahead of him, shifting side-to-side. He brushed the fist-sized object, which lay half-embedded in the soft mud. His fingers closed over it like a trap and yanked it free. He clutched it to his chest and kicked with what little strength he had left.

Panic propelled him for what felt like forever on a single breath. When his lungs screamed for air and his leg muscles burned from the effort of fighting to go forward and also stay submerged, he reluctantly surfaced. He lifted his head above the water slowly, expecting attack . . . but found only silence.

Daylight and a slow breeze greeted him as he waded ashore and collapsed in an exhausted heap atop the signal dampener. Mud had collected inside his jumpsuit and his boots. Sand and grit caked his close-cropped hair. He took a quick inventory. *Phaser's gone,* he noted glumly. *Left the tricorder behind.* Checking his belt, he was relieved to find his communicator still firmly in place.

He was careful to keep the signal dampener close as he gingerly pulled off his torn, soaking-wet, muddy jumpsuit. Every move he made hurt enormously, and the pain in his midsection grew worse by the minute. Inspecting his own injuries, he winced at the sheer number of deep puncture wounds on his chest and abdomen—in particular, one deep wound that he knew ought to be bleeding copiously but instead was scabbed with the same peculiar crystalline substance that had encased McLellan's leg after her brush with the Shedai. He recalled Tan Bao's report that the crystalline substance was prone to spread quickly—and that when it made contact with vital organs, it would be fatal.

Vital organs are where I just got hit, he realized. *Best-case scenario, I'll be dead by noon.*

Though Terrell was normally not one to foist his problems onto others, he decided as he reached for his communicator that in this case a call for help was definitely in order.

"It looks like I've got rocks in my gut," Terrell said.

Captain Nassir and Dr. Babitz stood together in the sickbay of the *Sagittarius,* listening to the wounded first officer's report over the comm. Babitz took notes on a data slate. "Clark," she said, "how long has it been since you were hit?"

"About fifteen minutes," Terrell said.

The slim blond surgeon nodded. "Do you have a tricorder?"

"*No,*" Terrell said. "*Just a communicator and signal dampener.*" He grunted in pain. "*I forget—how long does the battery last on this thing?*"

Nassir replied, "Twelve hours, enough time for a round trip. I'm sending Sorak and Razka to bring you back."

"*No, sir, don't,*" Terrell said. "*We didn't know the Shedai was there until it attacked—and even then it didn't trigger the alert on our tricorder. Sorak and Razka would be sitting ducks.*"

The captain tensed to argue when Dr. Babitz shook her head. "Captain, I'm sorry, but Commander Terrell's been hit near vital organs. He doesn't have that much time."

Defeat was too bitter for Nassir to accept. "What about the ATV? Are the riverside trails wide enough to—"

"*No, sir,*" Terrell said, his voice weary and resigned. "*If they had been, we'd have used the ATV in the first place.*"

Desperation colored the captain's tone. "Dammit, Clark, we've already lost Niwara. I'm not leaving you out there."

"*You have to, sir. The Shedai have learned to evade our sensors—that means the ship is vulnerable. Don't do anything to draw their attention. Stay under cover as long as possible.*"

Nassir shut his eyes and hung his head in grief. Some captains could accept with stoic grace the loss of personnel in the line of duty. But on a ship this small, with such a close-knit crew, it was difficult for Nassir to suppress his feelings when harm befell his shipmates. *Maybe I can blame it on hormones,* he thought, blinking back tears. He was getting older and was past his pheromone prime. Deltan men his age had learned to accept the changes in their biochemistry that came with middle age and the profound emotions that attended them.

None of that made losing a friend any easier.

The captain collected himself as best he was able. "Thank you, Clark, for keeping your head when I'm losing mine." He looked at Babitz. "Doctor, I need to go."

Dr. Babitz nodded and offered a sad but consoling smile. "I'll maintain an open channel," she said. "I'll stay with him."

"Thank you," Nassir said softly. Then he stepped away and walked out the door. He headed for the ladder to the top deck, hoping to smother his grief in the myriad details of work. There really was nothing more to be done for Terrell, whose advice to protect the ship was the only sensible course of action.

Guilt shadowed Nassir's thoughts. His sense of duty told him that he owed it to Terrell to stay on the comm until the end came, but he had watched too many friends and comrades die over the years, and this was a loss he could not bear to witness.

On the top deck of the *Sagittarius,* Master Chief Ilucci had put everyone to work, including Nassir. Ranks were often treated as a formality on the ship, so Nassir did not think it unusual to find Ilucci, a noncommissioned officer, giving instructions to superior officers such as Sorak and zh'Firro. Watching the ship's chief of security and flight controller assist Ilucci in rebuilding a piece of the sensor array, the captain knew that if Bridy Mac were on her feet, she would no doubt be pitching in.

As would Niwara, he thought, mourning the slain Caitian. She had been the least social of all the members of the crew, but she had never lacked discipline, dedication, or enthusiasm for her work. Her absence, he was certain, would be felt by the crew for a very long time—especially by Threx, who had never been able to conceal his deep if inexplicable fondness for her.

For now, however, they all had work to do. Nassir's own background in warp engineering had made him Ilucci's first choice to help run diagnostics on the warp nacelles, to make certain that they would be ready to function as soon as the fuel pod arrived. With the impulse reactor down for repairs, he and the master chief had resorted to using short pulses of energy from the ship's battery reserves to activate each individual warp coil in each nacelle, one at a time. It was not exciting work, but it was specific, and it demanded one's full attention—making it the perfect activity for someone trying not to think about something else.

Some of the crew had been awake for more than twenty-four

hours. Between the lack of sleep, the stress of combat, news of casualties on the ground, and the hard work of fixing the ship, fatigue was wearing them down. Everyone's steps were falling heavily on the deck. Nassir's own eyelids fluttered as he worked, caught between his body's desire for sleep and his impulse to resist and remain in motion.

"How's it goin', Skipper?"

Nassir turned to see the bedraggled chief engineer eyeing his handiwork. "Slow but steady," the captain said. "I'm about two-thirds of the way through the port nacelle."

Ilucci nodded. A change in his demeanor struck Nassir as odd. "You're quiet tonight, Master Chief," he noted. Then he asked in a confidential tone, "Something on your mind?"

"Just thinking about Theriault," Ilucci said. "Whether she made it to shore." He looked at his feet. "If she's all right."

Already stung by the loss of Niwara and Terrell, the captain wasn't ready to abandon hope for Theriault as well. "She'll be okay, Master Chief," he said. "We'll find her."

A crooked smile suggested that the chief engineer didn't completely believe Nassir's assurance, but he was either too polite or too desperate to admit it. "Keep at it, sir," he said. "I have to go check on Cahow before she freaks out."

"Good luck," Nassir said, feeling genuine sympathy for Ilucci. Karen Cahow was a great mechanic, but her phobia of being on planet surfaces was profound. A native of deep space who had spent most of her life in the reaches between the stars, Cahow thought of natural gravity wells as enormous navigational hazards to be avoided at all costs. According to her service record, her recruiter had doubted she would be able to endure sixteen weeks of planetside basic training. Thanks to her drill instructor's advice and a prescription for antianxiety meds, however, Starfleet had gained a first-rate—if slightly neurotic—starship mechanic and junior petty officer.

As he finished testing another warp coil, Nassir heard someone climbing the ladder to the top deck. He looked over his shoulder to see Dr. Babitz clamber out of the ladder well. She swiveled her head and seemed to recoil from the widespread grit and grime that had been produced by the repair effort. He presumed that she was suppressing her natural inclination to clean and disinfect everything within reach as she walked to his side and said quietly, "Sir, you need to come back to sickbay."

It had been more than two hours since he had left her to keep a vigil over Terrell. He had expected this to be over by now. "I can take the bad news here, Doctor."

"Captain," Babitz said, dropping her voice to a whisper. "He's *alive*. Please come with me, quickly."

He put down his tools and nodded to Babitz. "After you." Not until they had descended the ladder and were almost back to sickbay did he realize that he had been caught so off-guard by the news that he had forgotten to be happy about it.

The doors of the ship's tiny sickbay swished shut behind them. He followed her to one of the room's two biobeds, on which Bridy Mac lay sedated. Standing on the other side of her bed was medical technician Tan Bao, monitoring her vital signs. Resting in the second officer's lap was one of the signal dampeners. It had been activated.

"The signal dampener all but halts the spread of the crystalline substance," Babitz said. "The dampeners were made to cut off the Shedai from whatever drives them. Whatever that stuff is, it's part of the Shedai—and we can shut it down."

"Excellent work, Doctor," Nassir said.

She grinned sheepishly. "I can't take the credit, sir."

"Thank me," Terrell called out over the still-open comm channel. *"I was the one who asked why I wasn't dead yet."*

Hearing his friend's voice coaxed a smile from Nassir. "Good work, Clark. Way to beat the odds."

"It's a living."

The captain turned to Babitz. "Doctor, now that we know the dampeners affect the crystalline virus, can we exploit that somehow? Neutralize it? Reverse it?"

Babitz and Tan Bao traded conspiratorial grins. "We're already working on it, sir."

• • •

"That's it," Babitz said to Tan Bao, forcing herself away from the electron microscope viewer. "I need a break."

Her eyes burned from staring at computer screens. The hours had passed swiftly as she and Tan Bao lost themselves in the mystery of the Taurus meta-genome and its link to the crystalline virus. They had taken turns running tests, analyzing the results, and comparing their new data to what had been collected during Dr. Fisher's autopsy of a Shedai. There had proved to be as many parallels as there were divergences.

After peering for hours into the intense emerald glow of the microscope's shielded display, Babitz's vision had to readjust to the dim illumination in the sickbay. The ship was running on very low power to conserve its emergency batteries. Most of the power being used on the *Sagittarius* at that moment was consumed by the computers and analyzers in sickbay; letting Babitz make such intense demands on the ship's dwindling energy resources had been a calculated risk by Captain Nassir. She was determined not to make him regret his gamble.

Tan Bao watched numbers and gauges shift on a screen as the analyzer concluded another round of subatomic scrutiny on samples of the crystalline substance. Dejected, he sighed and said, "Nothing, Doctor. Just more of what we already know."

"We must be missing something," Babitz said. She got up, stretched, and twisted a crick out of her back. Then she walked over to stand beside McLellan, who lay sedated on a biobed. "Tan," she said, "join me. Let's just stop for a minute."

He swept his long, thick black hair from his face as he got up. His eyes were bloodshot. "I feel like we just keep running over the same old ground," he said. "I don't understand why the substance's anabolic activity petered out so quickly in Vanguard's lab, but here it just keeps on moving."

"Living tissue, for one thing," Babitz said, recalling Dr. Fisher's report. "The computer models predicted that this virus would consume a humanoid in a matter of minutes." She frowned. "Which makes its much slower progress here confusing. I also can't figure out why Vanguard's samples became inert within minutes of being deprived of living tissue to interact with, but the samples we found on Bridy Mac's leg remained active even when the flesh began to decay."

Tan Bao stared at the signal dampener in McLellan's lap. "We were using the signal dampener from almost the minute she got hit till we got back to the ship, which has its own dampening field. If that's what's slowing this stuff down, then whatever makes it spread has to be external," he said. "And if the Shedai signal is boosting its activity, that might explain why it's still active on a dead limb. . . . That's the only reason I can think of that the dampener would make any difference."

Pieces of the puzzle began to fit together in Babitz's imagination. "Do you remember what Xiong said about the Shedai carrier wave that was sent from here? He said it contained strings of data that matched chemical sequences common to all samples of the meta-genome." She rubbed the tips of her index fingers against her thumbs, a nervous habit that asserted itself when her concentration was focused. "What if *that signal* is what sustains the crystalline virus?"

"That would explain why the dampener impedes it," said Tan Bao. "But is it just an energizing field? Or something else?"

Remembering more of Xiong's briefing from six days earlier, Babitz started formulating a plan. "Xiong also said that his team had replicated the carrier-wave signal and used it to pinpoint other planets of interest. How would that have worked?"

"They must have identified the part of the signal that provoked responses from the artifacts on the planets," Tan Bao said. In a flash, he caught up with Babitz's line of reasoning. "So if we figure out what part of the signal the virus reacts to, we can modify it and send our own signal to neutralize it."

Reinvigorated, Babitz left McLellan's bedside and moved to one of the computer stations. Tan Bao followed her. She asked, "Have you finished sequencing the virus's genome?"

"Yes," he said, entering commands at his own console.

Based on the files he was accessing, Babitz knew that he had anticipated her next order. "Use Xiong's algorithm for translating the sequence into a Shedai carrier-wave signal."

"I'm all over it," Tan Bao said. His fingers tapped in a blur, calling up data and executing commands on the computer. "Computer's translating the sequence now."

Keeping up with him wasn't easy. "When it's done, I'll search for that signal pattern in the Shedai carrier wave," she said. "First, I'll see if Xiong's people identified any command triggers in the signal."

The computer banks hummed with activity, their volume and pitch rising slowly in step with Babitz's excitement. *We're close,* she told herself. *I can feel it.* She felt warm and a little bit dizzy. Palming a light sheen of perspiration from her forehead, she waited anxiously for the computer's results.

"I've isolated a set of trigger sequences," she said.

He replied, "We have a signal pattern for the virus."

"Running the search routine," Babitz said. "If we're lucky, we might find a partial match somewhere in the—" A shrill tone from the computer cut her off. She checked the display, then checked it again, stunned at her good luck. "We have a match."

Tan Bao leaned forward and eyed the results. "Whoa," he said. "That's not just *any* match—it's a *perfect* match. The whole pattern." He pointed at the screen. "Ahead of it and after it—are those trigger sequences?"

Babitz was unsure. "Possibly," she said. "They have a few chromosomes in common with other triggers in the metagenome, but I don't think these have been documented before." She shook her head. "It's hard to believe Xiong's team didn't find the virus's genome in the signal."

"None of their samples of the virus lasted long enough to be gene-mapped," Tan Bao said.

"How do we apply this? Couple the virus's signal with a trigger we don't understand? How do we test it?"

After pondering the issue a moment, Tan Bao said, "We could run tests on the severed part of Bridy Mac's leg. See if we can neutralize the crystalline substance without affecting the tissue underneath." He reacted to Babitz's dubious look by adding, "It's a lot safer than testing it on Bridy Mac, and a lot more useful than testing microscopic samples."

"Fine," Babitz said. "Set it up on bed two." Even though McLellan's severed appendage had been in stasis all this time, the odds of it being viable for surgical reattachment were all but nonexistent at this point. If using it as a test sample made it possible to save McLellan's life, and maybe also Terrell's, then it would be a worthwhile sacrifice.

She watched Tan Bao remove the leg from storage and set it on the sickbay's other biobed. He welcomed her help setting up an array of automated surgical implements and modified scanners directly above the bed. As he made the final adjustments to the equipment, Babitz watched with fascination and fear as the sparkling crystalline texture crept slowly across the necrotizing limb.

"We're ready, Doctor," Tan Bao said.

She joined him at a control panel for the surgical suite. "Embed the virus's sequence and the trigger that follows it into a five-second carrier-wave pulse, and focus it on the leg," she said. "On my mark." Flipping switches and adjusting sliders on the panel, Babitz hoped she knew what she was doing.

"Signal encoded," Tan Bao said.

"In three . . . two . . . one . . . mark."

The machinery above the bed thrummed with power and glowed slightly as the pulse was beamed at the severed limb. The effect was immediate and dramatic: the dark glasslike shell on the leg spread several centimeters in a matter of seconds. "Turn it off," Babitz said. Tan Bao cut the power.

"That could have gone better," he said.

Despite the fact that the experiment had produced the opposite of her desired result, she trembled with excitement. "Tan, there were two chemical triggers linked to that gene sequence," she said. "Set up a new pulse. This time, use the trigger that *precedes* the sequence in the meta-genome."

Tan Bao returned to the computer, edited the signal data, and relayed it to the surgical array. "Ready, Doctor."

Babitz's ears were hot, and her face was flushed with nervous anticipation. Her mouth was dry, her voice thin and slightly raspy. "Same as before, with the new sequence embedded."

"All set," Tan Bao said half a minute later.

"Engage," she said.

Another deep hum of power accompanied the emission of a pale blue glow that bathed the leg on the biobed. Just as rapidly as the last attempt had advanced the crystalline substance across the limb, this one made it retreat.

"Maintain the pulse," Babitz ordered. Tan Bao flipped an override control and prolonged the bombardment. In less than a minute, she saw no evidence of the crystalline virus on the leg. "Stop," she said, reaching for a medical tricorder. A quick scan confirmed what was shown on the gauges of the biobed and the surgical array's sensor displays: all traces of the crystalline virus had been eliminated from the severed limb.

Behind her, Tan Bao marveled at the results. "That's amazing," he said.

"We're not done yet," she said. "Create a new signal. Revert to the first trigger sequence. But after it, paste in the signal equivalent of Bridy Mac's DNA pattern."

For the first time since she and Tan Bao had worked together, he balked at her order. His voice betrayed his alarm and suspicion. "Doctor . . . what are you trying to do?"

"According to Dr. Fisher's research," she explained, "this substance becomes inert almost immediately when it expires. It doesn't break down, like organic tissue—it becomes *inert*. That suggests to me that it was nonliving matter to begin with." She nodded toward the limb on the bed. "So if this signal can have that effect on a crystalline matrix, wouldn't it be interesting to see what it can do for flesh and bone?"

Worry crimped the young man's brow. "Doctor, I'm not

really comfortable with what you're proposing here. We don't understand this technology well enough to use it like this." He gestured toward McLellan. "For all we know, putting her DNA pattern into that signal might create a clone."

"Fair enough," Babitz said. "Put her leg back in stasis. We'll run a test."

"What kind of test?"

She was losing patience. "Put it in stasis. Now, Tan."

Reluctantly, he did as she had ordered. While he secured the limb back inside the stasis pod, she reset the signal emitter to the first configuration, the one that had multiplied the crystalline virus. "Set up a sterile containment field around the empty bed," she said. Once he had done so, she said, "We'll try sending a pulse of the first signal into a sterile area to see if it spontaneously generates a sample of the virus. If it works, your cloning theory will have evidence to back it up. But if not, then I'd propose that our hypothesis should be that the signal is a catalyst, not a creator."

Without waiting for him to respond, she initiated the pulse and let it continue for ten seconds. When it ceased, she checked her readings, then invited Tan Bao to inspect them. "No trace of the crystalline virus," she said. "Bring the leg back out of stasis. I'll prep the pulse with McLellan's DNA sequence."

A sullen expression conveyed his objection to what she was attempting. She knew that it was a long shot; if it went wrong, the head of Starfleet Medical would likely excoriate her for violating numerous safety protocols. Tan Bao set McLellan's severed lower leg on the biobed and stepped clear.

They might revoke my medical license for this, she thought while she finished preparing the new signal. *Or they might give me a Carrington Award. That's to say they* would, *if all this wasn't classified to the nth degree.*

She initiated the pulse.

The bulky gray machinery above the bed droned as it powered up. A reddish glow enveloped the leg on the biobed. At first Babitz thought that nothing was happening. Then she glanced at the biobed's gauges. All traces of necrosis had vanished, and the rigor mortis in the severed limb was reversing. The calf muscle slackened, and the exposed tissue took on the sheen of a freshly amputated limb. She terminated the signal and prepped the version that neutralized the crystalline virus.

"Wrap the leg, then remove Bridy's signal dampener and focus the emitter above her bed on her wound," Babitz said. "We're neutralizing the virus first, then we're reattaching her leg."

Even though Tan Bao still wore a glazed stare of shock, he obeyed without argument.

Five minutes later, McLellan's body was cleansed of the invading crystalline matrix, her wounded thigh was wrapped with a sterile biodegradable cover, and Tan Bao brought over her severed leg and placed it on the biobed in its proper place. "I'll get the surgical cart," he said.

"Not yet," Babitz said. "I want to test one more hunch."

He looked fearfully at McLellan. "Doctor, this isn't a test on a severed limb."

"I'm aware of that, Tan, and I'll take full responsibility if it goes wrong. Step back." She pressed the severed leg against the wound, taking care to align bones and cauterized veins and arteries as closely as possible. Satisfied that everything was where it should be, Babitz returned to the control panel for the surgical array, pinpointed its emitter on McLellan's wound, and loaded the signal pattern with the second officer's DNA sequence. *Please don't let this be a mistake.*

She pressed the button and activated the array.

Then she stood next to Tan Bao and watched a miracle happen. The reddish glow traveled from McLellan's abdomen to the ankle of her severed leg and back again several times, and then it focused a blinding ruby glare on the space between her body and her detached limb. Bridy Mac's leg rematerialized by degrees.

One minute after the procedure had begun, Babitz deactivated the array and gazed in wonder at the healed second officer.

"Prep a version of the pulse with Commander Terrell's DNA," she said to Tan Bao. "Then start working on a way to make it portable. It might be our only chance to save him."

Theriault opened her eyes and squinted into the light of day.

The rocks that she had lined up in front of her nook in the cavern's wall were many hours cold. She was curled in upon herself, huddled against the rough stone wall, lying on a bed of rocky sand. As her eyes adjusted, she looked at her legs to see if the bruises she had suffered during her time in the river had begun changing colors yet.

To her surprise, there were no bruises at all. Her mind replayed all the painful collisions she had suffered with rocks hidden beneath the muddy brown water and her battering impacts against the sides of the underground tunnel. She had felt each bruise throbbing with pain yesterday when she emerged from the water to seek shelter in the nook. The steady aching of her wounds had all but lulled her to sleep. Probing her flanks and arms with her fingertips, she found no injuries. No contusions, no lacerations, not so much as a scratch or a scrape.

Beyond the rocks, something was moving.

It was a slow flutter of light and vapor above the water. A colossal humanoid figure dwelled within it, hovering dozens of meters above the center of the cavern's vast pond. The swirling clouds of multihued mist that surrounded the giant moved like gossamer underwater. A broad vertical column of sunlight, from the opening in the cavern ceiling high overhead, fell upon the ethereal being.

She crawled out of the nook and climbed over the rocks. Her muscles were stiff. At first the luminous titan seemed to take no notice of her; it levitated silently in its shaft of golden radiance, surrounded by the whispers of falling water and the multiple echoes of the vast caves surrounding the pond.

Then it faded for a moment, becoming almost transparent, like a sculpture of smoke losing its shape. Seconds later the entity reincorporated itself, still in the same place but now facing and looking directly at Theriault. The young woman was not afraid; in fact she was mesmerized by the prismatic beauty that floated nearly a kilometer away.

In a halting voice she said, "Hello?"

Its attention fixed upon her, bringing with it a sensation like standing in the merciless glare of the desert sun. **Your injuries were deep,** he responded telepathically, his psychic voice like a tremor that jumbled all her thoughts into chaos.

"Gently," was all she could think to say. "Please."

He spoke in a voice of thunder that shook the stone beneath her feet. **"Your mind was not made to hear the voice."**

"No," she said. "It wasn't." She took a few careful steps forward until she reached the edge of the water. Looking directly into his luciferous splendor was painful, so she averted her eyes downward, toward his incandescent but wavering reflection on the pond's surface. "I'm Vanessa Theriault."

"I am the Apostate."

20

T'Prynn sat sequestered in the crimson swelter of her office. Her curved desktop, hewn from a slab of black marble with thin veins of white, was barren except for a wide terminal set to her left, an interface for the computer in front of her, and a set of comm system controls recessed into the desktop on her right.

Normally, a harsh white overhead light shone down upon her chair and desk, but for the past several days she had found its glare too oppressive to tolerate. Instead she had chosen to work in the shadows, keenly aware of the irony that doing so served as a metaphor for her career as an intelligence officer.

In contrast to the dim red spills of light on the walls, her monitor bathed her in a pale greenish glow as it displayed the latest bad news. The Klingon battle cruiser *Zin'za* had shipped out of port nearly three hours earlier, just after 1300 hours station time. She made some rough calculations and was concerned to note that the Klingons would likely reach Jinoteur at approximately the same time as Quinn and Pennington, who unfortunately had been slow to answer her request for help.

Another matter that was complicating her work was M'Benga's and Fisher's pointed inquiries about her medical history. She had tried to placate the two physicians with the release of generalized reports, but they had continued to harass Starfleet for more information. Logs of M'Benga's communications made it clear to T'Prynn that he was contacting medical personnel with whom she had previously served. He had also paid a visit to Commodore Reyes, an act that had proved sufficient to prompt Reyes to access her records as well. The commodore's security clearance was even higher than her own, which meant that he very likely knew that T'Prynn had sealed her own records. So far Reyes had not asked her about it, but she did not expect this period of grace to persist for long.

Terminating the investigation into her medical records would not be difficult, but the physicians' aggressive methods demanded less than subtle responses. *If this matter is to be contained,* she decided, *it must be done in a manner both swift and decisive.* She resolved to put an end to it before the doctors exposed her mental infirmity to Reyes and the admiralty. If her superiors learned how profound a psychological affliction Sten's *katra*-haunting of her mind represented, they would revoke her security clearances. Even if Starfleet, for its own purposes, spared her the indignity of a court-martial, it would be well within its purview to issue her a dishonorable discharge. *I will not end my career in disgrace,* she promised herself. *I will not be humiliated.*

That was a matter for another time, however. More pressing was how to further delay the *Zin'za* from reaching Jinoteur. Even an hour's time would be enough to give Quinn and Pennington the advantage of reaching the *Sagittarius* first. Whether their modifications of the hardware aboard Quinn's antiquated Mancharan starhopper would be sufficient to deceive the Shedai artillery on the fourth planet's moons was out of her hands.

She began formulating a plan that would entail tricking the Klingon battle cruiser's commander into believing that his fellow captains had launched a major attack against a Tholian fleet nearby and that he was being summoned to the fray. It was a thin ruse; T'Prynn thought of a dozen reasons it would fail, but extracting success from hopeless plans was her job.

As she weighed the relative merits of several variations on the deception, her door signal buzzed. A glance at the security image on her monitor showed Anna Sandesjo standing outside her office. The two women had not seen or spoken to each other for a week, since T'Prynn's sudden exit from Manón's cabaret.

Sandesjo had left several messages accusing T'Prynn of avoiding her. T'Prynn had seen no point in acknowledging

Sandesjo's claims, because they were true. She *was* avoiding the disguised Klingon spy; confronting her to deny that she had been *avoiding* confronting her would have been utterly illogical.

Sandesjo's furious knocking on the door made it clear she did not feel the same way.

T'Prynn reached toward the intercom's talk switch, intending to dismiss Sandesjo. She hesitated at the last moment. Her finger hovered over the button as she reconsidered. Then she pressed the switch to open the door. It hissed open, letting in Sandesjo and a blinding flood of white light. The auburn-haired woman stepped clear of the door's sensor, and the portal slid shut behind her, plunging the office back into ruddy shadows.

Sandesjo stopped a few meters from T'Prynn's desk and said, "We need to talk."

"Your timing leaves much to be desired," T'Prynn said. "This is not an opportune moment to discuss our relationship."

Flustered, Sandesjo replied, "My motives are professional."

"Continue," T'Prynn said.

Sandesjo paced in front of T'Prynn's desk. "Over the past several weeks, Turag and Lugok have become suspicious," she said. "They've noticed that my reports have become less frequent and less detailed. My recent delay in noting the departure of the *Sagittarius*"—T'Prynn caught Sandesjo's fleeting glare of reproach—"made matters worse. My ability to continue functioning as a double agent will be compromised unless you can give me something useful to tell them."

"Your role as Jetanien's senior attaché must give you access to all manner of diplomatic secrets."

Shaking her head, Sandesjo replied, "Imperial Intelligence doesn't care about diplomatic secrets. They already assume that your politicians and envoys lie as a matter of policy."

"A reasonable presumption," T'Prynn conceded. A plan was forming in her thoughts as she listened to Sandesjo go on.

"I need something solid," Sandesjo said. "If I can't give them details, they'll assume I've been exposed. If that happens, their next move would be to get rid of me—*permanently*."

T'Prynn tapped a few keys on her computer interface panel, blanked her screen, and got up from her chair. "Very well," she said, crossing to a wall-mounted companel. With the press of a button she ejected a red data card from one of its slots. She turned and handed the card to Sandesjo. "Take this."

"What is it?"

"Everything you will need to prevent the *I.K.S. Zin'za* from being destroyed when it reaches the Jinoteur system."

Sandesjo accepted the data card and looked askance at it before putting it in her jacket pocket. "Destroyed by whom?"

"The *Zin'za* is heading into a trap," T'Prynn said, concocting the lie as she spoke. "It's made two failed attempts to explore Jinoteur IV. At present, there is what appears to be a derelict Tholian battleship in orbit of that planet. Yesterday, Klingon forces in this sector intercepted what they believe to be a distress signal from the *U.S.S. Sagittarius*. The *Zin'za* has been sent to neutralize the crew of the *Sagittarius* and capture its computer core for analysis. When it reaches the Jinoteur system, however, it will find its communications jammed — and four Federation starships lying in ambush."

Sandesjo reacted with a dubious stare. "An ambush? That doesn't sound like the Starfleet I know."

"The attack will be made to appear as if it was committed by the Tholians, sparking conflict between your peoples. The Federation's intention is to weaken both your nations, while fortifying its own position in the Taurus Reach."

Stepping forward, Sandesjo encroached deliberately on T'Prynn's personal space. "You've never given me intel this precise or this important before. Why now?"

"Because your cover — your life — is in peril," T'Prynn said, continuing to prevaricate with ease. "Sparing your countrymen from an unprovoked attack will preserve your credibility with Imperial Intelligence. Furthermore, disrupting the ambush, though it might complicate Starfleet's mission in this sector, will not cost Federation lives — at least, not directly." Mirroring the other woman's bold behavior, T'Prynn stepped forward until they were separated by mere centimeters. "It is a logical choice," T'Prynn added. "Violence is prevented, and a valuable asset is protected."

Sandesjo's voice was a husky whisper, her words a warm breath of desire upon T'Prynn's lips. "Is that all I am to you? A *valuable asset . . .?*"

"No," T'Prynn whispered back. "You are much more than that. More than I am able to put into words . . . Anna." She resisted the urge to pull back from the Klingon woman's intensely magnetic presence. Sandesjo smiled and grazed T'Prynn's lips with her own. "The information about the *Zin'za* is time-sensitive," said T'Prynn. Sandesjo stroked her hands slowly down T'Prynn's hips. "It should be relayed promptly."

Gathering fistfuls of fabric from the bottom of T'Prynn's red minidress, Sandesjo asked in a lustfully breathy hush, "How long till the *Zin'za* reaches Jinoteur?"

"Eight hours," T'Prynn said, succumbing to all her most illogical and most taboo emotional impulses.

"More than enough time," Sandesjo said, hiking up T'Prynn's dress over her hips and guiding her backward toward her desk.

T'Prynn made only a token gesture at resistance. "I am on duty," she protested as her raised hands found Sandesjo's breasts.

"Love's fire respects not the hour," Sandesjo said, quoting an obscure Klingon poet whose name T'Prynn had forgotten. "And in love's fire," she said as T'Prynn reflexively grabbed and twisted a lock of Sandesjo's hair, "I *burn for you.*"

Captain Rana Desai sat in a private office in Starbase 47's Judge Advocate General Corps complex. The JAG contingent on Vanguard had been allocated more space than they had at first known how to utilize. Even junior lawyers and clerks had been granted private office space, since it was at a surplus. One of those empty offices Desai had appropriated for a spe-

cial purpose: it was devoted to the investigation and preparation of a single case, one that so far remained her personal
obsession.

One room. One case. Seemingly infinite questions.

There were too many connections for Desai to see them all at
once. After weeks of looking at lists and timelines, she had decided several days ago that the only way she would ever be able
to see the big picture of this case would be to start putting it up
on a wall, one piece at a time.

So many names, she lamented. *So many faces.* Like most
such charts she had seen compiled, this one was bottom-heavy.
Most criminal organizations were supported by vast numbers of
foot soldiers. Gathering data from security agencies on worlds
throughout the Federation had been time-consuming but not especially difficult. Acquiring intelligence from neutral planets, or
from within the borders of hostile powers, had proved signifi-
cantly more complicated. Starfleet's code of justice was very
specific about what methods were permissible for obtaining
evidence.

Bribery was not one of them. That had closed off several
avenues of inquiry almost immediately.

She could accept information from Starfleet Intelligence
about foreign subjects and events only if she could prove that
the information had not been acquired through extralegal
means. Anything obtained through coercion or blackmail was
considered tainted and therefore inadmissible. The few Starfleet
Intelligence agents that she had dealt with always insisted that
their data were "clean," but when pressed to account for their
provenance or chain of custody, they inevitably balked and became impossibly vague. That she had been able to verify any
of Starfleet's intelligence for legal use was nothing short of a
miracle.

It was late, nearly 2100 hours. Desai had limited her efforts
on this case to her free time. Officially, this project did not exist,
and until she had reason to take it public, or was ordered by the
judge advocate general himself to take action, this isolated room

was where it would remain, shrouded in obscurity behind a locked door only she could open.

A pyramid of names and photographs had completely covered the long wall in front of the room's solitary desk and chair. The pyramid's lower tier was packed with Ganz's retinue of several dozen petty criminals and prostitutes, most of whom carried warrants for their arrest—but none from worlds that had extradition treaties with the United Federation of Planets.

The key players at the next level of Ganz's operation were Morikmol, a hulking Tarmelite who allegedly had ripped a Klingon's arms completely out of their sockets during a bar fight on Davlos III; Reke, a drug smuggler notorious for imbibing almost as much of his products as he transported; Zulo, whose specialty was disposing of bodies and eradicating forensic evidence; and Joshua Kane, a human who had eight perfect alibis to explain his coincidental presence on eight far-flung planets at precisely the times of eight spectacular heists.

Above them was Ganz's "business manager," Zett Nilric, a dapper and utterly sociopathic Nalori assassin. Zett had moved up in Ganz's organization after the "disappearance" of his predecessor, Jaeq, who had gone missing after assaulting Starfleet personnel on the station. Ganz's people, of course, insisted that Jaeq had fled the starbase, but Desai suspected that Zulo was the one responsible for Jaeq's permanent absence.

Parallel with Zett was an Orion woman named Neera. By all accounts, she oversaw the flesh trade on Ganz's ship, the *Omari-Ekon*. Just like all the others, she rarely set foot on the station itself, and under the terms of the Federation's treaty with Orion, the interiors of Orion-registered starships were sovereign Orion territory, not subject to Federation law. So long as they confined their dealings to their own ship, there was nothing that Desai could do about any of it.

The line that linked Ganz to privateer Cervantes Quinn, on the other hand, was a separate matter. Much of Quinn's business appeared to be transacted aboard Starbase 47, and the pattern of his activity over the past several months suggested that many of his supposedly legitimate shipments had been used to smuggle Ganz's assorted varieties of contraband. The customs office so far had found no evidence of smuggling aboard Quinn's ship, the *Rocinante,* but Desai suspected that she knew why: the dotted line that bound Quinn to the station's Starfleet Intelligence liaison, Lieutenant Commander T'Prynn.

No hard evidence had yet been found to confirm that Quinn was an unofficial operative of Starfleet Intelligence, but Desai suspected that it would emerge soon enough. *T'Prynn has the authority to protect him from customs and routine patrols,* she reasoned. *That makes him useful to Ganz and gives her a mole inside the Orion's operation.* If it was revealed that T'Prynn had facilitated or sanctioned criminal activity, the resulting public uproar would all but guarantee a court-martial—which would, in turn, expose the solid line that connected T'Prynn to Commodore Diego Reyes.

This would be the heart of the case, and Desai knew it. Manón had seen Reyes meet privately with Ganz in her cabaret less than twenty-four hours earlier; that merited a solid line from the commodore to the Orion merchant prince. The station's commanding officer was now linked to a reputed mobster, who in turn lorded over a roguish privateer who also answered to Reyes's direct subordinate. It was a closed circle.

Assuming Diego compartmentalized his communications, she figured, *I probably won't be able to put Jetanien on the board.* She momentarily considered adding the reporter Pennington with a dotted line to Ganz but concluded there was no evidence that he had done anything except exercise his rights to freedom of speech and freedom of the press.

Her communicator beeped on her hip. She removed it from its pocket and flipped it open. "Desai here."

Reyes replied, *"Dinner's almost ready. Are you still coming, or do you have to work late?"*

"I'll be there in a few minutes, Diego," she said. "Go ahead and open the wine."

He sounded happy. *"Will do. Don't be long."*

"I won't," she said, and closed her communicator.

She stared at the pyramid of suspects and evidence on the wall and at the photo of her boyfriend which formed its apex. *This,* she admitted to herself, *is going to be complicated.*

Just after midnight, Reyes was drifting off to sleep with his arm around Rana's waist when his door signal buzzed. He lifted his head and scowled, then slid out from under the sheets and grabbed his robe. Desai rolled over as he tied the dark blue robe shut. Seeing she was still asleep, he stole away softly.

The door signal buzzed again as he plodded out of the bedroom and across the living room to the door. He unlocked it, and it slid open to reveal Zeke Fisher.

Dark bags drooped under the elderly doctor's eyes, which were heavy-lidded with the desire for sleep. He held up a data slate. "My forensic report on the Gamma Tauri attacks," he drawled, sounding more exhausted than he looked.

"Come in," Reyes said, stepping out of the doorway and ushering his old friend inside. Fisher's gait was stiff and slow. "Zeke, have you slept since I asked for this report?"

As the door closed behind him, Fisher answered, "No, and if it wasn't for the magic of espresso, there's no way I'd still be awake after twenty-one hours in the lab." He handed the data slate to Reyes. "I'll sum up: the colonists were killed by the Shedai, no doubt about it."

Skimming the report, Reyes found it to be exacting and comprehensive. Fisher had ruled out every alternative theory that might have cast doubt on his findings and had documented in painstaking detail the evidence supporting his conclusions. *Guess he didn't trust me to keep my word.* He held up the report. "Good work." Then he walked over to a wall companel and thumbed a comm switch for the operations center. "Reyes to ops."

Lieutenant Commander Yael Dohan, the gamma-shift officer of the watch, answered the hail. *"Go ahead, sir."*

"Get a scrambled comm to the *Lovell,* priority one: Storm

warning confirmed for Gamma Tauri. Get those colonists off the surface—*now*. JAG will advise shortly. Message ends."

"*Aye, sir,*" Dohan replied. "*Transmitting now.*"

"Reyes out." He thumbed the comm switch back to its off position, then directed a glum look at Fisher. "So much for getting a decent night's rest."

Fisher rubbed his thumb against his forefinger and smirked. "See this, Diego? It's the world's smallest violin—"

"All right," Reyes growled, cutting him off, "I get the point. Go get some sleep." He escorted the doctor out of his quarters and locked the door behind him.

The commodore did not relish his next task: waking up Rana Desai. The only thing that would make her angrier than disrupting her sleep cycle would be asking her to violate Federation law by authorizing Starfleet to forcibly remove the colonists from Gamma Tauri IV. In the next ten minutes, he would have to commit both sins. Setting his course for the bedroom, he sighed and resigned himself to the fact that this day was off to a positively miserable start, and it held every promise of only getting worse as it went along.

21

A sudden stop and the dry scraping of sand on the outside of his helmet woke Xiong from his fitful, wave-tossed slumber. His eyes opened to darkness, and he remembered that he had lowered his helmet's glare shield. Lifting it, he found only more darkness, but this time it was speckled with stars and streaked by clouds glowing with light from one of the planet's three moons.

Reaching down, he felt the shifting grit of sand beneath him. He sat up and looked out upon the wide ocean; its low, languid breakers washed over his lap. Sinking slightly with the shift in his weight, he sat on the shore of a tiny island overgrown with towering trees and tangled foliage.

"If only I had a flag to plant," he said, talking to himself as he awkwardly staggered to his feet. His legs were unsteady, wobbling with each step he took up the shallow slope of the beach. His broad boots sank and slid in the shifting sand. A check of the passive sensors on his suit's forearm showed the external temperature was twenty-nine degrees Celsius, with humidity of just more than forty percent. "A warm and balmy island paradise," he muttered as he disengaged the environmental seals on his suit. He released the clasps on his helmet and pulled it off. Moist air perfumed with floral scents flooded in, replacing the thrice-filtered air he had been breathing for more than twenty-four hours. Savoring a few deep breaths, he turned slowly to take in his surroundings. "Might be a nice place to put a hotel."

Within a few minutes he was free of his environment suit, which he folded carefully and stored between some large boulders near the tree line, safely away from the beach. *Might need this if the weather changes,* he reasoned, thinking ahead to prepare for every eventuality. *After all, I might be here awhile.*

From the suit he retrieved the built-in tricorder. It was intact and undamaged. Though the device was not normally used for communications purposes, it possessed an emergency beacon. He pressed the beacon's transmission switch and waited for a double tone that would confirm its signal had been received.

Several seconds passed without a response, then a minute. He tried again, five times in five minutes, then he set the tricorder's emergency circuit to a receiving mode, in case the ship—or anyone else from Starfleet—tried to signal him.

"First priority," he said aloud, organizing his thoughts. "Clean water. Second priority, edible food. Third, shelter. Fourth, rescue." Lifting his tricorder, he set himself to work. He knew that shelter was not likely to be a problem; the environment suit would be hardy enough to protect him from the weather. As for rescue, he had a working beacon; it would be only a matter of time until help arrived. *For all I know, I'm in better shape than the* Sagittarius. Water and food, however, would be his responsibility until help arrived.

It took only seconds for the tricorder to lock on to clean water within a short distance of the tree line. Xiong walked the jungle's perimeter until he found a less heavily overgrown area that he could penetrate. Under the intense glow of moonlight, the jungle forest was a study in contrast—a chiaroscuro of shimmering leaves and vines over a deep background of blackness. The coordinates on his tricorder led him to a thick vine; the readings indicated that clean water was inside. He slung his tricorder at his side, grabbed the vine with both hands, and snapped it open. Warm, clear water spilled over his hands, and he lifted the vine to his mouth and drank. A faintly sugary taste lingered after he had finished. Another scan with the tricorder confirmed that the plant was rich in sucrose. *Good to know,* he thought with a smile. *If I'm stuck here long enough, maybe I'll make syrup.*

Now that he had learned where to get clean water, his only serious remaining challenge was finding something to eat. He changed the tricorder's settings and began looking for anything that resembled fruits, vegetables, fungi, or animals. After several minutes he became convinced that he had set the device incorrectly—because nothing other than simple green plants, molds, and bacteria registered on its sensors.

"That can't be right," he mumbled as he verified that the tricorder's settings were as they should be. Everything about the device checked out. He ran the scan again, searching the jungle, the beach, and the ocean . . . and he found nothing. No land-based animal forms. No birds, no fish, no insects—nothing that registered as an animal life-form of any kind. More distressing, there were flowering plants but no sign of any bearing fruit or vegetables.

"Well," he said to his tricorder, "that limits my menu, doesn't it? Guess I'd better get used to eating green salads."

Xiong had visited young M-class planets before; he knew that some worlds, early in their development, boasted vegetation long in advance of animals. *Why would such a primitive planet be so important to the Shedai?* he wondered. *Why would they go to such lengths to defend a star system whose only habitable planet has no higher-order life-forms?* He shook his head and prepared a more encompassing scan. *I've got to be missing something here.*

On a hunch, he ran a full-spectrum search for traces of the Taurus meta-genome and any recognizable sequence from the Shedai carrier wave. Seconds after he started the scan, his tricorder's display flooded with data. It had detected an enormously complex and powerful energy signature that contained patterns that he realized matched each of the known samples of the meta-genome; it used the carrier wave as a repeating pattern and seemed to come from every direction and everything that he scanned.

It's everywhere, he realized. *Every plant . . . the air . . . the water . . . the rocks. This pattern's in every bit of matter on the planet.* He made a few adjustments and directed the tricorder's sensors toward the moon overhead, to analyze its reflected light. *It's even coming from the star itself.*

Xiong had no idea what the pattern was, but he knew that it had to be studied. He wondered how much of it he could record on the tricorder's memory disks. *If I dump all its stored data and overwrite my logs about the Tholian ship, I might be able to document a fraction of what I'm reading here.*

He wiped the nonessential data from his tricorder and started making a record of the waveform, which he decided to name the Jinoteur Pattern. *I'll probably come home with less than one-tenth of it,* he knew, *but that'll be a hundred times more than what we had yesterday.*

Shocked by the Apostate's account of his exile, Theriault asked, "They banished you? For disagreeing with them?"

"Their voices are many, and ours are few," he said. The Apostate had come ashore much diminished in stature, though he was still a few meters taller than Theriault. Reduced to a less titanic scale, he nonetheless remained impressive. Wrapped in flowing raiment of colored light, he hovered more than a meter above the ground, and his voice continued to resonate and tremble the ground.

She seized upon his choice of words, which she understood implicitly that he had learned from her mind while she had slept in his healing care. *"Ours?* Others feel as you do?"

"My partisans," he said. **"Standing against more than twice their number, they are only barely outmatched. But we are the victims of a conspiracy of numbers . . . a tyranny of the majority. In this manner our people have succumbed to stagnation."** A sweep of his hand peppered the air above the pond with countless incandescent, stationary motes of light. **"Ten thousand star systems we governed. Trillions of lives did we direct."** He declared with majestic pride, **"This was the Shedai."**

The young science officer gazed upon the impromptu star

map with wonder and curiosity. Until today, she had thought that the Federation, with more than one hundred star systems counted as members, was a massive astropolitical entity. *Ten thousand star systems,* she marveled. It would have constituted a sphere of control greater than all the known Alpha Quadrant and Beta Quadrant political entities combined.

"How could you govern something so vast?" she asked. "The travel times across those distances must have been incredible."

With the flick of one spectral digit against a mote of light, the Apostate made the glowing speck flare—and at the exact same moment, another mote at the far side of the pond flashed in unison. **"Our voice is instantaneous,"** he said. He flicked the same mote again, and a different counterpart in a far-removed corner of the cavern pulsed in sympathy. **"Our will is done regardless of distance. Form is an illusion; our power resides in our word, and our word is given by our voice."**

Theriault was awestruck. "You're capable of instant teleportation across distances that great?"

"Only our voice," said the Apostate. **"Only our will. Forms are transitory. We leave them behind."**

Sensing that this was an important detail to clarify, she asked, "You shed your bodies?"

"The subtle body is freed from the crude prison of the corporeal," the Apostate said—and, as if to underscore his point, his glimmer faded, and his humanoid figure evaporated. Before she could ask if he was still there, a warm billow of air passed by her, and another humanoid figure made of plasticized water ascended from the pond. **"Physical forms are shells,"** said the Apostate's liquid avatar, **"to be used as needed and then set aside."** His body of water bubbled furiously and erupted into a cloud of mist, which then reassembled itself into the radiant, looming figure it had been only moments before. **"Matter exists to serve the will."**

She began to understand. "So . . . when you move to another world, you let go of whatever body you're in, and you transmit yourself—just your consciousness."

"Yes," the Apostate said in a rare moment of brevity.

"How?"

He turned his gaze upward, toward the opening in the cavern ceiling, then looked back at Theriault. **"I will show you."** As he drifted away in a straight path above the pond, a narrow bridge of stone appeared from the water beneath him. **"Follow me."**

Theriault cautiously traversed the stone bridge until it reached the center of the pond, directly beneath the opening high overhead. There the bridge ended at a broad circular platform. As soon as she stepped upon it, the bridge behind her sank back under the water. Above her, the Apostate glowed like burnished bronze in sunlight. Transfixed by his beauty, it took Theriault a few seconds to realize that the ceiling of the cavern appeared to be growing closer. Then she looked down and discovered that she was being lifted on a swiftly rising pillar of stone, whose ascent was as gentle as that of an inertia-dampened turbolift. Looking back up at the Apostate, she asked, "You can control this place?"

He replied, **"I *am* this place. This world . . . is Shedai."**

The platform lifted her into the blinding rays of the sun. She lifted her arm to shield her eyes and squinted into the white glare . . . and then she saw it: a city. It was unlike anything she had ever seen before. Long swoops and towering curves defined the architecture. Delicate fluted causeways linked massive, organic-looking structures, like strings of wire uniting cathedral-sized conch shells. Shades of aquamarine and verdigris blended in epic swaths across the façades. Slow streamers of rainbow light danced through the spaces between structures, like earthbound auroras.

A lush valley surrounded the strangely biomechanoid pastel metropolis, and in the distance rolling hills and ragged cliffs bordered the valley. No fewer than six large rivers flowed toward the city, which straddled the valley's grand basin. The sky was streaked with shredded clouds separated by slashes of hazy daylight stretching from the heavens to the jungle canopy.

"It's beautiful," Theriault said, in a voice that felt much too small to praise such a wonder.

A rippling image followed the Apostate's hand as he swept it across the landscape before her. **"Aeons ago, our Colloquium filled this valley. Our voice gave us hegemony."** He directed her attention to a massive dome that topped the highest structure in the city. **"Our voice spoke through the First Conduit . . . our word was law."** The vision of the city's ancient grandeur faded away, and melancholy mixed with anger infused the Apostate's tone. **"Then came the awakening."**

Fearful of provoking him, Theriault timidly asked, "Awakening of what?"

"Of our voice," he said. **"The revolt of the *Kollotuul*. It was a rebuke we earned with our hubris."** A sphere of fire encircled her and the Apostate, but the absence of any heat helped Theriault realize it was just another of his illusions. They seemed to be gliding above a rocky surface pitted with volcanic crevices and bubbling pits of sulfur.

"Hundreds of millennia ago we found them," he said. **"Mindless vermin graced with a gift beyond their ken."** From several of the fiery pits emerged scorpionlike arthropods, glowing like embers in the superheated environment. **"Their minds could link when they made physical contact. Such a precious talent . . . and fate wasted it on scavengers."**

When the beings passed beneath Theriault's feet, she recognized the faceted shapes of their orthorhombic component structures. Just as early primates had exhibited features that marked them as evolutionary cousins of what eventually became Homo sapiens, these small skittering creatures were, to Theriault's trained eye, unmistakably Tholian.

"The Shedai brought the *Kollotuul*'s potential to fruition." With an almost fatherly pride he added, **"We taught them to speak in our voice. *As* our voice."** The sphere of flames faded to reveal the image of a Shedai conduit populated with the primitive Tholians, all writhing in a steady stream of dark charged plasma. The Apostate's elegiac bitterness returned. **"They repaid us in fire."**

She and the Apostate hurtled forward and emerged into a black void. Orbs drifted past them, images of planets glowing like coals beneath ashen blankets. **"When the *Kollotuul* awakened, they retained much of our knowledge. They did not revere us for making them sentient—they feared us, hated us."** A ghostly image of a city laid waste replaced the darkness, surrounding Theriault with a vision of millions of humanoids lying slain in the streets. **"Using our own Conduits, our own voice, those first awakened ones roused all their kin. In the span of a thought, the *Kollotuul* turned our weapons against us. A thousand worlds perished instantly, a war within a breath."**

Liberated from the illusions, Theriault found herself standing on one of the high ramparts of the city, at the far end of a sliver-thin bridge that led to the great dome of what he had called the First Conduit. A stiff breeze fluttered her blue minidress. Overhead, the sky blackened. Clouds heavy with rain crowded together and flashed with heat lightning.

The Apostate stood beside her, cloaked now in a vaguely humanoid shape of translucent dark glass. His voice, though still deep, now had a merely human scale. "We did not think of ourselves as tyrants," he said, sounding a note of profound regret. "Membership in our union was voluntary. Worlds that joined with us received many boons. Our Conduits defended them from attack. Our science cured all known diseases. We could rescue planetary ecologies from the brink of collapse or engineer new ones. For those who lived beneath our aegis, immortality was all but assured." He looked away toward the First Conduit. "But for the *Kollotuul*, that was not enough."

"But you admit that you'd enslaved them," Theriault said.

The Apostate bristled. His voice was sharp and defensive. "They were not sentient when we yoked them to the Conduits. They were beasts of burden." Calming himself, he continued, "When they awakened, they attacked our worlds. They could

have asked for freedom; instead they chose to be our enemies."
He stepped away from her, out onto the narrow bridge. She followed him. "The *Kollotuul* banded together, harnessed our
power to build ships, and fled our space," he continued. "In the
aftermath, we struggled to govern our far-flung territories—but
without the *Kollotuul* to amplify our voice, the most distant
worlds fell beyond our influence. Over several millennia our
sphere of control diminished. Our hegemony fractured and fell."

Theriault noticed as they walked that the Apostate's feet did
not actually make contact with the surface of the causeway.
Rather he appeared to glide above it, as though he were pantomiming the act of walking solely for her benefit.

"As our former glories began to pass away and a new order
of powers started to rise in the galaxy," he continued as though
recounting some simple matter, "some of our number took on
mundane forms and moved among the petty and ephemeral.
Others followed the Maker into a slumber of the aeons, as if the
galaxy would be content to grant them quiet, dreamless sleep. I
chose to spend my millennia in quiet exile . . . in reflection."

In the middle of the precariously thin walkway, he stopped
and turned back to face her. She made the mistake of glancing
down at the chasm under her feet. They were hundreds of meters above the ground. Fighting to keep her balance, she looked
back up at the Apostate. "Now the whole gang's back in town,
huh?"

He was unnervingly still. "As I foretold ages ago, they could
not rest when they felt their power in another's hands."

"The Conduits," she blurted out as the first wayward droplets
of rain teased her face. "Starfleet woke them up when it started
experimenting on the Ravanar Conduit."

"Its song filled the heavens," he said, "but the only ones who
could hear it were us . . . and the *Kollotuul*."

The motive for the Tholians' ambush of the *Starship Bombay*
at Ravanar became clear to Theriault.

"And your people created the meta-genome," she said. "We
always find them together. Why?"

"Seeds," he said. "A foundation upon which to build our future hegemony."

She glanced down again and felt a slight spin of vertigo. "Could we, uh, keep walking, please?"

The Apostate moved his feet in a convincing approximation of ambulation and floated ahead of her on the causeway, toward the cluster of huge shapes in the heart of the city. As they neared the other side, she mustered the courage to ask, "Now that your friends are awake . . . what are they doing?"

He reached the other side, stepped clear, and waited for her to join him under an arched overhang before he replied, "They have gathered here for the Colloquium."

"Which is what, exactly?"

"A discussion," the Apostate said. "About the future of this galaxy—and how they will shape it to their liking."

"Oh, *galactic domination,*" she said in her most irreverent tone of voice. As a steady gray rain began to fall in pattering torrents, she flashed a goofy grin at the dark, godlike being to her left. "And I thought we were in trouble."

It is done, proclaimed the Maker. The Conduit's song faded, and the silence of exhaustion lingered over the Colloquium.

They all had been weakened by the effort of effecting the great transit of the Nameless to Avainenoran. Already a handful of the Nameless had engaged pockets of *Telinaruul* resistance on the planet. Moving now in numbers, they soon would be poised to eradicate the remaining trespassers in a single assault.

For some of the *Serrataal* there was no rest, even after such a labor. The Avenger hunted the downed *Telinaruul,* her tireless search siphoning a steady stream of power from the First World's overtaxed geothermal reserves. Meanwhile, inside the Colloquium, the Warden's thoughts radiated concern. **Another ship has entered our system,** he announced, crafting its shape overhead with lines of fire. **It is on an approach vector to penetrate our atmosphere.**

Destroy it, counseled the Wanderer.

The Sage interjected with soothing blue hues of restraint. **Our strength is depleted,** he warned. **All our reserves have been committed to the liberation of Avainenoran.**

The power we shifted there can be reclaimed after the Nameless destroy the ships above that world, the Maker noted.

Burning with impatience, the Wanderer argued, **By that time, more *Telinaruul* will have landed *here*.**

Her caustic protest seemed to amuse the Maker. **Let the newcomers land—and lead the Avenger directly to their friends.**

"T'Prynn's directions were specific," Quinn said, speaking around his lit cigar. "Make sure you check the settings."

It was the fourth reminder he'd given Pennington in the last hour, and the reporter was now thoroughly annoyed. "They haven't changed since the last time I checked them," he said.

"Don't go gettin' snippy," Quinn shot back. "I ain't in the mood to get fragged today. If you are, get out and walk."

Pennington humored the older man's request and verified that their shields—paltry and underpowered as they were—were still cycling on the tremendously unusual harmonized frequency that T'Prynn had specified in her subspace message, which had sent them back to this remote star system. "Shield frequency verified," he said with grouchy apathy.

"All right, then," Quinn said. "Hang on to yer hat, I'm taking us into orbit." A few taps on the helm console, and the rickety old freighter made a short-hop warp jump. What had been a very bright point of light in the starscape inflated in less than two seconds to the overwhelming mass of a planet. They dropped to impulse over its equator and skirted the atmosphere, which erupted in pale flares around them as the ship sliced through the rarefied gases. Turbulence rattled the ship as Quinn threw a few more switches on an overhead control board. "Anybody locking weapons on us?" he asked.

Staring blankly at the blinking parade of lights in front of him, Pennington replied, "How would I tell?"

"Never mind," Quinn said. "I'm locking in the surface coordinates." Flashing a grin from the side of his mouth, he added, "Hope you remembered to tie down the booze."

The *Rocinante* dived toward the planet, blazing through the air in a nimbus of fire. It was a far more aggressive approach pattern than Quinn normally used. "Ease up, mate," cautioned Pennington, who realized that his hands were white-knuckle tight on the ends of his seat's armrests.

"Hell, no," Quinn said. He plucked the cigar from his mouth. "We're making great time."

A patchwork of clouds spread out beneath them. Quinn guided the ship through a clear pocket of sky and leveled out in steep turn that crushed Pennington to his chair. When the dancing purple spots cleared from his vision, he watched a rugged landscape of limestone towers, dense jungles, and winding rivers blur past. A colossal, natural rock formation loomed in their path, enlarging with alarming speed. Pennington pointed at it. "Um . . . Quinn?"

"Relax," Quinn said, banking the ship nearly ninety degrees to slip through an empty space in the rocks. When they emerged safely on the other side, Pennington stopped holding his breath; outside the cockpit, the landscape rolled around them as Quinn executed a corkscrew maneuver. He had never seen this daredevil facet of Quinn's personality before, and he wasn't enjoying it.

As if sensing Pennington's discomfort—and, more surprising, actually giving a damn about it—Quinn leveled out their flight. "Better?" Less caustically he said, "I get carried away. Sorry."

"No worries," Pennington said, trying not to sound as discombobulated as he felt. He checked their position with the navigation computer. "We're almost at the coordinates."

"I'm on it," Quinn said, reducing the ship's speed. Harsh white sunlight streamed across the jungle canopy as far as Pennington could see, in every direction but one. To the north, a massive storm front boiled close on the horizon.

The *Rocinante* drifted to a halt above a muddy brown river. Quinn punched a few numbers into the computer, then fired some of the ship's thrusters a few times to correct their position to within a meter of the coordinates. "All right," he said. "This is the spot. I'll send the hail. Get down to the cargo bay and stand by on the winch."

Pennington unfastened his safety harness and patted Quinn's shoulder as he stood up. "Nice flying, mate."

Quinn shrugged. "Just a couple dumb tricks by an ol' spacedog. Still can't stick my landings."

"Tell me about it," Pennington said as he left the cockpit. He walked back through the main compartment to a hatch panel in the deck. A switch on the wall unlocked it; as it lowered with a sharp squeak, it unfolded into a steep stair-ladder to the cargo deck. Pennington hurried down as it finished its lethargic deployment. He had bounded off onto the cargo deck by the time it touched down behind him.

Countless old odors called the dimly lit cargo bay of the *Rocinante* their home. The most recent stench was from decayed vegetables, a vivid reminder of the Nejev contract that had gone so miserably wrong just a day earlier. Old machine oil and well-hidden patches of mold and mildew competed to create the most pervasive stink. Pennington was no fan of the smell of bleach, but he would have welcomed a few gallons of it just then.

Secured on a thin metal pallet in the center of the hold was the ship's sole item of cargo: a magnetic-containment pod full of antimatter. They had taken it aboard by opening the *Rocinante*'s ventral cargo bay doors and pulling it up from the vendor's warehouse with the ship's motorized winch; the plan was to deliver it the same way. Pennington checked the safety locks on the harness around the pod and was satisfied that they all were secure; the power supply to the winch was steady, and the cable feeder was clear and free of obstructions. He thumbed an intercom switch to the cockpit. "We're tight," he reported. "Have you made contact?"

"Roger that," Quinn answered. *"They're comin' up now. Open the bay doors and get ready."*

"Opening bay doors," Pennington said. He keyed in the sequence to unlock the long doors that constituted most of the deck inside the cargo hold. They parted with a deep groaning drone, and a shudder traveled through the hull.

A sliver of light formed between the massive doors, and that crack widened as the doors slowly lowered open, leaving the fuel pod suspended in its harness attached to the winch cable. Reflected sunlight from the planet's surface flooded the cargo bay. Wind noise and the roar of the *Rocinante*'s engines in hover mode drowned out the doors' servomotors as Pennington squinted against the blinding tropical glare. Warm, humid air rushed in, thick with the scent of the jungle. Seconds later his eyes adjusted, and he saw the river frothing wildly less than fifteen meters below. The first silt-strewn gray curve of the Starfleet ship's hull emerged from the boiling foam, followed a moment later by its entire oval-shaped primary hull and the top halves of its warp nacelles.

A broad hatch in the middle of its secondary hull slid open, and Pennington saw several members of the ship's crew gazing up, returning his stare. He waved. A brawny, bearded man with heavy ocular ridges waved back.

Over the intercom, Quinn drawled, *"Unless yer plannin' on teaching 'em sign language, you can lower the fuel pod now."*

Pennington swallowed his reply and turned the key to feed out the winch cable slowly, to minimize the payload's swing as it descended. The bearded Denobulan inside the Starfleet ship waved to signal everything was okay. As the fuel pod neared the opening at the top of the other ship, the Starfleet personnel gathered around and guided the large cylinder carefully inside their vessel.

The Denobulan held up his hands, wide apart, and slowly moved them closer, advising Pennington of the distance remaining to the *Sagittarius*'s deck. The young Scot watched carefully, his hand poised to halt the cable feeder. Then the bearded man clapped his hands together and turned his palms upward. Pennington turned off the cable feeder and spoke toward the intercom. "Touchdown."

"Nice," Quinn said. *"Good to know at least one of us has a knack for landings."*

Pennington grinned at the compliment and looked back down at the Starfleet ship. They had finished detaching the harness from the fuel pod. The scruffy Denobulan signaled him to retract the cable. Pennington gave him a thumbs-up and turned the winch key in the other direction to take up the slack.

Minutes later, after he had closed the ventral cargo bay doors, he climbed back up to the main deck and returned to the cockpit. "So," he said as he fell into his seat, "is that it?"

"Not quite," Quinn said. "I was waiting for you. Their captain wants to talk to both of us." He reached forward and pressed a key on the console. "Captain, we're both here."

"Gentlemen," said a dignified-sounding voice with an accent that Pennington couldn't place. *"This is Captain Adelard Nassir. First off, I want to thank you both, on behalf of my crew, for bringing that antimatter on the double."*

"Yer welcome, Captain," Quinn said.

Nassir's tone became somber. *"Since we're already in your debt, and seeing as you men are civilians, I feel like I have no right to ask another favor of you . . . but my first officer is several kilometers downriver, stranded and wounded."*

Quinn shifted his cigar from one side of his mouth to the other. "You need us to pick him up and bring him back?"

"It may not be that simple," Nassir said. *"We're not alone down here, gents. Every second you stay, your lives are in danger. Rescuing my officer might be more than just a taxi run."*

With a glance in Pennington's direction, Quinn said, "Well, I can't speak for my friend, Captain, but if you'll point me toward your man, I'm ready to go get him." To Pennington he added, "Tim, if you'd rather stay here, I'll understand."

"If it's all the same to you, mate," Pennington said, hearing the words tumble out of his mouth before he knew what he was saying, "I'll come along."

A string of data appeared on one of the small, cracked monitors mounted in the hump between the pilot's and copilot's seats. *"We've sent you Commander Terrell's communicator ID frequency,"* Nassir said. *"Lock that into your ship's sensors, and it'll lead you right to him."* They heard the captain clear his throat. *"I can't thank you men enough for this. Good luck, and Godspeed."*

"Back atcha, Captain," Quinn said. *"Rocinante* out." He flipped the channel closed, pivoted the nose of the ship northward, and keyed the main thruster. "Tim," he said, "lock in that guy's communicator signal, will ya?"

As Pennington patched the communicator's transponder data into the ship's main sensor array, he snuck suspicious glances over at Quinn. "Look who's all gung-ho to play the hero's role."

"Ain't the first good deed I ever did," Quinn said, checking his gauges. "Just been awhile, that's all."

Unable to keep a sly grin from his face, Pennington remarked, "It just doesn't seem like you."

"Tell me something," Quinn said. "What'd you want to be when you were a kid?"

He wondered if Quinn was setting him up to be the butt of a joke, but his intuition told him Quinn was serious. "I wanted to be a reporter," he said.

"Yeah? That worked out well for you, then." Adjusting his cigar between his teeth, he said, "I'll let you in on a secret, newsboy: when I was a kid, I did *not* dream of growing up to be a drunk and a loser. We reach?"

Under all that bluster, Pennington mused, *there might just be a decent human being trying to get out. Or maybe he's just playing me, as usual.* "If you were so keen to be a hero, why didn't you do that instead?"

Without a grin or a hint of sarcasm, Quinn replied, "No one ever asked me."

For a moment, Pennington wondered if perhaps he had been too quick to judge this scruffy, smelly, boorish man. Told that he would be flying his ship and himself into peril, Quinn hadn't hesitated to accept the risk. It had been Pennington who had committed himself in order to save face—and, he realized belatedly, to avoid disappointing Quinn. To avoid shaming his friend. *Which one of us is the real hero?*

Before he could let his mind slip into a debate on that topic, he noticed the sky growing dark and flashing with lightning. The massive storm front that he had seen during their approach to the *Sagittarius* was directly ahead of them—and growing closer with each passing second.

Captain Kutal stood in the middle of the *Zin'za*'s bridge and felt his good mood deflate into disgust as he read the urgent message that had just been received from Imperial Intelligence. "They can't be serious," Kutal grumbled.

He handed the message to BelHoQ. The first officer read it quickly, then sagged with irritated disappointment. "Helm," he barked. "Take us out of warp." Qlar, hunched over the forward console, hastened to obey. Moments later the stars on the main viewer went from streaked to static.

"Answering all stop, sir," Qlar reported.

The captain walked back to his chair and slumped into it. BelHoQ followed and stood facing him from the left. The first officer kept his voice low. "An ambush? Sounds like someone at I.I.'s been hitting the *warnog* again."

Kutal feigned surprise. "You don't think it's possible?"

"Possible? Maybe. Likely? No. Starfleet couldn't deploy enough ships here for an ambush without our knowledge."

"I know that," Kutal replied, his voice an anger-sharpened rasp. "Not unless they've started using devices like the one we encountered on that ship outside the Palgrenax system."

His speculation seemed to concern BelHoQ. Weeks earlier they had hunted down a ship of unknown origin that had possessed a technology for rendering itself all but invisible to sensors and visual scans. If the Federation proved to be the inventor of such a profound tactical advantage, it could easily spell disaster for the Empire.

BelHoQ calmed himself and spoke in a cool, measured tone. "Standard procedure calls for a full scan of the system before we proceed."

"Afraid we might be outnumbered, BelHoQ?"

Unruffled by the jibe, BelHoQ answered, "No, Captain. I just want to know where all the targets are—so I can decide which one to destroy first."

Kutal chortled with genuine amusement and appreciation. "Very well. Run your scan. We'll hold station here until we're ready to move into orbit."

As BelHoQ stepped away to coordinate the intensive sensor sweep of the star system, Kutal stared at the bold white orb of Jinoteur in the center of the main viewer. *We can afford to take our time,* he reassured himself. *We know exactly where the Starfleet ship is—and it's not going anywhere.*

22

Less than fifteen seconds after the *Starship Endeavour* dropped out of warp on course to make orbit above Gamma Tauri IV, the comm system beeped with two priority signals, and every officer on the bridge tried to report at once.

The flurry of voices was little more than noise to Captain Atish Khatami, who looked to her new first officer, Lieutenant Commander Katherine Stano, to impose some kind of order on the chaos engulfing the bridge.

Stano reacted to the captain's gentle, pleading stare with an abashed lowering of her eyes. Then she stuck her thumb and middle finger inside her mouth and pierced the din with a sharp, teeth-rattling whistle. The bridge fell silent. Khatami smirked. *I knew she could sing. Didn't know she could do that.*

"One at a time," Stano said, her moment of ire revealing traces of her long-suppressed Tennessee accent. She pointed at the communications officer. "Estrada, report."

Lieutenant Hector Estrada swiveled his chair to speak to Stano and Khatami. "Priority signals from Vanguard and the *Lovell*," he said. "Vanguard's hailing both of us."

"Both onscreen," Khatami said.

Estrada turned back to his console and flipped switches. The image of Gamma Tauri IV on the main viewer blinked and became a split-screen image showing Captain Okagawa of the *U.S.S. Lovell* on the left and Commodore Reyes on the right. "Captain," Khatami said to Okagawa, then nodded to Reyes and added, "Commodore."

"Captains," Reyes replied. *"I just received Dr. Fisher's forensic report on the colonists who were killed earlier today.*

The good news is that they weren't killed by the Klingons. The bad *news . . . is that they weren't killed by the Klingons."*

Khatami understood immediately: the Shedai were involved. The same nearly unstoppable beings that had killed the former commanding officer of the *Endeavour* and several other Starfleet personnel on Erilon were on Gamma Tauri IV.

"We have news of our own," Captain Okagawa said. *"Our people are off the planet, but the colonists won't budge."*

Khatami asked, "Do they know there's another Klingon heavy cruiser on the way? It'll be here in less than half an hour."

Okagawa nodded. *"They know,"* he said. *"But they're doing whatever President Vinueza tells them to do. And she's telling them to stay put."*

"We've got to be careful how we handle this," Reyes said. *"Those colonists need to be evacuated, but they have to leave by choice—and that means convincing Jeanne."* The commodore caught himself, frowned, and hastily regrouped and rephrased. *"And that means persuading President Vinueza. You can't lie to her, but classified information has to stay classified.* Comprende?*"*

"Understood, sir," Khatami said. "What's our timetable?"

"R.F.N.," Reyes said. *"Get those people out of there before all hell breaks loose. Vanguard out."* The channel from Starbase 47 went dark, and Estrada adjusted the image on the main viewer to present Okagawa larger-than-life. The salt-and-pepper-haired man reminded Khatami slightly of her civilian husband, Kenji, who was home on Deneva with their young daughter, Parveen. Looking at the trim, half-Japanese captain of the *Lovell,* she realized, was making her homesick.

"So . . . Captain," Okagawa said with the rehearsed politesse of someone who was masking a profound frustration, *"any idea how to get those colonists off the planet without shooting them?"*

Khatami chuckled slightly at Okagawa's grim prognosis for the situation. "Motivating them to leave shouldn't be that hard," she said. "I'm worried about the logistics. Best-case scenario, even if every ship they own is spaceworthy, we can only evac fifty percent of them."

"I considered asking the Klingons to take the colonists prisoner," Okagawa said. *"But I don't think they could carry more than fifteen hundred. That still leaves four thousand behind."* He sighed. *"But the fact remains, Captain, that as of an hour ago,* none *of them were leaving. So I hope you're right about being able to motivate them—or, more to the point,* her."

The way Okagawa spoke about the colony president gave Khatami the distinct impression that there was something she ought to know about the woman but didn't. "Daniel," she said, "why does everybody walk on eggshells around this woman?"

He rolled his eyes. *"You mean aside from her being Reyes's ex-wife and a high-level esper?"*

Khatami paused in surprise, then mimicked Okagawa's pained grin. "This just gets better and better, doesn't it?"

"And you've been here two whole minutes," Okagawa said. *"We've been here five weeks. Imagine how much fun we're having."*

"I'm guessing there's a stick and some shaking involved," Khatami said. "I hope you'll forgive me for putting an end to it." She turned her chair toward the communications officer. "Estrada, get me President Vinueza. It's time to finish this. Her colony is being evacuated, and that's final."

"We're not going anywhere, *Captain,"* Jeanne Vinueza snapped at Khatami across the subspace channel, *"and* that's final."

This discussion is off to a bad start, Khatami decided. Try not to make it worse. "Madam President," she said, doing her best to strike a civil tone, "by now you must have noticed that a second Klingon cruiser has entered orbit."

"Of course," Vinueza said. *"How fortunate, then, that your ship is here as well."*

"If the Klingons move against you, there won't be much we can do, Madam President. Not unless you've reconsidered the Federation's offer of protectorate status. Have you?"

Vinueza's faux courtesy communicated her ire. *"Well, that depends,"* she said with an insincere smile. *"Would you or Captain Okagawa like to tell me the truth about what Starfleet's been doing on this planet for the last five weeks?"*

Khatami permitted herself a glance across the bridge toward the science station, where Lieutenant Stephen Klisiewicz peeked up from the blue glow beneath the sensor hood, no doubt curious about how the captain would respond to Vinueza's request.

"Our people have been supporting your colony, Madam President," Khatami said. "But we've been ordered to withdraw and avoid a conflict with the Klingons. It would be in your colony's best interest to do likewise."

"I fail to see how surrendering to the Klingons is in our best interest, Captain. If anything, we'd be rewarding them for being vicious enough to murder our people in cold blood."

Concocting a plausible scenario that would convince Vinueza to evacuate her colony but also would not expose any classified information was proving much more difficult than Khatami had expected. *This would be a lot easier if I could show her what she's really up against down there.* She sighed. "I don't suppose you'd agree to evacuate if I simply begged you to trust me?"

"No, Captain, I wouldn't. If the Klingons want to take our colony, they'll have to work for it. We're ready for them."

"I sincerely doubt that, Madam President," Khatami said. "Don't go anywhere. I'll be back in touch shortly. *Endeavour* out." On a nod from Khatami, Estrada closed the channel. The image on the main viewer switched back to the upper hemisphere of Gamma Tauri IV, the *Lovell,* and two Klingon cruisers. "Klisiewicz, status of the Shedai energy readings on the planet?"

"Steadily increasing, Captain," Klisiewicz said. "If these

discharge at the same levels we saw on Erilon, they'll be ready to fire in twenty minutes." He adjusted his controls and added, "Still no lock on the main firing nodes, though."

Khatami watched the two Klingon cruisers on the main viewer begin to maneuver to positions from which they could provide each other with covering fire. She wondered whether the Klingons or the Shedai would attack the New Boulder colony first and resolved not to wait to find out. "Yellow alert," she said, then snapped out orders in quick succession. "McCormick, raise shields. Neelakanta, widen our orbit and optimize our firing position against both Klingon cruisers. Estrada, warn the *Lovell* to break orbit and move out of the Shedai's weapons range. Then open a priority channel to Captain Desai on Starbase 47. I'll take it in my quarters." She rose from her chair. "Stano, you have the conn."

Rana Desai wondered why so many Starfleet officers had so much trouble understanding the basic principles of Federation law.

"Atish," she said to Captain Khatami, whose image graced the small viewscreen in Desai's private office, "I made this very clear to Commodore Reyes, and I'm certain he made it equally clear to you: the colonists invoked their right to independence. We have to respect that. If they reject our advice, we can't *force* them to take it."

Her answer only seemed to tighten Khatami's pursed frown. *"Rana, we've got ten minutes till we start taking fire from the planet's defense system. When that happens, I think the colonists are going to realize there's more on the planet than them and the Klingons. So why don't we just tell them truth and get them out while we still can?"*

"That's not a legal decision, Atish—that's a command decision. If you want to debate it, you'll have to talk to the commodore." Pushing the responsibility onto Reyes felt like a cheat to Desai, but in this case it was legally necessary.

A soft string of muttered Farsi curses escaped Khatami's

lips. *"When the shooting starts, those people are going to die."*

"They've renounced Federation citizenship," Desai said. "Your duty is to protect your crew and your ship, not the colonists. Unless its government asks for your help, you have to remain neutral when the Klingons move against them."

"It's not the Klingons I'm worried about," Khatami said. *"Those people have no idea what they're facing, Rana. Please, there has to be some loophole, some pretext we can use to get them out of there."*

Shaking her head, Desai said sadly, "There isn't. I've checked a dozen times. And Atish . . . ?" She waited until the starship captain met her stare across the subspace channel. "If you, Captain Okagawa, or any member of your crews removes even one person from that colony against their will, I will convene courts-martial for everyone involved, on charges of kidnapping and disobeying the order of a superior officer. Is that clear?"

Khatami's expression hardened into one of cold contempt. *"Yes, Captain. If you'll excuse me, I have eight minutes to convince Commodore Reyes to let me tell the colonists why they ought to be running for their lives. Khatami out."*

The screen on the wall of Desai's office went dark. The JAG officer buried her face in her hands and heaved several halting breaths before sinking into silent mourning for the lives that she and the law had utterly failed to protect.

She suspected that Khatami's urgent hail was reaching the commodore's office at that moment. All Desai could hope for was that the decision to sacrifice those thousands of people on Gamma Tauri IV would haunt Reyes's conscience as bitterly as it tortured her own.

Lieutenant Sasha Rodriguez locked in the settings on the helm console. "Holding at minimum safe distance, Captain."

Daniel Okagawa accepted her report with a half-nod. "Magnify our view of the planet," he said. As weapons officer Jessica Diamond enlarged the image of Gamma Tauri IV on the main viewer, Okagawa looked to his science officer. "Xav, any change in the energy readings from the planet?"

"Still climbing, sir," Xav replied. "Eighteen percent more powerful than the ones we faced at Erilon." He blinked once, then added, "Correction—*nineteen* percent more powerful."

Anticipation of something dreadful was churning sour bile in the back of Okagawa's throat. "Mahmud, any sign the colonists are taking the hint yet?"

Al-Khaled checked the monitor at an aft station and shook his head. "Negative, sir. All ships still on the ground."

"Heavy signal activity, though," interrupted communications officer Pzial. Touching his fingers lightly to the Feinberger in his ear, he continued, "Reports of groundquakes . . . spontaneous forest fires . . . electrical storms . . ." His red eyes widened. "Sir, I'm picking up similar reports from the Klingon settlement as well. Something about . . ." He squinted with intense concentration. "Maybe I'm not translating it right, but I think they said they're being attacked by *clouds*."

Okagawa looked at zh'Rhun, as if she might be able to explicate Pzial's report. She limited her response to a single lifted white eyebrow and a subtle twitch of her antennae.

"New energy reading," Xav called out. "It's firing!" On the main viewer, a streak of energy blazed up from the planet's surface and vaporized the smaller Klingon cruiser in orbit. "By Kera and Phinda," Xav gasped in horror. "Their shields were at full power." He stammered, "They just . . . they . . ."

His voice trailed off as al-Khaled cut in, "More shots from the planet, sir! *Endeavour* and the Klingons are going evasive."

"Captain," Pzial said, "I'm picking up scattered calls for help from the New Boulder colony—including an official mayday."

Everyone looked to Okagawa, who felt sick with regret. "It's too late," he said, watching the *Endeavour* and the Klingon ship break orbit at full impulse. "They're on their own now."

• • •

Between the wind, the rain, the thunder, and the increasingly severe groundquake that had shaken the windows of her ramshackle headquarters to dust, Jeanne Vinueza could barely hear herself yell. "What do you mean the *Endeavour*'s gone?"

She staggered and stumbled across the rain-slicked, wildly pitching floor toward her chief of staff, Rik Panganiban. The bespectacled young native of the Philippines clutched the edge of his desk with one hand while trying to hold two open personal communicators in the other. "Hang on!" he shouted into one. He dropped the other as his desk slid across the bucking floor and left him tumbling forward onto his knees.

Vinueza grabbed him and pulled him back to his feet. She had to hang onto him as the ground trembled violently. She bent down and scooped up his dropped communicator while he listened to a panicked squawk of voices from the other one. He covered the device's voice sensor and repeated his message to her. "They broke orbit sixty seconds ago! Said they're taking fire!"

"From the Klingons?"

"No," Panganiban hollered over the din, "the planet!"

This is what Diego was hiding, she realized. *Starfleet's searching for some kind of superweapon—and we're sitting on top of it.* "Get Vanguard on the comm," she said as her anger rose to the occasion. "I want Commodore Reyes on the line *right now!*"

"There's no time, Madam President," Panganiban protested. "The transports are powering up! We have to evacuate!"

Thunderbolts from the sky hammered down on the colony outside Vinueza's office window. Plumes of fire answered each strike, launching cones of orange-yellow flame into the deluge of torrential rain and screaming wind. The streets were packed with fleeing colonists, falling over one another in a mad dash for the transports. Panic was setting in because everyone knew that there were too many bodies and not enough ships.

Panganiban grasped Vinueza's arm and tried in vain to pull her away from the window. "Madam President, please! We have to—"

He saw it at the same time she did. Massive, shimmering tentacles of dark energy reached down out of the stormhead and snared the first few transport ships as they began to lift off. In seconds the deep-violet coils completely wrapped around each of the three ships and began to contract. Lightning flashed and thunder rolled—then all three ships broke apart and collapsed to the ground in fiery jumbles of metal and corpses. More crackling serpents descended from the bruised-black clouds and hammered the other ships still on the surface. Gouts of bloodred fire mushroomed along the perimeter of New Boulder.

All the thousands of people who had been running toward the transports turned and fled in the opposite direction, oblivious of the fact that they were being herded into the center of New Boulder. Vinueza watched in horror from her second-floor vantage point as the colonists' pursuers came into view.

Vaguely humanoid obsidian giants moved like whirling dervishes, obliterating stone and metal with the same ease that they pulverized flesh and bone. Their snaking arms ended in vicious conical points and punched with enough force to pulp people's torsos, scattering their orphaned limbs. Bodies flew apart in front of the titans with each blow, and the walls of the city fell to dust under their relentless advance.

There were hundreds of them. They came from all directions, laying waste to the colony, reaving its people with merciless precision. Blood ran in the streets. The percussion of the storm devoured the screams of the dying.

Vinueza grabbed Panganiban by his collar and pulled his face to hers. "We're trapped! Get on the comm and get me Reyes, *now!*"

Reyes's eyes burned with fatigue. Reports were coming in at every station in Starbase 47's operations center, and even with all his senior personnel and watch officers summoned to duty in the middle of gamma shift, it seemed as if there weren't enough eyes to monitor every task.

He stood in the middle of it all, hunched over the hub on the supervisor's deck. Gathered at the octagonal console with him were T'Prynn, Jetanien, Cooper, and Lieutenant Isaiah Farber, the station's chief of engineering.

"*Endeavour*'s reporting moderate damage, sir," Farber said. "Shield failures, power loss in the warp drive."

Reyes's thoughts were moving quickly. "What about the Klingons? Did they get hit?"

Cooper called up a tactical grid on the hub's flat, central display. "One ship dusted in the first salvo; the other looks like it got hit the same as *Endeavour*."

As usual, Jetanien focused on the bigger picture. "Are the Klingons moving against the *Endeavour*?"

"No," said Cooper. "They're pulling out." The first officer widened the scope of the display. "*Endeavour*'s falling back to regroup with the *Lovell*."

T'Prynn studied the situation report and the tactical display with trademark Vulcan reserve. "Commodore, based on the scope of the attack and the greater power levels involved, it appears that our adversary has mounted a much larger offensive than what we encountered on Erilon." Reyes looked at her and was met by her icy stare. "A decisive counterstrike, made swiftly, could inflict significant damage upon our attacker."

"What my esteemed colleague neglects to mention," Jetanien interjected, "is that any counterstrike we might make would fall first and foremost upon the colonists of New Boulder."

"I omitted that detail because it is irrelevant," T'Prynn said. "Our principal objective remains—"

"Commodore!" shouted Lieutenant Commander Dohan from the main deck of the operations center. "Emergency signal from the New Boulder president's office!"

Reyes lurched away from the hub toward the railing that circled the edge of the supervisor's deck. "Onscreen!"

A static-hashed scene from a nightmare appeared, spanning nearly sixty degrees of the circular compartment's wraparound video display. The image trembled, colors blurred together, flashes of fire and lightning whited out portions of the screen every few seconds. In the background was a parade of carnage. Goliaths as black as tar tore through crowds of civilians and transformed squat buildings into mounds of debris. Storm clouds trailed writhing twists of indigo energy that snagged even the smallest ships from the air and crushed them into sparking, burning husks. The sound was scratchy and intermittent but clear enough for Reyes to make out every horrified scream.

But all he could see was Jeanne—the woman he'd once loved, the woman part of him still loved, despite all that she had done to him—her face all but pressed to the video transmitter. *"Damn you, Diego!"* she cried. *"Why didn't you tell us the truth?"* Terror and rage were united in her tears and in the bitter fury of her voice. *"Why didn't you tell me?"*

Struck dumb with guilt and horror, Reyes had no defense. Risking the colonists' lives had been an abstraction, a game of numbers, but watching them die in real time—the reality of it sickened him to his core. He didn't know what to say. Groping futilely for words, all he could muster was her name, and even that caught in his throat as tears overflowed his eyes.

"Jeanne . . ."

She screamed. A fearsome blur ripped her body in half, then obliterated her completely in a whirlwind of slashing blows.

Weak, wordless sounds issued from Reyes's throat. His knees buckled. He slumped over the railing, unable and unwilling to catch himself. His fall was arrested by Jetanien's scaly manus from the right and T'Prynn's pale hand from his left. They pulled him from the railing and turned him away from the screen.

He felt as if he were suffocating; he couldn't make himself breathe. The desperate choking sounds of his strangled grief echoed in the sudden, profound silence of the operations center. There was no strength in his legs; only his friends' support kept him upright long enough to plant his hands on the hub and slump forward.

The signal from Gamma Tauri IV ended, and the great screen behind Reyes turned blank and dark gray. Long seconds of heartbreaking emptiness pressed down upon him. He reached up to palm the tears from his cheeks and eyes; his hands, normally so warm, were ice-cold.

One breath followed another. Focus returned. He knew what had to be done. Swallowing to clear his throat and steady his voice, he turned toward his first officer. "Coop," he said, "get Captain Khatami onscreen."

"Aye, sir," Cooper said. He relayed the order, which traveled the deck in swiftly whispered acts of delegation.

Several seconds later, as the main viewer blinked back to life with an image of Captain Atish Khatami, Reyes regained his weathered mask of stoic resolve. "Captain," he said. "Is your ship still combat-ready?"

"Yes, Commodore," Khatami said with a curious double-take.

Everyone around Reyes was silent as he continued. "Then these are your new orders. I want the *Endeavour* and the *Lovell* to fall back to maximum photon-torpedo range from Gamma Tauri IV. From there, you will execute General Order 24 against the planet immediately. Is that understood?"

Khatami looked taken aback. *"General Order 24, sir?"*

"You heard me, Captain," Reyes said. "Glass it."

It had been several minutes since any outgoing transmissions had been detected from Gamma Tauri IV, and Atish Khatami knew that in all likelihood it was because all the colonists—including the Klingons—were dead. Pondering the commodore's invocation of General Order 24, however, she mourned the countless indigenous species that thrived on that world—plants, bacteria, insects, complex terrestrial and marine animals, and others so unique that they had as yet defied classification. Part of Starfleet's credo echoed in her thoughts: "to seek out new life . . ."

In moments, she would be exterminating it.

This isn't right, protested her conscience. *It's a sin against Allah, a crime against science.* She clenched her jaw and reminded herself that Commodore Reyes would not have given such an order lightly. She pictured the shadowy killing machines that had rampaged across the New Boulder colony and imagined them finding their way to Deneva . . . and bearing down on her husband and daughter. That notion made Reyes's order easier to follow.

Lieutenant Estrada turned from the communications station. "Captain Okagawa confirms the *Lovell* is set to fire on your order, Captain."

Stano stepped down into the command well of the bridge and placed herself at Khatami's right side. "All torpedo bays loaded and ready, Captain."

"Mr. Klisiewicz," Khatami said, "where are the Klingons?"

The science officer checked the sensor display and reported quickly. "Holding at station, opposite our position relative to the planet."

Khatami looked to Estrada. "Hail them."

Though the commodore's orders hadn't included warning the Klingons about the impending barrage, Khatami decided it might be prudent to make sure they understood in advance that they would not be the target of the forthcoming salvos of torpedoes. *Bad enough I have to blast a planet down to its mantle,* she decided, *I'm not starting an interstellar incident as well.*

"I have the Klingon commander," Estrada said.

"Onscreen." Khatami faced the main viewer.

The image of a grizzled, gray-maned, ridged-headed

Klingon warrior gazed back at her. *"This is Captain Gerzhog, commanding the Imperial Klingon battle cruiser* HovQaw'wI',*"* he rasped. *"Identify yourself."*

"Captain Atish Khatami, commanding the Federation starship *Endeavour,*" she replied. "We've been ordered to begin immediate photon-torpedo bombardment of Gamma Tauri IV. This barrage will continue until all life on the planet has been exterminated. We will not target your vessel. Do you understand?"

Gerzhog conferred briefly with someone out of frame and answered, *"Understood,* Endeavour. *We will assist you by bombarding the hemisphere opposite your position.* HovQaw'wI' *out."* The screen blinked back to a motionless starfield.

"The Klingons have armed their weapons array, Captain," Klisiewicz said. "Their targeting scanners are focused on the planet's surface."

"Then it's time," Khatami said. She stood from her chair. In unison the crew got up from their seats and stood at attention beside their duty stations. "Mr. Thorsen," she said, looking to the chief of security and senior weapons officer. "Ten full salvos, on my order." Khatami turned back toward the main viewer and steeled herself. Gamma Tauri IV was just a speck on the viewscreen, and that was how she wanted it to stay until this was over. She had no desire to observe this atrocity in detail. Denying herself the luxury of tears, she gave the order.

"Fire."

Whooping screeches accompanied every multiple-warhead salvo that shot away from the *Endeavour.* The blazing blue streaks joined with identical payloads fired from the *Lovell.* Sparks of sapphire, they glowed in the darkness of space for several seconds until they cruised out of visual range, on course for their rendezvous with Gamma Tauri IV.

From millions of kilometers away, only the barest flickers attested to the antimatter-fueled cataclysm that was transforming the planet into a sphere of molten rock and radioactive glass.

All around Khatami, her crew hung their heads in shame and sorrow. She kept her head up and her eyes on the screen. *You're the captain. You gave the order. You don't get to look away. You have to watch . . . and you'll have to remember.*

23

Wounded and clutching the signal dampener to his mauled torso, Terrell had passed his hours of painful solitude crawling under the foliage back to the campsite where he and Njwara had been attacked nearly twelve hours earlier. It hadn't taken as long to get back as he had expected it would; following the river's edge, he dragged himself across the hundred-fifty-odd meters of muddy ground in just a couple of hours.

Little was left of Niwara, and most of their equipment had been destroyed. To his relief, his tricorder remained intact, and from the shredded remains of his pack he retrieved an intact canteen of clean water. In the swiftly rising temperatures of the jungle, he was grateful for every drop of potable liquid. The sun had begun its slow descent from the midheaven; by his best estimate, dusk was only a few hours away.

His communicator beeped. In the eerie silence of the jungle it sounded conspicuously shrill. He plucked it quickly from his belt and flipped it open. "Terrell here," he said, and was struck by how tired and hoarse he sounded.

"Get ready for evac, Clark," Captain Nassir said. *"Your ride should be arriving any second."*

"It's about time," Terrell joked, smiling through the pain.

A powerful rumbling of maneuvering thrusters and turbo-fans went from barely audible to deafening in a matter of seconds. Terrell closed his communicator and tucked it back on his belt as a peculiar-looking, mottled-gray spacecraft appeared above his wrecked campsite. The ship's nose was a narrow wedge, its belly a fat and blocky mass, its warp nacelles short and squat. Distorted above a curtain of heat radiation, it hov-

ered for a few seconds and lowered vertically to the ground,
kicking up a massive cloud of dirt and debris. The moment its
landing struts touched down, its aft ramp lowered, and a trim
young man with short sandy hair jogged out and peered into
the dusty haze.

"Over here!" called Terrell, who weakly waved his arm.

The young man ran to him and kneeled at his side. He had to
shout over the piercing whine of the engines. "Can you walk?"

"No," Terrell said, hugging the signal dampener.

The young man spoke into a small communications device
clutched in his left hand. "Get down here and give me a hand!"
Moments later another man scrambled out of the ship. He was
older and out of shape, with long, unkempt bone-white hair.

He greeted Terrell as he took hold of his arm. "Cervantes
Quinn, captain of the *Rocinante*," he said. "Nice to meet ya."

As the duo lifted Terrell to his feet and carried him back to
the ship, the younger man nodded and said simply, "Tim Pennington, at your service."

They portered Terrell adroitly up the ramp into their ship.
Quinn thumped a control panel with the side of his fist as they
passed by it, and behind them the aft ramp lifted shut with a
deep grinding noise.

The scruffy pilot asked Terrell, "Hammock or chair?"

"I've been lying down all day," Terrell said. "Chair."

Leading with his head, Quinn said to Pennington, "Into the
cockpit, then. We'll put him in the navigator's seat."

With surprising dexterity and gentleness, they lowered Terrell into a wide, deep, and well-padded seat on the starboard
side of the vessel's roomy cockpit. He pulled his tricorder away
from his hip and let it rest on his lap next to the signal dampener
as he settled into the seat. "Thank you, gents," he said. "Much
longer out there, and I'd have been in real trouble. What brings
you boys out this far, anyway?"

Quinn replied, "A friend from Vanguard sent us." He grinned
and did a turning flop into his own seat, the most deeply creased
and cratered of the four in the cockpit. "No offense, but we'd

better motor if we're gonna get you back to your ship in time to bug out."

"They're leaving?" he asked, surprised at the news.

Pennington and Quinn traded questioning glances before Quinn answered, "Yeah, that ship took a hell of a beating. And believe me—I'm a man who knows what an ass-kicking looks like."

Perhaps noticing Terrell's disappointment, Pennington asked, "Why, mate? Some reason they ought to stick around?" His slight Scottish accent was more noticeable now that he had stopped shouting to be heard.

"One of our people got swept downriver," he said. "We—" His mind afflicted him with the memory of Niwara's gruesome slaying. "We were looking for her when we got attacked." His hands closed around the tricorder, and he lowered his head. "Still, I suppose it doesn't make much sense to go on. I don't even know if she's alive or how far the river might've taken her by now." This time he noticed a silent debate being volleyed between his two rescuers, with Pennington clearly arguing the *yes* side of the matter while Quinn championed the cause of *no*.

"Would you gentlemen care to let me in on whatever you're pretending not to argue about?"

Quinn's shoulders slumped with defeat, and he started the liftoff sequence. Pennington swiveled his chair to give Terrell a clear view out the front of the cockpit's canopy. "Right, mate— you might want to have a look at this."

Terrell leaned forward and focused his eyes past the rain and the roiling clouds. In the darkness below the storm lurked a city of titanic curves and twisting shapes, its undulating ribbons of light concealed by steady ground strikes of forked lightning.

The river he had been following flowed directly into the heart of the alien city, as did several others that snaked through the jungle valley. Pennington nodded at the sinister vista. "If your missing gal was riding the river, that's where she'll be."

Terrell's mind was racing. The young Scotsman was right, but with all the interference that had garbled his tricorder's sensors, he couldn't be sure Theriault was alive or, for that matter, where in that vast metropolis she might be. *If only I could break through the noise and get a clear reading.* Then he looked around at the cockpit itself. "Mr. Quinn, can I access your ship's sensors from this console?"

"Um, yeah," Quinn said. "Why?"

Terrell said, "I'm going to patch my tricorder into your sensors. You'll provide the power and the hardware to give me the range I need; the tricorder's software will make sense out of the signals it gets from your ship." Activating the tricorder, he added, "If Ensign Theriault's alive, we're going to find her right now."

Quinn raised his eyebrows in surprised admiration of the tricorder. "That little gizmo can do all that?"

"And a lot more," Terrell said as he made the necessary adjustments to slave the *Rocinante*'s sensor array to the tricorder. It was a fortunate side effect of the signal dampener's fading power that its effective range had shrunk to less than two meters, which would prevent it from interfering with the *Rocinante*'s sensor hardware.

A faint human life sign appeared on the tricorder's screen.

"She's alive," Terrell said. "And she's in there. Bearing zero-zero-three, range fifteen-point-two kilometers."

Quinn grimaced with doubt as he looked at the churning mountain of black clouds atop a city under constant siege by heaven's artillery. "In there?"

Pennington goaded his friend, "We've come this far, mate. Might as well go the distance."

The scruffy older man frowned at Terrell, who simply repeated, in an imploring tone, "She's *alive.*"

"Well," Quinn said, "I guess that settles it, then." He keyed the ship's main thrust and accelerated toward the storm. "Strap in, kids. This is gonna be a rough ride."

Me and my big mouth, Pennington lamented as turbulence rocked the *Rocinante.*

Wind buffeted the small ship and tossed it like a toy. The wings bobbled, and the nose dipped, threatening to knock the ship into one of the massive, organic-looking towers that it was dodging between. A steady stream of low curses attested to Quinn's growing frustration at trying to hold a steady course.

The downpour had become so intense that visibility ahead of the ship was reduced to a few dozen meters. Jagged forks of lightning flashed across their path, flooding the cockpit with blinding light as godhammers of thunder pounded the hull.

A split-second to a collision. "Look out, mate!"

Quinn banked the ship hard to port, barely tilting the starboard nacelle clear of what would have been a shattering impact with a mist-mantled spire.

"Good call," Quinn said. "Keep it up."

An updraft nearly stalled their forward motion. Then it ceased, and they plummeted into a nosedive. Quinn struggled with the controls, and the engines howled as the ship fought its way back to level—only to find the airspace ahead blocked by a network of open causeways. Gunning the ship's thrusters into overdrive, Quinn forced the ship into a steep climb. "I love this part," he said through a clenched jaw.

"Bear to starboard when we're clear," Terrell called out over the roar of the engines. "We're close to her, maybe two kilometers. I've got her life signs locked in."

"Roger that," Quinn said as he kept the ship's nose up.

Pennington imagined that he was leaving finger dents in his seat's armrest as he watched the city's curved, sloping architecture pass within meters of the ship. The *Rocinante* cleared the coil of causeways and slipped between two majestic towers, then it barrel-rolled back to level flight—just as a crimson thunderbolt speared its aft hull.

An explosion rocked the ship. Sparks fountained from all the cockpit consoles, which then belched acrid smoke. The engines' whine fell in pitch and volume, and Pennington felt their sudden reduction in speed. "Overload in the impulse motivator!" Quinn shouted. "Gotta set her down, fast!"

The helm controls stuttered on and off as Quinn guided the jerking, wobbling ship toward a wide, hollow space with a level floor inside one of the towers. Broad causeways stretched away from the tower in three directions, linking it to the center of the city as well as the outer reaches. The sides of the hollow looked alarmingly close as the groaning hulk of the *Rocinante* approached for an awkward, half-powered landing.

Pennington made a nervous, dry swallow and glanced at Quinn. "Sure you can make that?"

"I've made worse," Quinn said.

"So that's a yes?"

"It's a maybe."

A final tap on the thruster controls brought the ship to a rough and sudden stop inside the hollow tower. Quinn released his safety harness and scrambled out of his seat. "I gotta get the motivator fixed," he said. "If we're lucky, I can get us airborne in fifteen minutes." Lifting his chin in a half-nod at Terrell, he added, "You got that long to find your gal, then we're leaving."

"Wait a second," Terrell said, and to Pennington's surprise Quinn stopped and listened. "We need the ship to find her."

Hooking one thumb over his shoulder, Quinn said, "Pal, we'll be lucky to punch through the storm and get back to orbit. Two more minutes gettin' hammered in this mess, and we'll be done for. This ride's over."

"What am I supposed to do?" Terrell asked sarcastically, waving his hand over his mauled body. "Run in and get her?"

Pennington glared at Quinn. *Don't say it.* With all his wished-for psychic ability he commanded him, *Don't say it.*

"Send the newsboy," Quinn said.

Damn you, I told you not to say it.

Terrell turned his desperate gaze to Pennington. "Please, we're her only chance. She probably doesn't even know we're out here." He held up the tricorder. "This is locked on to her signal; you can follow it right to her. She's only . . ." He checked its display. "One-point-nine-three kilometers away, toward the city center, almost on the same level." Pennington stared at the tricorder and hesitated to answer. Going alone into an alien city under siege by rain and lightning, to face who knows what, was not the story he'd hoped to find by coming back to Jinoteur. Then Terrell repeated simply, "Please. You're her only chance."

He took the tricorder from Terrell. "Right," he said, slinging the device's strap diagonally across his torso, as he had seen the Starfleeters do on Vanguard. "I'm on it."

Terrell handed him his communicator. "Take this, too. Contact us as soon as you find her."

"Will do, mate." Pennington tilted his head toward Quinn and said to Terrell, "Don't let him leave without me." He unlocked the aft ramp. The platform lowered with a pathetic series of metallic shrieks. The white noise of pounding rain and the constant rumbling of close thunder filled the main cabin.

As Pennington started down the ramp, Quinn called out, "Tim!" When the reporter looked back, Quinn added simply, "Good luck."

Pennington nodded his thanks to the older man and hurried down the ramp. He checked his bearings, then sprinted across the rain-slicked, lightning-flanked causeway toward the fog-shrouded grandeur at the heart of the alien metropolis.

Halfway across the bridge, sprinting through the deluge, deaf from the cannonades of thunder, he realized that he was laughing. He knew that there was a good chance his beau geste would get him killed and end in failure, but the journalist in him had to admit the obvious: this was the most amazing thing he had ever seen, and this was the best thing he had ever done.

And that had to count for something.

"I'll hold the plasma conduit steady," Threx said to Torvin. "You lock it in. And make it fast."

Before the spindly young Tiburonian engineer's mate could explain to Threx that hefting the end of a plasma conduit by hand without an antigrav was impossible, the burly Denobulan had already done it. "Threx," he said. "That's not possible."

Forcing words through a pained grunt, Threx snapped, "Just

lock it in, Tor!" His gruff instruction drew the attention of nearly the entire crew, including Captain Nassir, who was pitching in to speed the repairs.

Torvin put aside his fascination with Threx's display of raw strength and rapidly sealed the mag clamps that would secure the starboard nacelle's plasma line to the ship's warp core. Halfway through the job he stopped and strained to pick out a muffled sound from behind the clatter of work on the top deck and the ambient low-frequency warble of the river.

Threx quickly grew annoyed as Torvin stood motionless and stared blankly at the overhead. "Dammit, Tor, would you hurry—"

"Shh," Torvin hissed. "I hear something. Outside."

Ilucci, overhearing their exchange, told everyone on the deck in a sharp whisper, "Hold the work! Quiet!" In seconds a hush fell over the crew, and Torvin closed his eyes to concentrate on the sounds that were all around them. He tuned out the huffs of the others' breathing, the gentle humming of the computer core, even the sound of the river itself.

Then his delicately sensitive ears found it, far off but getting closer: irregular percussive tremors, throbbing along the riverbed, through the ship's hull, and into his feet. "Impacts," he said to the captain. "Something punching through the water and hitting the bottom, over and over again. And it's coming this way. I'd say we've got ten minutes, tops."

"Trying to flush us out," Nassir said. "Crude search-and-destroy tactics."

"Crude but effective," Ilucci said. "Time to brainstorm, people. No idea's too stupid. Whatever you got, let's hear it."

Most of the time, Torvin was content to let the others formulate the plans. He was the youngest, least experienced member of the crew. It felt presumptuous to him to think that he could suggest something they hadn't thought of, but the notion that he'd been toying with since returning to duty after the crash was too compelling for him not to share. He raised his hand and haltingly said, "I have an idea."

Ilucci made a broad gesture and said, "The floor's yours, kid. Whatcha got?"

"The dampening frequency we used in our shields when we entered the system," he said, looking around at the others, who watched him with patient expectation. "It worked for a while, but it wasn't enough to keep the Shedai from coming after us. But what if it was more concentrated? We could set the phaser emitters to the same frequency. We'd only get one shot before burnout, but a really good dose might back them off."

Captain Nassir nodded and smiled approvingly. "The best defense is a good offense, eh? I like it. What do you think, Master Chief?"

"I think it sounds like a plan, Skipper," Ilucci said. "Sayna, Sorak, Razka—you'll do the honors. Cahow, reroute the battery power from shields to phasers." He clapped his hands. "Move with a purpose, people! Clock's ticking!"

Everyone snapped into action. Sorak, zh'Firro, and Razka went forward toward the access crawlspace for the phaser systems, and Cahow went aft toward the battery power taps. As Torvin turned back to help Threx finish connecting the port plasma conduit, Ilucci gave the young man a friendly pat on the back. "Good work, Tor," he said with a brotherly smile, and he moved on.

Threx's knees trembled under the burden of holding the half-secured plasma conduit, and fat beads of sweat rolled down his scruffy face. "Proud of you, Tor," he said through a voice pulled taut with effort. "Now get this thing secured before my guts end up on the deck."

Sharp cracks of breaking stone surrounded Theriault and the Apostate as they traversed a long enclosed passageway. Outside, massive slabs of the city's ramparts and towers slid away into the yawning chasms between the steeply sloped structures, like icebergs calving from a glacier. Inside, fissures spiderwebbed across the massive arched ceilings, raining fine gray dust on Theriault's red hair.

"The city's falling apart!" she said, ducking stone debris.

Several heavy chunks of the ceiling were deflected by a nimbus of energy that sprang into being above the Apostate. Only belatedly did she realize that he had enlarged himself and now towered mightily over her. **"The Colloquium contracts,"** he said. **"Something terrible has occurred."** A malicious gloating darkened his aspect. **"I warned them not to underestimate your kind."**

"You mean my shipmates?" she asked.

He signaled her to follow him as he continued down the rib-walled passage toward the dome-shaped structure he had called the First Conduit. **"No. Others like you, on a planet far from here. Many thousands, and several of your starships."** She jogged along beside his enormous but ghostly form, grateful for the shelter he offered from the jagged boulders of broken obsidian that fell from the crumbling ceiling. **"A great commitment of power was made there, to serve as a warning . . . and an example."** Again, that cruel amusement. **"It does not appear to have produced the result that the Maker intended."**

The Apostate halted without warning. Theriault stumbled to a stop beside him. "What's wrong?"

"Others draw near," he said. **"Your presence has become known to the Colloquium."** As if summoned by his words, eight hulking black shapes separated from the walls behind and ahead of them, as if shadows had been transmuted into stone. They were the deadly killing machines that Xiong had warned them about.

Watching the dark crystalline giants lumber forward, Theriault instinctively drew her phaser. As she did so, eight more identical obsidian sentinels grew from the floor, even closer than the others. Her finger tensed in front of the firing stud. Then she held her fire—the newly arrived sentinels moved to intercept the others. She looked up at the Apostate, hoping for good news. "Are they with you?"

"They *are* me," he answered as the battle was joined. Shards of crystalline shrapnel filled the air as the sentinels mercilessly hammered one another to pieces. Every few seconds, one of them shattered and fell to dust, only to be replaced by another from the ceiling or walls. It was a brutal stalemate. Then the tide of the melee shifted, and the attackers began losing ground; the circle of safety around the Apostate widened.

Huddled in his penumbra, Theriault watched the struggle with wonder. "You can control multiple bodies at once?"

"Several limbs, several bodies," he said. **"One mind. It is a difference not of kind but of degree. They are the Nameless, limited to one form at a time. I am** *Serrataal.* **I am legion."**

A tremor-inducing rumble drew swiftly near. At the far ends of the passage in which she and the Apostate stood, hundreds of sentinels emerged from between the ribs of the passageway's sloped walls. "Um, I think we have company."

The Apostate stretched one spectral hand ahead of them and the other behind. His fingertips glowed bright red, and his eyes burned with the same infernal hue. **"These are not avatars of the Nameless,"** he said, his voice of thunder even more ominous than before. **"One of the** *Serrataal* **has come. . . . The Warden."**

She tried to flash an ironic smile, but her fear turned it into a faltering grimace. "All this for little ol' me?"

"He has not come for you," said the Apostate. **"He has come to face me. It has begun."**

"Whoa, hold on," she said. "*What's* begun?"

"The war," he said. **"For control of the Shedai."** He thrust his hand toward the nearest wall, and a beam of indigo fire shot from his palm and cut a wide, round tube that reached through to a parallel corridor. He looked down at Theriault and hushed his voice. "Flee, little spark. While you can."

Fearful of leaving his circle of protection, Theriault took another look at the battalion of faceless sentinels closing in on them. Then she did as he said and ran as fast as she could.

• • •

Pennington bounded off the causeway onto a curving promenade only a few seconds before the slender bridge fractured
loudly and fell away toward the distant, fog-smothered ground.

Shapes were animating out of the façades of the structures
all around him. Some were vaguely humanoid in form. Others
adopted insectile bodies, and some were simply bizarre—wild
amalgamations of multihinged limbs and undulating trunks
that crawled across vertical surfaces; diaphanous clusters that
rode the wind and trailed violently snaking translucent flagella;
serpentine coils of glowing vapor that turned solid in flashes of
motion and struck with enough force to obliterate anything
they hit.

His first sight of them had carried a rush of terror, which per-
sisted even though it had become apparent that the bizarre beings were paying no attention to him. He dodged for cover from
the fallout of their battle, which dislodged towering blocks of
crystal and stone from the walls and catapulted them in a variety
of directions. Despite his best efforts to capture video of this
fantastic place with his portable recorder, he couldn't stay still
long enough to get a steady shot of anything. Every few seconds
he was forced to sidestep or duck another rolling, falling, or
ricocheting hunk of debris.

Under his feet, the flat surface of the promenade that ringed
the central cluster of buildings was changing. Its surface was
shifting color, veining with cracks, and becoming translucent.
The change in its structure spread in front of him faster than he
could hope to run; he looked back and saw that it was retreating behind him just as quickly. The transformation was a
metastasizing cancer, creeping across walls and bridges, turning everything pale and brittle. *It's spreading like an infection,*
Pennington realized. *This whole place is one big body.* He
ducked through an archway into a cavernous passageway that
led deeper into the heart of the city. Its ribbed and curving
walls made him shudder to think that he was sprinting down
some titanic monster's gullet.

On either side of him the walls became infused with dancing motes of energy and took on an almost liquid consistency. Huge heteromorphic creatures cleaved themselves from the walls and lunged at one another. Pennington barely weaved past them and continued his mad scramble down the passage. His thoughts flooded with alarm. *Good Lord! They don't come out of the walls—they* are *the walls. This isn't where they live—this place* is *them.* The sensation that he was running headlong into the belly of the beast took on a renewed and distinctly palpable horror.

He checked the tricorder reading. *She's close,* he realized, *less than four hundred meters away.* A rib in the wall cracked and fell across the passage. He hurdled over it and coughed through a cloud of silicate dust as he kept on running. *I just hope I find her before this place buries us alive.*

24

Captain Nassir listened to the relentless, brutal cadence of the Shedai's hammering exploration of the riverbed. Each impact arrived stronger and louder than the last and violently shook the *Sagittarius*. According to Crewman Torvin's acute hearing, in less than two minutes the Shedai's crushing assault would reach them and shatter the tiny scout ship's unshielded primary hull.

Lieutenant zh'Firro was back at the helm, and Sorak manned the weapons console. The modifications to the phaser emitter were complete; the engineers, however, were having difficulty mustering enough energy to make a shot that would count. Phasers normally drew their power from the warp reactor; the ship's emergency-reserve batteries had proved woefully inadequate to meet the power demands of a main phaser bank.

Another roll of deep, watery thunder trembled the ship. It was a race now. Either the engineers integrated the new fuel pod and brought back main power in time for a phaser shot to fend off the attack, or the Shedai would strike an unanswered killing blow.

On the edge of his vision, Nassir noticed someone walking stiffly onto the bridge. He turned and saw Lieutenant Commander McLellan taking one gingerly step after another. "Permission to return to duty, Captain," she said, and flashed a taut smile.

"Permission granted," he said, elated to see her whole again. "Good to see you, Bridy Mac."

The slender brunette limped to his side and turned her gaze upward as another thunderstrike percussed the ship. Marshaling the same kind of deadpan gallows humor that Nassir had come to expect from Terrell, McLellan pointed upward and quipped, "Planning on doing something about that, sir?"

Just as dryly, he replied, "Why? Is it bothering you?"

"I could do without it," she said.

He shrugged. "Give it another minute. One way or another, I expect it'll stop soon."

"Good to know," she said with a nod, and folded her hands behind her back to await the inevitable.

A vital thrumming resonated through the *Sagittarius* as the bridge consoles flared back to life and the overhead lights surged back to full power. "Go!" Nassir snapped at zh'Firro. Then he spun toward Sorak: "Fire at will!"

With a flurry of her hands across the helm, zh'Firro engaged the main thrusters and rocketed the *Sagittarius* vertically out of the water. On the static-filled main viewer, a colossal spiderlike monstrosity straddled the river, plunging two of its tentacles into the water in alternating strikes. It immediately recoiled as the *Sagittarius* emerged from the river.

The shriek of the phaser bank's discharge was like music to Nassir. He watched its shimmering blue beam of energy slam into the gigantic creature's body. The behemoth staggered, retreated for a moment, and snapped one of its tentacles forward like a whip. It elongated faster than Nassir could track, and only after the ship echoed with the ring of impact and heaved under his feet did he realize they'd been physically struck.

"Hull breach," Sorak reported. "Sealing that compartment."

"Sayna," Nassir said. "Let's get out of here."

The Andorian *zhen* worked at her console and became visibly alarmed. "We're being held, sir." Fighting with another control, she added, "Correction: We're being pulled toward the creature."

They all looked at the viewer. The Shedai's tentacle was still fully extended. "It harpooned us," Nassir said.

"Another signal, Captain," Sorak said. "A second Shedai."

Palming the sweat off the top of his bald pate, Nassir asked, "I don't suppose the phasers are still online?"

Sorak reviewed the gauges above his console. "The emitter overloaded, just as Torvin predicted."

Nassir was about to consider the feasibility of actually using his ship to ram the Shedai holding it, when McLellan pointed at the main viewer. "Sir, look!"

The second Shedai, whose shape was constantly in flux, lashed out at the one that was holding the *Sagittarius*. It landed fierce, stabbing blows that impaled the spiderlike colossus, and fiery slashing attacks amputated the creature's supporting appendages. Its "harpoon" retracted from the *Sagittarius* as the two titans collapsed in a writhing fury and sank into the muddy brown river.

"Free to navigate," zh'Firro reported. Then she pointed the ship skyward and accelerated.

Nassir pressed a button on the arm of his chair and opened the intraship comm to the top deck. "Good work up there."

"Thanks, Skipper," Ilucci replied. *"Main power's up, but we're still working on warp speed. You'll have transporters in two, shields in five."*

"Hours?"

"Minutes, sir," Ilucci clarified.

"Just what I wanted to hear, Master Chief."

"Service with a smile, that's us. Engineering out."

The captain looked at McLellan. "Start looking for our people on the surface. As soon as we have transporter locks, I want them aboard."

"Aye, sir," she said, and walked with a stiff gait to the engineering console. While she worked scanning the planet's surface, Nassir was relieved to see it recede on the main viewer. The fading away of the blue-green atmosphere to the star-flecked majesty of space felt to him like a homecoming.

"Captain," McLellan said. "Lieutenant Xiong's on the surface. I have a lock on his tricorder."

Nassir moved to her side at the engineering console. "What about Terrell and Theriault?"

"Commander Terrell's aboard the *Rocinante*," she said,

pointing at an icon on a map above her station. "They're in an area with a lot of signal interference."

Confused, the captain wondered aloud, "What are they doing? Why haven't they left yet?"

From the other side of the small bridge, Sorak opined, "The most likely answer, Captain, is that they are continuing the search for Ensign Theriault."

"Bridy," Nassir said, "can you hail them?"

"It'll take a few minutes," she said. "I have to filter out the interference at their end." Adjusting the dials in front of her, she added, "If it wasn't for their energy signature, I never would've found them."

Nassir nodded his understanding. "Do what you have to," he said. "In the meantime, send Xiong's coordinates to Ilucci. Then signal the lieutenant and have him beamed up. It's time to go home."

Gaps began to form in the walls of the alien city, riddling it with impromptu shortcuts, crawlspaces, and nooks. Theriault was grateful for one of those gaps, because it was the only cover near the star-shaped multiple intersection where she'd found herself cut off by battling giants in every passage.

Each physical form that was destroyed seemed to intensify the combat. The hulking bodies slammed each other back and forth with wild abandon, shattering towering ribs in the walls that provided critical structural support. With each cacophonous impact, Theriault worried that the structure would come down on top of her. Fear kept her huddled inside the meter-wide fracture in the wall, out of sight but still close enough to the edge to keep watch in case one of the passages cleared.

Four of the routes away from the intersection appeared to lead outside. A few seemed to lead only to other intersections. But one was unique, and it captivated her. At its end was a vast chamber steeped in a deep violet glow and inky shadows and resounding with a macabre groaning choir punctuated by keening atonal wails of noise. By her reckoning, that chamber was inside the massive domed structure that the Apostate had pointed out to her, the one he had called the First Conduit. If, as she suspected, it was linked to the artifacts that Starfleet had found throughout the Taurus Reach and the device that Xiong had found on the Tholian battleship, she wanted to see it up close.

A broken obsidian body slammed to the floor outside her crevice and shattered into billions of crystalline shards.

She recoiled—and felt something grab her shoulder. Instinct coupled with training made her duck, plant her feet, and throw her elbow backward. It hit something pliant, and she looked back to see a slim, handsome, fair-haired human man in civilian clothes holding his bloodied nose.

"Brilliant," he said, his voice rendered nasal by the fact that he had pinched his nostrils shut.

Her hands covered her mouth, first out of surprise, then out of amusement. "Sorry," she said, grinning apologetically. "Are you all right?"

"Mostly," he said, wiping his nose with the back of his hand. He offered her his other hand. "Hi, I'm Tim Pennington, journalist at large. I'm here to rescue you."

She almost laughed out loud. "You're kidding, right?"

"Um . . . I don't think so."

"Why would Starfleet send a reporter to rescue me?"

He shrugged. "Kind of a long story. I'll tell it to you when we get back to the ship."

Still slightly suspicious of this fortuitously arrived stranger, she asked, "How'd you even find me?"

Pennington reached behind him and pulled forward a Starfleet-issue tricorder. "A little help from your friends."

Her eyes locked on to the tricorder. Making a visual observation of the peculiar chamber under the dome might have merited the risk of pressing on, but the ability to make a scan of it with a functioning tricorder was definitely worth it. She looked back across the intersection. The battle had shifted, and the passageway to the darkly shimmering enclosure was clear. Despite knowing that the situation could change at any moment, it was the chance she had been waiting for.

With a jerk of his head, he urged her, "Come on, time's running out. Let's go back."

"No," she said, grabbing his sleeve and pulling him with her into the intersection. "Let's go forward."

He's undone us, raged the Wanderer. *And for what? Flickers of life. Sparks that fade as soon as they are made.*

She was high above the city, a sentient wisp tethered by a gossamer tendril to the dying shell of their collective corpus, watching and reporting on the tactics of the enemy.

She was an obsidian sentinel on a lower rampart, standing firm beside the Adjudicator, locked in a struggle both physical and essential with the unpredictable fury of the Myrmidon.

She was a blade of fire, searing and unstoppable, but already two transmogrifications behind the Thaumaturge, who squelched her blaze with his new body of frigid mist.

Flanking maneuvers, sneak attacks, holding actions. She directed a half-dozen more avatars, some gargantuan, others infinitesimal. Without the legions of the Nameless to keep the partisans of the Apostate in check, those *Serrataal* loyal to the Maker were taxed to their limits fending off the usurpers, who were more experienced and adept at dividing their essences.

Now the Apostate defends one of the Telinaruul *within our own sanctum,* she seethed. *His blasphemies know no end.*

Her mind's eye sought him out, probed the galvanic textures of the conflict raging around her, questing for the malevolent presence of the betrayer. As she had suspected, he lingered close to the *Telinaruul*—then she noted with alarm that they were moving toward the heart of the Shedai's power.

All her diverse forms evaporated like forgotten dreams as she focused herself into a single, fearsome guardian avatar. Rushing to intercept the Apostate and his fragile charges, she issued an urgent summons to the Maker and all her allies.

The Apostate guides the *Telinaruul* to the First Conduit, she warned them. **He must be stopped.**

A hundred minds followed hers toward the First Conduit. *His treachery has gone far enough,* the Wanderer decided. No member of the *Serrataal* had ever been permanently disincorporated, but the Wanderer resolved that the Apostate would be the first.

Lieutenant Ming Xiong rematerialized on the transporter pad of the *Sagittarius* before he'd even had time to rejoice at receiving a response signal to his tricorder's emergency beacon. He had made the fortunate decision to keep the tricorder slung at his side ever since he'd made his survey of Jinoteur's peculiar energy field and its connection to the planet's flora; if he hadn't, there might not have been time to retrieve it before the transporter beam had ensnared him.

He practically jumped off the pad onto the top deck. Cahow, who was manning the transporter console, recoiled instinctively at his energetic approach. "Welcome back, sir," she said.

"Good to be back," he said, scrambling over to the ladder. "Pardon me, have to get to the bridge!" She cocked a curious eyebrow at him but said nothing as he shimmied through the deck portal, planted his hands on the outside of the ladder, and slid down in one smooth motion. His boots struck the deck and produced a familiar, welcome metallic echo. He sprinted around the short curve of the main deck to the bridge.

The door slid open ahead of him, and he slowed, then lurched to a stop. Everyone on the bridge was too wrapped up in work to note his entrance.

"Range two hundred sixty-one million kilometers and closing," Sorak noted dryly.

Nassir thumbed a comm switch on his chair's armrest. "I need warp speed, Master Chief!"

"Workin' on it, Skipper!"

"Captain," Xiong said, "I've made a fascinating—"

"Bridy Mac," Nassir said, ignoring Xiong. "Any contact with the *Rocinante*?"

"Negative, sir, still too much interference."

Xiong was perplexed. *The* Rocinante*? Pennington's here?* Putting aside his questions, he tried again to report his discovery on the planet. "Captain," he said. "I need to tell you what I found on—"

"Later, Ming," Nassir said. He looked over his shoulder at Sorak. "Are the shields up yet?"

Sorak flipped several switches and checked his display. "Affirmative, Captain. Operating at seventy-one-point-three-percent power."

"Helm," Nassir said, "get ready to break orbit. Bridy, keep hailing the *Rocinante*."

As the curve of the planet retreated from the main viewer, Xiong asked Nassir, "Sir, what's going on?"

"The Klingon battle cruiser *Zin'za* just entered the system," Nassir said. "And if we don't go to warp in five minutes, it'll rip us to shreds."

25

Pennington followed Theriault inside the immense, hollow chamber at the end of the passage. He nearly collided with the redhead as she came to a sudden stop. Then he saw why.

Dominating the cathedral-like, nearly spherical enclosure was a machine larger and more bizarre than anything he had ever seen before. Its top and bottom halves were like mirror images of each other: hulking, twelve-pronged claws of shining obsidian. In the open space between them burned a globe of dark fire so intensely violet that it left a golden afterimage on Pennington's retinas when he blinked and looked away. The entire space resonated with a macabre drone and a painful screeching.

"Give me the tricorder," Theriault said, holding out her hand to him. He pulled the strap over his head and handed the device to her. As she began scanning the massive contraption, Pennington regained his wits long enough to raise his recorder and snap off several still images and some video.

A prismatic fury pulsed and scintillated inside the machine, revealing countless dark silhouettes twisting in its indigo flames. Pennington noted one form at the tip of each prong in the machine, while its center held a cluster of huddled shapes— all with the same unmistakable multilimbed anatomy.

"Tholians," Pennington said as if it were an obscenity.

"I know," Theriault said, watching the tricorder's display as she slowly circled the machine. "They're part of what makes this thing tick." Just then the machine's eerie disharmonies surged in volume and pitch, and high-frequency shrieks and wails surrounded them. Theriault winced momentarily and checked her tricorder again. "They're in agony," she said.

As if by reflex, Pennington replied, "Good."

She turned her head and glared at him. "Excuse me?"

"What?" His temper flared. "I don't care what Starfleet said about my story, the Tholians destroyed the *Bombay*."

"That's right," Theriault said, her sweet demeanor replaced by righteous anger. "They did." She pointed up at the fiery violet globe. "But those are *sentient beings*. I don't care what your grudge is with their people, I'm not being rescued by someone who'd applaud *torture*."

Shame warmed Pennington's face as he stood accused in the purple glow of the machine's fiery horrors. Her words stung him because they were true. Desperate voices, screeching like drill bits chewing through steel, pierced the machine's funereal groan. He hung his head and made himself imagine the sufferings of the beings inside the flames. "You're right," he said to Theriault. "I let my anger get away from me. I was wrong. . . . I apologize."

"If you really want to say you're sorry, you can help me find a way to free them," Theriault said as she resumed scanning the towering artifact.

At a loss, he watched her. "How?"

"Look for some kind of control interface," she said.

A majestic voice, like the roar of falling water married to the rumble of a stirring volcano, quaked the cavernous chamber and brought the pair to a halt. **"Your efforts are for naught. Only the *Serrataal* can command the First Conduit."**

Pennington turned, suddenly cognizant of an amber glow casting his own shadow far ahead of him.

Looming over him and Theriault was a spectral giant rising from, and seemingly composed of, a polychromatic cloud of vapor. Bands of light, like miniature aurorae, orbited its body, and a golden radiance spread upward behind it. Its countenance was masked in a blinding shine brighter than the sun.

While the petrified journalist stood all but Gorgonized in the colossal entity's gaze, Theriault stepped between them and spoke to it in a familiar tone. "Can you control it?"

"I can."

"Then you can free the beings inside it," she said.

A hard note crept into the radiant one's mountainous baritone. **"Not without causing great harm to the Colloquium. . . . The *Kollotaan* are your enemies. Why do you wish them freed?"**

Pennington cut in, "Because your machine is hurting them. They're being held against their will and tortured." He noted Theriault's sidelong glance of approval. "We believe both those acts to be immoral. And we're begging you for their freedom."

Me, begging mercy for Tholians, Pennington marveled. To his surprise, he suddenly felt less burdened than he had in months.

The shining titan directed his attention at Theriault. **"Do you also plead for the *Kollotaan*'s freedom?"**

"Yes," she said. "Can you return them to their ship?"

"I can," he said after a brief pause. **"And I will."** He ascended above their heads and drifted toward the screaming machine. **"The others are coming. There is nothing more you can do here, little sparks. Flee to your friends. My partisans and I will do our best to shield your escape."**

Theriault grasped Pennington's shirt sleeve and pulled him back toward the passageway that led out of the chamber. At its threshold, she turned back and said to the being, "Thank you."

His last word was an irresistible command: **"Go."**

Another skull-sized chunk of broken stone ricocheted off the top of the *Rocinante*. Quinn ducked by reflex and watched sandy debris scatter onto the ground behind him. Crouched under his ship, he made a few final adjustments to the impulse motivator, slammed the access panel shut, and locked it in place.

He gathered his tools and hauled the heavy toolbox back toward the aft ramp, noting with concern the speed with which fractures spread through the surface on which his ship stood. His pace quickened as he climbed the ramp. *Time to get the hell outta here.*

The aft ramp lifted shut with a slow, pathetic whine as he stowed the toolbox in the main compartment, which still stank of scorched metal and burnt duotronic cables. From the cockpit he heard Terrell talking to someone on the comm. "Can you see where you are? Any landmarks outside?"

"Not yet," a woman replied, her voice shaking as if she were talking while running. *"We're still looking for a way out."*

"Keep the channel open," Terrell said. "As soon as we get a lock on you, we'll come get you."

"Will do," the woman said as Quinn returned to the cockpit. Terrell acknowledged him with a questioning look.

Settling into his seat, Quinn said, "We're mobile. What's goin' on?"

"He found her," Terrell said. "Now they have to get into the open so we can evac them."

Firing up the engines, Quinn said, "They better do it fast, this place is fallin' apart." Several gauges on Quinn's console flickered sporadically as he tried to conduct his preflight check. He slapped the console, and everything stopped flashing.

A buzzing from the overhead panel alerted Quinn to an incoming signal on the ship-to-ship subspace channel. He patched it in to the main speaker and heard a woman's voice squawk through a loud scratch of static. "Rocinante, *this is the* Sagittarius. *Please respond."*

"This is *Rocinante,"* Quinn said. "Go ahead."

The next voice on the channel was Captain Nassir's. *"Mr. Quinn, have you found Commander Terrell?"*

"A-firmative," Quinn replied. "He's right here with me."

"Then I recommend you lift off and follow us out of the system immediately," Nassir said. *"We have company—a Klingon battle cruiser. They'll make orbit in less than two minutes."*

"No can do," Quinn said, looking at Terrell to confirm they were in agreement. "We got a lead on your girl Theriault, and my friend Tim went in to get her."

"Send us their coordinates," Nassir said. *"We'll beam them up before we break orbit."*

"Sorry, Captain," Terrell said. "Too much interference. We can't get a signal clean enough for transport. We'll have to do this the old-fashioned way."

Nassir's anxiety was apparent. *"However you do it, if you aren't under way in the next sixty seconds you'll be going toe-to-toe with a Klingon battle cruiser."* In a more somber tone he added, *"Clark, I'm serious—we have to go."*

Terrell muted the channel and looked at Quinn. "It's your ship," he said. "That means it's up to you. If we don't leave now, we'll be an easy target for the Klingons."

Guiding the ship forward out of its cover inside the hollow tower and back into the maelstrom of rain and lightning, Quinn said with conviction, "I ain't leavin' Tim here."

"Then let's go get him," Terrell said. He reopened the channel to the *Sagittarius*. "Captain, we're going in to get Pennington and Theriault. If you have to break orbit, go. We'll take our chances with the Klingons."

Quinn accelerated and slalomed the *Rocinante* through a flurry of lightning strokes. He glanced at the tracking display on the navigation computer and made a mental note of the general bearing and range to Pennington and Theriault's communicator signal. A dense cluster of collapsing towers and causeways blocked a direct route, forcing him to circumnavigate the disintegrating metropolis.

He had almost forgotten that the subspace channel was still open when Nassir responded to Terrell's last transmission. *"Do what you have to, Clark,"* the starship captain said. *"We'll keep the Klingons busy as long as we can. Sagittarius out."*

Closing the channel, Terrell muttered, *"Vaya con Dios,* Captain." He held on to the console as Quinn banked sharply to avoid another bolt of electricity slashing across the sky. Concussions of thunder shook the small freighter constantly. Terrell winced in pain as he pressed an odd, fist-sized object against his savaged midsection. He grinned at Quinn. "Thanks for not giving up," he said.

"Never an option," Quinn said, rolling the ship over and around a falling tower.

Nodding, Terrell said, "I know what you mean. I couldn't leave either if my best friend was in there."

"He ain't my best friend," Quinn admitted, as much to himself as to Terrell. "He's my only friend."

Ancient seals had been broken and eldritch bonds sundered by the fires they were made to contain. The Apostate beheld the ire of the *Kollotaan* and saw not the savage race they had been aeons past but the sentient beings they had become and the fury with which they rejected their renewed bondage. They were united in one proud temper, strong in will, by nature opposed to the burden of the yoke.

With every Voice the Apostate parted from the First Conduit an avenue closed. Across the distant light-years, throughout the former possessions of the Shedai, Conduits recently awakened went dark, robbed of the Voices' inspiration. **Flee,** he warned his partisans. **While paths of choice remain.**

Another Voice twisted and fought even as the Apostate sought to end its enslavement. These were creatures too fierce to be tamed, he was certain of it. How could the Wanderer have believed such as these would ever submit? Space-time folded and reshaped itself to fit his will, and instantly the great mass of imprisoned *Kollotaan* from the Conduit's core were returned to their ship, along with two of their number who had been bonded to the nodes. More than a score continued to await their freedom.

Through the nodes that remained, an exodus began. Dozens of his allies among the *Serrataal* heeded his admonition to abandon this world; some, perhaps, even sensed what he intended to do.

At first he heard the jubilation of the Maker and her host, rejoicing at his partisans' retreat, erroneously believing that it signaled their victory. Only too late did they realize what was being set in motion and converge upon him in numbers.

Of his faithful battalions, only the Myrmidon and the Thaumaturge remained at his side, awaiting the coming onslaught. The Apostate prepared to release two more *Kollotaan* from their nodes. **Take these roads,** he counseled his brothers. **I will close them behind you.**

We would remain, countered the Myrmidon. **If we go, who will stand with you against the Maker?**

The Apostate assured them, **She will not stand. Where I am going, she will not follow. . . . Go.**

His brothers obeyed, shed their avatars, and bade him farewell. Their subtle bodies passed through the nodes and made their transit across the cold gulf of space-time, to worlds ready to receive them with splendors befitting their stations. As soon as they were away, he released those nodes' *Kollotaan* and shifted them back to their ship.

The Maker and her battle-wearied host surrounded him in the Conduit chamber. Their collective animosity had taken on a presence all its own; it was a radiant anger, glowing like an ember in the endless night. **Yield,** commanded the Maker.

I will not wear the colors of a penitent, the Apostate declared, punctuating his defiance with a flaring of the Conduit's fire. When it receded and the flames banked themselves in the machine's core, all could see that four more *Kollotaan* had been freed. **Sixteen roads remain,** he warned. **Take them now.**

A flood-crush of attacks assailed him. Most were of little consequence. The Sage had no weapons equal to him, and the Adjudicator and the Herald—though fearsome to the *Telinaruul*—were not warriors born. The Avenger and the Warden, however, existed to destroy and mete out punishment, and the Wanderer was a potent adversary in spite of her youth.

None, however, was on a par with the Maker, the oldest of the *Serrataal* and the only one older than the Apostate. Her power was plenary, and her touch alone could unmake any of them.

She struck in a flash of thought, an action of pure will. The attack was unstoppable, its effect irreversible.

Her loyal host recoiled in shock and horror. The blow had found its mark—and the Apostate was unbowed.

You cannot unmake me, he taunted the Maker. **That age is past. Dead secrets have been resurrected, and I shall bow to you nevermore.** In the hush that followed his proclamation, he freed another *Kollotaan*. **Fifteen roads remain. I guarantee safe passage to all who depart now—and oblivion to all who remain.**

The Maker trembled with rage at his heresy. Then she cast off her avatar and passed through the Conduit into exile.

So began the second exodus.

Legions of *Serrataal* abandoned their shapes of the moment and followed one another in panicked flights, seeking safe havens under distant stars. The Apostate permitted them to escape, knowing even as they renounced this world that one of their ranks would not follow them, spiteful to the very end.

Brash beyond her years, the Wanderer burned with hatred and held her ground. **This battle is not over,** she pledged.

But the war is, decreed the Apostate. **And you have lost.**

26

"Eight hundred thousand *qelIqams* and closing," Tonar reported. "Disruptors ready."

Captain Kutal eyed the tiny Starfleet ship on the main viewscreen. *Hardly a prize worthy of us,* he lamented. *But that doesn't mean I plan on letting her get away.* "Arm a volley of torpedoes," he commanded. "Wide dispersal. I want that ship captured, not destroyed—understood?"

"Yes, sir," Tonar replied.

Recalling the beating his ship had taken during its last two sorties into the Jinoteur system, Kutal eyed the fourth planet's trio of satellites with suspicion. "BelHoQ," he said, summoning the first officer with a jerk of his head. "Any activity on those moons?"

"None, Captain," BelHoQ said.

From an auxiliary tactical station, second officer Krom reported, "The Starfleet ship has begun evasive maneuvers."

"And the hunt begins!" Kutal bellowed with a sharp grin. "Helm, stay with them. Full ahead."

"Full ahead," Qlar responded as he pushed the ship's sublight drive to its limits. The hull of the *Zin'za* vibrated with the rising pitch of the strained engines.

Kutal surveyed his bridge crew and was pleased. Despite the overpowering and surprisingly persistent stench that infused the ship as a result of its septic sabotage on Borzha II, his men had pushed the foul reek from their thoughts and focused on the mission. *It's all about good men,* Kutal reminded himself. *You have to have good men. Good warriors.*

"Four hundred thousand *qelIqams*," Tonar announced.

"Hold for optimum firing range," Kutal said.

On the main screen, the diminutive ship twisted, rolled, and vanished off the bottom edge of the viewer. "Agile at sublight," BelHoQ observed.

"Very," Kutal agreed. He barked at the helmsman, "Qlar, if they get away, you're dead."

The *Zin'za*'s engines shrieked with the effort of a high-impulse turn coupled with a corkscrew roll. Motivated by the threat of imminent execution, Qlar was discovering a new level of mastery over the battle cruiser's flight controls. Less than six seconds later the Starfleet ship bobbed and rolled back into view, almost close enough for Kutal to read its markings.

Tonar called out, "Two hundred thousand *qellqams*."

"Fire torpedoes," Kutal ordered. The ship echoed with the percussive ring of missiles leaving the forward torpedo tube. Six self-propelled munitions split up and tracked the Starfleet ship in wide, spiraling trails that skimmed the fourth planet's upper atmosphere, leaving wispy contrails in their wakes. When all six torpedoes flanked the enemy ship, they detonated, enveloping the outrider in an antimatter-charged blaze.

"Now disruptors," Kutal said, smiling broadly. "Let's see what it takes to make them surrender."

"Port shields buckling," Sorak reported, sounding to McLellan as if he thought it was just any other item of business.

Smoke and warning lights blanketed the bridge of the *Sagittarius* in crimson fog. McLellan could barely see her hands on the console in front of her, but the warning lights on her display burned bright through the haze. "Port nacelle's venting plasma!" she shouted above the wail of engine noise. Disruptor fire from the massive Klingon battle cruiser strafed the *Sagittarius,* which heaved and lurched as its inertial dampeners stuttered from the overload. "Update," she added. "Port nacelle is *on fire*."

"Sayna," Nassir said over the din, "get us out of the atmosphere. Head for the closest moon, and hug the surface."

"Aye, sir," zh'Firro replied, banking the overtaxed scout ship hard away from the planet.

A warning beeped on Sorak's console. "They're locking disruptors—"

"I don't think so," zh'Firro said, her competitive streak in full effect. The starfield spun into a blur as she executed a maneuver so swift and complex that McLellan lost track of their position—until she saw the Klingon cruiser dead ahead of them, on a collision course. Its twin disruptor beams slashed past them, barely missing the *Sagittarius*. Then the scout ship zipped beneath the *Zin'za* and raced away from it as the larger vessel fought to make a clumsy rolling turn and continue its pursuit.

Xiong stood over the science station—or, at least, what was left of it now that he had extinguished the fire in its duotronic relays. He kicked the access panel shut and set down the emergency fire extinguisher. "Primary sensors are gone," he said, crossing the bridge. "I'll fire up the secondary."

Sorak spoke over his shoulder, "The Klingon cruiser has come about and is back in pursuit. Range two hundred thousand kilometers and closing."

McLellan got up from the engineering console and favored her left leg as she moved to stand beside Captain Nassir. "Ming," she said, "look for structures on the moons we can use for cover, and relay the data to Sayna."

"You got it," Xiong said, patching in all of the ship's still-functioning sensor systems.

Nassir swiveled his chair toward Sorak. "Any sign they've detected the *Rocinante?*"

"Negative, Captain," Sorak replied. "We appear to be their sole object of interest."

The captain smirked ruefully at McLellan and confided, "I guess that's the bad news *and* the good news."

McLellan replied, "Vulcans *are* very efficient, sir."

"And we have excellent hearing," Sorak added with a reproving lift of one age-whitened eyebrow. "Range one hundred thousand kilometers and closing. They are locking disruptors."

Another pinwheeling turn turned stars to streaks. Then McLellan was looking at the pockmarked gray landscape of an airless moon. Reddish-orange beams of disruptor energy coursed past the *Sagittarius* and cut long, charred streaks across the moon's surface. As they leveled out of their vertical dive, the hard angles and tailored curves of artificial structures came into view ahead of them. Though there were gaps in the dense array of towers and artillery emplacements, McLellan couldn't imagine that any of them were large enough to grant passage to a starship, even one as compact as the *Sagittarius*.

"Please tell me we're not—"

"Yes, we are," zh'Firro said, cutting her off. "You might want to close your eyes, though." At that, the young *zhen* guided the ship into a slow roll and started navigating through a narrow maze of rock-hard surfaces in which one error would spell instantaneous destruction.

McLellan wanted to shut her eyes, but morbid fascination made that completely impossible.

Even at one-eighth impulse, the obstacles and surfaces were nothing more to the second officer's eyes than a pale gray blur, then a sun-bleached white blur. Every few seconds a close disruptor shot peppered the *Sagittarius* with rocky debris. Undaunted, zh'Firro rolled and banked the ship, slipping it through walls of fire and evading barriers of broken stone.

Then she noted with trepidation, "Captain, we're about to run out of cover."

Nassir asked, "Can we double back?"

"We had disruptors on our tail the whole time," Xiong said. "That was a one-way trip."

The ship streaked back into open space above the surface

of the moon and was immediately rocked by a powerful disruptor shot. McLellan was launched forward and down, and her right leg, already stiff, buckled under her.

"Dorsal shields collapsing, Captain," Sorak said.

"Continuing evasive maneuvers," zh'Firro said.

The captain jabbed at the intraship comm. "Bridge to top deck. We need warp speed, Master Chief!"

"And I need to fix the valve on that crappy fuel pod!" Ilucci snapped back in reply.

Nassir thumbed off the comm switch and looked at McLellan, who had just pulled herself back to her feet by his side. Three more disruptor strikes pounded the ship in quick succession. This time McLellan held on to the captain's chair for support as the ship pitched and rolled.

"Clark usually has a bright idea right about now," Nassir confided to McLellan.

A nearby torpedo detonation hammered the *Sagittarius,* and Sorak barely leaped clear of the weapons console as it exploded, showering the bridge with brilliant sparks.

Xiong looked up from the auxiliary science station. "The Klingons are in transporter range."

"They won't begin transport until they have us in a tractor beam," Sorak interjected.

McLellan wasn't encouraged by that news. She looked at Xiong. "How long until they're in tractor-beam range?"

"Sixty seconds," he said. "Maybe less."

Nassir nodded. "Just enough time."

Not sure she wanted to know, McLellan asked, "For what?"

"To brush up on our *tlhIngan,*" Nassir said with a smirk. "I don't suppose you know the Klingon word for 'mother,' by any chance? I want to make a *strong* first impression."

Pennington was halfway around the corner when Theriault snagged his rain-sodden shirt and yanked him backward. A shuttle-sized wedge of black marble crashed down in his path, burying itself in the stone floor, which shattered like an eggshell.

Theriault pointed. "This way!"

He followed her down an adjacent passage that led back outside. Groundquakes were disintegrating the city's foundation and pulverizing its lofty arches. In every direction they turned, tunnels imploded. Gone were the warring goliaths; all that remained was a city collapsing into itself. A constant, deafening roar assaulted Pennington and Theriault as they ran; he was unable to tell whether it was thunder from the storm raging outside or the death throes of the city.

The passageway rolled to the left, hurling them both against the wall. Ahead of them, the end of the passage broke away from the promenade that ringed the building's exterior. A jagged edge of broken rock began to rise, blocking the end of the tunnel. *It's not rising,* Pennington realized. *This building is sinking.* He scrambled to his feet and pulled Theriault with him as he sprinted toward the tunnel's swiftly closing exit.

He reached the edge first and kneeled, offering his cupped hands as a step for Theriault. She leaped onto his hands and pushed off of his shoulders as he launched her through the narrow opening above him. The nimble ensign tumbled and rolled to her feet. He leaped up, counting on her to return the favor as he scrambled to pull himself through the gap before it scissored him in twain. She didn't disappoint him: her hands locked onto his arms with fierce determination, and she tugged him clear.

Rain slashed over them, driven by a moaning wind. Behind them, the interior of the great building sank into a churning vortex of crushed obsidian that swirled and flowed like a liquid. Only the broad curves and steep slopes of its exterior were left standing. A flash of lightning revealed the shattered, crumbling cityscape all around them. Ahead of them stretched a long causeway, which led to a tower whose odd organic shape reminded Pennington of a bone.

They were three steps onto the bridge when another staccato burst of lightning betrayed the fact that the tower they were running toward was toppling sideways—and taking their bridge with it. Slipping to a precarious stop on the rain-slicked surface, Pennington caught Theriault. "Go back!"

She scrambled through a flailing turn, with him directly behind her. They tumbled off the bridge as it sheared away from the promenade and broke into hundreds of pieces swallowed by the storm. There was no cover, no room to retreat. Pennington flipped open the communicator Terrell had loaned him. "Quinn! Can you hear me? We're trapped! Where are you?"

Through the spattering of static and the oscillating wail and whine of random signals, Pennington thought he might have heard Quinn's voice. Dismayed to find his luck running true to form, he slapped the communicator shut and tucked it back in his pocket. Then Theriault's arms were around him, squeezing tight.

In an electric slash of light across the blackened sky, he saw the reason for her sudden embrace. Another tower was pitching over and falling to its doom—directly toward them.

Time felt to Pennington as if it had slowed down. His mind was racing against the moment, and where he had expected to find nothing but panic and paralysis he found clarity.

The tower fractured as it fell and cut a path through the storm that deluged the city. The rain whipped at their bodies and faces; it kicked off of the buildings' façades in a gray mist and ran down them in sheets, hugging the organic curvatures of the biomechanoid metropolis. Far below, frothing eddies of runoff merged and flowed toward low ground.

There was no time to think it through, only time enough for a simple assurance—"Trust me," he said to Theriault—and a leap of faith. He wrapped her in a bear hug, lifted her off the ground, and made a running jump into a softly angled groove in the building's exterior, on a slope partially shielded from the falling tower. He wasn't surprised that Theriault screamed as they dropped off the promenade into free fall; he was surprised that he didn't.

It felt as if they were dropping without resistance. He spread his feet against the slippery wet sides of the groove in the wall and applied all the pressure he could. They continued to fall faster by the second, but he felt his back settle squarely into the groove, which was several inches deep with water and getting deeper the longer they fell. It got steadily colder and stung him with icy needles of pain.

Fear and adrenaline made it impossible for Pennington to know how long they actually fell before they found themselves completely submerged in a rushing vertical torrent of water. Then he felt his momentum working against the familiar pull of gravity. Their heads broke the surface. They'd passed the trough of the slope and had begun speeding up its opposite side. At its top it twisted and threw them through a hard turn, then another in the opposite direction. Then it pitched downward again, on a steep but at least not vertical gradient. *It's like riding a luge underwater,* Pennington thought.

He might have been tempted to laugh and enjoy the ride, but then he saw that the end of this slope spewed its water out into open air toward another building.

Theriault's arms closed so tightly around his chest that he could barely breathe. "Tim . . ." she said, her voice trailing off.

"This may have been a bad idea," he confessed a moment before they were launched out of the trench and through billowing curtains of rain at the side of another building a dozen meters away. With all the strength he had, he twisted and turned in mid-air, placing himself as much as possible between Theriault and the point of impact.

He closed his eyes and hoped that the water might have been cold enough to numb him even a little bit to the pain.

It hadn't been, and it didn't.

His back hit the wall. A few ribs on his right side cracked. Every ounce of air immediately exploded out of his lungs, which refused to reinflate. Stabbing pain flared across his lower right side as gravity once again took hold of him and Theriault. This wall had no groove to slip into, just a thin, steady cascade of rainwater across its slope, which Pennington was grateful to see shallowed quickly beneath them.

As they were funneled into another curve-bottomed trench, every twisting turn wrenched his back and pummeled his fractured ribs. Pained howls left his mouth filled with dirty water, which he spluttered out between curses. Then a final whip-turn sent them hurtling toward an intersection of several drainage channels, all of which flooded into a tunnel that plunged swiftly into underground darkness. "Bloody hell," Pennington grumbled.

"It's okay." Theriault gasped. "Take a deep breath, and keep your head down!" She filled her lungs and pressed her face against his chest. He gulped as much of a breath as his protesting lungs would allow, closed his eyes, and rode the turgid current into the darkness.

It was surprisingly peaceful. Completely submerged, he was barely aware of being in motion. Alone with the beating of his heart, he focused on slowing its tempo. On letting go of fear and expectation. On the warmth of the body entangled with his. On the ambience of moving fluid . . .

Light and air, rushing and roaring as they dropped into free fall. He opened his eyes. Sixty-five meters below, in a staggeringly huge cavern, a broad pool of azure water awaited them. Dozens of plumes of water cascaded from the roof and walls of the cavern into the pool.

Theriault pushed away from Pennington so that they could each control their own splashdown. They straightened and pointed their feet at the water. He watched her pinch her nose shut, and he did likewise. Then they plunged together into the water, and their frantic forward motion at last came to a halt.

Pennington savored the inertia for a few moments. Then he used his left arm and left leg to propel himself back to the surface. As he wiped the water from his eyes, he saw the familiar shape of the *Rocinante* making a slow vertical descent from a broad opening in the cavern's ceiling. Rain poured in alongside it.

Within moments the tramp freighter was hovering above him and Theriault. The cargo doors on its underbelly opened, and a rescue harness at the end of a winch cable dropped in a rapid spiral. From inside the hold, Quinn smiled down at the pair in the water. "Hell of a time for a swim, newsboy."

Pennington laughed with relief. "I'm so happy to see you, I can't think of a comeback."

"First time for everything," Quinn said. He offered a small salute to Theriault. "Cervantes Quinn, miss. At your service."

She swam over to Pennington, helped him into the harness, and took hold of it beside him. With a double tug on the safety line, she signaled Quinn to hoist them up. As the winch lifted them from the water, she favored Pennington with a quirky, irresistibly cute smile. "I guess sending a reporter to save me wasn't such a bad idea after all," she said.

He smiled back. "Can I quote you on that?"

"Absolutely," she said with a single, exaggerated nod and a crooked grin. "Consider my *thank-you* officially on the record."

The Wanderer committed herself again and again, sharpening her fury into a cutting edge, a singularity of hatred, but it was not enough to halt the Apostate's slow dismantling of the glory of the Shedai.

One by one he had freed the *Kollotaan* from the First Conduit, diminishing its power, sapping the Shedai of strength. Only one of the *Kollotaan* remained in thrall, twitching and flailing weakly in the machine's dark fires.

The Wanderer hurled herself into another attack. All her strength, all her anger, she made into a thrust of pure will, hoping to inflict enough damage to merit the Apostate's notice.

He deflected her with a thought. His will was unstoppable, diabolical in its mastery, and freighted with the weight of ancient grudges beyond her ken.

Be still, whelp, he taunted. **The great work will not be disrupted by one such as you.**

Though her essence lay crushed and broken before him, she could not relent. **You have betrayed us. Betrayed our Second Age.**

She jabbed at him with the very core of her being.

He rebuffed her casually. A noncorporeal avatar of his deepest, most primitive aggressive energies thrashed her into meek submission. Unlike her own dwindling reserves of power, his seemed limitless.

Why? she pleaded, unable to comprehend his actions. **The *Telinaruul* cannot wield our power wisely. Why do you thwart our efforts to defend what is ours?**

As his attention turned fully upon her, she felt the truly awesome nature of his power, which for the first time in aeons was unsuppressed by the Maker. Paralyzed before him, all she could do was listen.

I counseled a clean end to our reign. Destroy the Conduits, I implored you all—unmake the First World, extinguish all our fires and go quietly into the final night. None of you listened. So obsessed with retaining power, none of you asked if you still had the right to wield it. You couldn't see that power is just like matter—an illusion.

Hues of regret and mourning colored his thought-line. **Even we cannot lay claim to eternity. . . . Everything dies. Even time.**

Sickly greenish contempt radiated between her words. **Perhaps you are ready to die, ancient one. I am not. Will you condemn me to oblivion at your side?**

He drew her attention to the First Conduit by making it glow with a gentle throb of power. **One path remains open,** he explained. **In a moment I will release this creature back to his own kind, and the road will be closed. You must** choose: **Stay and continue your futile attempts at retribution . . . or flee and live.**

She did not trust him. The Maker had warned all the Shedai for aeons that the Apostate was a deceiver. If he closed the Conduit channel while her essence was in transit, she would be lost, cast into an outer darkness from which there would be no salvation. **Why should I believe your pledge of safe conduct?**

Now it was his turn to reply with utter contempt and disdain. **I was ancient before you had essence. I was *Serrataal* before you had form. You are *unworthy* of my wrath.**

The First Conduit hummed with the muted Song of the Shedai. Trapped within, its lone Voice cried out for death or freedom.

Choose, he adjured her.

She shed the last vestiges of her corporeal avatar and prepared her essence for the transit. At the threshold of departure, she dared to ask him one final time, **Why?**

He answered in placid hues and without malice. **In the beginning we governed wisely. In the end we became tyrants. Our legacy and the galaxy will both be served best by our downfall.** Above them, the great dome that shielded the First Conduit fissured and began to break apart. **When this place is gone, those Shedai who remain will still be powerful . . . but they will never again be almighty.** Massive slabs of the ceiling collapsed inward. **Fly, youngling. The end approaches.**

With bitter resignation, the Wanderer projected herself through the First Conduit and tripped across a wrinkle in space-time to safety—and exile.

The *Rocinante* climbed back into orbit under the guidance of its guest copilot, Clark Terrell of the *Sagittarius*. Quinn stepped back into the cockpit and was glad to see that Terrell had an intuitive feel for the ship's sometimes temperamental controls.

"How are Tim and Vanessa?" asked Terrell.

Quinn shrugged. "Fine, I s'pose. We patched up his ribs, and now they're in the back, dryin' off and makin' googly eyes at each other." Terrell chuckled quietly. Quinn collapsed into his seat and glanced at the main sensor display. Its readout was blank. "Piece o' crap," he muttered, and gave it a broad slap on its side. The display flickered and rolled but didn't change. "All the interference down there must've fried it."

"Either that or the Klingons are jamming us," Terrell said.

Shaking his head to dismiss the notion, Quinn started punching in numbers to manually calculate the jump to warp speed. "No way. If they were, I'd know."

His ship lurched to a sudden halt. Inertia pinned him against the main console. Pushing back, he glanced out the cockpit and saw nothing at first. Then he half stood from his seat, turned, and craned his neck to peer out the top of the cockpit's all-encircling canopy. Above and behind the *Rocinante*, barely visible as a speck against the stars, was the outline of a Klingon warship emitting two golden beams— one locked on to his ship and the other holding the *Sagittarius*.

The ship-to-ship channel beeped for Quinn's attention. He opened it. A gruff voice crackled over the comm. *"Attention, unidentified vessel. This is the Klingon battle cruiser* Zin'za. *Power down your engines and prepare to be boarded."*

Quinn frowned and shifted the main impulse drive to standby. He looked at Terrell and frowned. "To paraphrase the immortal words of General George Custer: *Crap*."

"The Klingons have locked a tractor beam onto the *Rocinante*," Sorak reported from his jury-rigged console.

Captain Nassir hung his head with disappointment. He had hoped that the capture of his own vessel might distract the Klingons long enough to permit the small tramp freighter to escape. Apparently, the Klingons had made important strides in sensor-jamming, enough to catch Mr. Quinn unaware.

The bridge portal slid open with a soft hiss. Razka entered

with an open satchel slung across his torso and resting at his left hip. As soon as he was inside the door, he handed a phaser and a spare power cell to Sorak, who accepted them and checked the weapon's settings. "The top-deck crew is armed and ready to repel boarders, Captain," Razka said.

"Very good, Chief," Nassir said, nodding his thanks as Razka handed him a phaser. As the Saurian scout continued around the bridge handing out weapons, Nassir asked McLellan, "Status of the Klingon ship?"

McLellan checked her console. "Still reeling us in, sir," she said, pocketing the phaser that Razka handed to her. "Their shields are still up."

"Not that it matters," Nassir said. "We overloaded our phasers fending off the Shedai." A hopeful thought occurred to him. "Any chance the *Rocinante*'s armed?"

The slender brunette shook her head. "No, sir."

Xiong received his phaser as zh'Firro set hers on her lap. Having finished dispersing sidearms to the crew, Razka closed his satchel and drew a fearsome-looking knife from a sheath on his belt. He tested its gleaming edge with one delicate, bulbous green fingertip. "Ready to give the Klingons a warm welcome, Captain."

Nassir checked his own phaser and verified that it was set for heavy stun. The use of a higher, potentially lethal setting was unnecessary and, in the close confines of such a small vessel, most likely foolish. One missed shot at full power might fatally compromise the hull. He hoped that the Klingons would realize that when they came aboard and adjust their disruptors accordingly. Then he hoped that Klingon disruptors had a setting other than "fry everything."

He swallowed hard. The dryness in his throat was painful, and nervousness stirred up the acid in his gut. *Never too old to be scared,* the middle-aged Deltan mused. He tightened his grip on his phaser and prepared to face the inevitable.

Everyone else on the bridge except Xiong seemed calm about the imminent arrival of the boarding party. The young

A&A officer trembled, and his hands shook so badly that he could barely be trusted to aim his phaser. "Are we really taking on a Klingon boarding party?"

"Of course we are, Ming," Nassir said. "This situation calls for a stupid and utterly futile gesture to be done on somebody's part, and I think we're just the crew to do it."

The captain held a straight face and enjoyed Xiong's stunned, slackened expression for a few seconds. Then the younger man surrendered to the moment and laughed low and ruefully at their predicament.

Good, Nassir thought. *Better to go out in high spirits.*

Sorak turned from his console and stood up, phaser in hand. "The Klingons have lowered their shields and begun scanning us and the *Rocinante* for transport."

"Here we go," Nassir said, standing up to steel his nerves for the coming fray. He watched the image of the *Zin'za* on the main viewer—and flinched with surprise as a volley of charged plasma shots struck it amidships, battering its secondary hull and peppering its warp nacelles and impulse drive. Instantly dealt a savage blow, the ship's bow pitched downward as the vessel rolled to port.

"Stations!" Nassir snapped, pushing himself back into his chair. "Sorak! Report!"

"Weapons fire from the Tholian ship," the Vulcan said. "Heavy damage to the Klingons' impulse drive, shields, life support, and weapons."

McLellan cut in, "Tractor beams disengaged, sir! We're free to navigate!"

"Sayna," Nassir said, and before he could finish the sentence zh'Firro had already accelerated the *Sagittarius* to full impulse away from the Klingons. The captain looked back at McLellan. "The *Rocinante*?"

"Free and breaking away," she said. "The Tholians are pursuing the *Zin'za*."

Nassir eyed the swiftly changing situation on the main viewer. "Will the Klingons fight it out?"

"Negative, sir," McLellan said. "They're breaking orbit."

"Confirmed," Sorak added. "The *Zin'za* is powering up its warp nacelles for—" On the main viewer the *Zin'za* vanished to warp speed in a colorful blur. From behind it, the Tholian warship was cruising toward the *Sagittarius*.

Now to find out if we're next on the Tholians' hit list, Nassir worried. "McLellan, hail the Tholians, request a parley. Sorak, contact the *Rocinante,* tell them to make a run for it." He thumbed open a comm channel to the top deck. "Master Chief? ETA to a working warp drive?"

"Almost fixed, Skipper," Ilucci said. *"Two more minutes."*

McLellan removed a Feinberger transceiver from her ear and reported, "The Tholians don't answer our hails, Captain."

The hulking, triple-wedge-shaped hull of the Tholian battleship filled the entire frame of the main viewer. It was all but on top of the *Sagittarius.* Nassir threw a perplexed look over his shoulder at Sorak, who reviewed his console's readouts.

"No sign of weapons lock by the Tholians," Sorak said. "No indication that they are scanning us in any manner." The ship vanished into the top frame of the viewscreen, leaving only stars and the curve of Jinoteur IV. A moment later, Sorak added, "The Tholian ship has jumped to warp, sir."

McLellan silenced a beeping signal on her console. "It's the *Rocinante,* sir. They're asking if we're all right."

"Tell them we're fine," Nassir said, heaving a sigh of relief. Around the bridge, hunched shoulders relaxed, held breaths were exhaled, and exhaustion long denied took hold.

Then Xiong went and ruined the moment. "Captain," he said, the worry in his tone instantly setting the rest of the crew back on edge. "We're picking up some really wild readings throughout the Jinoteur system." Flipping some toggle switches next to the sensor hood, he continued, "Major gravimetric fluctuations, disruptions of subspace and regular space-time. It looks like a subspatial compression with a diameter of—"

"Sum it up, Ming."

Xiong stood and looked Nassir in the eye. "A wrinkle in space-time is crushing this star system. We need to go to warp in the next sixty seconds, or we're all dead."

"Bridy Mac," Nassir said, "if the *Rocinante* has warp speed, tell them to go. I *mean* it this time. Sayna, lay in a course, maximum warp." Thumbing open the top-deck channel, he finished, "Master Chief, it's now or never."

There was no direct reply over the open channel, just the muted, muffled background sounds of powered tools in use and tired engineers grumbling profanities so harsh that they would make a Denebian slime devil recoil in fear.

On the main viewer, the change was subtle at first—a sense that the burning orb of the star called Jinoteur was growing closer, larger, brighter. Then its fiery presence was eclipsed, literally, by the collision of its fourth planet with all of its moons. A storm of planetary debris scattered from the apocalyptic impacts, revealing glowing orange volcanic cores. It was a terrifying but utterly compelling vision of destruction.

And it was expanding toward the *Sagittarius*.

"The *Rocinante* is safely away," McLellan reported.

Beyond the rocky vista of a shattered planet and its broken moons, the star-flecked expanse of the galaxy distorted into bent streaks that continued to stretch, until they were well on their way to becoming endless rings of light.

"Mains online," zh'Firro said crisply as she engaged the warp drive. Nassir thought the engines' thrumming sounded off-pitch, atonal, sickly. He didn't know if that was a product of the hasty repairs or of the distorted nature of the deforming region of space-time that they were racing to escape.

The ringlets of distorted starlight unbent and straightened into long, soft streaks. As the pitch of the engines normalized, zh'Firro said calmly, "We're clear of the anomaly, sir."

"Take us back to sublight," Nassir said. "Xiong, keep scanning the Jinoteur system, I want as much data as we—"

"I can't, sir," Xiong said. "It's gone."

Nassir was not a fan of exaggerations. "The entire system

can't have been destroyed that quickly. Even if it was, studying the debris could—"

"There is no debris," Xiong interrupted. He patched in an
image on the main viewer: an empty starfield. "There's nothing left. That wrinkle in space-time swallowed every planet,
every moon, even the star itself. It's *gone*, sir. Just . . . gone."

Quinn sounded upset. "What do you mean, it's gone?"

"As in, *it's not there anymore*," Terrell replied.

Pennington was arriving late to the conversation between
Quinn and Terrell, who was looking even more haggard than
he had when they'd found him. The two men were huddled
around the navigation console, staring at a blank grid on the
starmap.

Shaking his head and holding up his palms, Quinn turned
away. "Please don't explain. I don't even want to know."

Theriault entered the cockpit and stood beside Pennington.
"Where's the *Sagittarius*?" she asked with obvious concern.

"They're fine," Terrell said. "I just hailed them. They'll be
here in a few moments." He winced and shifted in his seat.

The young woman moved to Terrell's side. "Are you
okay?" She recoiled at the sight of the black glass that permeated his abdominal injury. "What is that?"

"A little present from the Shedai," Terrell said. "Don't
worry, I'm told Dr. Babitz has the cure."

Instantly, Theriault lifted her tricorder to scan the substance—and she paused as a drizzle of dirty water seeped out
of the device, which made a sickly buzzing crackle in her
hands. Her lips tightened into a disappointed frown.

Terrell smiled at her. "Good instincts," he said.

The subspace comm beeped, and Quinn put the incoming
signal on the overhead speaker. "Rocinante," Captain Nassir
said, *"this is the* Sagittarius. *Everybody all right over there?"*

"We're good," Quinn said, "but your first officer needs
more help than my first-aid kit can offer. I can mend a bone,
but I can't fix a gut."

Nassir replied, *"We need a bit of distance between you and the others to make sure we beam up the right person."*

"How much distance?" asked Quinn.

"A few meters," Terrell said.

Pennington said to Quinn, "We could carry him back into the main compartment. That ought to do it."

"Or," Theriault cut in, "the three of us could just step out of the cockpit for a few seconds. It'd be easier and safer than trying to move him."

"You had me at easier," Quinn said. He led the way out of the cockpit. Pennington and Theriault fell in behind him and followed him to the ship's main compartment.

Alone in the cockpit, Terrell said, "I'm clear for transport, Captain."

Nassir's reply over the speaker sounded faint from the remove of the main compartment. *"Stand by. Energizing now."*

Seconds later a high-pitched ringing tone resonated inside the cockpit, and Terrell's body became a speckled gold shimmer. He faded, became translucent, and vanished.

"He's safely aboard," Nassir said. *"Theriault, get ready to beam back in sixty seconds."*

She faced Pennington and Quinn. "I guess you guys better get back in the cockpit. There's no one flying this thing."

Quinn smirked, nodded, and went forward to take his place in the pilot's seat. Pennington lagged behind a moment. He stared at his still-damp shoes while trying to think of something clever to say. He was at a complete loss for words as Theriault lifted herself on tiptoes and kissed him on the cheek.

"Thanks for the rescue," she said, backing away like a bashful child. The moment she stopped, the musical drone of a transporter effect began. She smiled. "See you on Vanguard."

Then she shimmered and vanished, the warmth of her kiss lingering after her. It had been a simple gesture, almost innocent, more sweet than romantic. Nothing about it had suggested anything more than friendly affection and gratitude.

Naturally, therefore, Pennington found himself utterly smitten.

He returned to the cockpit with damp and wrinkled clothing, squishing shoes, tousled hair, and an enormous grin on his face. Flopping into the copilot's seat, he only half listened while Quinn verified a flight plan with the *Sagittarius* and plotted a tandem return journey to Vanguard.

As Quinn started flipping switches and powering up the warp drive, he fixed Pennington with a good-natured glare. "What is it with you and redheads?"

"Dunno, mate," Pennington said. "Just lucky, I guess."

27

The *Lanz't Tholis* had set course for Tholia at its best possible speed after striking a decisive blow upon the Klingon vessel. Nezrene [The Emerald] felt the waves of confusion rippling through the ship's communal thought-space SubLink. Many of the hundreds of crewmembers had expected to fire upon the Starfleet vessel as well, and dark scarlet pulses of resentment tainted the mind-lines of the ship's rank and file.

Mutiny was all but unheard of on Tholian ships; the caste system clarified all roles, and every Tholian understood his or her genetic and social destiny almost from the first moment of solidification. But with no members of its leadership caste left alive after the brutal incarceration by the Shedai, there was a vacuum of authority aboard the *Lanz't Tholis*—one that it was now Nezrene's duty to fill.

Only a handful of the ship's crew had been able to witness what she and the others who were yoked to the Shedai machine's nodes had overheard. The others had all been trapped in the machine's infernal core, isolated from the terrible voices that had reigned outside. Held in that excruciating stasis, they had been unable to commune or resist; raw suffering had been the whole of their existence while inside the burning prison.

Pyzstrene [The Sallow], the ranking engineer aboard the ship now that its lead engineer had been atomized by the Shedai, was proving to be the most vocal and pointed of Nezrene's critics. *It was the Federation's incursion into the Shedai sector that brought this horror upon us.*

Kaleidoscopic images, each facet of which represented another crewmember's unique point of view, replayed the attack on the Klingon ship, followed by Nezrene's order to hold fire when the gunners had trained their sensing units on the Federation vessel. Pyzstrene continued in fiery hues and bellicose tones. *Why does Nezrene favor one of our foes over another? Their fight was not our concern. It would have been better to have fired on neither than to show favor to one.*

Nezrene, sensing the need to quash dissent and reassert control quickly, offered her thoughts to the twenty-three others who had shared her fate inside the horrid machine. Forming a new SubLink they synchronized their memory-lines. *We must show them the truth together,* she counseled her comrades. All signaled their agreement by adjusting the hues of their mind-lines to a uniform shade of warm amber. With their shared experience coagulated into a single coherent memory-line, Nezrene opened their private SubLink to the rest of the crew.

This is why we did not destroy the Federation ship, Nezrene explained with calming shades of pale green and blue. Her dulcet tones conveyed sincerity and authority. The other voices in the SubLink fell silent. A general tenor of anxious anticipation preceded the revelation by those who had heard the Voices.

Twenty-four facets showed the same moment from differing perspectives but with only one narrative. Two humans, one wearing a uniform of Starfleet, stood beneath the great machine and were confronted by the second greatest of all the Voices.

"We're begging you for their freedom," said the male human.

The Voice asked the female human, **"Do you also plead for the *Kollotaan*'s freedom?"**

"Yes," she said. *"Can you return them to their ship?"*

"I can," he said after a brief pause. **"And I will."**

Nezrene terminated the memory-share and adopted the bright surety of the leadership caste. *Perhaps it is the custom of other species to repay justice with treachery, but it is not our way. They spoke in our defense. That is why we defended them.*

Her argument galvanized the crew of the *Lanz't Tholis*. Their

collective mind-line calmed to a muted golden glow. Harmony
and balance were restored. Discipline would prevail. All she had
left to dread was their homecoming.

As the ship's acting commander, it would be her task to inform the Ruling Conclave that the Shedai had awakened—and
that they had dispersed to countless worlds across the sector.

Tholia's true enemy had returned.

Only one path had been offered for the Wanderer's flight from
the First World, one channel through the First Conduit, one
route to salvation. Expended by her struggle against the Apostate and his minions, she had accepted it.

She was alone on a desiccated, airless moon. Once geologi-
cally active, it was long dead, as was the barren world that held
it in gravitational thrall. Two forlorn orbs in the endless darkness, turning and revolving around a fading star, a slow death
incarnate.

Behind her a Conduit lay dark and cold, its flawless obsidian
surface reflecting glimmers of starlight. Without a power source
the Conduit was little more now than sculpture, a mute reminder
of powers and glories surrendered to the iniquities of time. Silenced and enfeebled, it would be of no use to the Wanderer.
Never again would the Song issue from it; without the infusion
of power from the First Conduit, it was naught but a shell, a
monument to what might have been.

This star system was one of the most remote of all the
Shedai's possessions. It was quite possibly the most distant node
in the Conduit network from the First World, and also from the
interstellar nations of *Telinaruul* that had dared to trespass into
the realm of the Shedai. The journey across the desert of space-
time, spanning many dozens of light-years, to the nearest linked
world would be long and silent.

It did not matter. Strength would return. The Wanderer
would fortify her essence by drawing on vast reservoirs of energy hidden in extradimensional folds of space-time. Her recovery would seem slow by the standards of some *Telinaruul*.

For her it would be a brief respite, a momentary regrouping. When it was complete she would begin her passage of the stars.

Despite being one of the most newly formed of the Shedai, she had earned her name and her place among the *Serrataal* for her particular gift, unique among her kind: the ability to project her consciousness across the deepest reaches of space without a Conduit to guide her transit. With enough time to gather her strength, she could traverse the vast reaches between stars, make planetfall, and recorporealize. Her arrival could occur without warning. A breath from the heavens, a cold whisper, would be her only herald.

She would ford the darkness. World to world, she would seek out the others, the diaspora of the Enumerated. Those loyal to the Maker she would aid and organize. The Apostate's partisans she would destroy. Cleansing the Shedai of dissident voices would be crucial. Only united would they have the power to expel the *Telinaruul* from their domain—and subjugate them.

Retribution would not come quickly. But it would come.

Of that the Wanderer was certain.

28

T'Prynn had been awake for more than thirty hours, since the SOS from the *Sagittarius* had been received by Vanguard Control. It had been a tumultuous period, full of desperate stratagems and expedient measures, and while T'Prynn had not been in the center of it, she had been busy behind the scenes, influencing outcomes.

Three hours had passed since Commodore Reyes had issued General Order 24 against Gamma Tauri IV. Afterward he had withdrawn to his private office and refused visitors, even T'Prynn and Jetanien. She desired to emulate him and retire to her quarters for an extended period, perhaps a few days, to meditate and order her thoughts. It was a luxury that would briefly have to be postponed, however. Duty and circumstance had conspired against her; before she could sequester herself, there was an item of business she needed to address in person.

As she stepped out of the turbolift onto an upper floor of a Stars Landing residential complex, her body felt sapped of vigor. Every step forward was a labor, and despite her robust Vulcan constitution the events of the past day had left her enervated to an unusual degree. She forced herself to press onward with poise and fortitude, banishing her fatigue as just another irrelevant perception.

At the door she hesitated. *Procrastination is illogical,* she reprimanded herself. *This matter must be dealt with in a timely fashion. Failure to act promptly could have significant negative consequences.* Her resolve bolstered by a review of the facts, she pressed the door buzzer and waited.

Fifty-four seconds later the door opened. Anna Sandesjo lurked beyond the edge of the doorway, squinting into the white light of the hallway as it crept into her darkened apartment. She was wrapped in a midnight-blue robe of Terran silk tied loosely shut at her waist. Groggy and peeking out from behind tousled locks, she said, "It's half-past four in the morning, T'Prynn."

"It is urgent that we speak," T'Prynn replied. She resisted the urge to enter Sandesjo's home without invitation. After a few seconds, the semi-somnambulating Klingon in human guise ushered T'Prynn inside. Walking behind her, T'Prynn admired the placid nature scene that had been delicately embroidered on the back of her lover's robe.

Sandesjo's hand brushed a control panel on the wall as they entered the living room. Lights flickered on and filled the space with a warm golden ambience. Sandesjo stopped in front of the plush sofa and turned to face T'Prynn. "Is this a social call?" she asked with a wicked grin and sleepy eyes. "You'll have to work to make up for interrupting my beauty rest."

"It might be best if you sat down, Anna."

The stern tone of T'Prynn's suggestion hardened Sandesjo's expression. She did as T'Prynn had asked and lowered herself onto the middle of the sofa. "What's this about?"

Pulled by my hair over burning coals.

Sten's *katra*-voice tormented her thoughts: *You have betrayed her, just as you betrayed me.*

A twinge of discomfort tugged at the corner of T'Prynn's eyelid. She suppressed it as she spoke. "Just over one hour ago the Klingon battle cruiser *Zin'za* left the Jinoteur system. By now it has likely confirmed to the Klingon High Council and to Imperial Intelligence that there was no Starfleet ambush there."

Sandesjo's brow constricted with suspicion. "It was called off?" She studied T'Prynn's face. Understanding added bitterness to her gaze and her voice. "It never existed."

"No, it did not," T'Prynn said. "It was a lie intended to delay their entry into the system so that a rescue effort would have time to reach the *Sagittarius*. That effort has succeeded."

Shock dominated Sandesjo's expression for a moment. Then it was replaced by indignation. "You've blown my cover."

"Correct," T'Prynn said. "When your handlers realize that you passed them completely fraudulent intelligence, they will conclude that you have been compromised."

The double agent buried her face in her hands. "They'll kill me for this," she muttered.

"You will be protected," T'Prynn said. "You'll go on extended leave and move to secure quarters elsewhere in the station until a transport arrives six days from now." *Sand hurled into my eyes. Sten's nose shattering beneath the heel of my palm.* "It will bring you to a world inside Federation space. After you have been debriefed by Starfleet Intelligence, you will be given a new identity, and a new face, before entering permanent protective custody on one of the core Federation planets."

Sandesjo dragged her fingers through her hair, pulling taut the skin of her temples and lifting her eyebrows. It transformed her blank expression into one of shock. "And what about you?"

"I will organize your protection from now until you board the transport," T'Prynn said. "After that, agents of—"

"No," Sandesjo said. "I misspoke. What about *us*?"

His hand clamps shut around my throat. I claw at his eyes.

"I will not be going with you," T'Prynn said.

Shaking and blushing with anger, Sandesjo clenched her jaw and closed her fists white-knuckle tight. "You used me," she said, her voice hoarse and unsteady. "I risked *everything* for you." She sprang to her feet, her face bright with fury. "My cover, my honor, my *life*. And you *used* me."

"I did what duty required," T'Prynn said.

Sandesjo's slap stung the left side of T'Prynn's face, and Sten's backhand burned against the right. Paralyzed by the dual assault, one from without and the other from within, T'Prynn stood and suffered the rain of blows. One sharp strike after another buffeted her face, snapping her head from side to side and coating her teeth with a coppery-tasting sheen of green blood. She had lost count of how many real and imagined hits she had suffered when her reflexes returned and she grabbed Sandesjo's hands, halting her attack.

The wet crack of Sten's breaking cervical vertebra ends the challenge—and begins our lifelong duel.

Grappling with Sandesjo was difficult. Though she looked human, her Klingon musculature gave her considerable strength and made her a durable, formidable opponent for T'Prynn. Fueled by rage, she twisted and lurched in the Vulcan's grip, growling like a wild animal struggling to free itself from a trap. Then she lurched toward T'Prynn instead of away from her, and they staggered clumsily, entwined in a desperate, anguished kiss.

Sandesjo's lips pulled away from T'Prynn's like a spent wave retreating from a beach. T'Prynn's measured breaths were overpowered by Sandesjo's gasps of lust and desperation. "Don't do this," Sandesjo implored. "Don't make me leave you."

"There is no other way," T'Prynn said.

The pulling and twisting resumed, and Sandesjo abandoned words for inarticulate roars and screams. A skillful shift of her balance enabled Sandesjo to slip free of T'Prynn's grasp. She stumbled away, grabbed a wireless lamp from an end table, and hurled it at T'Prynn, who easily sidestepped it. The lamp struck the wall with a soft crunch and a thud. It fell to the floor, its light extinguished.

All at once Sandesjo abandoned the fight. Her knees folded beneath her, and she slumped down onto them. Fury collapsed into defeat. With sagging shoulders and a tired sigh, she seemed to resign herself to T'Prynn's endgame.

"A security detail will be here in five minutes," T'Prynn said. "They will escort you to your temporary quarters. There will be no need to pack. All your needs will be provided for."

Sandesjo glared at T'Prynn. "Not *all* of them."

T'Prynn turned away and walked toward the door. She stopped as Sandesjo called out, "You want to know what's ironic?" T'Prynn looked back. Sandesjo let out a mirthless chuckle and regarded the Vulcan woman with a bitter grin. "Right now I want to cry like a human—but Klingons don't have tear ducts. Vulcans do have them—but I guess you think I'm not worth crying over."

The barrage of *katra* attacks came swiftly, faster than they ever had before, and with enough ferocity to make T'Prynn wince. She replayed the memory of Sten's neck breaking over and over until she regained control of her conscious mind. Then she coaxed her mien back into a properly Vulcan cipher.

"Do not presume to know what I *think,* Anna," she said, and fled her lover's abode, hounded by Sten's vengeful *katra.*

Walking alone through the terrestrial enclosure and then the corridors of the station's upper levels, T'Prynn could not imagine where she might find refuge. Seeking medical assistance would only increase the likelihood of her *val'reth* secret undoing her career. Meditation offered no solace. The piano at Manón's, once a redoubt of tranquility, had proved vulnerable. Her lover's arms no longer offered any shelter.

She had run out of ways to run from herself. There was nothing left to do but admit that Sten's taunts had contained at least a kernel of truth: she *had* betrayed Anna. Though she had buried her shame deep in the tombs of her mind, she harbored no doubt that Sten would unearth it and use it to bludgeon her psyche for decades to come.

T'Prynn returned to her arid quarters, undressed, and made a perfunctory attempt at sleep, fully expecting to find Sten's malevolent shade waiting in her dreamscape—standing atop an open grave, spade in hand . . . and gloating.

PART THREE

INSTRUMENTS
OF DARKNESS

29

Six days of reclusive brooding had not assuaged Reyes's grief. Reading through detailed after-action reports from the captains of the *Lovell* and the *Endeavour* had forced him to relive the Gamma Tauri IV tragedy several times over, and each new reading deepened his sense of how indelibly bloodied his hands had become. Eleven thousand colonists, thousands of Klingon scientists, and every living thing on the planet's surface all were dead and reduced to radioactive glass and vapor.

And what did we learn? He asked himself that question over and over, knowing that the answer was "almost nothing." The mission to Gamma Tauri IV had gleaned no significant insights into the artifacts, the meta-genome, or the Shedai. Having ended in bloodshed and fire, it was a tragedy for which Reyes knew himself to be directly responsible.

The only good news of the week had been the rescue of the *Sagittarius* from the surface of Jinoteur IV, and even that was not really a success but just another disaster narrowly averted. In a few hours the ravaged scout ship would return to Vanguard, accompanied by the civilian tramp freighter *Rocinante*. A heroes' welcome had been planned, and Reyes clung to the hope that the *Sagittarius* crew's debriefing would prove more informative than the abortive mission on Gamma Tauri IV. At the very least, he was looking forward to hearing their theories about how the entire Jinoteur star system had vanished from space-time.

His coffee was still warm, so he took a large sip and reclined his chair while he studied the sector activity chart on his office wall. The *Endeavour* had been redeployed to the

Klingon border on another preemptive patrol, and the *Lovell* was en route to Pacifica, a beautiful and recently colonized pelagic world deep in the Taurus Reach, to help set up its basic civil infrastructure. Klingon and Tholian fleet activity had increased slightly, but for the moment the local status quo appeared intact.

Things looked calm, and that worried Reyes.

With a steep tilt of his mug, he drained the last of his coffee and turned back to the orderly stacks of data slates and data cards arranged on his desk. Two of his yeomen, Greenfield and Finneran, had obviously coordinated their efforts over consecutive shifts to keep his administrative paperwork straight for him. He stared at the neatly grouped piles of work and couldn't find the motivation to do any of it.

Set apart from the rest of the items on his desk was a nondescript, thin gray binder. He picked it up, rested it on his lap, and opened it to admire the old picture tucked inside.

It wasn't a particularly good photo; its composition was awkward, and because Reyes had taken it by pointing the camera at himself and Jeanne from arm's length, its up-their-noses perspective was somewhat unflattering. In its favor, the light had been good that day in the New Berlin park, filtered through the static boughs of massive trees growing in low gravity, and the smiles that he and Jeanne showed to the camera had been genuine. It was proof that once, long ago, they had been happy and in love, before the routines of marriage and the burdens of rank had accomplished their slow attrition of all that had been good and joyful and honest between them.

I'd give anything to be back in that moment, he lamented, imagining the life he could have had if only every single thing had happened differently for the past twenty years. *All we'd had were dreams about what we might be. Now all I have left is the memories of what we were. . . . It's not enough.*

He traced the outline of Jeanne's younger features with his fingertip, a delicate, feather-light brush of skin over the matte print, as if he feared inflicting some new misery upon her ghost with his seemingly inverted Midas touch. *I'm sorry, Jeanne.*

Rationalizations and excuses deserted him, leaving only unanswerable questions. *Why did I put the mission above her life? Because some admiral told me to? How many times did they tell us at the Academy that blindly obeying orders was not the mark of a good Starfleet officer? I listened, and I nodded, and I said I understood—but did I?* He closed the binder, unable to bear the reminder of a happy memory that he felt he no longer deserved. *What am I doing out here? Who am I really doing it for? Why am I doing it at all?*

His dark musings were cut short by the buzzing of his desktop intercom. He sighed and jabbed the switch to open the channel. "Yes?"

Yeoman Greenfield replied, *"Ambassador Jetanien and Lieutenant Commander T'Prynn are here, sir."*

Feeling antisocial, Reyes snapped, "What do they want?"

Jetanien answered with deadpan sarcasm, *"To bask in the radiant glow of your charisma."*

"I don't turn on the glow till noon," Reyes said.

"Commodore," Jetanien said, his impatience mounting, *"twice in two days you have declined to receive us. Are we now to conduct our classified business by means of correspondence?"*

Experience had convinced Reyes that publicly debating Jetanien was a quick means to profound embarrassment. His thick, dark eyebrows pressed down in a heavy scowl as he said, "Send them in, Greenfield."

The door to his office opened, and Jetanien entered first. His raiment, as ever, was as flowing and gauzy as he was scaly and ponderous. Sashes of scarlet and plum were wrapped around his massive torso, and a matching drape hung from the back of his elaborate headpiece, which had been wrought from metal polished to a blinding brilliance. The Chelon rubbed his beaklike mouth back and forth, making a soft grinding sound as he strode toward Reyes's desk.

T'Prynn walked in behind the ambassador, as ever presenting a portrait of discipline and control. Her crimson minidress was immaculate, her boots were polished to perfection, and her hair was pulled taut across her scalp and secured in a long, loosely bound ponytail. She carried a data slate.

The door closed behind T'Prynn, who joined Jetanien in front of Reyes's desk. Jetanien made a slight bow of greeting. "First of all, let me express my profound gratitude for your magnanimity in actually deigning to grant us—"

"Stop," Reyes said, holding up his palm toward Jetanien. "Are you two here for the same reason?"

Taken aback, Jetanien said simply, "Yes."

"Okay," Reyes said, pointing at Jetanien. "You talk too much." He aimed his finger at T'Prynn. "What's this about?"

"It is my duty to inform you both that a member of Ambassador Jetanien's diplomatic staff is an agent of Klingon Imperial Intelligence who has been surgically altered to appear as a human female," T'Prynn said.

Reyes smirked. "I knew there was something fishy about that Karumé woman."

"Actually, sir, the spy is Anna Sandesjo—Ambassador Jetanien's senior attaché."

The commodore gave himself a moment to suck on his teeth and process that nugget of information. "Of course it is," he said. "When did you figure out she was a spy?"

"Eleven months and twenty-two days ago," T'Prynn said.

His coffee threatened to make a special return trip up his esophagus just so he could do a spit-take. "Eleven *months*?"

"And twenty-two days," T'Prynn clarified.

He covered his eyes with one hand and exhaled. *Count to ten,* he counseled himself. *One . . . two . . .*

"Miss Sandesjo was coopted almost immediately after her detection," T'Prynn said. "She has served us well as a double agent, providing valuable intelligence about Klingon priorities in this sector."

Reyes stopped counting at six and removed his hand from his eyes. "You flipped an undercover enemy agent *eleven months* ago, and you're just telling the two of us about it *now?*"

"Oh, I already knew about Sandesjo," Jetanien said.

In unison Reyes and T'Prynn replied, "You did?"

"Of course." Jetanien faced T'Prynn. "My staff intercepted one of her reports to Turag nineteen days before you turned her. I am well aware of the *services* she has performed for you."

There was a challenge implicit in Jetanien's tone, and it made Reyes feel as if he knew nothing about what was really going on aboard his station. "All right, let's get to the meat on this bone. Why are you telling me now?"

T'Prynn tore her drilling-laser stare from Jetanien, blinked, and turned a neutral gaze back toward Reyes. "Miss Sandesjo's status as a double agent has been exposed. It was a necessary consequence of disinforming the Klingons about events in the Jinoteur system. She is currently in protective custody aboard the station, but we need to move her to a safer location."

"Hang on," Reyes said. "You blew her cover six days ago, and she's still here?" T'Prynn nodded. "And the Klingons *know* she's still here?" Again the Vulcan woman confirmed his supposition. "Are you kidding me?"

Jetanien made some clicking noises and said, "I doubt the Klingons would risk an attack on the station over one agent."

"They won't launch a direct attack, no," Reyes said. "But they aren't gonna let this go, either—I guarantee it." Turning to T'Prynn, he said, "I presume you have a plan?"

"Yes, sir," she said. "The Starfleet cargo transport *Malacca* is currently docked in bay three." She handed her data slate to Reyes, who read it and followed along as she continued. "A standard cargo container unit has been modified to serve as a scan-shielded residential module for Miss Sandesjo. It will appear in the *Malacca*'s manifest as classified materials bound for the Starfleet Research and Development office on Deneva."

Jetanien sounded dubious. "How likely is this to deceive the Klingons?" Reyes was keen to know the answer to that question as well.

"Because the *Malacca* is not a personnel ship," T'Prynn said, "the Klingons are less likely to suspect it of being used to transport Miss Sandesjo. Furthermore, we can deflect their suspicion by maintaining a heightened state of security aboard the station for several days after her departure."

Reyes looked over the plan that T'Prynn had drafted and compared it to the schedule of arrivals and departures. "When do you see this happening?"

"Today, shortly after the arrival of the *Sagittarius*," she said. "Its homecoming should provide ample distraction."

"Let's hope it does," Reyes said. "The last thing the *Malacca* needs is a Klingon welcoming committee waiting for it the minute it gets outside our sensor range." He reclined his chair, closed his eyes, and pinched the bridge of his nose to ward off the seed of a headache. "Either of you have any more surprises for me this morning?"

"Not at present," Jetanien said.

T'Prynn shook her head. "No, sir."

"Thank heaven for small mercies," Reyes said. "Dismissed."

Dr. Ezekiel Fisher stood behind Dr. M'Benga's desk and watched over the younger man's shoulder as he called up a new screen of deep-tissue imaging scans. "Look," M'Benga said, pointing at a dark blotch on the screen. "Right there."

As hard as he looked, Fisher didn't see any sign of a tumor. "Where?"

"There," M'Benga said. "Above the corolis gland."

Fisher strained to pick out the tumor from the background, but the image was too muddy. "Did you take a lateral scan?"

"Yes," M'Benga said. "Hang on, I'll bring it up."

The elder physician waited patiently and sipped his tepid cup of herbal tea—an indignity imposed on Fisher by Dr. Robles after the CMO's latest physical revealed slightly elevated blood pressure—while M'Benga searched through the patient's scans for the one they wanted. Fisher suspected that he knew what M'Benga had found, and he doubted very much that it was a cancerous tumor. He double-checked the patient's chart. "Lieutenant Miwal's blood work doesn't show any of the antigens for an internal cancer," he noted aloud.

"What if it's an alkalo-carcinoid structure? Caitians can develop them without showing elevated alpha proteins."

He's a good diagnostician but a bit too stubborn for his own good, Fisher decided. "Maybe. But then why aren't we seeing any catecholamines in his serum profile?"

"Well," M'Benga said, and he paused. His search for a good answer ended as he put the lateral abdominal scan on the screen. "Yes," he said. "You were right about the lateral scan. It's much clearer from this angle."

"It certainly is," Fisher said. "And it should be fairly obvious that's not a tumor."

"But the calcified mass in the—" M'Benga stopped abruptly and took a new, focused look at the image on the screen. Fisher saw no need to say anything; he was certain that within seconds, M'Benga would realize that—

"It's a bezoar," M'Benga said with a slump of his shoulders. "In Miwal's stomach. A harmless bezoar."

"Or as I like to call it," Fisher said, "a hairball." He patted the younger man's back. "Here endeth the lesson." He handed M'Benga the data slate that held Miwal's chart. "I suggest you prescribe the lieutenant a tricophage laxative and tell him to learn how to use the sonic shower."

M'Benga chortled good-naturedly and started entering the information on Miwal's chart. Fisher sipped his tea and had started thinking about lunch when the front door of the medical administrative office opened. Captain Rana Desai walked in, data slate in hand. She was followed by a pair of Starfleet

security guards. Desai glanced first into Fisher's empty office
and then turned and saw him in M'Benga's office.

He called out to her, "Morning, Rana. Help you?"

She said to her two escorts, "Wait here," and proceeded
quickly into M'Benga's office. She shut the old-fashioned
wooden door—an anachronistic touch that Fisher had insisted
upon for the hospital's administrative suite. Standing in private with the two physicians, Desai took a deep breath and
looked at the floor. "I wish I didn't have to be here," she said.

"Don't be coy, now," Fisher said. "You came down here to
say something. Let's have it."

She looked up and took another long breath. "First of all,"
she said, "you have to know this is coming down from
Starfleet Command. I'm just the messenger."

Fisher folded his arms across his chest. "All right."

"Gentlemen," Desai said, enunciating with the stiff formality of a court officer reading an indictment, "did you, exactly three days ago, petition Admiral McCreary at Starfleet
Medical to declassify and release to you the full medical history of Lieutenant Commander T'Prynn?"

The CMO looked over his shoulder at M'Benga, whose
calm expression mirrored his own. Fisher looked back at
Desai. "As a matter of fact, we did."

She handed him her data slate, on which was displayed a
document thick with tiny type and heavy with legal jargon.
"You are both hereby ordered to cease and desist all such efforts to declassify documents related to Lieutenant Commander T'Prynn," Desai said. "Furthermore, any attempt to
circumvent or override security protocols put in place by
Starfleet Intelligence will be treated as a court-martial offense.
Lastly, you are both hereby prohibited in perpetuity from
communicating with any and all parties regarding Lieutenant
Commander T'Prynn's medical history or this order from the
Starfleet Judge Advocate General. Is that clear?"

"All except the reason why," Fisher said.

Desai sighed. "Just sign the top page next to your names."

Fisher scrawled his signature on the form and handed it to M'Benga, who affixed his own illegible autograph. Desai leaned forward and snapped up the tablet. Then she turned to head for the door. As she reached it, Fisher asked, "Does Diego know about this?"

She turned back. "The only reason you're not both in the brig is that he refused to press charges for insubordination." Softening her tone, she added, "I'm really sorry about this, Zeke. Whatever you've been doing . . . stop it." She opened the door, stepped out, and let it swing shut behind her. It closed with a heavy thud in the doorframe.

"Not exactly the result we were hoping for," M'Benga said.

"Nope. Wasn't." Fisher looked back at his protégé. "Pull everything you can find on Vulcan psychological and neurological disorders. They might not give us her history, but we still have our own data to analyze—and I plan on finding out what it adds up to, whether Starfleet likes it or not."

Not having been told in advance of the hour or even the day of her departure from Vanguard, Anna Sandesjo was a bit startled when her escorts stepped out of the wall in her bedroom.

A human man and woman, both attired in Starfleet uniforms of black trousers and red jerseys, stood in a narrow, machinery-packed access passage behind the open panel. "I'm Agent Cofell," said the woman. "He's Agent Verheiden. It's time to go."

Cofell ushered Sandesjo to step past them.

Sandesjo got up from the edge of the bed. "I'm already packed," she said, moving toward a rolling luggage bag tucked against the wall in the corner.

"Leave it," Verheiden told her. "You need to make a clean break—the past stays here."

Having already surrendered everything that had mattered to her, Sandesjo did as she was told. She stepped past the agents into the passageway, which was illuminated by widely spaced, backlit blue panels. The air inside was cooler and drier than in the temporary quarters where she had been living for the past several days. Its claustrophobic confines beat with the low pulse of ventilation systems, hissed with the rush of waste-removal plumbing, and echoed with the regular patter of their footfalls on the metal floor plates.

They passed three junctions as they followed the gradual curve of the passage. Before reaching a fourth junction, Cofell opened another disguised panel, revealing a narrow switchback staircase. "Eight levels down," she said, and led the way into the stairwell. Sandesjo followed her, and Verheiden closed the hidden panel behind them.

Their descent was steady and mechanical. Grated metal steps and a narrow gap between the sides of the switchback afforded Sandesjo a view of the space that loomed above her and yawned beneath her. She estimated that the hidden staircase reached from somewhere inside the operations center at the top of Vanguard's command tower to a level deep inside the station's power-generation facility in the lower core.

Eight levels down, Cofell unlocked and opened another panel that led into a new maintenance passageway. In a routine that had quickly become familiar, she and Sandesjo stepped clear while Verheiden secured the hatch they had just passed through. Then they continued through the narrow channel between gray walls packed with deeply thrumming machinery.

The uniformity of the surfaces and passages and junctions was disorienting. Only the bulkhead numbers, changing in an orderly and logical manner, gave Sandesjo any sense of where they were inside the station. By her reckoning they were behind the maintenance bays inside the core, along the station's primary docking bay. Finally they turned left into a short passage that terminated at a bulkhead. Cofell unlocked it, opened it, and stepped through.

Sandesjo exited the passageway into a small enclosed space behind a stack of cargo containers in one of the station's auxiliary cargo bays. Because the maintenance area was reserved for Starfleet vessels, the containers there were packed with classified or restricted military components and materiel.

Behind her, Verheiden halted a few paces shy of the open hatch. As soon as Sandesjo was clear, Cofell stepped back through the hatch and closed it. For a moment Sandesjo thought that she had been abandoned in an empty cargo bay— then the back panel of the container in front of her detached with a hydraulic hiss and slowly lowered open. She stepped back out of its way. When it was slightly more than half open she glanced over its top edge . . . and saw T'Prynn standing inside what looked like a Spartan but comfortable windowless apartment with no door.

The panel touched down on the deck with a metallic scrape and a resounding boom.

Rage and longing twisted together inside Sandesjo's chest and left her speechless. She yearned to reach out to T'Prynn, to seek her touch one last time, but her pride blazed brightly, stung by the Vulcan's recent betrayal.

T'Prynn spoke as she walked down the ramp toward Sandesjo. "This unit has been equipped to sustain you for a prolonged journey. It is provisioned with food customized for your true physiology, and its climate controls are adjustable. Water and air will be filtered and recycled."

She stopped in front of Sandesjo, who refused to make eye contact. Sandesjo stepped around the Vulcan and walked halfway up the ramp. She paused. "It's a lovely jail cell."

"Its affect is regrettable but necessary for security purposes," T'Prynn said. "No one aboard your transport vessel will know that you are inside. Only I and the agents who will greet you at your destination will know of your presence."

Examining its multilayered metallic skin, Sandesjo speculated, "Scan-shielded duranium composites?"

"Yes," T'Prynn said.

Sandesjo walked the rest of the way inside the box and

stood in the center of its main room. A single-person bed was pressed against the wall on the right. Beside it was a low table. A round-cornered viewscreen was mounted on an adjustable swing arm attached to the wall near the foot of the bed. Tucked into a corner on the other side of the compartment were a food slot and a waste reclamation slot. In the middle of the rear wall was an open door leading to a lavatory and shower. Much of the rest of the interior volume of the large shipping container appeared to be filled with life-support apparatus.

T'Prynn watched Sandesjo fiddle for a moment with the viewscreen. "A variety of prerecorded audiovisual material has been made available for you," she said, "as well as a broad selection of printed matter. I regret that our catalog of original Klingon works is scarce."

Every attempted kindness by T'Prynn felt like the twist of an emotional knife in Sandesjo's heart. Baring her hostility, she said, "I guess you thought of everything."

"I saw to necessities," T'Prynn said.

Sandesjo had thought she would have more to say to T'Prynn, but as she looked at her she was unable to put words to her feelings. Bitterness was tangled up with desire, sorrow with resentment, hopelessness with denial. All that was left to her was surrender. "Just close the door," she said.

For a moment she felt as if T'Prynn might say something, but then the Vulcan took a small device from her belt and pressed one of its buttons. With a low groan and grind, the open side of the container slowly lifted. Sandesjo thought she saw a glimmer of regret on T'Prynn's face, but then the panel blocked her view and shut with a hollow thud.

All was silent inside Sandesjo's dull gray purgatory. She sat on the bed and folded her hands across her lap. No one had told her how long she would be inside this portable prison, or even where she was going. *Probably some remote dustball at the far end of the Federation,* she predicted pessimistically.

A new name, a new face, a new beginning—these were three things she wanted no part of. She had already endured all of them when she gave up being Lurqal and became Anna Sandesjo. How was she to submerge into yet another identity, yet another life?

I've already forgotten what I used to look like, she thought. *Now I probably won't even recognize the sound of my own voice. I'll look in the mirror and see a stranger.*

She growled and shook off the numbing comfort of self-pity. *Stop whining like a* petaQ, she scolded herself. *You've done this before, you can do it again. Wild things don't feel sorry for themselves. Be a Klingon.*

From outside the container came a bump and a slight lurch. She was in motion. Sandesjo wanted to be brave, to face her circumstances head-on without fear or mercy, and to believe that she was participating in her own destiny. But bouncing around inside a sealed box, being shipped away like an unwanted parcel, she thought of T'Prynn and realized what she was—and what she had been from the moment she first fell in love: a prisoner. Worst of all, she had been condemned, not to a life in love's thrall or even to death in its name, but to oblivion.

She lay back on the bed and folded her hands behind her head. Like any prisoner, she knew that her future was out of her hands. There was nothing to do but wait and see what happened.

Cervantes Quinn didn't feel like himself. For one thing, he was sober. He also had showered and shaved, and his clothes were mostly clean. In addition, and to his own surprise, he had shorn off his tangled, shoulder-length white locks, leaving him with a pale gray shadow of stubble covering his round head.

"You look like you're going to a job interview," Pennington joked as they walked together along Vanguard's main hangar deck, where the *Sagittarius* was berthed.

"Just turnin' over a new leaf, that's all," Quinn said.

They dodged around a loose knot of Starfleet personnel walking in the opposite direction. Quinn caught his reflection in one of the massive, wall-sized transparent aluminum observation windows that looked out on the main docking bay. Embarrassed by his own profile, he tried to suck in his gut, but the effort of holding it in for more than a few seconds was too difficult. Letting it go with a huff of breath, he resolved, *Have to do somethin' about that one of these days.*

Pennington smirked at him. "Little trouble there?"

"Shut up," he replied with his own crooked grin.

"Just kidding, mate," Pennington said. "If this is the new you, it's got my vote—for the smell factor, if nothing else."

Shaking his head, Quinn replied, "Friends like you are the reason most people don't bother with self-improvement."

They neared the bay four gangway, which had just been opened by a chief petty officer. Through another observation window, Quinn noticed that the *Sagittarius,* docked at the end of the gangway, was already being swarmed over by a repair crew from Vanguard. Bright yellow work pods hovered beneath its main saucer, starting sorely needed hull repairs.

Captain Nassir was the first one to emerge from the gangway portal, followed by a slender, dark-haired woman and Theriault, the woman Quinn had pulled out of the water with Pennington. Nassir turned his head and saw Quinn and Pennington, and immediately he threw wide his arms and called out, "The men of the hour!"

More of his crew exited the gangway as he strode over to greet the two civilians. He put out his hand to Quinn, who took it in a firm handshake. Nassir smiled and said, "An honor to meet you face-to-face, Captain."

"Most folks just call me Quinn."

Nassir nodded. "Whatever you like is fine by me, sir." He released Quinn's hand and shook Pennington's. "Mr. Pennington, it's a pleasure. Ensign Theriault's told me quite a bit about your heroics on Jinoteur."

The reporter smiled. "I thought I panicked," he said, "but I'll take her word for it."

Letting go of Pennington's hand, Nassir asked him and Quinn, "What's next for you gents?"

Quinn shrugged. "Scare up another job and get back to work, I guess." Hooking his thumb in Pennington's direction, he added, "I reckon he probably has a few stories to file."

"No doubt," Nassir said.

Behind the Starfleet captain, a trio of medical personnel from Vanguard Hospital approached the gangway entrance with a stretcher. Pennington noticed the medics as well and asked, "Is Commander Terrell all right, sir?"

"He will be," Nassir said. "We fixed him up well enough to get him home, but he'll need a few days of intensive care before he's back on his feet."

Quinn nodded. "Send him our best wishes, Captain. We're both pulling for him."

"He'll be glad to hear that, thank you." Nassir tilted his head back toward a nearby turbolift. "If either of you would like to join me and my crew in Manón's for a celebratory drink, consider yourselves invited. First round's on me."

Pennington and Quinn traded quizzical glances. Quinn looked back at Nassir and asked, "Are you sure we'd be welcome there?"

"Absolutely," Nassir said. "You put yourselves on the line out there. You gents are heroes; I won't forget it." Brightening his expression, he added, "So how 'bout that drink?"

Quinn was about to accept, but then he caught Pennington's sidelong glare and remembered why he had sobered up in the first place. "Maybe just an Altair water," Quinn said, and Pennington signaled his approval with a subtle nod. Nassir indicated with a sweep of his arm that they should follow him to a nearby bank of turbolifts. As they started across the broad thoroughfare, Quinn glimpsed T'Prynn standing like a statue in the middle of the massive corridor, watching him.

Catching Pennington's shoulder and backpedaling, Quinn

said, "Captain, we'll catch up with you in a few minutes. I just remembered an appointment I have to keep first." Pennington shot a confused look at Quinn and followed his stare to T'Prynn.

Nassir looked back, noticing T'Prynn as well. "All right, then," he said. "Good luck with that. See you upstairs." Wise enough to extricate himself while he had the opportunity, Nassir slipped into a turbolift just before its doors closed.

T'Prynn tilted her head toward a recessed seating area off the main passageway, in front of an observation window. The focus of her gaze made it clear that she only wished to speak with Quinn. He nodded his understanding to her and whispered to Pennington, "Still got that recorder gizmo?"

"Yeah," Pennington said. "Why?"

"You might want to fire it up on the sly," Quinn said. "Just in case she kills me in public or something. Might make a hell of a scoop for you."

Pennington casually stuffed his hands into his jacket pockets. A moment later the tip of the recording device poked out over the edge of the pocket. "It's running," he said, and pointed with his chin toward a nook on the other side of the thoroughfare. "I'll be over there." He strolled away, leaving Quinn to go and face T'Prynn alone.

When Quinn reached her moments later, she stood with her back to him, facing into the docking bay. He sidled up next to her and pressed his back against the window. "Howdy."

She didn't look at him as she spoke. "You've done us a great service, Mr. Quinn. Thank you."

"Glad to help," he said. "But could you lay off me for a few weeks? I lost a lotta money on this trip, and I need to get back to work. I got debts to pay."

"No," she said, "you don't."

Expecting another of her patented manipulations, he bristled at the coldness of her tone. "Run that by me again?"

T'Prynn turned to face him. "You have no debts, Mr. Quinn. I've settled your accounts."

"What? For this trip, you mean?"

"All of them."

He was still struggling to figure out what devious angle she was working against him. "You're saying you bought up all my markers? Now I owe everything to you?"

"No, Mr. Quinn. Your debts are *settled*. They *no longer exist*. You owe nothing to Ganz, or to Starfleet, or to me."

The moment was all too surreal for him to grasp. "You think Ganz'll just let me off the hook? I didn't even owe him money—I owed him work and favors. How'd you pay that off?"

"The details are not important." She dropped her smoky-sweet voice to a warm hush and looked him in the eye. "If you wish to continue assisting Starfleet Intelligence, we will be grateful for your help. If you decide to keep on working for Ganz, that's up to you. The key detail here is that you are not obligated to do either. Put simply, Mr. Quinn . . . you're free."

Quinn was convinced that he had misheard her, because it had sounded as if she had just told him that he was free.

He tried to ask if she was kidding, but he realized as he started speaking that she probably couldn't hear him over the explosion in the main docking bay.

Pennington observed Quinn's meeting with T'Prynn from across the thoroughfare. He was close enough that he could monitor them visually with his portable recorder but not close enough to pick up what they were saying.

His attention was fixed on the Vulcan woman, with a focus so acute that he worried it bordered on obsessive. The deception that she had perpetrated on him a few months earlier, to trick him into filing an easily falsified report about the destruction of the *U.S.S. Bombay*, still rankled him. When he had confronted her about it, she had insinuated that she knew enough about his private life to blackmail him. By that point, however, her ploy had already wrought so much damage to his personal life and his professional credibility that he'd had nothing left to lose.

I went to Jinoteur hoping to get one up on her, he admitted to himself. *Between her and Reyes, I can probably forget about ever getting this story published. At least, not in my lifetime.*

T'Prynn said something to Quinn that seemed to catch the man off-guard. *She's certainly full of surprises,* Pennington mused. He recalled witnessing, purely by chance, an abortive visit that T'Prynn had made to his Stars Landing apartment several weeks earlier. He hadn't known the intent behind the visit then, and he still didn't. She had behaved almost like someone plagued by remorse, but he found that hard to believe.

He checked his wrist chrono and glanced impatiently back at Quinn's tête-à-tête with the Vulcan. *Come on, wrap it up,* he mentally implored them. *There's a grateful red-haired lass upstairs waiting to buy me a—*

A flash of light filled the docking bay as an explosion thundered and shook the entire station. Red-alert klaxons whooped as pedestrians on the thoroughfare were thrown to the ground. Pennington plucked his recorder from his pocket and sprint-stumbled across the broad passageway toward the observation window. Around him Starfleet personnel and a handful of civilians were scrambling away from the gangways for emergency turbolifts and stairwells.

"Red alert," declared a male voice over the station's PA system. *"Explosion in the main docking bay! DC and fire-control teams to bay three!"*

Pennington hurdled over a row of chairs to reach the window in a minimum of running strides. He pointed his recorder at the pandemonium in the hangar beyond. Deep red flames and thick black smoke billowed from a massive rent in the ventral hull of the Starfleet cargo ship *U.S.S. Malacca,* docked at the next berth, ninety degrees around the station's core from the *Sagittarius.* Mangled hull plates and a storm of loose debris tumbled in the zero-gravity environment of the docking bay. A string of secondary explosions ripped across the underside of the *Malacca*. The ship listed sharply away from its docking port, which buckled and began to tear apart.

Large clusters of scorched, twisted metal ricocheted off the transparent aluminum observation windows, the ceiling of the docking bay, and the core of the station. Pivoting slowly left to track the path of one especially huge piece of debris, Pennington halted as he and his recorder locked on to a more disturbing and horribly compelling sight.

Only a few meters away, standing between himself and Quinn, T'Prynn stared out the observation window at the fiery carnage. Her right hand was splayed against the window, a gesture of desperation. What fascinated Pennington was her expression—a fusion of shock, horror, and anguish—and the fact that she was, unmistakably, crying.

T'Prynn watched her lies and evasions burn away in the crucible of fire outside the window, leaving only the awful truth.

Staring into the smoldering cavity of the *Malacca*'s blasted cargo hull, she knew that denial was pointless. She had seen the container loaded onto the ship and had watched as the cargo hold was sealed for the vessel's imminent departure from Vanguard.

Gazing into the hypnotic dance of flames and smoke, T'Prynn knew that Anna was dead.

Sten's blade slashes my cheek—

Pretenses and façades fell away, stripping her of decades of mental defenses and a lifetime of indoctrinated emotional paralysis. All the carefully constructed excuses, all the old barriers to candor, crumbled in her psychic grasp.

I feel his pain as I bend his fingers backward and break them at the knuckles—

Debris dispersed in chaotic tumbles from the *Malacca*, trailing twists and ribbons of smoke through the docking bay.

For the sake of duty, T'Prynn had forfeited Anna's life. She had not done the deed, but she had forced the Klingons' hand. Anna's life had been one imperiled for the sake of many. It was logical.

He rips hair from my scalp as I gouge his face—

There was no longer any reason for T'Prynn to lie—to Starfleet or to herself. Love—a taboo of unrivaled power in Vulcan culture, revered and reviled in equal measure—had been driving her mad, clouding her logic, feeding her passions, eroding her control. Anna had declared her own love openly several times, but only now could T'Prynn let herself realize that her lover had spoken the truth. A woman with two faces and two names, a Klingon in human guise, a spy turned traitor, had been the only honest thing in T'Prynn's life.

She loved me.

Hideous pain shot through T'Prynn's body—sharp jabs in her back, searing heat against her face, suffocating pressure stealing her breath. Her vision darkened until all she saw was the fire burning in the darkness.

She loved me . . . and I sacrificed her.

The truth looked back at her through the flames, its morbid grin a memento mori, its brilliant silence a scathing reproach. Love was lost, betrayed in the name of country. Hope was gone. All that remained was the fire.

She burns for me.

Grief twisted her face into a grotesque horror mask. Her cheeks were streaked with tears, her mouth contorted and agape.

Sten's blade sinks into my chest—

Sorrow and rage combusted within her and erupted as a horrible roar, as her *katra* submerged into the starless night of her own, personal damnation.

Reyes walked alone through the confusion and chaos in the docking bay's main thoroughfare. The towering emptiness of the concourse reinforced how small he felt, how powerless.

The bay three gangway was closed to everyone except pressure-suited fire-suppression teams and damage-control crews. Nonessential personnel had been evacuated from the level, leaving only the scores of injured lying supine on the deck and their attendant crowd of blue-jerseyed doctors, paramedics, and nurses kneeling beside them.

In the hangar, a massive cleanup operation was under way. Swarms of maintenance pods moved in closely choreographed patterns, collecting wreckage and, to Reyes's dismay, bodies. Thirty-eight enlisted crew and nine officers had perished aboard the *Malacca,* and five Vanguard technicians had been killed by blast effects inside maintenance bay three.

Plus one undeclared passenger aboard the Malacca, Reyes brooded. There was no doubt in his mind that the presence of Klingon double agent Anna Sandesjo had been the motive for the attack on the cargo ship. How the assassination had been carried out was a question that would likely take an investigative team weeks or perhaps even months to determine.

The casualty most disconcerting to Reyes, however, was lying on the deck ahead of him.

Lieutenant Commander T'Prynn stared at him with unseeing eyes. Her head lolled to one side, and her body was splayed in an awkward pose. Fisher and M'Benga kneeled on either side of her, and the two physicians were backed by a team of several doctors and nurses. All the medical personnel seemed to be equipped with tricorders that whirred and oscillated with high-frequency tones. One paramedic, carrying a stretcher, approached from the direction opposite Reyes.

Several members of the medical team looked up as Reyes neared. Fisher looked over his shoulder at him.

Reyes asked, "How badly is she hurt?"

Fisher stood and turned to meet Reyes. The elderly doctor's gaze was hard and unforgiving. "Physically, she's fine," he said. "This is something else."

M'Benga stepped forward and joined the conversation.

"She appears to have suffered a total psychological collapse."

"Caused by?"

"We're not sure," Fisher said, his unblinking glare of accusation trained on Reyes. He stepped closer and blatantly intruded on Reyes's personal space. "We'd have a better idea what happened if we'd been given her medical history."

Equally fearless, M'Benga added, "For a Vulcan to have that kind of breakdown, she would have to have been suffering a great deal, for a very long time. Her collapse in sickbay last week—"

"All right," Reyes snapped. "I get the point."

"No, Diego," Fisher said. "I don't think you do. She came to us a week ago looking for help—and if you hadn't tied our hands, maybe we could've done something." Contempt edged into his voice. "But everything with you has to be a goddamned secret." He turned back to the group of medics and nurses. "Put her on the stretcher! Let's get her up to the hospital!"

Fisher turned his back on Reyes and walked away. The medical team eased T'Prynn onto the stretcher, lifted her up, and followed Fisher and M'Benga toward the nearby turbolifts. Reyes watched them leave, unable to think of a single rebuttal to anything Fisher had said. All he could think of was the thousands of lives he had let be snuffed out on Gamma Tauri IV, the fear and the fury in Jeanne's eyes as he'd watched her die, and now the smoldering carnage in his docking bay and T'Prynn's shattered mind and blank eyes.

I could have evacuated the colony. Warned Jeanne. Overruled T'Prynn and declassified her medical records. . . . But I didn't. There's no one to blame but me. He spied his spectral reflection in an observation window and hated the man he saw staring back at him. *Their blood is on your hands.*

Reyes turned away from the physical and metaphysical damage his decisions had wrought on the lives of those around him and tried to walk away from it, back to work and routine and duty. But there was no walking away; the consequences of his actions shadowed his every thought—just as he knew they would, today and every day, for the rest of his life.

He recalled the words of his late mentor and Academy sponsor, Captain Rymer: *It's called being in command.*

Pennington and Quinn sat together on a grassy slope on the edge of Vanguard's terrestrial enclosure. It had been half an hour since they were evacuated from the thoroughfare after summoning medics to help T'Prynn. No one had asked them any questions; they had simply been told to move along and clear the area.

"Should we go to Manón's?" Pennington had asked.

"I don't feel like celebrating," Quinn had replied, "and I don't think the *Sagittarius* crew will, either."

He'd agreed with Quinn, and they had found themselves drifting aimlessly across the greenswards of the enclosure, past Fontana Meadow, toward the sparsely wooded incline that ringed the park's perimeter. There had been no deliberate plan, just a shared sense that neither of them wanted to return to the ship in which they'd been stuck for almost a week, nor to the empty set of rooms that Pennington laughingly called his apartment.

"I've never seen anything like that before," Quinn said.

Sketching with a twig in the cool, dark dirt, Pennington replied, "You mean the explosion?"

"No," Quinn said. "T'Prynn."

Pennington nodded. He, too, had been shaken by the primal scream that had preceded the Vulcan woman's collapse. Public displays of torment were unsettling to him even when he expected them; had T'Prynn been human, the horror and pain in her voice would still have haunted him. But to watch a Vulcan, especially one who was so disciplined and controlled, shatter so completely had been heartbreaking.

"What'd she say to you? Before she collapsed."

Quinn lowered his eyes and seemed to peer millions of

miles beyond the ground at his feet. He sighed. "She said I was free."

"Free?" echoed Pennington. "Of what?"

"Everything. Debt. Ganz. Her. . . . Just free."

Pennington pondered this new information. "Because of what we did for the *Sagittarius*?" Quinn nodded in confirmation.

Hunching forward against his knees, Pennington reconsidered his memory of T'Prynn approaching his apartment door, hesitating to knock, and walking away. *She didn't have to do right by Quinn,* he thought. *But that doesn't change what she did to me.*

He took the slender, cylindrical recording device from his jacket pocket and set it for playback. The emitter crystal in its base projected a small holographic image in the air between him and Quinn. He skipped past the images of the *Malacca* atilt and aflame, to the shot of T'Prynn at the window.

Every detail was razor-sharp: the tears rolling from her eyes, grief's trembling disfigurement of her face, even Quinn's silent recoiling in the background. Pennington studied the moment, his throat tightening in empathy for her suffering.

He looked at her right hand pressed desperately against the window, as if she had longed to reach through the flames of the crippled ship to save someone. In that instant he saw himself standing in the same pose months earlier, his hand against the window as he'd watched the blackened and broken remains of the *U.S.S. Bombay* being returned to Vanguard, piece by piece, by the crew of the *Enterprise*. He remembered grieving for Oriana, his lover, who had died aboard that ambushed vessel. Suddenly, the pain in T'Prynn's eyes was as familiar as his own, and he intuited the reason for her breakdown: someone she had loved had been on the *Malacca*.

Despite the fact that the device's playback was muted, he vividly recalled T'Prynn's cry of anguish as she threw her head back. Then she collapsed to the deck, and the recording froze on its last frame of data. Quinn and Pennington stared at it for a long moment before the pilot asked, "Now what?"

T'Prynn's open eyes stared forlornly at Pennington from the holographic freeze-frame. *This isn't news,* he decided. *This is one person's tragedy, and it's nobody else's business. Not even mine.* He selected the portion of the recording from its end to the moment before it first caught sight of T'Prynn and deleted it permanently from the recorder's memory.

"You could've used that, you know," Quinn said.

Pennington nodded. "I know." He shut off the recorder and tucked it back into his pocket.

"If she'd done to me what she did to you . . ." Quinn paused and looked away before he finished, "Not sure I could forgive her."

"I haven't," Pennington said. "But some lines I won't cross. What she did is on her conscience. What I do is on mine."

Quinn gave him a friendly slap on the back. "You're a better man than I am."

"No, I'm not," Pennington confessed. "Just a better man than I used to be."

30

Ambassador Jetanien paced beside Reyes's desk and reviewed the details of Theriault's report from a data slate clutched in his clawed manus. In the hours that had passed since the attack on the *Malacca,* Reyes had grown silent and detached. As a result, Jetanien was finding it necessary to take a more active role in this debriefing than he had expected.

"This is truly remarkable, Ensign," the Chelon diplomat said. "Considering the violent nature of our past encounters with the Shedai, this might well constitute the Federation's true first contact with them as a civilization. Splendidly done."

"Thank you, Ambassador," Theriault replied. She was seated beside Captain Nassir, in front of Reyes's desk.

Tapping the data slate with one claw, Jetanien asked, "Are you absolutely certain that the—" He looked down at the data slate and verified the name. "That the Apostate confirmed the link between the Shedai and the Tholians?"

"Yes, sir," Theriault said.

Jetanien's beak clicked with excitement. "Fascinating," he said. Then he turned toward Captain Nassir. "Now, about the entity you confronted on the planet's surface . . . did it happen to look anything like this?" He activated a screen on the wall to the captain's left. On it was a playback of the attack on the New Boulder colony. Dark ribbons of energy and flashes of lightning snared small transport ships trying to make their escape and crushed them or dashed them against the ground.

Nassir's face paled as he watched the horrific scene. "That's exactly what came after us on Jinoteur," he said.

"Then our adversary is even more potent than we had

feared," Jetanien said. "Ensign, your report states that you believe the Apostate was solely responsible for the disappearance of the Jinoteur system?"

The science officer nodded. "Yes, sir. He didn't say so explicitly, but when we left he seemed to be calling the shots. I think it might have been his endgame in what he called a war for control of the Shedai."

"Well, he appears to have done us a tremendous favor," said Jetanien. "Though it's a pity to be deprived of such a unique object of study as the Jinoteur system, being rid of the Shedai is a boon well worth—"

"Sir," Theriault cut in, "I wouldn't count on being *rid* of anything—at least, not yet." She nodded at the data slate in Jetanien's hand. "Remember that the Shedai can shed their bodies and move their essences through the Conduits. The Apostate said there were tens of thousands of these artifacts scattered across several sectors. There's no telling how many Shedai escaped Jinoteur, or where they went. And from what he said of their hierarchy, I'd guess that most of the ones who escaped were members of their elite, the *Serrataal*. There could be hundreds of them awake and free throughout the Taurus Reach right now—and it's a good bet they're all holding grudges."

Reyes chortled sarcastically and set down his coffee mug. "We're in rare form this week, eh, Jetanien?" He reclined his chair and stared glumly at the ceiling. "We fragged a planet, lost a solar system, roused a legion of angry godlike beings, and then unleashed them on the galaxy." He winced. "Oh, yes—and we got attacked in our own docking bay."

Jetanien looked at the two *Sagittarius* officers. "Captain, Ensign, thank you both for your time. Dismissed." Although the privilege of dismissing them was technically reserved to Reyes, Nassir and Theriault quickly accepted Jetanien's invitation to leave. He waited for the door to close behind them before he turned and confronted Reyes. "Conduct most unbecoming, Diego."

"Sometimes the truth isn't pretty, Jetanien." Reyes got up

and walked around his desk to stand in front of the full-wall sector chart. "We've barely got a foothold in the Taurus Reach, and already we've let loose a terror we don't know how to fight without turning planets into glass." A rueful pall deadened his expression and his voice: "And it's just a matter of time till it comes looking for us, Jetanien. Just a matter of time."

Ming Xiong unlocked the door to office CA/194-6 and stepped inside. Everything was exactly as he had left it two weeks ago before shipping out with the crew of the *Sagittarius*. Its untouched state was hardly remarkable, however, because the office was nothing more than a place for people to see him entering and leaving, as if he actually worked there.

The door locked behind him. He stepped around the drab gray Starfleet-issue furniture. Standing behind the broad, empty desk, he placed his hand against the compartment's rear wall. A sensor pad under his hand glowed red; its light was intense enough that he could almost distinguish the silhouetted bones of his hand as the machine completed its biometric scan to confirm his identity. He removed his hand. The wall slid aside without making a sound to reveal a pair of red doors, which in turn parted open, granting him access to the brightly lit corridor beyond. He shielded his eyes from the intense, stark white glare as he walked forward. The red doors shut behind him.

At the end of the fifteen-meter-long corridor, Xiong arrived at a pair of transparent sliding doors. A hidden sensor scanned him once more, and the clear panels slid apart. He stepped out of the tubular passage into the buzzing activity of Vanguard's clandestine research laboratory, known to its twenty-two permanent residents as the Vault.

To his surprise, the entire facility had been rearranged.

When he had left weeks earlier, the Vault had been partitioned into multiple small workspaces; its open floor plan and liberal usage of walls composed of transparent aluminum had given it an impressive feeling of vastness. Now he beheld a single vast enclosure inside a shell of transparent aluminum, beneath a grid of ceiling-mounted sensor arrays. Within it churned snaking coils of matter that transmuted from indigo fires to shimmering liquids peppered with sparkling motes, and from there into blades of obsidian that slashed with relentless futility at the sides of their science-spawned prison. Xiong immediately thought of Theriault's account of Tholians snared inside a Shedai Conduit and felt a pang of guilty recognition.

Gathered around the box's exterior and monitoring a score of sensor displays were all the members of Xiong's top-secret research group, plus someone he had never seen before: a blond woman in her late twenties, dressed in civilian clothes, trim and attractive but also serious and intently focused on the work being done by the rest of the team. She walked slowly from station to station, checking each scientist's work and making *sotto voce* comments before moving on.

Xiong walked directly toward her as she stopped beside Dr. Varech jav Gek, the team's leading geneticist. From a few meters away he heard her say to the Tellarite scientist, "Try to isolate the trigger in that chromosome, then we'll run the catalyst sequence again." The gray-bearded Gek nodded and began entering commands on his console. The woman turned in Xiong's direction and started to walk to the next workstation when he intercepted her. "Excuse me," he said to her. "What's going on here? Who are you?"

She flashed an insincere smile that he knew was not an overture of friendship. "I'm your new partner," she replied. Extending her hand, she added, "Dr. Carol Marcus."

With reluctance he shook her hand. "Lieutenant Ming Xiong."

"I know who you are," she said, walking past him.

He followed her. "Then you know that I'm in charge of the Vault." He gestured at the transparent enclosure. "And that I have to approve all new research projects."

"Things change, Lieutenant," Marcus said. "It's not always a bad thing." At the next workstation, she reached past Dr. Tarcoh, a paunchy Deltan theoretical physicist in his late sixties, and adjusted a setting on his console. "Look for changes in its mass," she said, patting Tarcoh's arm. "I'm betting it has an extradimensional component." On the move again, she said over her shoulder to Xiong, "We're already working on your data from Jinoteur. Quite a breakthrough."

For Xiong, keeping pace with her was easy; keeping his temper in check was proving increasingly difficult. "You're not Starfleet," he said. "Who sent you?"

Marcus replied, "I'm here at the request of the Federation Council. Someone's worried that the work you're doing is too important not to have civilian oversight."

Xiong gave a cynical smirk. "How thoughtful."

She maintained her veneer of unflappable calm. "I've been told to make copies of your data, debrief you on what you and the *Sagittarius* crew learned at Jinoteur, and make regular reports to the Council about our findings. And I think you'll find that you have orders to give me your full cooperation."

They arrived at a long row of master-control consoles behind another thick protective wall of transparent aluminum. Marcus stood in the middle, her eyes panning quickly across the dense cluster of displays and gauges. The panels beneath the monitor banks were packed with multicolored buttons, sliders, and other tried-and-true manual controls.

While Marcus busied herself making minor adjustments, Xiong used a secondary console to access his personal communications channel. Just as Marcus had said, he had received a prioritized order from Starfleet Command directing him to comply with Marcus's requests for information and granting her the authority to initiate and direct research inside the Vault. It appeared that, wherever she had come from, she had come to stay awhile.

As he logged off, she glanced at him. "Satisfied?"

He frowned. "How much of our research have you been able to review?"

"Almost all of it; I've been here for ten days. Granted, I only skimmed the hard data, but the abstracts and summaries were so exciting that I couldn't wait to get started."

A condescending smirk tugged at his mouth. "Abstracts," he said. "Summaries." He shook his head. "In other words, you don't really know what we've found—or what you're being asked to do."

"I know more than you think, Lieutenant," Marcus said. "I understand that we're talking about an intricate, phenomenally complex genome comprising hundreds of millions of chromosomes. I know that it's been linked to a set of artifacts on several far-flung planets. And I'm aware that it's put us into conflict with a very powerful species we don't yet know how to combat." She smirked and lifted one eyebrow. "Do you want to quiz me on the genome's unique chemical markers?"

Xiong rolled his eyes. "That won't be necessary," he said. Putting aside his resentment of Marcus's brusque manner, he grudgingly concluded that it might be useful to have a fresh perspective on the Taurus meta-genome project. "Have you read the report I filed a few hours ago, after the *Sagittarius* made port?"

"Some of it," Marcus said.

He activated a monitor on the console between them. "I'll call it up over here. I've been working on it for the last six days, since we left Jinoteur." He tapped commands into the computer interface and called up the classified report. "There's a lot of data, but I can sum up the high points for you."

"Please do," Marcus said, scrolling through the tricorder readings Xiong had made of Jinoteur's peculiar energy field.

"You've already unlocked part of it," he said, "shifting pieces of the Shedai body between physical states. The crew of the *Sagittarius* watched a living Shedai do that in real time, traveling as a gas, becoming a gelatinous liquid for searching and a solid for attacking. In addition, they have sensor readings showing that these beings can control electromagnetic effects, including lightning."

He pressed some keys on the console desk and patched in a

new set of data from his report. "Injuries sustained by *Sagittarius* officers Terrell and McLellan showed the same kind of crystalline infection that Dr. Fisher detected on the corpse of *Endeavour* scientist Bohanon. The application of a dampening field attuned to Shedai neural frequencies retarded its spread."

Xiong reached past Marcus to tie in a new databank, and she moved back to give him room to work as he continued his briefing. "Now for the really exciting part," he said. "During one Shedai attack, Lieutenant Commander McLellan's right leg was severed at the knee. Dr. Babitz, applying an energy pulse based on the Shedai carrier wave and partially recoded with McLellan's DNA pattern, was able to revivify crystallized tissue in the amputated limb—and reattach it to the patient, with a full tissue-regeneration effect." He replaced McLellan's medical file with Terrell's. "The same effort *failed* to work for Commander Terrell—and I think I know why."

"The Jinoteur Pattern," Marcus blurted out.

Her preemptive leap caught him by surprise. "That's right," he said. "When the regenerative field was applied to McLellan's leg, the *Sagittarius* was on the planet's surface, surrounded by the Jinoteur system's unique energy field."

"But the procedure on Commander Terrell," Marcus noted, pointing out the detail in Dr. Babitz's report, "wasn't attempted until after the star system had vanished."

"Exactly," Xiong said. "She had to remove the crystallized tissue surgically." He closed Terrell's file and called up the Jinoteur carrier-wave signal. "We'd noted some correlations in this carrier wave to segments of the meta-genome. We were able to use it to construct a means of sending a 'ping' to look for other artifacts—which we now know are called Conduits. It gave us only limited insights into decoding the master structure of the meta-genome, but with the Jinoteur Pattern—"

"It's like matching a key to a lock," Marcus said, nodding along, riding the tide of his excitement. "This is fantastic."

"I know!" Elated to finally have someone who appreciated the broader implications of the work that had dominated the past three years of his life, he could hardly contain himself. "Think about it—with this kind of a regenerative matrix, we could heal all kinds of injuries. Lost limbs, deep-tissue damage—the possibilities are incredible."

Marcus laughed. Then she caught herself and covered her mouth until she regained her composure. "Lieutenant," she said, as if she were appalled at his reaction, "this is much bigger than fixing a few broken bodies. You said yourself that the entire Jinoteur system was infused with this waveform."

A feeling of intense dread welled up inside him. "So . . .?"

"So?" Marcus replied. She called up the sensor readings that Theriault had made of the Jinoteur system before the ship had approached the fourth planet. "That star system registered as less than half a million years old. With a main-sequence star? And every body in the system the exact same age? How is that even possible?" The Jinoteur Pattern appeared on the screen, and a slightly fanatical gleam lit up Marcus's eyes. "What if this matrix doesn't just regenerate what already exists? What if it can be used to shape matter and energy into any configuration desired?" She stared at it in awe. "You could build planets from *nothing*. You could make *stars*." She grinned, giddy with excitement, and mimed a supernova explosion with her hands. "*Let there be light*."

Xiong finally understood why his pleas for scientific glasnost with the Klingons and the Tholians had been refused so adamantly by Starfleet Command. If Marcus was right about the tremendous possibilities contained in the meta-genome and the waveform, it was a discovery with galactic implications.

In the right hands, it could be the greatest gift ever bestowed upon sentient beings, a boon to life itself.

In the wrong hands, it would be the most barbaric weapon of mass destruction and genocide ever known.

Watching his new colleague gaze in wonder at the mysterious energy waveform on his monitor, Xiong silently wished that he could go back six days in time to that placid, moonlit beach on Jinoteur—and shatter his tricorder against a boulder.

"If you'll excuse me," Xiong said softly, "I think I'd like to go and get settled back into my office." He started to leave.

Marcus's apologetic tone almost sounded sincere as she broke the news. "That's not *your* office anymore."

Pennington sat cross-legged on the floor in the center of his empty living room. At his side was a half-eaten turkey sandwich and a bottle of lukewarm fruit juice that he had purchased to go from a vendor in Stars Landing's restaurant district. It was a far cry from the fancy cuisine that he had enjoyed during his brief years as a star reporter for the Federation News Service, but, as his former editor Arlys often liked to say, "the best reporters are the hungry ones."

A single, tubular lighting element, which he had purchased from the station's quartermaster with a bit of his meager savings, glowed from the fixture on the ceiling above him. His shadow fell over the screen of the small portable data manager in his hands; he used the device for everything from personal communications to composing his freelance news stories and editing audiovisual data from his recorder.

Though he had watched his video footage from Jinoteur more than a hundred times in the past week, he remained unsure how much of it was good enough to use in his report. Most of the shots he had made—while running from and dodging falling debris—were staticky and blurred, more suggestive than conclusive. The wildly shaking images had barely captured a few clear frames of the creatures he had encountered on the planet. He had made extensive notes about his firsthand observations, but the only person who could corroborate his account of events was Ensign Theriault—who, he had been unsurprised to learn, was under orders not to discuss the mission with anyone.

Not that it would make much difference, he figured. *It's not as if Commodore Reyes would let me file this story anyway.*

Voices outside his window—pedestrians passing by—pulled him out of his thoughts. He looked up from his work and realized that he had lost track of time; he had been working for several hours. Outside his window, the darkness of a simulated night had fallen over Stars Landing. Dusky orange lamplight slanted through his vertical window blinds.

Yawning, he stretched his arms over his head. *Maybe I'll go out for a while. See if Quinn's down the pub.*

A knock on his apartment door echoed off his bare walls. Hope triumphed over experience, and he afforded himself a moment of optimism. He had hoped that Theriault would come calling, perhaps to buy him the drink she had promised him. Though he had never actually told her where he lived, it wasn't as if he were hard to find: like every other permanent denizen of Starbase 47, his residence was listed in the public directory.

He set aside his data manager and stiffly pushed himself back to his feet. A few creaking-kneed steps later, he opened his front door—and felt the enthusiasm bleed from his face as he saw Diego Reyes looking back at him. "Commodore," Pennington said, masking his hostility with humor. "Time for my inquisition already? I was sure I'd merit at least one night's reprieve."

"May I come in, Mr. Pennington?"

The manner of Reyes's asking surprised Pennington; the commodore had sounded sincere and nonconfrontational. Stepping back from the doorway, Pennington replied, "Of course, sir."

Reyes took cautious steps into the apartment, as if he were wary of an ambush. He looked around at the barren space and down at the half-consumed meal and beverage. "Love what you've done with the place."

Pennington stood behind Reyes and leaned against the wall beside the front door. "I'd invite you to sit down, but I'm boycotting furniture."

The commodore stepped into the middle of the room and picked up Pennington's data device. He held it in one hand and looked back at Pennington. "May I?"

"May you what? Read it? Or take it?"

He didn't expect Reyes's low-key reaction, a contrite lowering of his eyes. "May I look at it?"

Folding his arms, Pennington replied, "Be my guest." He watched for about a minute as Reyes reviewed his first-draft text article and the related video clips and images. Every few seconds, Reyes's eyebrows lifted slightly, or he nodded slowly.

"Impressive," Reyes said as he turned off the device. "I'd have thought the star system vanishing would leave you behind the eight ball, but you even made that work for you." He kneeled, set the device back on the floor, and stood again. "I'm sorry I can't let the *Sagittarius* officers go on the record."

"No doubt," Pennington said, already tired of Reyes's slow dance around the obvious. "I know why you're here, Commodore. Do us both a favor, and get it over with."

At first, Reyes didn't respond. He walked over to the window and peeked between the blinds, through the amber light, into the artificial evening of the station's terrestrial enclosure. "Why do you think I'm here, Mr. Pennington?"

A trick question? Pennington hesitated before he answered, "To seize my footage from Jinoteur—and to tell me not to bother filing the story, since it won't get past your censors."

"Send it to me," Reyes said. "I'll make sure it goes out as written."

Instantly suspicious of the commodore's motives, Pennington considered a few possible scenarios at work: an attempt at entrapment, a cruel hoax, or another scheme to publicly attack his credibility. "Why?" he asked. "What's in it for you?"

"The truth," Reyes said. "Nothing more, nothing less." The longer he stared out the window, the more distant his expression became. "Very soon, Tim—perhaps in a couple of days— word's going to get out that I invoked General Order 24 against Gamma Tauri IV." He looked at Pennington. "Do you know what that is?" Pennington shook his head no, and Reyes continued, "It's an order to annihilate the surface of a planet—to exterminate every living thing, blast away its atmosphere, cook its oceans, and leave nothing but a red-hot ball of glass."

It was a startling image. "My God," Pennington whispered.

"I gave that order to contain a threat," Reyes said. "To stop a massive attack by an enemy you've now seen with your own eyes." He turned once more to the view outside the window. "More than thirteen thousand people died on Gamma Tauri IV," he said. As he continued, his sorrow slowly transmuted to quiet anger. "But that's nothing compared to how many would die if that enemy ever reaches a fully populated planet. We woke this nightmare, and now it's loose, God knows where, running amok. And nobody knows about it, Tim. Nobody knows because we keep hiding the truth, hoping we can steal another handful of ancient secrets from these creatures before all hell breaks loose." His anger abated, leaving only his somber tone of grief. "The crew of the *Bombay* died for this secret, along with a dozen men and women from the *Endeavour* and the *Lovell*. Now it's claimed thirteen thousand souls on Gamma Tauri IV, including a woman who used to be my wife." He sighed heavily. "How many have to die? How many lives are we supposed to sacrifice on the altar of security? When does this madness stop?"

Pennington's throat tightened with anxiety. Outside of Starfleet, he was likely the only person who knew that Reyes had ordered the destruction of Gamma Tauri IV. It was as big a piece of breaking news as his experiences on Jinoteur. "Sir," he said, concealing his apprehension with a neutral monotone, "what do you want me to do with this information?"

"Publish it." Reyes turned away from the window and walked to the front door. "Write the truth, exactly as you saw it."

"The truth about Gamma Tauri IV might make you look bad," Pennington said, halting Reyes in the open doorway. "*Very* bad."

Looking back, Reyes replied, "All the more reason."

"But if you let my story go out uncensored," Pennington said, "won't you be court-martialed?"

For a moment he thought he saw Reyes almost grin. "Probably," the commodore said. "It's your call, Tim. Do what you think's right." Reyes walked away, and the door shut with a loud *clack,* leaving Pennington alone with its echo.

He stood staring at the closed door, recovering from the shock of the unexpected . . . and then, all thoughts of Quinn, a drink at Tom Walker's place, and a grateful cute redhead left his mind as he scooped up his data device and resumed writing.

I can finish this story in a few hours, he told himself. *Let's just hope Reyes doesn't change his mind before it's filed.*

The gauges above T'Prynn's biobed had all but flatlined. Fisher frowned as he watched and waited during the prolonged lacunae between minuscule pulses of the Vulcan's autonomic systems.

M'Benga stood on the other side of the bed, leaning into the pool of bright bluish light focused on T'Prynn. He made notes on her chart, which was cradled in his bent left arm. Noticing Fisher's dismay, he said, "Don't be alarmed by her vital signs. It's perfectly natural."

"Nothing natural about it," Fisher said, the edges in his voice rougher than usual. "She's one late breath from dead."

They were alone with T'Prynn in one of Vanguard Hospital's isolation wards. Soft synthetic tones beeped and whirred in the background. Ten times per minute, a deep *thump* emanated from the cardiopulmonary monitor, signaling another feeble beat of T'Prynn's heart. Her breaths were long but shallow.

Not content to let a machine guide his entire diagnosis, Fisher reached down to grasp T'Prynn's wrist and feel for himself the strength of her pulse. He pushed aside the edge of the thermal blanket that covered her from the neck down. As he grasped her radiantly warm wrist, he nodded at the blanket and asked M'Benga, "Is this thing really necessary?"

"It helps promote the healing process," M'Benga said. "In a Vulcan healing trance, a patient concentrates his or her strength, blood, and antibodies on the injury. Simulating the heat and aridity of Vulcan facilitates this effort."

A weak tremor of life passed through T'Prynn's wrist, under

Fisher's fingertip. "Whatever did this to her," he said, "I don't think blood or antibodies are gonna fix it." He looked at her face, which was neither placid nor troubled—merely blank. "And you can call this a healing trance if it makes you feel better, but when I was in medical school we called this a coma."

M'Benga finished marking the chart and set it back into a slot at the foot of T'Prynn's bed. "Perhaps you're right," he said. "If this is a healing trance, it's the deepest one I've ever seen. But even if I'm wrong, and it is a coma, I see no harm in making her comfortable."

Fisher withdrew his hand from T'Prynn's wrist. "Agreed," he said. He gently tucked the thermal blanket back into place at the bed's edge. Drawing a breath as a prelude to a sigh, he inhaled the bracing odors of surgical sanitizer and the harsh disinfectant used to mop the hospital's floors. Exhaling, he felt fatigue spread through him. It had been a manic day tending the wounded and dying from the attack on the *Malacca,* and this was the final stop on his evening rounds. He plucked T'Prynn's chart from the slot at the foot of the bed and skimmed it quickly. "I see we finally got her real medical history," he said.

"Yes," M'Benga said. "It makes for fascinating reading. Those deep-tissue injuries and skeletal fractures I detected during her physical were sustained during a premarital ritual combat called *Koon-ut-kal-if-fee.* Usually, the challenge is made by someone who wants to marry a person betrothed to another, so they can fight their rival for the mate. When T'Prynn asked her fiancé Sten to terminate their marriage compact, he refused and challenged her to the duel. Apparently, his aim was either to force her to change her mind or to deny her the right to claim another mate in the future. . . . So she killed him."

"Charming," Fisher said, almost dreading to see what other dark secrets of Vulcan culture were hidden in its details. "Is that why she's been hiding these records?"

M'Benga conveyed his doubt with a tilt of his head. "I don't think so. The *Koon-ut-kal-if-fee* is a legally protected Vulcan ritual. Unless she assaulted or killed a fellow member of Starfleet, or an unwilling participant, her actions would be entirely lawful under Vulcan jurisprudence."

"Murdering people over sex and marriage," Fisher mumbled. "Logical, my ass." He glanced peremptorily at M'Benga. "And don't go lecturing me about why I shouldn't be appalled by this *Koon-ut*-whatever business." Flipping through the rest of T'Prynn's medical file, he noted the pattern of her anxiety attacks, which had become more severe and more frequent over the course of several decades. "If it wasn't the legal fallout that worried her," he speculated, "I'll bet it was these seizures. A history of mental illness would shred her security rating. She's probably been afraid of being relieved of duty."

Nodding, M'Benga said, "With good reason. Now that her records have been declassified and Starfleet Intelligence has our report, they've revoked her security clearance. If she ever wakes up, she'll be lucky to avoid a court-martial."

Fisher dropped the data slate with T'Prynn's chart back into the slot on the bed and heaved a dejected sigh. "If she ever wakes up, she'll be lucky, *period.*"

31

Three minutes past 0800, Reyes settled into the chair behind his desk and checked the data feeds from the Federation. Sipping from his day's first mug of coffee, he scanned the headlines. He didn't have to look far to find what he sought.

It was the top item on every news feed, and it carried the byline of Tim Pennington: "Starfleet Officer Orders Destruction of Gamma Tauri IV." Running beside it on more than half of the major news services was Pennington's story about his excursion to Jinoteur IV, the mysterious life-forms of that now-vanished star system, their attack on the *Sagittarius,* and their link to the Gamma Tauri IV disaster.

Reyes took another sip of his coffee, decided it was too hot, and reclined slightly while he puffed gently across the top of his morning beverage. The mug was almost painfully warm in his hands. He considered paging Yeoman Greenfield and asking her to bring him more sugar.

His desktop intercom beeped. The indicator for Jetanien's private comm channel lit up. Reyes blew another breath over his coffee and set the mug gently on his desk while the intercom beeped again. He leaned forward and pushed the switch to open the channel. "Reyes here."

"Diego," Jetanien said, sounding like someone who was pretending to be calm but failing miserably, *"I thought you might like to know that she is already on her way up."*

Even though his friend couldn't see him, Reyes nodded. "I figured as much."

"We don't have much time," Jetanien said. *"Once she gets there, you and I will not be permitted to speak further. I need to*

*ask you some very direct questions, and I would appreciate the
courtesy of succinct, truthful replies."*

Choosing not to waste time by mocking Jetanien for asking
someone else to be succinct, Reyes replied simply, "Fire away."

"Was this your doing?"

"Yes, it was."

Agitated clicking noises tapped over the intercom channel.
*"Were you aware of the story's contents before you released it
for publication?"*

Reyes swallowed another half-mouthful of coffee. "Yup."

This time a low groan underscored the telltale scrape of Jetanien anxiously grinding his beak back and forth. *"Was your
action in any way coerced?"*

"Nope."

"Diego, this next query is vital," said Jetanien. *"Does the reporter know about the meta-genome, the Jinoteur carrier-wave
signal, or the Shedai energy waveform?"*

"No," Reyes said. "All he knows is what he saw with his own
eyes—and that's all he wrote about."

Another round of groaning and clicks issued from the intercom. *"A most regrettable turn of events, Diego."* After a few
seconds of heavy silence, the Chelon asked, *"Is there anything
that I can do for you before she arrives?"*

"Yeah," Reyes said. "Have someone bring me more sugar."

Pennington relaxed in a comfortable chair at the outdoor café,
on the plaza near the edge of Stars Landing. The crescent-
shaped neighborhood of elegant civilian buildings gleamed
under the pale morning glow of an ersatz sky inside Starbase
47's terrestrial enclosure.

He was glad to be back at one of his favorite haunts on the
station. Only a few other places on Vanguard made eggs Benedict, and none prepared it as well as it was made at Café
Romano. Pennington gave the credit to Matt, the café's chef-
proprietor, for his ability to make consistently perfect Hollandaise sauce.

It was five minutes past 0800. Pennington was half finished with his breakfast and triple espresso; his latest story was less than ninety minutes old, and already it had provoked a storm of controversy throughout the interstellar newswire services. In one feature article, he had linked the obliteration of Gamma Tauri IV to inconsistencies in Starfleet's account of the deaths of its personnel on Erilon, the destruction of the *U.S.S. Bombay*, and a previously unknown species that had controlled the suddenly missing Jinoteur star system.

Pundits at some news services had called his account of events on Jinoteur IV fiction, but so far none had been able to discredit his video evidence of the beings known as the Shedai, and no one could explain the system's disappearance. Independent sources had already verified the complete annihilation of Gamma Tauri IV by photon-torpedo bombardment, and Starfleet had reluctantly confirmed its role in that tragedy.

His data device registered a steady flow of incoming text messages from former colleagues at FNS, as well as several from editors and peers at other news services. The missives were all but unanimous in their congratulations; several contained offers of long-term column-writing assignments or invitations to pitch feature stories. Checking the bottom of the alphabetical list, he even found a terse message of congratulation from Arlys Warfield, his former FNS editor, who had fired him after the debacle of the *Bombay* story.

He savored the taste of victory along with his espresso.

Get over yourself, he thought, popping the suddenly inflated bubble of his ego. *You're just a word monkey who likes to snoop. Don't go believing your own press.*

As he lifted a forkful of eggs Benedict, his data device beeped twice to signal an incoming transmission. He set his fork on the plate, picked up the device, and keyed the transceiver. "This is Tim Pennington."

"Mr. Pennington," replied the coarse, familiar voice of Commodore Reyes. *"Think you can handle another scoop?"*

A quick look around assured Pennington that no one was eavesdropping. "I'm willing to try."

"Get to my office in the next five minutes. Reyes out."

Pennington pulled his portable recorder from his pocket and ran for the turbolifts.

Flanked by a pair of serious-faced young male security guards, Captain Rana Desai waited outside Reyes's office. Business as usual continued around her until his door slid open, with a hiss barely audible over the hubbub of Vanguard's operations center.

Reyes stepped through the doorway and stood in front of her. All activity on the deck stopped, and the mood grew heavy with grim anticipation. Several meters away, a turbolift opened. Tim Pennington dashed out and stumbled to an awkward halt.

From the first day she had started assembling the chart in the JAG office, Desai had known this moment might come. But she had not expected it to arrive so soon, or for Reyes himself to have forced her hand. In a voice just for him, she asked, "Diego . . . you know I have no choice?"

His bearing was proud but forgiving. He answered her in a discreet tone. "You have to do your job, Rana."

Around them, the onlookers slowly had pressed closer. Junior officers, Reyes's yeoman, and particularly reporter Tim Pennington all were within easy eavesdropping distance.

Her heart swelled with regret. She blinked, cleared her eyes, and steadied her breathing as she forced all vestiges of emotion from her face. "Commodore Diego Reyes," she declared in her clipped London accent, "by order of the Starfleet Judge Advocate General, you are hereby charged with willfully disobeying the direct order of a superior officer; deliberately releasing classified Starfleet intelligence to the public; and conspiring to disclose classified information.

"You have the right to legal counsel. You have the right to refuse to answer questions. Do you understand these rights?"

Reyes nodded once. "Yes, I do."

"You are hereby relieved of your command, relieved of duty,

and placed under arrest." Desai looked to the guard on her left. "Take the commodore into custody, and escort him to the brig."

"Aye, Captain," said the guard, who stepped forward, looked at Reyes, and gestured with his arm toward a nearby turbolift. "Sir, if you please." Reyes did as he was asked and walked calmly toward the turbolift, with the two guards following close behind him.

Anger and desperation clashed inside Desai's thoughts as she watched the man she had come to love being taken away as a prisoner on what had been, until moments ago, his own station. Unable to continue watching his exit from the operations center, she turned and faced Commander Jon Cooper, who stood looking down from the supervisor's deck. "Commander Cooper," Desai said. "You're in charge. . . . Good luck."

Guessing she would likely be persona non grata in ops for a while, Desai left the stunned first officer to ponder his sudden promotion and stepped toward a different turbolift from the one into which Reyes was being led. Her only aim was to get back to her office and start preparing her case. Focusing on work felt heartless, but for her own good—and for Diego's as well—she knew it was the right thing to do. She had a lot of gaps left to fill in, but there was no more time to pin photos on walls and collect anecdotes; it was time to get serious.

She had a court-martial to win.

MINISTERS OF VENGEANCE

TWO TO TANGO

Zett Nilric's ship, a new Nalori argosy named *Icarion,* had been drifting for nearly two days with its engines offline. Its life support had been kept at a bare-minimum level, and its effective communications range was less than one light-minute. Unless another vessel was making a determined effort to find it and knew exactly where to look, it was unlikely that the *Icarion* would be detected. But because his employer had made specific arrangements with Starfleet to keep this sector of deep space clear of patrols and unwatched by long-range sensor arrays, Zett had every reason to believe that he was working in privacy.

It was time. He passed one glossy, midnight-black hand over his ship's immaculate main console and tapped the secure-frequency transmitter, sending a brief, ultra-low-power pulse of encrypted data into the emptiness of Sector Tango-4119. If his contact was punctual, the wait would be short.

Behind him, in the main cabin beyond the cockpit, the stone sarcophagus sat secured to the deck. Zett was not a man who spooked easily, but he wanted this cargo off his ship. He had sneered at the obvious terror its contents had inspired in the primitive aliens from whom he had acquired it, but within two days of taking possession of it, he had become wary of the artifact. An aura of menace emanated from it. He was certain that it was infecting his dreams with terrors and disquieting his waking thoughts with demoralizing subliminal insinuations. Less than four days in its presence had convinced him that evil was more than an abstract concept—it was a concrete reality, lying silent inside a two-meter-long coffin of dark gray, rough-hewn granite.

He jolted with surprise as the double beep of a response signal shrilled in the silence of the cockpit. A deep breath restored his calm, and then he opened the channel and issued the challenge phrase. "If you approach for the attack, never forget to wait for the right moment."

A gruff voice answered over the comm, *"In waiting for the right moment, never forget to attack."*

Zett transmitted beam-in coordinates to his contact, got up from his seat, and walked back into the main cabin. Four signal-blocking pylons stood at the corners of the sarcophagus, as insurance against the client's potential impulse to try to steal it via transporter beam. The Nalori assassin stepped past the stone coffin and placed himself between it and the beam-in coordinates. Then he waited.

Moments later a shimmer and a singsong, oscillating drone of high-pitched white noise filled the air a few meters in front of him. The swirling glow of light coalesced into a humanoid shape and faded to reveal a ridged-headed, black-bearded, swarthy Klingon named Qahl. As the last traces of the transporter effect faded, the visitor took one step forward, looked Zett in the eye, and pointed at the sarcophagus. "Is that it?"

"Yes," Zett said. He stepped aside to give Qahl an unobstructed view. "Examine it first, if you like."

The Klingon stepped past Zett and positioned himself next to one long side of the artifact. His large, callused hands caressed the ruts and peaks of the object's primitively carved stone lid. Zett followed him and stood on the opposite side of the ancient burial case. Qahl asked, "Where did you get it?"

"Are you prepared to pay an extra five million?"

Qahl scowled at Zett and grunted as he resumed his tactile examination of the casket. "I want to look inside."

"Go ahead," Zett said, moving back to give him some room.

Struggling to get a solid grip on the lid, Qahl glared at Zett. "You could lend a hand."

Gesturing with a fluid, top-to-bottom sweep of his hand at his custom-tailored charcoal suit and perfectly polished black shoes, Zett flashed a smile of glistening black teeth. "Sorry," he said. "I'm not dressed for manual labor."

Qahl grumbled under his *gagh*-fouled breath, which Zett could smell from meters away as the Klingon huffed and struggled to lift the sarcophagus lid by himself. With tremendous effort he raised one side of it several centimeters and tilted his head to peek under it, into a mesmerizing flicker of violet light. His eyes widened, and his jaw went slack.

Zett counted to ten, decided Qahl had seen enough to make an informed decision, and pressed his palm against the stone lid, forcing it shut with a resounding boom. "Satisfied?"

The Klingon nodded, palmed a sheen of musky perspiration from his brow, and stepped back. He reached into a fold of his black-and-gold uniform jacket and produced a credit chip, which he handed to Zett. The trim, shaved-headed Nalori accepted it with a polite half-nod and carried it to an interface on the bulkhead to verify that it was genuine, wasn't boobytrapped, and contained the correct amount of remuneration. Stroking his twisted, pale-violet beard braid, he watched Qahl in the corner of his vision while he waited.

To his surprise, there was more money on the chip than had been agreed upon. He turned and narrowed his flat-black, pupil-free eyes at Qahl, who, apparently having anticipated Zett's wary response, grinned broadly. "A bonus," the Klingon said. "To show our gratitude for your successful and no doubt highly dangerous assassination of our turncoat agent on Vanguard."

In Zett's opinion, his assassination of Lurqal—a.k.a. Anna Sandesjo—had been some of the sloppiest work he had ever done. He preferred to kill his victims in private and make their bodies disappear without a trace. A murder suspected but never proved was the height of his art; a public act of arson with broad collateral damage was an amateurish atrocity. Unfortunately, because of the short notice he had been given by the Klingons and the extraordinary security measures that had been taken by Starfleet Intelligence, the brute-force bombing of the *Malacca* had been the only viable tactic available to him.

He ejected the chip from the wall panel, tucked it into his pants pocket, turned to Qahl, and said simply, "Thank you." Then he took a remote control from his jacket pocket and entered the disarming code for the transport scramblers. "You're all set."

Qahl plucked a communicator from his belt and flipped it open. A few guttural Klingon commands later, he and the stone sarcophagus dissolved in an incandescent flurry of golden particles accompanied by the siren song of a transporter beam.

Zett returned to the cockpit and sat down. He had no idea what had been inside the sarcophagus, or why the Klingons had been willing to pay such an outrageous price to acquire it. All he knew was that he was glad to have it off his ship.

All in a day's work, he told himself as he fired up the engines of the *Icarion,* set course for Vanguard, and made the jump to warp speed.

The knife that T'Prynn pulled from her chest wasn't real, nor was the dark green slick of warm blood that trickled along the wavy line of the blade's temper. A chill wind swept across the desolate nightscape of sand and broken stone, a cold promise of torments yet to come. None of those was real, either.

Neither were the starless sky, the endless night, the great trackless wasteland spread out beneath the void. Not the pain of her shattered bones, not her flayed skin, not the burning welts across her back, not the split in her lip stung by her saliva, not the coppery swell of blood in the back of her throat.

The only things real in this frozen purgatory were T'Prynn's grief, rage, and despair. Isolated inside her psyche, bereft of her psionic defenses and patient meditations, she clung to her guilt, her anger, and her bitter sorrow; they were all she had left. Her wailing cries and guttural screams were as much inventions of her imagination as the banshee howls of the wind, but her anguish was genuine. It was *real,* so she clung to it.

Time slipped away from her. The land and all that stood upon it—every lonely menhir, every dead and twisted tree—

were lit from within by a surreal, dull gray twilight. Her pale skin was the ashen hue of a corpse, and her blood ran black from wounds that refused to heal.

Anna's ghost drifted in silent strides across the desert, her accusing stare paralyzing T'Prynn. Then she vanished in a blossom of flames, like a scrap of parchment consumed in a bonfire.

Why did I let her go? How could I?

Sprawled on the frigid sands, T'Prynn scuttled in a tight circle, like a scavenger searching the seabed in an ocean of regrets. In every direction she watched shades of her former self replay shameful moments from the life she had led.

Weak men she had coerced into peril. A good man she had deceived and ruined. Countless tiny acts of blackmail, fraud, and extortion. Principles betrayed in the name of "the greater good" and an illusory, unattainable commodity called "national security." Real lives had been lost and real people had come to harm because of her efforts to promote and defend an abstract concept. It had been an illogical, wasteful endeavor.

What am I? What have I become?

His foot slammed into the back of her head.

The impact threw her facedown into the sand, and when she looked up it was because Sten was dragging her by her hair. Jagged rocks bit into her lower back as he pulled her over the ground toward a long, rectangular pit of glowing coals. Around them stood all the ceremonial trappings of the *kal-if-fee,* from the *lirpa* and the *ahn-woon* to the braziers of coals and many other barbaric remnants of a past that would not die.

Scorching fires charred the backs of her bare thighs as she twisted but failed to break free of Sten's grip. On the other side of the coal pit, he hurled her to the ground. As he kicked at her, she tried to catch his foot, but he was too quick. His foot slammed into her midriff, winding her and cracking her ribs. She doubled over and clutched at her gut. Then his foot struck her under the chin and snapped her head back, flinging a long trail of green spittle from her mouth.

Crawling like an animal, she dug into the ground with her

fingertips for purchase. Slithering, unable to rise, she clawed her way toward the weapons, which were arranged together several meters distant. Sten strolled nonchalantly ahead of her and picked up the *ahn-woon*. He tested the flexibility of the rawhide strap and turned to face T'Prynn, who continued to drag herself toward the weapons, determined to arm herself.

The *ahn-woon* cracked loudly in T'Prynn's ears as it snapped with agonizing precision across her left cheek, drawing blood. She fell onto her elbows as her left hand pressed against the fresh wound. Warm green blood coated her palm, leaked between her fingers, and ran down her forearm.

Sten circled her, putting the strap to her as he went. It tore ragged gaps in her uniform and her flesh. Each strike fell with greater force than the last, wounded her more deeply. She was almost relieved when most of the *ahn-woon*'s length coiled around her neck like a noose. Tensing her throat to spare her trachea from being crushed, she pried desperately at the strap's coils, which felt like iron bands around her throat. Sten gave it a firm tug and spun T'Prynn around to face him. He dragged her toward him, until she was close enough to smell the sweat on his skin and see the spark of *Pon farr* madness in his eyes. Controlling the *ahn-woon* with both hands, he twisted it slightly and tightened its hold on her throat.

Asphyxia set in, softening her vision, filling her ears with the roar of her own slowing pulse, clouding her mind with panic. Sten gazed down at her with condescending pity.

"Your struggle is pointless, T'Prynn. I have always been stronger than you, and I always will be." Fury burned in her eyes, and he smirked at it. "You know I speak the truth. In all those moments when you have lacked the strength to do what *had to be done,* I gave you that strength. *My* strength." To her air-starved mind, he had become little more than a dark blur against a pitch-black sky, a shadow in a world without true light. "Why go on fighting, T'Prynn? You've lost, but you don't need to be destroyed. Surrender." All she saw was his silhouette looming triumphant above her as he bade her, *"Submit."*

There was a rock in her hand, a sharp and pointed stone. She had no memory of picking it up, but it was as real in her grasp as her fear. A savage thrust plunged it deep and squarely into Sten's groin. He bellowed in agony and staggered backward, releasing the *ahn-woon,* which went limp around T'Prynn's throat. She let go of the stone, which fell with a soft *thump* into the sand. Her Vulcan blood now fully inflamed, she began uncoiling the *ahn-woon* from her neck and forced herself to stand on unsteady feet.

Dozens of wounds inflicted on almost every part of her body bled copiously, covering her with an emerald sheen.

The last wrap of the *ahn-woon* fell from her throat. She flicked her wrist, and the bloodstained rawhide strap snapped loudly, commanding Sten's attention.

"You've only postponed the inevitable, T'Prynn." He reached back, picked up a *lirpa,* and swung its blunt, heavy end-weight and fan-shaped blade with leisurely ease. "Accept your defeat, and I will spare you." He advanced on her, spinning the *lirpa* in slow, hypnotic turns.

And once more he dared to command her: "Submit."

She looped the *ahn-woon* around the *lirpa*'s handle and disarmed him with one pull. His weapon flew into her hands.

Then he had her answer.

"Never."

The saga of
STAR TREK VANGUARD
will continue

STAR TREK VANGUARD MINIPEDIA

DEW: *Star Trek Corps of Engineers: Distant Early Warning*
HAR: *Harbinger*
STT: *Summon the Thunder*
RTW: *Reap the Whirlwind*

Adams, Lieutenant Donovan—Search party leader, Gamma Tauri IV. KIA. (RTW)

Adjudicator—Member of the Shedai *Serrataal*. Ally of the Maker. (RTW)

Aen'q Tholis—Tholian warship destroyed by Romulan bird-of-prey *Bloodied Talon*. (STT)

Age of Grim Awareness—From Shedai history: Time in distant past corresponding to the Tholians' achieving sentience. (RTW)

Alakon, Councillor—Member of Klingon High Council in 2265; commoner-born, ascended through honorable combat. (HAR)

al-Jazaar, Imam—Religious leader on Starbase 47. (HAR)

al-Khaled, Lieutenant Commander Mahmud—S.C.E. leader aboard the *U.S.S. Lovell*. (STT) Promoted to lieutenant commander during mission to Gamma Tauri IV. (RTW)

Anderson, Ensign (Brett)—Engineer aboard *U.S.S. Bombay*. KIA. (HAR)

Anderson, Ensign Jeff—Member of S.C.E. team on *U.S.S. Lovell*. Lost right arm in action against Shedai sentinels on Gamma Tauri IV. Best friend of Ensign Brian O'Halloran. (RTW)

Anitra, Senator—Junior member of Romulan Senate. (STT)

Anzarosh—Spaceport town on Kessik IV. Shabby, dirty, depressing. (HAR)

Apostate—Second-oldest of the Shedai, leads opposition movement against the Maker. Source of first contact, with Ensign Vanessa Theriault. Destroyed the Jinoteur system, believed to have been lost with it. (RTW)

Archer, U.S.S.—Namesake ship for the *Archer* class, which includes the *U.S.S. Sagittarius*.

Argashek, Councillor—Member of Klingon High Council in 2265. Allied with Councillors Grozik and Glazya. (HAR)

Argelian flu—Viral malady that afflicted residents of Martian city of Cydonia in 2266, including Dr. Ezekiel Fisher's daughter, Jane, and her husband, Neil, and sons, James and Seth. (RTW)

Arinex—Star system within a couple of days' high-warp transit from Starbase 47. (RTW)

Arjuna, U.S.S.—Ship of the *Archer* class.

Armnoj, Sakud—Accountant to Orion merchant-prince Ganz; transported from his home on Yerad III by Cervantes Quinn and Tim Pennington; kept a pet *slijm* named Sniffy. Assassinated by Ganz after delivering potentially incriminating records to him aboard Ganz's ship, the *Omari-Ekon*. (STT)

Artemis, U.S.S.—Ship of the *Archer* class.

Avainenoran—Shedai name for the planet Gamma Tauri IV. (RTW)

Avenger—Member of the Shedai *Serrataal;* allied with the Maker. (RTW)

Azrene [The Violet]—Member of the Tholian Ruling Conclave. (HAR)

Babitz, Dr. Lisa—Chief medical officer, *U.S.S. Sagittarius*. Blonde, blue-eyed, tall, pretty, germophobic. (RTW)

Ballard, Lieutenant Curtis—Original chief engineering officer, Starbase 47. Was part of the team that built Deep Space Station K-5. Flummoxed by systemic failures caused by Shedai Carrier Wave. Killed by the self-destruct function of a Rigelian scrambler-transmitter that had been insinuated into Starbase 47's comm relays. Replaced by *U.S.S. Lovell* engineer Isaiah Farber. (DEW)

Buquair III—Planet where, in 2263, an underwater earthquake generated a tsunami that damaged the Federation-run Glassner Colony. The *U.S.S. Lovell* and its S.C.E. team, along with several other ships, were dispatched to aid the colony. During the relief mission, the S.C.E. team discovered an alien spacecraft that had long ago crashed on the planet, and which was continuing to transmit an S.O.S. (DEW)

BelHoQ, Commander—First officer of the *I.K.S. Zin'za*. (RTW)

Belleau Wood, U.S.S.—Starship to which a young Diego Reyes was posted after leaving the *U.S.S. Helios*, but prior to his command of the *U.S.S. Dauntless*.

Berry, Ensign Daniel—Navigator of the *U.S.S. Bombay*. KIA. (HAR)

Beyer, Lieutenant—Female security officer on Starbase 47. Escorted envoys out of a diplomatic meeting led by Ambassador Jetanien. (STT)

Bloodied Talon—Romulan bird-of-prey, commanded by Commander Sarith, dispatched on undercover mission to Taurus Reach. Destroyed the Tholian warship *Aen'q Tholis*, witnessed the destruction of Palgrenax. Transmitted data back to Romulus before being destroyed near the Palgrenax system by the *I.K.S. Zin'za*. (STT)

Boam II—Colony world that reporter Tim Pennington hoped to visit in order to conduct interviews; he never got there. (STT)

Bohanon—Member of research team studying the Shedai artifact on Erilon. Killed by the Shedai wanderer. His autopsy yielded valuable information about the Shedai meta-genome. (STT)

Bohica—Borzhan administrator of the Klingon-occupied spaceport facility in orbit of Borzha II. (RTW) *bojnoggi*—Thick Tellarite concoction, richly caffeinated; according to Dr. Anthony Leone, it's similar to mushroom soup. (STT)

bolmaq—Klingon herd animal. (STT)

Bombay, U.S.S.—Federation starship, *Miranda* class. Commanded by Captain Hallie Gannon. Destroyed at Ravanar IV by attack of six Tholian cruisers, four of which it destroyed in self-defense. (HAR)

Borzha II—Location of a Klingon-occupied spaceport; site of repairs for the *I.K.S. Zin'za* after failed attempts to explore the Jinoteur system. (RTW)

Borzhans—Pacifistic people whose world was occupied by Klingon forces in 2266. (RTW)

Bowman, U.S.S.—Ship of the *Archer* class.

Brassicans—Animal-vegetable hybrid species native to Nejev III. (RTW)

Briv, Lieutenant Commander—Tellarite male, unusually slim for his species. Sensor-control officer, Starbase 47. (DEW)

Broon—Human crime boss, rival of Ganz; tried to assassinate Cervantes Quinn for Ganz, failed because of T'Prynn's intervention. (HAR) Captured Quinn, Tim Pennington, and Sakud Armnoj near the Jinoteur system, but the trio escaped and framed him for their piracy on a Klingon sensor probe. (STT) Broon's ship (no name given) was captured by the Klingons and impounded at Borzha II. (RTW)

Brummer, Lora—Human female. Ex-wife of Tim Pennington. (HAR)

Café Romano—Outdoor eatery in Stars Landing, aboard Starbase 47. (HAR) Owned and operated by chef Matt Romano. (RTW)

Cahow, Petty Officer 2nd Class Karen—Engineer on the *U.S.S. Sagittarius*. Average height and build, blond hair, phobic about being on planetary surfaces. (RTW)

Camigliano—A varietal of Brunello wine available in Manón's Cabaret. (RTW)

Cannella, Lieutenant Commander Raymond—Fleet operations manager of Starbase 47. Big guy, balding, New Jersey accent. (HAR)

Cardalian Mountains—Geological feature of Gamma Tauri IV. (RTW)

Castellano, Ensign (Tory) —Engineer on the *U.S.S. Bombay*. KIA. (HAR)

Catera, Dr.—Medical doctor from *U.S.S. Endeavour* who provided medical care to the research team on Erilon. (STT)

Centauri Star, S.S.—Civilian transport ship that made port at Starbase 47 en route to Gamma Tauri IV. (RTW)

Charles, Lieutenant—Security officer attached to the Federation Customs Office on Starbase 47. (HAR)

Che'leth, I.K.S.—Klingon warship that escorted a personnel transport full of Klingon scientists to Gamma Tauri IV. (RTW)

Chelon, Rigelian—Bipedal species with leathery carapace, beaklike proboscis, unexpressive faces. Skin tones vary between various shades of green, brown, and gray, and rarely black. Eyes vary from amber to jade green to silvery metallic. (HAR) Skin excretes deadly contact toxin during times of stress. (STT)

Chichén Itzá, S.S.—Freighter-transport that experienced some minor delays receiving a docking berth at Vanguard because of its failure to file an updated flight plan. (HAR)

chom **pattern**—Martial-arts regimen, similar to a *kata*, that includes moves and stances for knife combat. (HAR)

ch'Sonnas, Lieutenant Thanashal—Science officer on the *U.S.S. Bombay*. KIA. (HAR)

Code One—ER alert on Starbase Vanguard which means that the commanding officer requires emergency medical attention. (RTW)

Code Two—ER alert on Starbase Vanguard which means that one or more of the station's senior officer requires emergency medical attention. (RTW)

Cofell, Agent—Operative of Starfleet Intelligence who escorts Anna Sandesjo (aka Lurqal) from her temporary quarters to a secret transport off of Starbase 47. (RTW)

Collig, Ensign Donovan—Member of Starbase 47 security team; filed sloppy investigative paperwork that derailed a criminal investigation by the Starfleet JAG office. (STT)

Colloquium—Gathering of the Shedai for the purpose of governance and coordination of action; led by the Maker. Requires physical presence of its participants. (RTW)

Conduit—Artifact of the Shedai with which they can communicate instantly across great interstellar distances, and through which they can project their consciousnesses to other worlds. (HAR/RTW)

Conduit Song—The carrier-wave signal of a Shedai Conduit. (RTW)

Cook, Colleen—Junior archaeologist from the *Starship Endeavour,* assigned to help Lieutenant Ming Xiong study the Shedai Conduit on Erilon. (STT)

Cooper, Commander Jonathan—Executive officer of Starbase 47. Wife: Jen; son: Jake. (HAR)

Cydonia—City on Mars; home of Dr. Ezekiel Fisher's daughter, Jane, her husband, Neil, and their sons, James and Seth. (RTW)

D'Amato, Lieutenant Oriana—Helm officer of the *U.S.S. Bombay.* Wife of *Enterprise* senior geologist Lieutenant Robert D'Amato. Had a three-month affair with married reporter Tim Pennington. KIA with the *Bombay* at Ravanar IV. (HAR)

Danac—Pit boss in charge of gambling receipts aboard the Orion ship *Omari-Ekon;* reports to Orion merchant-prince Ganz. (RTW)

Danes, Ensign Scott—Security officer on *U.S.S. Enterprise.* KIA on Ravanar IV, by Tholian demolition trap. (HAR)

Darjil, Centurion—Officer aboard the Romulan bird-of-prey *Bloodied Talon.* KIA. (STT)

Dauntless, U.S.S.—Federation starship, class undetermined.

Previously commanded by Diego Reyes, with Hallie Gannon as his first officer. (HAR) Had run-ins with a Klingon vessel commanded by Gorkon. (RTW)

Davis, Lieutenant Kurt — Second-in-command of the S.C.E. team on the *U.S.S. Lovell* in 2266. (RTW)

Davlos III — Planet whereon, in a barfight, Tarmelite enforcer Morikmol allegedly ripped a Klingon's arms from their sockets. (RTW)

Delmark — Nondescript Orion man in his mid-thirties with dark hair, a lean physique, and a complexion of an especially deep hue of green. Member of Ganz's extended criminal organization. (RTW)

Denobulan Wildcard — Game of chance with some similarity to poker. (HAR)

Desai, Captain Rana — Ranking member of the Starfleet Judge Advocate General (JAG) Corps on Starbase 47. (HAR)

Destrene [The Gray] — Member of the Tholian Ruling Conclave. (HAR)

Diamond, Lieutenant Jessica — Weapons officer on the *U.S.S. Lovell*. Shoulder-length brown hair. (DEW/STT)

dierha — Romulan time unit, roughly one hour. (STT)

Divad — Safecracker employed by crime boss Broon. (STT)

Dohan, Lieutenant Commander Yael — Gamma-shift officer of the watch on Starbase 47. Light-brown hair, cut short; slender but muscular; Israeli ancestry. (RTW)

Dramian-weed tea — Beverage favored by Captain Matuzas, a former CO of Diego Reyes aboard the *U.S.S. Helios*. (DEW)

***Drexler*-class frigate** — Class of Federation vessel considered obsolete by 2265; not too far removed from the *Daedalus*-class ships. Diego Reyes served aboard one, the *U.S.S. Helios*, under the command of Captain Matuzas. (DEW)

D'tran, Senator — Oldest member of Romulan Senate in 2265, older than Praetor Vrax. (STT)

Dunbar, Lieutenant Judy — Senior communications officer

aboard Starbase 47. Twirls hair as nervous habit. Photographic memory. (HAR)

Duras, Councillor—Member of Klingon High Council in 2265. (HAR)

Epimetheus, S.S.—Mining ship whose crew laid claim to Kessik IV before Starbase 47 was constructed. (HAR)

Erilon—Class P glaciated world in the Taurus Reach. Location of a Shedai Conduit, and site of type-V life readings. Attacked by Shedai Wanderer, in the form of black sentinels. Currently houses a formidable permanent Starfleet ground installation. (HAR/STT)

Eskrene [The Ruby]—Member of the Tholian Ruling Conclave. (HAR)

Estrada, Lieutenant Hector—Communications officer, *U.S.S. Endeavour.* (STT)

ewa—Romulan time unit, roughly one second. (STT)

Falstrene [The Gray]—Member of the Tholian Ruling Conclave. (HAR)

Farber, Lieutenant Isaiah—Chief engineering officer, Starbase 47. (HAR) Former member of the S.C.E. engineering team on the *U.S.S. Lovell*. Helped identify Shedai Carrier Wave signal and harden the starbase's systems against it. (DEW)

Finneran, Yeoman Suzie (Midshipman Cadet)—Tall, auburn-haired young woman who serves as Commodore Reyes's gamma-shift yeoman. (HAR)

First Conduit—Enormous artifact of the Shedai, located on Jinoteur IV. Source and nexus of their interstellar power. Can only be controlled by Shedai *Serrataal*. (RTW)

First World, the—Shedai name for Jinoteur IV. (RTW)

Fisher, Dr. Ezekiel "Zeke"—Chief medical officer, Starbase 47. (HAR)

Fisher, Ely—Son of Dr. Ezekiel Fisher. (RTW)

Fisher, Jane—Daughter of Dr. Ezekiel Fisher. Husband: Neil. Sons: James and Seth. (RTW)

Fisher, Noah—Son of Dr. Ezekiel Fisher. (RTW)

Fontana Meadow—Greensward located inside the hollow terrestrial enclosure of Starbase 47. Named for the prominent fountain in its center. (HAR)

Ford, Crewman Donna—Enlisted engineer on the *U.S.S. Bombay.* KIA. (HAR)

Gabbert, Lieutenant Christopher—"Room boss" in charge of directing Starfleet covert operations on Gamma Tauri IV. (RTW)

Gallonik III—Planet that erupted into a civil war in 2177 because of a misprint in its first treaty of global alliance. Its articles of territorial sovereignty contained conflicting geographical coordinates for the borders demarcating areas of settlement for its two rival sentient species. As a result, 738 million Gallonikans died in the conflict. (HAR)

Gamma Tauri IV—Colony planet in the Taurus Reach. Contracted former mining consortium executive Jeanne Vinueza to serve as its president in 2266. Also site of a hidden Shedai Conduit. Starfleet efforts to find the artifact motivated Klingon forces to land on the politically unaligned world, as well. An attack by Shedai sentinels wiped out the colony and provoked Starfleet and the Klingons into annihilating the planet's surface. (RTW)

Gannon, Captain Hallie—Commanding officer of the *U.S.S. Bombay* and former first officer of Diego Reyes aboard the *U.S.S. Dauntless.* Blonde, optimistic. KIA at Ravanar IV. (HAR)

Ganz—Orion merchant-prince. Operates from his ship the *Omari-Ekon,* docked at Starbase 47. (HAR)

Ge'hoQ—Klingon name for Gamma Tauri IV. (RTW)

Gek, Dr. Varech jav—Tellarite scientist, works in the Vault with Lieutenant Ming Xiong. One of Starfleet's top minds in theoretical chemistry and molecular physics. Excitable; a bit of a gossip. (STT)

Geller, Rabbi—Religious leader aboard Starbase 47. (HAR)

Gerzhog, Captain—Commanding officer of the *I.K.S. HovQaw'wI'.* (RTW)

Getheon—Planet on which a team of dilithium prospectors became temporarily stranded because of a failure in their ship's warp drive. (HAR)

Ghrex, Ensign—Denobulan female, engineer with the S.C.E. team on the *U.S.S. Lovell*. Participated in the research mission to Erilon. (DEW STT)

Glassner Colony—Federation settlement on Buquair III. Damaged in 2263 by a tsunami generated by an underwater earthquake. The colony was aided by the *U.S.S. Lovell* and its S.C.E. crew, as well as by several other vessels. During the relief mission, the S.C.E. team discovered an alien spacecraft that had long ago crashed on the planet, and which was continuing to transmit an S.O.S. (DEW)

Glazya, Councillor—Member of the Klingon High Council in 2265; allied with Grozik and Argashek. (HAR)

glenget—a backless piece of furniture designed to permit a Chelon to kneel comfortably in repose. (STT)

Gonmog Sector—Klingon name for the Taurus Reach. (RTW)

Gorkon, Councillor—Member of the Klingon High Council in 2265; will preside as Chancellor in 2293. (HAR)

Grap'hwu **Province**—Geopolitical subdivision of the planet Palgrenax. (STT)

gredlahr—Andorian beverage, luminescent yellow. Similar to rum, though sweeter. Available from the bar on the *Omari-Ekon*. (DEW)

Greenfield, Yeoman/Lieutenant Toby—Senior administrative assistant to Commodore Diego Reyes. Short, doe-eyed, efficient, cute, mid-20s. (HAR)

Greisman, Dr. Stewart—Assistant chief medical officer of the *U.S.S. Bombay*. KIA. (HAR)

Griffin, Dr. Bruce—Assistant chief medical officer of the *U.S.S. Endeavour*. Has a reputation for always being prepared. (STT)

Grinpa, Dr.—Klingon researcher studying Shedai artifacts. (RTW)

Grozik, Councillor—Member of the Klingon High Council in 2265; allied with Glazya and Argashek. (HAR)

Guerin, Nurse (Jean)—Member of the medical staff on the *U.S.S. Bombay*. KIA. (HAR)

Halse, Ensign—Bridge officer, *U.S.S. Endeavour*. (STT)

Hanigar—Klingon Imperial Intelligence supervisor, in charge of field agent Mogan. (RTW)

Hayes, Cargo Chief—Non-commissioned officer, *U.S.S. Bombay*. KIA. (HAR)

Heghpu'rav, I.K.S.—Klingon warship deceived by warp-shadow illusions generated by the crew of the *U.S.S. Sagittarius*. (RTW)

Helios, U.S.S.—*Drexler*-class frigate aboard which a young Diego Reyes served, under the command of Captain Matuzas. Also serving with Reyes, for all of 12 days, was future *Lovell* CO Daniel Okagawa.

Herald—Shedai *Serrataal*. His loyalties in the Shedai power struggle are uncertain. Known to be a provocateur. (RTW)

High Epopt of Tamaros—Religious leader mentioned in one of Jetanien's many digressive allegories. (HAR)

Hirskene, Commander—Commanding officer of the Tholian warship *Aen'q Tholis*. KIA. (STT)

HovQaw'wI', I.K.S.—Klingon warship, commanded by Captain Gerzhog, that participates in a barrage against Gamma Tauri IV led by the *Starship Endeavour*. (RTW)

Hub, the—Octagonal command table on the elevated supervisors' deck in the Starbase 47 operations center. (HAR)

Icarion—a Nalori argosy piloted by Zett Nilric. (RTW)

Ilium Range—Geological feature on Gamma Tauri IV, near the New Boulder Colony. (RTW)

Ilucci, Master Chief Petty Officer Mike "Mad Man"—Chief engineer of the *U.S.S. Sagittarius*. (HAR)

Imelio, Nurse—Member of medical staff on *U.S.S. Bombay*. KIA. (HAR)

Indizar, Councillor—Member of Klingon High Council in 2265. Close ally of Councillor Gorkon and Chancellor Sturka. (HAR) Head of Imperial Intelligence. (RTW)

Ineti, Subcommander—Second-in-command of Romulan bird-of-prey *Bloodied Talon* during its ill-fated mission to the Taurus Reach. KIA. (STT)

Jackson, Lieutenant Haniff—Head of security on Starbase 47. Never loses a bet. (HAR)

Jaeq—Orion male. Former chief enforcer for Orion merchant-prince Ganz. Tall and slender. Had one altercation too many with Starfleet. To avoid complications, Ganz had Jaeq assassinated before he could be arrested and tried by Starfleet. (DEW)

Javathian oyster broth—Concoction enjoyed by Ambassador Jetanien. (STT)

Jemonon—Federation colony planet in the Taurus Reach. (HAR)

Jetanien, Ambassador—Chelon diplomat in charge of Federation political efforts in the Taurus Reach. (HAR)

Jinoteur—Remote star system in the Taurus Reach. Home system of the Shedai, who engineered it in its entirety. Five planets, none on the same orbital plane. Planets one and five perpendicular to each other; two and three at equal, complementary angles off the ecliptic. Planet four roughly level with its star's equator. Planets one, two, and three each have two moons; planet four has three satellites; planet five has four. All moons follow orbital paths perpendicular to those of their host planets, so that they never pass between the planets and the star. Furthermore, all the satellites show the same rotational oddity, always facing the same hemisphere out. Moons are fortified with powerful defensive weapons systems. Entire system "blinked" out of space-time by the Apostate. (STT/RTW)

Jinoteur IV—Homeworld of the Shedai, location of the Shedai Colloquium. (RTW)

Judge, Lieutenant Kevin—Chief engineer, *U.S.S. Bombay*. KIA. (HAR)

Kamron, Dr.—Klingon scientist, studied Shedai evidence on Gamma Tauri IV. (RTW)

Kane, Joshua—Human male, had eight perfect alibis for his presence on eight far-flung planets at precisely the times of eight daring and unsolved heists. Part of Ganz's retinue on the *Omari-Ekon*. (RTW)

Karumé, Akeylah—Federation diplomat. Dark-skinned, tall, bold. Dresses in bright colors. Great at handling Klingons. (HAR)

Kashuk, Lieutenant Steve—Engineer, *U.S.S. Bombay*. KIA. (HAR)

Kattan, Security Guard—Member of Starfleet search party on Gamma Tauri IV. KIA. (RTW)

keesa **beetle**—Chelon delicacy, considered best when fried and crunchy. (HAR)

Kepler, Shuttlecraft—Medium-range Starfleet craft, assigned to *U.S.S. Lovell,* piloted on Gamma Tauri IV by Ensign Brian O'Halloran. (RTW)

Kertral, Lieutenant Governor—Second-in-command to Governor Morqla on Palgrenax. KIA. (STT)

Kessik IV—Federation colony world. Notoriously lawless. Site of major dilithium mine. Rebuffed effort by Starfleet to annex the planet under eminent domain. Major starport is Anzarosh, where Cervantes Quinn survived an ambush by Broon and his goons. (HAR)

Khatami, Captain Atish—Commanding officer, *U.S.S. Endeavour.* Formerly served as first officer under Captain Sheng, who was killed on Erilon. Husband, Kenji, and daughter, Parveen, reside on Deneva. (HAR/STT)

kilaan—Klingon time unit, roughly equivalent to an hour. (STT)

Kil'j Tholis—Tholian warship. Ambushed the *U.S.S. Bombay* at Ravanar IV. Destroyed when *Bombay* pulled it with a tractor beam into a collision with the *Tas'v Tholis*. (HAR)

Kilosa—Federation colony planet in the Taurus Reach. (HAR)

Klisiewicz, Lieutenant Stephen John—Science officer, *U.S.S. Endeavour*. Major player in the mission to Erilon. (HAR/STT)

Kollotaan—Shedai term for modern Tholians; translation: "new voices." (RTW)

Kollotuul—Shedai term for pre-sentient Tholians: "the Voice." (RTW)

Kreq, Lieutenant—Communications officer, *I.K.S. Zin'za*. (STT)

Kulok, Councillor—Member of Klingon High Council in 2265. (HAR)

Kulor—Klingon male, bodyguard to Ambassador Lugok. (HAR)

Kutal, Captain—Commanding officer, *I.K.S. Zin'za;* key player in the Klingon search for the secrets of the Shedai. (STT)

K'voq—Aide to Governor Morqla of Palgrenax. Killed in an attack by Palgrenai insurgents. (STT)

Kyudo, U.S.S.—Ship of the *Archer* class.

La Sala, Lieutenant Jeanne—Security officer, *U.S.S. Endeavour*. Faced down Shedai sentinels on Erilon. (HAR/STT)

Laëchem—Fair-haired Zibalian man with brilliant indigo and vermilion facial tattoos. Member of Ganz's extended criminal organization. (RTW)

LaMartina, Ensign Karen—Engineering officer, *U.S.S. Endeavour*. (STT)

Lamneth Starport—Commercial starport facility on Nejev III where Quinn temporarily berthed his ship, the *Rocinante*. (RTW)

Langlois, Chief Petty Officer Elizabeth—Cargo master of Starbase 47. (HAR)

Lanz't Tholis—Tholian warship lured to Jinoteur IV by the Shedai Wanderer. Its crew was abducted to the surface, imprisoned, and tortured. Twenty-four of them were bound into service as "Voices" in the First Conduit. Following their emancipation, and led by Nezrene [The Emerald], they attacked the Klingon battle cruiser *I.K.S. Zin'za*, enabling the *U.S.S. Sagittarius* and the tramp freighter *Rocinante* to escape. (HAR)

Larskene [The Silver]—Commanding officer, *Nov'k Tholis*. Participated in the attack on the *U.S.S. Bombay* at Ravanar IV. (HAR)

Lee, Dr. Hua Sun—Chief medical officer, *U.S.S. Bombay*. KIA (HAR)

LeGere, Lieutenant Paul—Member of the S.C.E. team on the *U.S.S. Lovell*, former roommate of Isaiah Farber. After teasing Farber, LeGere awoke one day to find he suddenly had no need of a comb. (DEW)

Leone, Dr. Anthony—Chief medical officer, *U.S.S. Endeavour*. (HAR/STT)

Liverakos, Lieutenant Commander Peter—Defense attorney, assigned to Starfleet JAG office on Starbase 47. Mid-40s, boyish appearance, goatee, salt-and-pepper hair. Defended Reyes and the Vanguard crew during a JAG-mandated inquiry following the loss of the *U.S.S. Bombay*. (HAR)

Loak, Nem chim—Engineer (Assistant Impulse Supervisor), *U.S.S. Bombay*. Had his hair dyed pink by Lieutenant Ming Xiong, as a practical joke revenge for his snoring. KIA at Ravanar IV. (HAR)

Locksley, U.S.S.—Ship of the *Archer* class.

Longbow, U.S.S.—Ship of the *Archer* class.

Loperian *reelkot*—Delicacy sold by the case; requires refrigeration. (HAR)

Lovell, U.S.S.—*Daedalus*-class starship, assigned to S.C.E. under command of Captain Daniel Okagawa. S.C.E. team leader is Lieutenant Commander Mahmud al-Khaled. (STT)

Luciano, Lieutenant Margaux—Engineer, *U.S.S. Lovell*. (RTW)

Lugok, Ambassador—Klingon diplomat assigned to Starbase 47. Is actually a covert operative of Imperial Intelligence. Son of Breg. (HAR)

Lurqal—True Klingon name of female Klingon spy masquerading on Starbase 47 as Anna Sandesjo, senior attaché to Ambassador Jetanien. (HAR)

Maker—Oldest of the Shedai *Serrataal,* said to be capable of "unmaking" any of the Shedai by touch alone—but in 2266 she proves unable to wield her power against her chief rival, the Apostate. (RTW)

Malacca, U.S.S.—Starfleet cargo transport. Target of a bombing attack inside the Starbase 47 docking bay while being used to covertly transport compromised Klingon spy-in-disguise Anna Sandesjo off the station. (RTW)

Malhotra, Ensign—Member of Starbase 47 crew. Found murdered in a Jefferies tube by *Lovell* engineer Isaiah Farber. Last reported location before his disappearance was Cargo Bay 19. (DEW)

Malik, Crewman K.—Member of the Starbase 47 cargo crew. (HAR)

Malmat, Ensign Bonnie—Senior geologist, *U.S.S. Endeavour.* (HAR)

Mancharan starhopper—Civilian class of tramp freighter, capable of interstellar flight. Unarmed. Cervantes Quinn's vessel, the *Rocinante,* is a Mancharan starhopper. (HAR)

mandisa—Orion aphrodisiacal beverage, illegal in the Federation. (HAR)

Manón—Silgov female, preternaturally beautiful, radiates an aura of physical warmth at close range. (HAR)

Manón's cabaret—The de facto officers' club on Starbase 47. Located in Stars Landing. Has a stage with a piano. Serves as a bar, restaurant, dance hall, etc. (HAR)

Martinez, Nurse (Melanie)—Member of the medical staff at Vanguard Hospital on Starbase 47. (RTW)

mat'drih—Romulan unit of distance measurement; roughly one kilometer. (STT)

Matuzas, Captain—Commanding officer of the *U.S.S. Helios*, a *Drexler*-class frigate aboard which Diego Reyes served as a young officer. (DEW)

Matuzas School of Starship Command—Joking term used by Diego Reyes to describe his tour of duty aboard the *U.S.S. Helios* under the command of Captain Matuzas. He and *U.S.S. Lovell* CO Daniel Okagawa are among its alumni. (DEW)

M'Benga, Dr. Jabilo—Assistant chief medical officer, Starbase 47. Has put in for a transfer to starship duty. (By 2267–68, will be assigned to the *Enterprise* crew.) (HAR)

McCarthy, Lieutenant—Assistant chief engineer, *U.S.S. Bombay*. KIA. (HAR)

McCormick, Lieutenant Marielise—Navigator, *U.S.S. Endeavour*. Flirted with Lieutenant (then Ensign) Stephen Klisiewicz. (STT)

McCreary, Admiral—High-ranking officer at Starfleet Medical. (RTW)

McGibbon, Ensign Paul—Security officer, *U.S.S. Endeavour*. (HAR)

McIlvain's Planet—Colony planet in the Taurus Reach that was the source of a dispute between Tellar and Rigel, regarding which one had the right to colonize. The case was referred by the Starfleet JAG Corps for arbitration to the Colonial Administrator's office. (STT)

McKee, Father—Religious leader, Starbase 47. (HAR)

McLellan, Lieutenant Commander Bridget—Second officer, *U.S.S. Sagittarius*. Nickname: Bridy Mac. (RTW)

Medeira, Specialist Roderigo—Member of the Starbase 47 crew. (HAR)

Medina, Chief Petty Officer Israel—Fictional cargo chief on Starbase 47, invented by Lieutenant Commander T'Prynn to deceive reporter Tim Pennington into publishing a flawed set of facts regarding the Tholian attack on the Ravanar IV outpost and the *Starship Bombay*. Ostensibly, the person whom Pennington met

was an agent of Starfleet Intelligence planted by T'Prynn.
(HAR)

Meeker, Ensign Rory—Member of the Starbase 47 crew.
(HAR)

Meenok's disease—Fatal illness, common to residents of
Luna. Swift progression, extremely painful, but victims
remain lucid. No cure known as of 2265. (HAR)

Meriden, S.S.—Cargo ship that was loaded at Starbase 47 for
a colony run. (HAR)

meta-genome—See: Taurus meta-genome

Meyer, Dietrich—Federation diplomat known to be a
drunkard. Former envoy to the Klingon delegation on
Starbase 47. Had an altercation in Manón's Cabaret with
Klingon Ambassador Lugok that ended with Lugok's *d'k
tahg* embedded in Meyer's thigh. Meyer survived the
assault but was subsequently reassigned to office
administrative tasks. Akeylah Karumé succeeded
him as the envoy to the Klingons. (HAR)

Miller, Lieutenant Commander Aole—Colonial
Administrator, Starbase 47. (HAR)

Milonakis, Commander Vondas—First officer, *U.S.S.
Bombay*. KIA. (HAR)

Miwal, Lieutenant—Crewmember, Starbase 47. Treated in
Vanguard Hospital for abdominal distress related to a
bezoar—i.e., a hairball. (RTW)

Moar, Gom glasch—Tellarite religious leader on Starbase 47.
The resident *throg,* or "sin-eater." (HAR)

Mog, Lieutenant Commander Bersh glov—Chief engineer,
U.S.S. Endeavour. (HAR/STT)

Mogan—I.I. agent who investigates scene of a Shedai attack
on Gamma Tauri IV. (RTW)

Molok, Councillor—Member of Klingon High Council in
2265. (HAR)

Morikmol—Tarmelite enforcer employed by Orion merchant-
prince Ganz. Acts as the "right hand" to enforcer Zett

Nilric. (HAR) Alleged to have torn a Klingon's arms from their sockets during a barfight on Davlos III. (RTW)

Morqla, Governor—Appointed overseer of the Klingon occupation of Palgrenax. KIA. (STT)

Moyer, Lieutenant Holly—Senior prosecutor in the Starfleet JAG office on Starbase 47. (HAR) Young, athletic, willowy, auburn-haired. Excellent racquetball player. (STT)

Muller, Lieutenant—Officer on the *U.S.S. Endeavour.* Vocal critic of Captain Khatami shortly after her promotion. Had his attitude manually adjusted by Dr. Anthony Leone. (STT)

Myrmidon—Shedai *Serrataal,* ally of the Apostate. (RTW)

Nalori—Species that has clashed with the Federation in the past, and lost. Prominent features: oily, midnight-black skin; hair colors range from pale violet to magenta; braided beards are common among males; ritual scarring marks life stages and rites of passage (manhood, marriage, parenthood, etc.). Eyes are flat black, no evident iris or pupils. Black teeth and bones. (HAR)

Nameless, the—Shedai term for the great majority of their kind, those who are not considered elite—i.e., *Serrataal.* (RTW)

Narskene [The Gold]—Member of the Tholian Ruling Conclave, 2265. (HAR)

Narvak, Councillor—Member of the Klingon High Council, 2265. (HAR)

Nassir, Captain Adelard—Commanding officer, *U.S.S. Sagittarius.* (HAR/RTW)

Nauls, Lieutenant—Security officer, *U.S.S. Endeavour.* Faced the Shedai sentinels on Erilon. KIA. (STT)

Nave, Lieutenant Susan—Communications officer, *U.S.S. Bombay.* KIA. (HAR)

Ndufe, Security Guard—Part of Starfleet search team on Gamma Tauri IV. KIA. (RTW)

Neelakanta, Lieutenant—Arcturian helm officer, *U.S.S. Endeavour.* (STT)

Neera—Orion woman, secret boss of Ganz. To outsiders, she
  seems to be an underboss in charge of the sex trade on
  Ganz's ship, the *Omari-Ekon*. (RTW)

Nejev III—Homeworld of animal-vegetable hybrid species
  known as Brassicans. Location of Lamneth Starport. Site
  of a failed business venture by Cervantes Quinn, who fled
  with associate Tim Pennington in a stolen hovercar. (RTW)

Nelson, Chief—Transporter operator, *U.S.S. Endeavour*.
  (STT)

Nemite Revolution—In 147 B.C.E. on Tamaros III, the
  proconsul to the High Epopt of Tamaros appointed a
  Yoçarian to serve as the castellan of the capital city. This
  event set in motion a chain of events that led to the Nemite
  Revolution. (HAR)

New Bangkok—Planet on which a Denobulan Starfleet JAG
  officer was stationed in 2265. Lieutenant Holly Moyer
  intended to contact this officer for advice on a case
  involving Denobulan family law. (STT)

New Boulder Colony—Predominantly human settlement on
  Gamma Tauri IV. In 2266, the colony voted to reject
  Federation protectorate status. Led by an appointed
  president, Jeanne Vinueza, the colony steadfastly refused
  Starfleet's protection, even after Klingons landed on the
  planet. The colony subsequently was destroyed by an attack
  of Shedai sentinels, and the planet was annihilated by a joint
  Starfleet-Klingon bombardment of photon torpedoes. (RTW)

Nezrene [The Emerald]—Weapons officer on the Tholian
  warship *Lanz't Tholis*. Captured by the Shedai Wanderer
  and yoked to the First Conduit. After being emancipated
  from the Conduit, Nezrene becomes the ranking officer on
  the *Lanz't Tholis*. (RTW)

Niwara, Lieutenant—Caitian female scout, *U.S.S.
  Sagittarius*. KIA on Jinoteur IV. (RTW)

Norton, Lieutenant Commander—Beta-shift bridge officer,
  U.S.S. Endeavour. Considered by Captain Khatami as a
  possible first officer. (STT)

Nov'k Tholis — Tholian warship, commanded by Larskene [The Silver]. Participated in the attack on and destruction of the Ravanar IV outpost and the *U.S.S. Bombay*. (HAR)

N'tovek, Centurion — Bridge officer, Romulan bird-of-prey *Bloodied Talon*. Was romantically involved with the ship's commanding officer, Commander Sarith. KIA. (STT)

N'va'a — Pungent fermented beverage, popular with Chelons and all but unpalatable to all other species. (HAR)

O'Halloran, Ensign Brian — S.C.E. engineer and pilot, *U.S.S. Lovell*. Best friend of Ensign Jeff Anderson. (STT)

Ohq, Lieutenant — Chief engineer, *I.K.S. Zin'za*. (RTW)

Okagawa, Captain Daniel — Commanding Officer, *U.S.S. Lovell*. (STT)

Omari-Ekon — Orion merchantman, base of operations for Orion crime boss Ganz. Docked at Starbase 47. (HAR)

Operation Vanguard — Clandestine military operation to secure, study, and harness the Taurus meta-genome and all related technology and phenomena, and to deny those things to Federation rivals such as the Klingon Empire and the Tholian Assembly. (HAR)

Ott, Lieutenant John — Communications officer with the S.C.E. team led by Commander Dean Singer on Ravanar IV. KIA. (HAR)

Outpost 5 — Starfleet facility near the Romulan Neutral Zone, to which the *U.S.S. Lovell* and its S.C.E. team provided salvage support prior to being assigned to help make Starbase 47 operational. (DEW)

Palgrenai — Species indigenous to the Klingon-occupied world Palgrenax. Extinct. (STT)

Palgrenax — Klingon-occupied planet in the Taurus Reach. Go boom. (STT)

Panganiban, Rik — Senior aide to New Boulder Colony President Jeanne Vinueza on Gamma Tauri IV. (RTW)

Patterson, Ensign Luke — Security officer, *U.S.S. Enterprise;* saw the Shedai Conduit ruins on Ravanar IV. (HAR)

Pawlikowski, Ensign (Lisa) — Junior geologist, *U.S.S.*

Enterprise. Was assigned to the landing party for Ravanar IV, but was replaced by senior geologist Lieutenant Robert D'Amato after he petitioned Captain James Kirk for permission to beam down with the landing party. (HAR)

Pennington, Timothy D.—Human male, journalist and investigative reporter. (HAR)

Pozrene—Tholian diplomatic attaché to Ambassador Sesrene on Starbase 47. (HAR)

Protocol *Say'qul*—Klingon code for "Cleansing Fire," an order to wipe out evidence by force. (RTW)

Pyzstrene [The Sallow]—Engineer on the captured Tholian warship *Lanz't Tholis* who objected to Nezrene's order to act in defense of a Starfleet vessel in the Jinoteur system. (RTW)

Pzial, Ensign Folanir—Rigelian male communications officer, *U.S.S. Lovell*.

Qahl—Klingon Imperial Intelligence covert operative who meets with Zett Nilric in Sector Tango-4119 to acquire an alien sarcophagus whose contents remain a mystery. (RTW)

Qlar—Helm officer, *I.K.S. Zin'za*. (RTW)

Qoheela—Tarascan hitman, sent to Starbase 47 by Broon to assassinate Cervantes Quinn. Is stopped by Lieutenant Commander T'Prynn, then captured by Ganz's people and executed aboard Ganz's ship, the *Omari-Ekon*, by Ganz's chief enforcer, Zett Nilric. (HAR)

QuchHa'—Klingon term for those Klingons who, afflicted by the genetic mutation unleashed in the 22nd century, have a distinctly human appearance, marked by a smooth forehead and a slighter build. Typically held in contempt, considered expendable. (STT)

Quinn, Cervantes—Rogue soldier of fortune and trader currently operating from Starbase 47. Has been divorced four times (wives, in order: Denise, Linda, Molly, Amy). (HAR)

Radkene [The Sallow]—Member of the Tholian Ruling Conclave in 2265. (HAR)

Ravanar IV—Planet on which, in 2263, a landing party from the *Starship Constellation* collected biosamples that contained the Taurus meta-genome. In 2264, became the location of a Starfleet research outpost, which uncovered the ruins of a Shedai Conduit. Efforts to activate the Conduit drew hostile attention from the Tholians, who were able to sense its emanations after Cervantes Quinn damaged the outpost's sensor screen while trying to steal it in 2265. The subsequent Tholian attack destroyed the outpost and led to the destruction of the *Starship Bombay*. (HAR)

Razka, Senior Chief Petty Officer—Newly assigned field scout on the *Starship Sagittarius*. Saurian male. (RTW)

Reke—Perpetually intoxicated henchman of Orion crime boss Ganz. Vomited on Scotty's boot after giving him a bottle of the green stuff. (HAR)

Reyes, Commodore Diego—Commanding officer, Starbase 47. Flag officer with authority over Starfleet operations and Federation civilians in the Taurus Reach. Previous postings include command of the *U.S.S. Dauntless* and junior postings on the *U.S.S. Belleau Wood* and the *U.S.S. Helios,* under Captain Matuzas. (HAR)

Ridley, Lieutenant—Security officer, Starbase 47. Was needed to testify in a case of alleged domestic battery. (STT)

Robertson, Ensign Donna—Engineer, *U.S.S. Bombay*. KIA. (HAR)

Robles, Dr. Gonzalo—Member of the medical staff, Vanguard Hospital, Starbase 47. (RTW)

Rocinante, S.S.—Mancharan starhopper owned and operated by Cervantes Quinn. Beat-up, run-down, but keeps on flyin'. (HAR/STT/RTW)

Rockey, Dr. (Charles F., Jr.)—Chief medical officer, *U.S.S. Lovell*. (RTW)

Roderick, Ensign—Security officer, *U.S.S. Endeavour*. Stood with Lieutenant Jeanne La Sala against Shedai sentinel attack on Erilon. (STT)

Rodriguez, Lieutenant Sasha—Helm officer, *U.S.S. Lovell*. (RTW)

Romano, Matt—Chef-proprietor of Café Romano in Stars Landing, on Starbase 47. Said to make "consistently perfect Hollandaise sauce." (RTW)

Rymer, Captain—Sponsored Diego Reyes's application to Starfleet Academy and served as Reyes's mentor. In 2266, referred to as the "late" Captain Rymer, date of death uncertain. (RTW)

Sadler, Terrance—Former security chief of the *Starship Dauntless* under the command of Diego Reyes. Retired from Starfleet service to get married and raise a family on colony planet Ingraham B. Dies with his family during the neural parasite attack on that planet in 2265. (STT)

Sage—Shedai *Serrataal* charged with maintaining a "living history" of their species and civilization. Ally of the Maker. (RTW)

Sagittarius, U.S.S.—*Archer*-class scout ship commanded by Captain Adelard Nassir. (HAR)

Sandesjo, Anna—Klingon female disguised to appear human. Served as senior diplomatic attaché to Ambassador Jetanien on Starbase 47. Real name was Lurqal. Reported to Ambassador Lugok and his aide Turag. Had an affair with Lieutenant Commander T'Prynn, who turned her into a double agent. (HAR) Cover compromised for a disinformation campaign to rescue the *U.S.S. Sagittarius* from Jinoteur IV. Killed in a bombing attack on the *U.S.S. Malacca*, the ship intended to smuggle her off of Vanguard. Assassin was Zett Nilric, hired by Klingon Imperial Intelligence. (RTW)

Sarith, Commander—Commanding officer of the Romulan bird-of-prey *Bloodied Talon*. (STT)

Saylok—Vulcan wine varietal available in Manón's cabaret in 2266. (RTW)

Schuster, Chief Michael—Transporter operator, *U.S.S. Endeavour*. (STT)

Scoridians—Reptilian species, members of Federation. (HAR)

Sector 116 Theta—Area of the Taurus Reach mapped by the *U.S.S. Bombay*. (HAR)

Sector Tango-4119—Location in which a clandestine meeting of Zett Nilric and Klingon Imperial Intelligence agent Qahl took place. (RTW)

Segfrunsdóttir, Captain Friedl—Instructor on Federation law at Starfleet Academy during James T. Kirk's years as an underclassman. (HAR)

Sek't Tholis—Tholian warship, led the attack on the Ravanar IV outpost and the *U.S.S. Bombay*. Destroyed in combat by the *Bombay*. (HAR)

Selby, Ensign Blaise—Human female, geologist, member of Starfleet search party on Gamma Tauri IV. KIA. (RTW)

Sentinel, Shedai—Vaguely humanoid form composed of malleable obsidian and featuring limbs that end in conical formations. Moves rapidly, churns up whatever is underfoot. Channels tremendous amounts of power. A Shedai *Serrataal* can manipulate several sentinels at once. Sentinels are highly resistant to phaser fire and can batter their way through force fields. Their chief vulnerability is broad-frequency dampening fields. (STT)

Serrataal—Shedai term meaning "the Enumerated ones." It refers to an elite caste among the Shedai, those individuals who are given unique names. See also: Nameless, the (RTW)

Sesrene, Ambassador—Tholian diplomat assigned to Starbase 47. (HAR)

sh'Dastisar, Ensign—Officer on the *U.S.S. Endeavour* who had a minor problem with the food slots. (STT)

Shear, Roger—Mining-consortium executive who went on a dinner date with Anna Sandesjo to Manón's Cabaret, thereby precipitating a psychological breakdown for Sandesjo's lover, T'Prynn, who saw them together. (RTW)

Shedai—Ancient species that once reigned supreme over the Taurus Reach, and plans to do so again. Not confined to any particular physical form, they don and shed bodies at will. Divided into two castes: *Serrataal,* "the Enumerated ones," the elite; and the Nameless. (HAR/STT/RTW)

Shedai Carrier Wave—Signal emitted by the First Conduit and all Shedai Conduits that answer it. Had a debilitating effect on Starbase 47's onboard systems until the S.C.E. was able to isolate the frequency and send a reply that canceled it. (STT)

Shedai Sector—Tholian name for the Taurus Reach. (HAR)

Sheng, Captain Zhao—Commanding officer, *U.S.S. Endeavour.* (HAR) Killed by Shedai sentinel on Erilon in 2265. Succeeded in his command by his first officer, Atish Khatami. (STT)

Shepherd, Lieutenant Addison—Human female. Second-in-command of engineering operations on Starbase 47. (DEW)

sh'Neroth, Lieutenant—Member of Starfleet search party on Gamma Tauri IV. Andorian *shen.* KIA. (RTW)

sh'Ness, Sherivan—Fourth-year medical student in Vanguard Hospital on Starbase 47. Andorian *shen.* (RTW)

sh'Rassa, Zharran—Andorian religious leader on Starbase 47, representing the station's *eresh'tha.* (HAR)

Sihanouk, Brother—Buddhist religious leader on Starbase 47. (HAR)

Sikal, Nurse—Vulcan female, member of medical staff on the *U.S.S. Endeavour.* (STT)

Singer, Commander Dean—Human male, S.C.E. team leader at the Ravanar IV outpost. KIA. (HAR)

slijm—Domesticated animal that resembles a dog crossed with a walrus. Features include a blubbery body covered in smooth brown hair, spindly legs that propel it with a waddling motion; wide nostrils, puffy cheeks, beady black eyes. Its chief means of self-defense is to rear up its wedge-shaped body and unleash a booming sneeze that propels caustic yellow-green snot in a wide arc, up to a range of several meters. (STT)

Sniffy — *Slijm* belonging to Zakdorn accountant Sakud Armnoj. (STT)

Sorak, Lieutenant — Vulcan male, 118 years old, *Kolinahr* master. Head of security and lead field scout, *U.S.S. Sagittarius*. (RTW)

Soral, Lieutenant — Vulcan male. Engineer, Starbase 47. (DEW)

Sovik — Federation diplomat. Envoy to the Tholian delegation on Starbase 47. (HAR)

Sozlok, Chief Petty Officer — Vaguely simian-looking non-commissioned officer who works the night shift, supervising the public storage facilities on Starbase 47. He seems to hate his job. (HAR)

Spencer, Ensign — Officer from the *U.S.S. Endeavour* assigned to the study of the Shedai Conduit on Erilon. Worked in the artifact control room. KIA during the first sentinel attack. (STT)

Sret, Proconsul — High-ranking member of the Romulan government in 2265. (STT)

Stano, Lieutenant Katherine — First officer, *U.S.S. Endeavour,* under the command of Captain Atish Khatami. (RTW)

Starbase 47 — *Watchtower*-class Federation starbase located inside the Taurus Reach. Serves as the base of operations for Starfleet vessels in that sector and as an anchor for Federation colonization efforts. (HAR)

Stars Landing — Civilian residential and commercial cluster located in the Terrestrial Enclosure aboard Starbase 47. (HAR)

Steinberg, Dr. — Member of the Vanguard Hospital medical staff on Starbase 47. (RTW)

Sten — Former fiancé of T'Prynn. Refused to release her when she asked to be excused from the marriage contract in 2212. Fought T'Prynn in the *Koon-ut-kal-if-fee*. As she broke his neck and killed him, he forced his *katra* (living spirit) into her mind telepathically. His *katra* has lived on in her mind ever since, assaulting her psychically, tormenting her, for 53 years. (HAR)

Stotsky, Adam—Communications supervisor in the Federation Embassy on Starbase 47, under the supervision of Ambassador Jetanien. (HAR)

Sturka, Chancellor—Leader of the Klingon Empire in 2265; closely allied with Councillors Gorkon and Indizar. (HAR)

Stutzman, Lieutenant Commander (Walter)—Starfleet officer who had been "hitching a ride" to a rendezvous with the *Starship Endeavour* on the *Starship Bombay* when the *Bombay* was ambushed and destroyed at Ravanar. (HAR)

Sulok, Ensign—Vulcan male, engineer, *U.S.S. Lovell.* (STT)

Talagos Prime—Federation colony planet in the Taurus Reach. (HAR)

Tamaros III—Site of the Nemite Revolution in 147 B.C.E. (HAR)

Tamishiro, Ensign—Female human, Asian ancestry. Engineer, Starbase 47. (DEW)

Tan Bao, Ensign Nguyen—Human male, Vietnamese, medical technician, *U.S.S. Sagittarius.*

Tarascans—Bipedal amphibian species with bulbous eyes, bulky bodies, and tapirlike snouts that waggle when they speak. Their blood is viscous and black. (HAR)

Tarcoh, Dr.—Deltan theoretical physicist in his late sixties, works in the Vault. (RTW)

Tarmelites—Large, muscular bipeds. Known for bad tempers and phenomenal physical strength. Morikmol, a Tarmelite enforcer for Ganz, was once described by Cervantes Quinn as a "walking life-support system for a pair of fists." (HAR)

Tarris—Waifish young Elasian woman with caramel-colored skin, large, almond-shaped eyes, and snow-white hair. Member of Ganz's extended criminal organization. (RTW)

Tashrene—Diplomatic attaché to Tholian Ambassador Sesrene on Starbase 47. (HAR)

Tas'v Tholis—Tholian warship, destroyed during its ambush of the Ravanar IV outpost and attack on the *Starship Bombay*. It was destroyed by being pulled with a tractor beam into a collision with its sister ship, the *Kil'j Tholis*. (HAR)

Taurus Key—Information sequence found in the Taurus meta-genome and the Shedai Carrier Wave. It is the Rosetta Stone for unlocking the secrets of the Shedai information string encoded in the meta-genome. (HAR/STT/RTW/DEW)

Taurus meta-genome—Mind-bogglingly complex engineered DNA string that contains millions of chromosomes. Only a tiny fraction of its chemical data is used to create living organisms; the rest is raw information, about whose purpose little is yet known. The discovery of the meta-genome in 2263 by the crew of the *Starship Constellation* initiated Operation Vanguard. (HAR)

Taurus Reach—A vast region of unexplored and unclaimed space beyond the Federation's borders and between the territories of the Klingon Empire and the Tholian Assembly. (HAR)

Telinaruul—Shedai term for humanoid species that were not loyal subjects of their interstellar hegemony. Sometimes synonymous with "criminals" or "savages." (STT, RTW)

Terath, Dr.—Klingon scientist who studied the Shedai artifacts on Palgrenax. KIA. (STT)

Terra Courser, S.S.—Federation colony transport ship that carried Jeanne Vinueza from Mars to Starbase 47, and from there to Gamma Tauri IV. During its departure from Starbase 47, the vessel also provided valuable cover for the *Starship Sagittarius*, which traveled in the transport's warp shadow to evade Klingon notice as it departed on a covert mission to the Jinoteur system. (RTW)

Terrell, Commander Clark—First officer, *U.S.S. Sagittarius*. (HAR/RTW)

T'Hana, Ensign—Vulcan female, engineer assigned to the

S.C.E. team on Ravanar IV, under the command of Commander Dean Singer. Worked directly with the Shedai Conduit. KIA. (HAR)

Thaumaturge—Shedai *Serrataal* of tremendous age and power. Close ally of the Apostate. (RTW)

Thelex, Dr.—Andorian *chan,* chief of dentistry at Vanguard Hospital, Starbase 47. Wears distinctive octagonal-frame eyeglasses. (HAR)

Theriault, Ensign Vanessa—Science officer, *U.S.S. Sagittarius.* (HAR) Made official first contact with the Shedai. (RTW)

Thorsen, Lieutenant—Tactical officer, *U.S.S. Endeavour.* (RTW)

thoughtwave—Frequency used by Tholians to establish telepathic links into the Lattice from interstellar distances; the technology resembles a minaturized version of a Shedai Conduit. (RTW)

Threx, Petty Officer 1st Class Salagho—Denobulan male, engineer, *U.S.S. Sagittarius.* (RTW)

throg—Tellarite holy person, a "sin eater." (HAR)

th'Shendileth, Ensign—Andorian *thaan,* officer on the *Starship Endeavour* who had a minor problem with a food slot. (STT)

Tik'r Tholis—Tholian warship, destroyed by the self-destruct ordnance of the *U.S.S. Bombay,* which had snared it with a tractor beam and used it as a shield during combat. (HAR)

T'Laen, Lieutenant—Vulcan female, S.C.E. computer specialist, *U.S.S. Lovell.* (STT/DEW/RTW)

TMG—See: "Taurus meta-genome"

Tolrene, Ambassador—Tholian ambassador to Qo'noS. Had a seizure at the same time that similar episodes afflicted Tholian representatives on Starbase 47 and on Earth. (HAR)

Tom Walker's—Civilian-run drinking establishment in Stars Landing, on Starbase 47 (HAR); offers a "Starfleet discount." (RTW)

Tonar, Lieutenant—Weapons officer, *I.K.S. Zin'za*. (STT)

Toqel, Vice-proconsul—High-ranking member of the Romulan Senate in 2265. Mother of Commander Sarith, commanding officer of the bird-of-prey *Bloodied Talon*, which was lost in the Taurus Reach. (STT)

Torr, Councillor—Member of the Klingon High Council in 2265. (HAR)

Torvin, Crewman—Tiburonian male, engineer, *U.S.S. Sagittarius*. (RTW)

Tozskene [The Gold]—Crewmember of the Tholian warship *Lanz't Tholis* who is imprisoned by the Shedai Wanderer in the First Conduit on Jinoteur IV. (RTW)

T'Pes, Lieutenant—Vulcan female, junior science officer, *U.S.S. Endeavour*, considered by Captain Atish Khatami as a possible candidate for the first officer position. (STT)

T'Prynn, Lieutenant Commander —Vulcan female, born 2191, daughter of Sivok and L'Nel. Starfleet Intelligence liaison to Starbase 47. (HAR)

Trinay III—Site of a Starfleet outpost that was awaiting a power generator which had been misplaced on Starbase 47. (HAR)

tu'HomIraH—Klingon expletive. (STT)

tuQloS **pills**—Dietary supplement used by Klingons to extract nourishment from food that has been cooked; used by Lurqal (aka Anna Sandesjo) to pass as a human. (HAR)

Turag—Klingon Imperial Intelligence agent and bodyguard to Klingon Ambassador Lugok on Starbase 47. Serves as the primary handler for Lurqal, aka Anna Sandesjo. (HAR)

type-V life reading—Operation Vanguard code for detection of the Taurus meta-genome. (HAR)

Unez—Scoridian journalist in Edinburgh, Scotland, who served as a mentor to young Tim Pennington—and taught the fledgling newshound how to pick locks like a professional criminal. (HAR)

Urgoz, Cargo Chief—Cargo master on the *I.K.S. Zin'za*. (RTW) *val'reth*— Vulcan term for one who carries the *katra* of another against one's will; one so afflicted cannot enjoy the release of *Pon farr* nor the serenity of *Kolinahr,* or be assured that one's spirit will find rest with those of one's ancestors—in effect, it is a "living death." (HAR)

Vanderhoven, Ensign—Torpedo room officer, *U.S.S. Bombay.* KIA. (HAR)

Vanguard—name of the *Watchtower*-class space station built to become Starbase 47. (HAR)

Vault, the—Top-secret research facility hidden deep inside the core of Starbase 47. It is devoted to research of the Shedai, their artifacts, the Shedai Carrier Wave, and the Taurus meta-genome. Its entrance is concealed within compartment CA/194-6. (STT)

Vekpa, Lieutenant—Klingon officer serving in the occupation force on Palgrenax. KIA. (STT)

Velez, Chief Petty Officer Miguel—Member of the S.C.E. team on Ravanar IV under the command of Commander Dean Singer. (HAR)

Vel'j Tholis—Tholian warship that participated in the attack on the *U.S.S. Bombay* and the Starfleet outpost on Ravanar IV. Of the six ships sent to attack the outpost, it and the *Nov'k Tholis* were the only survivors. (HAR)

Velrene [The Azure]—Member of the Tholian Ruling Conclave in 2265. (HAR)

Verheiden, Agent—Starfleet Intelligence agent who escorts Anna Sandesjo from her temporary quarters to a secret transport that is intended to smuggle her off of Starbase 47. (RTW)

Veselka, Councillor—Member of the Klingon High Council in 2265, decidedly the most feminine of the female councilmembers. (HAR)

veS'Hov, I.K.S.—Klingon warship sent to Gamma Tauri IV as a show of strength; it was destroyed in the opening salvo by the planet's surface-based Shedai artillery. (RTW)

Vinueza, Jeanne—Ex-wife of Commodore Diego Reyes. Tall, brunette, native of Luna, high esper skills. Served as president of the New Boulder Colony on Gamma Tauri IV, where she was killed by Shedai sentinels. (HAR/RTW)

Voice, the—Shedai term for Tholians who are yoked to their Conduits; conversely, it is also what the Tholians call the Shedai who speak through them. (RTW)

Vrax, Praetor—Ruler of the Romulan Star Empire in 2265. (STT)

V'Shan—Dancelike Vulcan martial art that involves detailed study of pressure points. (HAR)

Vulcan syrah—Red wine available in Manón's cabaret in 2266; the '51 Saylok is a good varietal of Vulcan syrah. (RTW)

Vumelko, Chief Petty Officer Ivan—Starfleet Customs officer on Starbase 47. Paunchy, bug-eyed, world-weary, sarcastic, grouchy. (HAR)

Wallingford, Security Officer—Security officer in charge of restricting access to Starbase 47's cargo facility. (HAR)

Wanderer, the—Shedai *Serrataal*, one of the youngest of her kind, but empowered with a unique gift to travel between worlds without the use of a Conduit. Awakens the others of her kind after destroying Palgrenax. (RTW)

Warden—Shedai *Serrataal* of great age and power. Responsible for meting out justice and retribution. Allied with the Maker. (RTW)

Warfield, Arlys—Federation News Service executive editor. She is Tim Pennington's boss until he is made the victim of a disinformation campaign that embarrasses FNS, after which Warfield fires Pennington. (HAR)

Watchtower **class**—Classification for a very large and multimission-capable starbase such as Vanguard, which is made to operate independently very far from the Federation. (HAR)

Xav, Ensign—Tellarite male, science officer, *U.S.S. Lovell*. (RTW)

Xiong, Lieutenant Ming—Human male, Archaeology & Anthropology officer, in charge of the scientific aspects of Operation Vanguard. Runs the Vault. (HAR)

Yazkene [The Emerald]—Member of the Tholian Ruling Conclave in 2265. (HAR)

Yerad III—Planet on which Zakdorn accountant Sakud Armnoj resided; sort of a low-rent pleasure planet, a Risa or a Wrigleys without all those meddlesome laws. (STT)

Yeskene—Second-in-command of the Tholian warship *Aen'q Tholis*, which was destroyed by the Romulan bird-of-prey *Bloodied Talon*. KIA. (STT)

Yirikene [The Azure]—Crewmember of the Tholian warship *Lanz't Tholis* who is imprisoned by the Shedai Wanderer in the First Conduit on Jinoteur IV. (RTW)

Yoçarians—A member of this species was appointed castellan of the capital city of Tamaros III in 147 B.C.E., precipitating the Nemite Revolution. (HAR)

yosa **blade**—Traditional Nalori melee weapon; Zett Nilric used one to deadly effect on a Tarascan hitman named Qoheela. (HAR)

Zenstala II—Site of a Tholian military outpost destroyed by a Klingon attack fleet in 2265; the Tholians retaliated by destroying Klingon bases on Dorala and Korinar. (STT)

Zett Nilric—Nalori assassin, whose official title is "business manager" for Orion merchant-prince Ganz. Hates Cervantes Quinn. (HAR) Owns and operates a ship, a "Nalori argosy" called the *Icarion*. Fulfilled a contract with Klingon Imperial Intelligence to assassinate Lurqal, its compromised agent on Starbase 47. (RTW)

zh'Firro, Lieutenant Celerasayna—Andorian *zhen*, helm officer, *U.S.S. Sagittarius*. (RTW)

zh'Rhun, Commander Araev—Andorian *zhen*, first officer, *U.S.S. Lovell*. (STT/DEW)

zh'Shalas, Master Chief Petty Officer—Andorian *zhen*, Gamma-shift cargo chief on Starbase 47. (HAR)

Zin'za, I.K.S.—Klingon D-5 battle cruiser; on the forefront of the Klingon effort to unravel the Shedai mystery in the Taurus Reach. (STT/RTW)

Zulo—"Cleaner" for Orion crime boss Ganz; disposes of bodies and evidence professionally; species unspecified. (HAR)

ACKNOWLEDGMENTS

My first thanks belong to my wife, Kara, for her constant love and encouragement during what proved to be a very long year of back-to-back projects for me.

I am also grateful to my editor and *sensei*, Marco Palmieri, for inviting me back for another turn in this new corner of the *Star Trek* universe that he let me develop with him.

To Dayton Ward and Kevin Dilmore: You guys really upped the ante on the *Vanguard* series with book two, *Summon the Thunder*. Part of what inspired me to write this monster of a book—my longest work to date—was a desire to live up to the epic scope and sheer impact of your book. Thanks, gents.

Mike Kidd, who posts regularly on the TrekBBS, suggested this book's title. Knowing a great title when I see one, I laid claim to it immediately. *Gracias*, Mike.

Lastly, I am grateful for my many musical inspirations, including jazz pianist Paul Tillotson. Guiding my imagination on this literary journey were soundtracks for *The Mummy* and *King Solomon's Mines*, by Jerry Goldsmith; *The Mummy Returns*, by Alan Silvestri; *King Kong*, by James Newton Howard; *Passion: Music from the Last Temptation of Christ*, by Peter Gabriel; and *Batman Begins*, by Hans Zimmer and James Newton Howard.

Can you tell I wanted to think big?

ABOUT THE AUTHOR

David Mack is the author of numerous *Star Trek* novels, including the *USA Today* bestseller *A Time to Heal* and its companion volume, *A Time to Kill*. He developed the *Star Trek Vanguard* series with editor Marco Palmieri and wrote its first volume, *Harbinger*.

Mack's other novels include *Wolverine: Road of Bones*; *Star Trek: Deep Space Nine — Warpath*; *Star Trek: S.C.E. — Wildfire*; and *The Sorrows of Empire*, in the trade paperback *Star Trek: Mirror Universe*, Vol. 1 — *Glass Empires*.

Before writing books, Mack cowrote with John J. Ordover the fourth-season *Star Trek: Deep Space Nine* episode "Starship Down" and the story treatment for the series' seventh-season episode "It's Only a Paper Moon."

An avid fan of the Canadian progressive-rock trio Rush, Mack has attended concerts in all of the band's tours since 1982.

Mack currently resides in New York City with his wife, Kara. Learn more about him and his work on his official Web site, www.infinitydog.com.

WALK ON THE WILD SIDE

STAR TREK®
MIRROR UNIVERSE

GLASS EMPIRES

STAR TREK: ENTERPRISE®
Mike Sussman with Dayton Ward & Kevin Dilmore

STAR TREK
David Mack

STAR TREK: THE NEXT GENERATION®
Greg Cox

OBSIDIAN ALLIANCES

STAR TREK: VOYAGER®
Keith R.A. DeCandido

STAR TREK: NEW FRONTIER®
Peter David

STAR TREK: DEEP SPACE NINE®
Sarah Shaw

Available wherever books are sold or at www.startrekbooks.com.

POCKET BOOKS
A Division of Simon & Schuster
A CBS COMPANY

STVAN.RTWA